Thief's
Revenge

To Cheryl,

Enjoy the

Story!

Other Books by Jeffrey S. Crawford

<u>Fiction</u>
Finding Eden (Phineas Crook #1)
The King's Disease (Phineas Crook #2)

The Journal of Meshach

<u>Non-Fiction</u>
Image of God
On a Ship to Tarshish

www.jeffreyScrawford.com

Thief's Revenge

Jeffrey S. Crawford

HILLSIDE HOUSE
PUBLISHING

Thief's Revenge
Jeffrey S. Crawford
Hillside House Publishing

Published by Hillside House Publishing, Springdale, AR
Copyright © 2022 Jeffrey S. Crawford
All rights reserved.

Cover: ©2022, Ivan Zanchetta & bookcoversart.com

Library of Congress Cataloging-in-Publication Data

Library of Congress Control Number: 2022935844
Jeffrey S. Crawford

Thief's Revenge
ISBN: 978-1-7327596-6-4

Printed in the United States of America.

For my son,
Grayson
From a very proud father

Prologue

Jerusalem – August, 328 AD

The sun hung high in the cloudless sky. Its rays scorched the dry ground and the exposed skin of the men working to clear the rubble of limestone. A dry breeze did little to cool the air, serving instead to stir up dirt and dust, at times almost to the point that it was suffocating to anyone near the worksite.

A lone figure stood close, eager with anticipation, impervious to the heat and the dust. Her nose and mouth were covered with a purple veil, but her light gray eyes squinted with intensity as the sacred moment was drawing near.

"It is almost time, Empress." Marcarius, Bishop of Jerusalem, broke away from a large flat stone that eight men were currently working to move from the pit in the ground. He hobbled over to the figure who stood tall in her

1

supervision of the work that she, herself, had ordered. Marcarius was a short man, who appeared even shorter next to the very tall woman, whose royal robes flowed off of her slender form with grace and elegance.

This was Helena. Empress of Rome. Mother to Constantine, emperor of a newly reunified Roman Empire.

But royalty did not equate to softness when it came to Flavia Iulia Helena Augusta. She was a formidable woman. At the age of eighty, not many women, or men for that matter, could have undertaken the two-year journey that had brought the Augusta Imperatrix from Rome to the holy city of Jerusalem. The fact that Helena was standing here at all was testimony in itself as to the inner and outer power of the emperor's mother.

"The final slab is set for removal. It is a large stone and will take many men to move. But once it is cast aside, we will be free to enter." The bishop's eyes bulged as he rubbed his fatty hands together like a small child before the beginning of a great feast.

Helena only nodded, her gaze continually fixed on the work in the pit.

The lack of response served to make the nervous Marcarius all the more antsy. He let out a timid chuckle and continued to chat, as if to unburden himself of the moment. "We've all heard the story, of course. Of what is buried at the site. But that horrible temple has stood in its place for over one hundred and fifty years, and well...you understand how time has a way of turning stories into myths until one no longer knows where the truth lies. But soon, because of you, Oh Empress, we will finally know. We will finally know the truth."

Marcarius was referring to the pagan temple of Venus, which had stood on the site of the excavation since 130 AD. Emperor Hadrian had ordered its construction in an attempt to wipe away the memory of Jesus Christ and Christianity itself. Well, Hadrian was now gone and Christianity still remained, and thanks to a vision given to Constantine as well as the prowess of his mother, the temple had been ordered destroyed so that the secret it covered could finally be revealed.

The sound of metal on stone pinged through the dirty air as the men toiled to crack the seal held fast by the final block of stone.

"Come on you lazy fools!" shouted a foreman as he walked briskly around the slab, using force to position each man strategically. "Put your legs and back into it now."

Each man worked to wedge his iron pry bar into the seam where slab met foundation stone.

"Let's do this all together. On three. One. Two. Three!" He cracked a leather whip into the hot air by way of encouragement. Each man powered into the limestone slab, bare backs glistening with sweat as muscles strained and bulged.

"Yes, that's it! Keep going. Keep pushing. Do. Not. Stop!" Another crack of the whip drove the men harder still. Their grunts and groans gave way to another sound. A low moan stirred beneath the earth. It was as if the ground itself was fighting back, a tug of war between flesh and rock.

And then the sound gave way to what could only be described as a sigh. As if one side had finally yielded. Sensing the end was near, the foreman cracked his whip in a frenzy and shouted more commands of appeal, or perhaps threats.

Helena's eyes widened. She too sensed the ground was yielding to the strength of Roman will. And also slave labor.

"Yes, yes," Marcarius whispered.

As if willing the limestone rock to submit, Helena reached up and unfastened the side of her veil, letting it drop. Her lips pursed into a fine tight line, eyes growing wider still.

And then a mighty WHOOSH issued forth. From a crack. Yes! A crack had been achieved. The earth exhaled and air from within pushed a cloud of dust and vapor out and around the legs of the men. One fell back and away, clearly frightened.

"No! Do not yield!" The wicked whip landed on the back of the poor soul who scrambled to re-insert his pry bar and continue the push. The foreman screamed, "Everyone to this side! Hurry! The seal has been broken. Now is the time to finish." Men from the far side rushed around, slamming their bars into the smallest of cracks which immediately caused the crevice to grow.

"More men!" The whip cracked. A second wave of laborers rushed onto the scene, and that is when the stone gave up the fight. Slowly, it was lifted. The crack growing to an opening. Grappling hooks and ropes were attached so that men could pull from the far side while others continued to push and lift. The limestone lid moved up and up until it was finally standing on its side, vertical and pointed at the sky. And then it carried on over until it slammed back to the earth with a sickening thud.

4

"Ahhhhhhh!"

A man let out a scream as the slab landed on his lower half, crushing him. He had tragically slipped in his attempt to get away from the falling stone. Like ants, his co-laborers descended on the stone once again, lifting it just enough to pull him out. It was clearly too late.

As if nothing at all had happened, the foreman marched the short distance to Helena with Marcarius at her side. Bowing on one knee he said, "Empress, the chamber is open. Your will be done."

"Excellent." It was the first word Helena had spoken since arriving early that morning. "Marcarius. Come. Let us see what history has hidden but what God has revealed to us today. Ladders, torches, ropes. Let us not waste another moment." She was a commanding presence indeed.

The foreman went to work barking orders, echoing the queen mother's wishes. In short order, supplies had been gathered and assembled at the opening of the pit. Torches were tossed down to ascertain the depth, and two ladders, one on each side of the opening, were affixed into place.

The workers parted to each side, opening a pathway for Helena to come forward. And she did. Her majestic appearance caused the men who had toiled for many days to breach the pit to step back even further. She seemed to glide forward until she came to a halt at the edge of the pit. The fire flickering from the torches below could be seen burning on a rock floor, but their light betrayed nothing of the contents Helena hoped she was about to discover.

The Augusta Imperatrix had come a long way, all leading up to this moment. If the earthen chamber were empty or turned out to be a common storehouse for pottery and other such mundane items, then the whole venture would be a colossal failure. She was counting on the contents below to solidify her son's hold on the Roman Empire. To serve as a symbol that God himself had put his holy hand on Constantine, and that to fight the new emperor would be to fight God.

While she looked calm and in utter control on the outside, Helena's octogenarian heart was beating out of her chest. She felt like a young girl once again, about to uncover some hidden treasure. Well, that was exactly what might be about to happen. And not just any treasure, perhaps the greatest treasure known to mankind in all of history.

Helena was done waiting. She grabbed the post of the ladder and swung her body around. Marcarius came forward to offer assistance, but the short bishop was too late and it was obvious the queen mother needed no help. The earth appeared to swallow her as she slipped out of view. Not wanting to be left behind, the bishop of Jerusalem joined in the descent.

It was only a few minutes later that a team of five - Helena, Marcarius, and three priests hand-selected in advance - had gathered at the base of the two ladders, each having taken up one of the torches.

They found themselves in a large domed chamber at least twenty feet high. It was a simple room, clearly having been hewn from rock as the walls betrayed a slight curve that ran into the darkness on each side. A small shaft of sunlight from the opening above did little to illuminate the chamber, but after a few minutes the group's eyes began to adjust.

"Let us spread out." Helena's voice bounced off the hard surface of the room. "If you find anything, anything at all, do not touch it. Call for me immediately." And with that, the five members of the dig began moving in opposite directions.

It did not take long. The chamber turned out to be simply not that large and there were no antechambers or tunnels branching off. This was a single room put here for a single purpose.

"Empress!" a voice cried out.

Helena responded with swiftness, rushing toward the voice of the priest. The man's torch showed the way but revealed nothing more. But as Helena came upon him, joined simultaneously by the others in the room, their collective breath caught in their throats. The power of their five combined lights brought remarkable clarity to what was in front of them.

Three large wooden beams. Perhaps five feet long, propped up neatly against the wall, evenly spaced, one from another. No, not propped up...placed there intentionally.

And there was more.

In front of each wooden beam, on the rock floor of the chamber, was a large iron nail. Large enough to match the gauge of the holes on either end of each wooden beam.

And one other item. This one causing Helena's blood to rush.

A wooden placard. Set up neatly on a small easel in front of the whole display of beams and nails. The placard contained three lines of ancient script. Each line the same but in a different language: Greek, Hebrew, and Latin.

Marcarius fell to his knees. The priests followed suit.

Helena stood in awe. She had found it. There was no doubt. The message on the placard confirmed it.

But she had seen many forgeries along her way to Jerusalem the past two years. In Egypt, she was led to the remnants of Moses' famous burning bush. She had her doubts. And not far from here, she had been handed what she was told was the cloth used to swaddle the baby Jesus in the manger. Clearly a fake.

She had to know. She could leave nothing to chance.

"Marcarius!" she snapped. "Bring the woman."

"Yes, Empress, of course." The little man hurried to the ladder and called up. A slight figure appeared, silhouetted by the bright light of the opening. It took a few minutes that seemed like an eternity, but a frail and obviously weak woman made it to the bottom of the ladder with great effort. The three priests joined Marcarius and took the woman by the arms as she was near collapse from the effort.

Bringing her to the display of beams, nails, and placard, Helena moved to stand in front of the woman. Even in the firelit dimness of the chamber, the queen mother's features could be seen to soften.

"Sister." Helena reached up and laid her wrinkled hand on the side of the woman's face. "You are not well. Is this true?"

"Yes, Empress. I feel my days are short."

"She is riddled with sickness, Empress," inserted Marcarius. "Alma has worked in my home for many years and in the last year she became increasingly ill and, as you can see, has shriveled to near nothing. The Lord will take her soon, unless there is a miracle."

8

"A miracle, yes," replied Helena. She stared into woman's eyes. "You are a good woman, Alma. I can see it in you. Perhaps the Lord will grant the miracle Marcarius speaks of today." She glanced over at the wooden beams. "Sister, go...and lay your hands against the wood, one at a time. Take your time. Go slowly."

Alma nodded and moved away from Helena's gentle touch. She walked to the first post. Taking a deep breath and holding it, she leaned in, laying both hands on the coarse wood. The room held its breath with her.

Nothing.

It was but ordinary timber from a local grove of trees, no doubt.

Alma pulled away and looked back at Helena, who only nodded for her to continue. She moved to the second beam and leaned into it in the same manner.

Again, nothing.

This time the woman's shoulders sagged. Why was she here? What kind of miracle was she looking for? This felt like a cruel game for queens and priests and she felt like a disposable pawn. But there was one more beam of wood.

She shuffled over to it, her strength waning, her body calling out to her to just give up and die. But there was an audience. She had to perform. She took one more deep breath and leaned in. This time closing her eyes.

The moment she touched the splintery wood of the beam, the power shot through her. She gasped and almost fell backward.

Helena's eyes grew wide and she took her own step forward. "What is it?" she asked excitedly. "What is happening?"

The dim lighting of torchlight made it difficult to see clearly, but it appeared as if the woman's stature grew as they looked on. Her back straightened, vanishing the slump that had been so obvious before. As she stood tall, the tone of the muscles in her arms sharpened and it looked as if the sheen of her hair even brightened. Alma lowered her hands from the wooden beam and turned with confidence toward the party of five. Her face shown in the dark, as if her skin itself was glowing.

"It's a miracle," she gasped. "The Lord has answered."

"How do you kno-," Marcarius began.

"Because I know," she cut him off. "The disease is gone."

"Yes," Helena responded. She stepped forward and put her hand once again to Alma's cheek. The woman smiled. "I believe it is."

"Marcarius," she barked, causing the little man to flinch. "One more test. We must know with certainty."

"Another test, Empress?"

"The man crushed by the stone slab. Bring him."

"But...Empress...he is dead. How can we...."

"Just bring him, Bishop," she said with less force. "We must know."

He nodded and sent the instructions to the surface. A wrapped body was lowered to the rock floor, the lower half of the binding soaked in blood. The priests took the body and laid it in front of the third beam of wood that had healed Alma.

"Unwrap the body. Let us see this brother's face," Helena instructed. The priests relented to the gruesome task.

"And now..." Helena walked forward. She took the third beam of wood in her grasp and slowly lowered it to the ground, letting it rest alongside the body of the dead man. "Yes, yes," she whispered as she touched the wood. And then, getting on her knees in a most unroyal position, she shoved the beam until it came in contact with the body of the man.

And they waited.

One minute.

Then two.

And then...

The man's eyes opened.

She had done it! There was no doubt.

Helena of Rome had found the cross of Jesus Christ.

Chapter 1

Turin, Italy – 2:00 a.m., Present Day

The figure in black darted through the Giardini Reali, blending in perfectly with the shadows cast by the massive stand of trees. Breaching the old fortified ramparts to the garden had been easy. Security in the rear part of the complex was almost nonexistent.

The sky was blanketed in clouds and there was no moon. The conditions were ideal for what the thief had in mind this night. With the exception of ground lighting placed sporadically throughout the garden, there was no ambient illumination from above.

It was time to go up.

Flying from tree to tree, the figure arrived easily at the rear of the Royal Palace, a massive square building with a large open-air courtyard in the middle. Two trees nestled up next to the ancient brick of the building provided the cover needed. Removing one of two black packs from his back, the figure knelt and extracted a thin rope and firing mechanism with a spiked expansion anchor attached to the end.

Using compressed air, the intruder silently fired the anchor, with rope attached, toward the top lip of the outer wall. The only sound was a soft *WHOOSH*, followed by a grainy thud as the anchor took hold. It was a perfect shot.

Wasting no time, the figure left the first pack behind and, using only his arms, scaled the wall in less than thirty seconds. Had anyone been watching, they would have been impressed with the strength and agility of the climb, almost effortless in appearance, a testimony to a cat-like fitness and skill. But no one was watching. At least not this part of the complex, and certainly not once the figure gained the roof. Now the inky blackness of this particular night - a night so carefully chosen and planned - could be taken full advantage of.

Clad all in black and wearing shoes with thin pliable rubber soles, the figure glided across the clay roof tiles like a shadow moving noiselessly from one end to the next. Arriving at the pointed spire that rose up into the night sky, the figure paused to rest and take in his surroundings. There was no movement below, either in the courtyard of the palace behind him or in the plaza of Saint John the Baptist Cathedral which now lay before him. All was well and going according to plan.

But now came the more difficult part.

The spire of the palace with its impressive rotunda lay almost flush to the smaller dome of the cathedral itself. The dome would be his access point of entry. A bank of windows evenly spaced around the circumference of the dome designed to let natural light into the cathedral by day would serve to let the thief in by night. The challenge was the score of floodlights that up-lit the white stone blocks of the cathedral from below. He would be no more exposed at any time during the whole operation than when he was cutting his way through the glass of the dome window.

But the black clad figure had come prepared for this moment as well. Reaching up to a tiny clasp on the top of his head, he grabbed hold and pulled. A slender zipper parted the spandex fabric of his black bodysuit and, like a magician, he instantly appeared clad in an opaque suit of the same type, but now blending perfectly with the stone of the cathedral.

The off-white clad figure went to work on a pre-selected window of the dome. Attaching a set of cutting tools from his pack, he made quick work of the glass. Next, he attached a second rope and anchor and then, with another quick glance at the plaza, launched himself over the edge and into the cathedral.

Descending like a spider, the thief touched quietly down onto the marble floor at the front of the chapel, coming to rest behind a huge wooden altar of sorts that held six impossibly tall candles and a gold crucifix. He crouched down to listen. All was quiet and dark. The security cameras, which were surely pointed toward the front of the cathedral's chapel, would likely have only caught a vague image dropping from above. A blur really. Unless the security guard monitoring the cameras happened to be looking at a particular screen at a particular moment and been paying close attention, nothing out of the ordinary should have been detected. At least that's what he was counting on.

Lack of movement and alarm confirmed that he was correct.

The doorway to his final destination lay to his right. The thief smiled behind his spandex-covered face. Just as he had hoped and expected, there were no security guards present in the chapel itself. This was a quiet part of Italy and with the exception of what he had come to steal, there was nothing remarkable about this little town at all. As such, it was truly amazing that security for such an important relic was so minimal. Not that he was complaining. There would be challenge enough waiting for him on nights soon to come.

But now was the moment of action. The next ten minutes had to be perfectly timed. The thief had practiced this moment at least a dozen times and executed it to perfection each time. But those were simulations and this was the real thing. As he had so harshly learned in the past, anything can go wrong when it comes time for the execution of a heist. There were simply too many variables to account for no matter how comprehensive a simulation might be. Not that he was planning to turn back. Not now. Not after all that had brought him to this very moment.

Checking his equipment one final time, he set the timer on his watch to ten minutes precisely. Then he pressed START.

He quickly set a small rectangle box on the marble floor and pressed the black button on top. He counted to five in his head. Exactly as planned, there was a flicker of light that could be seen through the windows of the cathedral.

The small box on the floor looked unassuming, but what it had actually done was emit a high powered EMP – a short burst of electromagnetic energy. This particular EMP only had a range of about one hundred meters in every direction, but that was enough. Enough to disrupt every electrical signal within range. About right now, a security guard sitting in front of his display of monitors would be on his feet, feverishly working to reboot the entire system of cameras and sensors. It would take just over nine minutes to do so.

The beige figure bolted to the heavy wooden door. A combination of traditional and electronic mechanisms held the entrance fast. This was expected. In fact, everything the thief had seen thus far was expected. He'd done his homework in the weeks leading up to the operation, having joined multiple public tours of the cathedral and its attached complex, all incognito of course.

The analog bolts were easily dispatched via manual skill. A decoding device was needed for the more advanced lock. But exactly eighty-three seconds after engaging the door, the intruder was on other side.

A very short hallway led to a set of circular stone steps that carried down to a crypt of sorts, except this small grotto contained no corpses. A second hallway continued on, ending in what was clearly a wall of modern construction. A steel door of impossible strength barred access to the treasure on the other side. But the door was no match for the skill of the thief. It took a bit longer due to the sophistication of the locking system, but exactly one hundred and twelve seconds of work yielded the *THUNK* that made the masked figure smile for a second time.

A heave on the door and the final goal was within reach. A muted steel box the size of a coffin lay before him. He walked up to the container and stared down through four layers of bulletproof glass at the contents within. His breath caught in his chest and for the first time this night, the thief found himself paralyzed...caught off guard as it were. The holiness of the moment, or maybe it was the sacredness of the object in front of him, sucked the air out of the hermetically sealed chamber. Whatever the cause, it was for but a moment. A moment he didn't have. Glancing at his watch, he confirmed that the unplanned moment had spanned thirty seconds.

Not good.

Not good at all.

He was behind schedule.

The security system would be up and running again in only five-and-a-half minutes. Then the place would be descended upon by guards like vultures diving on a fresh kill.

In one fluid motion, he withdrew the fist-sized pyramid from his bag, slapping it onto the glass, right in the middle as best as he could eyeball it. One at a time, he pulled on each of the four corners at the base of the device. An attached wire uncoiled, which he fastened to each corner of the container's top. Satisfied the wires were properly connected and the device was secured according to the instructions given to him, he stepped back and withdrew a small remote control.

The sonic disrupter had cost him a small fortune and had not been easy to acquire. One doesn't just walk into Walmart and purchase a high-end security-busting device such as this. It was illegal to say the least. But he'd obtained this one. It could only be used once and then it was useless. No opportunity to test it. Only faith guided him now. If it didn't work, then all his effort leading to this moment will have been for naught. And he would still have to escape, even without the contents of the steel container.

No more time to contemplate.

He pressed the button on the remote.

A buzzing sensation filled the chamber. And then a sound like cracking ice when stepping onto a frozen pond. That was the only thing the burglar could liken it to. He'd expected something more dramatic. Stepping back up to the bulletproof glass, he smiled for a third time in the early morning hour. All four layers of bulletproof glass were compromised with cracks. So many that he could no longer see what lay behind them. It looked very much like the windshield of a car having taken an impact from some heavy object.

Three minutes to go.

He extracted a simple hammer and chisel from his pack. The simplest of instruments but sufficient for the final phase. A fire broke out in the cathedral in 1971 and a team of firefighters were forced to work like mad with sledgehammers to breach the glass and save the container's contents. But thanks to the sonic disrupter, the work this night would be light by comparison. The thief went to work, and with great ease removed the chunks of splintered glass in only a minute and a half.

There was now nothing between him and his bounty. Few human beings throughout history had been this close to this object. It was truly beautiful in a macabre sort of way. The cloth itself was a full fourteen feet in length with the bottom half folded under and onto a shelf positioned below the top half. And it was the top half that threatened to mesmerize anyone who dared to look.

Mostly at the face.

Or an impression of a face left behind by the seepage of blood. And following the clear outline of the torso, the unmistakable imprint of arms folded across the figure's midsection...a bloody hole in the palm of each hand.

But there was no time.

The clock was near expiration. It took the thief only forty-five seconds to extract a thin linen cloth from his pack, lay the cloth over the ancient relic, and then, using a three-and-a-half-foot wooden dowel matching the width of the cloth, roll all fourteen feet into a tight coil, placing the whole thing in a black cardboard tube with an attached sling.

He was done with seconds to spare.

The opaque clad figure darted back the way he'd come: up the stairs, through the security door and into the chapel, racing at full speed down the side of the building, flying by row after row of dark brown pews and the six stone pillars marking off alcoves on the sides of the chapel. His arrival near the front door of the cathedral coincided perfectly with the entrance of at least a dozen armed security guards. Just as he'd expected, the gaggle of troops stormed right past him toward the front of the chapel and the crypt from which he'd emerged only seconds earlier. They were in such a rush to secure the chapel's most famous treasure and to catch what they knew by now was a thief in their midst, that they never suspected that same thief would be standing – yes, just standing – feet from the front door, blending in perfectly with the stone column of the first alcove.

As the men thundered past him and toward the security door, the figure reached up for a second time this night and took hold of another clasp on the top of his covered head. As the spandex fell away, a head appeared, covered in a common stocking cap. The figure stepped fully out of the bodysuit wearing khaki shorts and an untucked black t-shirt. With the cardboard tube in hand, he strolled casually out the front door of the Cathedral of Saint John the Baptist, sauntered across the plaza to the corner of Via della Basilica and Via Porta Palatina where a motorcycle was propped and chained to a tree.

As if unhurried, the man pulled a set of keys from his pocket and unchained the cycle. He glanced back at the cathedral as he mounted and started the bike. Sirens in the distance brought another smile to his face. This time it was a smile of satisfaction.

Mission accomplished.

He gassed the throttle and shot off down the dark street in the opposite direction of the sirens.

The stolen Shroud of Turin slung over his shoulder.

Chapter 2

Alexander Pontia did not believe in God. He did not believe in man either. Truth be told, Alexander Pontia believed only in himself.

The answer as to why was simple. Neither God nor man had ever done anything to help Alexander in his struggle to become the man that stood in front of the mirror straightening his tie, assessing his perfectly manicured nails, finishing with a gentle pat of his freshly cut hair.

"You are pleased?" came the question from the stylist.

"Quite. Thank you, Maria. As always." He gave a curt nod as if to communicate that she was free to excuse herself.

"Very well, then. Next Tuesday? As always?" The young stylist finished packing her sheers into her travel bag and bent to gather the plastic onto which Alexander Pontia's jet black hair clippings had fallen.

"Not next Tuesday, no. I will be traveling. We will have to schedule for the following week. On Tuesday as normal, eight thirty sharp, right after my breakfast." Alexander did not like having to wait two weeks between groomings, but sometimes it was unavoidable.

Maria finished with the cleanup and silently left Alexander Pontia standing in front of the plate glass window of his cabin, looking at the majestic peaks of the Grand Tetons. Alexander loved the view. He never tired of it. It was an ever-present reminder of how far he'd come in his forty-two years of life.

All on his own.

No one had helped him find the acreage in this lovely corner of Wyoming. He'd found it on his own. And he'd commissioned the construction of the private log cabin home that sat on the property. Cabin was really not the best descriptor. More like a private lodge.

The money that had been generated to pay for the property and the residence had all come from Alexander's vast bank account. Actually, just one of his many bank accounts. All paid in cash. Alexander Pontia was in debt to no one. He was a true self-made millionaire. Oh, it wasn't because he didn't come from money. The Pontias were a wealthy family. But Alexander's father gave him none of it. Once the young Pontia turned sixteen, his father had cut him off. Completely. There would be no more weekly provision or financial allowance. There would be no inheritance. Whatever Alexander had going forward would come from his own, self-generated resources.

His father had prepared him for the moment. It was the way of the Pontias, a family with a proud Italian heritage. "A man is only worth as much as he can produce on his own," his father had drilled into him. "Expect no help from me. In the same way that my own father gave me no help. You will make it on your own...or you won't." And with that, Alexander was *on* his own. He'd had very little contact with his father since that day. His mother would reach out from time to time, on holidays and birthdays, and he suspected she wanted more, but he also knew his father forbid it. It was a strange sort of love, but it was the only love Alexander knew, from his parents that is.

Alexander felt a warm presence enter the room. The scent of lavender came with it and he relaxed a bit as a woman took his arm.

"Are you leaving soon?"

"In a bit."

"When will you come back to me?"

Alexander smiled. The sound of Maria's Jeep starting and of her driving down the gravel path to the exit of the property broke the trance he was in. He pulled his eyes from the Tetons and looked down at the one person who loved him more than any other. Jillian was his soulmate, and he had convinced himself that what he did, he did for her. But deep inside, Alexander knew he was motivated most of all by allegiance to self. But he truly did love this woman as much as she loved him.

They met while Alexander was still trying to claw his way up from nothing. He was only eighteen and working at a local pizza restaurant doing deliveries with occasional duties in the kitchen. Jillian worked across the street at the

Dairy Queen. They met one day when he was on break and had decided to walk over for a Butterfinger Blizzard. She caught his eye and he hers. The next day, she walked into the pizza place and ordered some breadsticks to go. They eventually exchanged names and numbers. That led to the regular swapping of burgers and ice cream for pizza. From there, love blossomed.

They moved in together, reasoning two incomes applied to one rent payment made sense, and shortly after that, decided to get married. He'd never had eyes for another woman.

One night, while lying in bed together, sick of going nowhere with their minimum wage income, not to mention being sick of eating free fast food, Alexander had an idea: What if they robbed a bank?

It sounded crazy at first. Who robs a bank? Druggies, losers, bad people, desperate people. Well, Alexander wasn't any of the first three categories, but he was quickly growing desperate, or at least dissatisfied. They could do it, he was convinced. They may not have college degrees, but they were smart. They'd pick a small branch of a local bank one town over. Alexander would let his beard grow in preparation. He'd wear a hat and oversized clothes. Jillian would go along pretending to be just another customer. Once Alexander slipped a note to the teller explaining he had a gun and wanted two bags stuffed with hundreds, she would cry out and pretend to have a panic attack, yelling that the bank was being robbed. She would fall down and sob and flail and beg for her life. This would create a panic. People's memories become fuzzy when they are panicked. That was the point. Alexander would take the bags of money and run to a waiting bicycle as people rushed to comfort and tend to Jillian. Once the commotion was over and the police were called, Jillian would simply disappear before they could question her. Alexander, having ditched the bike, would be waiting in their car one block away and they would calmly drive back home. He would shave his beard just in case anyone posted security footage on the news, and then they would lay low.

The plan worked like a charm. The couple pocketed just under ten grand and the police never came knocking.

And so it began. A new "career" of sorts.

As he looked into Jillian's eyes an idea came to mind. "I probably need eight or nine days and then I'll be home. You shouldn't stay here alone waiting on me. Why don't you fly to the house in Cancún? Invite a few of your girlfriends you haven't seen in a while. My treat, of course." He winked at her and she squeezed his arm tight, smiling.

"You take great care of me."

"None of this would be possible without you by my side." He leaned down and gave her an affectionate kiss.

An approaching thumping pulled them apart as the blue and white Sikorsky S-76 swooped in and landed on the Pontia's helipad just off to the right of their view from the windows.

"Time for you to go, Love."

"Yes, it is. I will see you next week."

With that, Alexander turned and left the room, headed for his private helicopter, which would carry him to the airport in Jackson Hole where his private jet would carry him to New York City. The airport wasn't really that far, only a twenty-minute drive. But Alexander liked to show off.

He needed no bags. His nondescript residence on the upper east side of Manhattan had all the clothes and belongings he would need. As always, his office in New York would be the staging point for another operation. His next operation.

Yes, it all started with a small bank in a rural town. But banks were a thing of the past. Too easy and the payoff too small. What Alexander Pontia was involved in now was bigger. Much bigger.

Chapter 3

Just over three hours later, Alexander Pontia's Learjet 75 delivered him to the Sheltair FBO at La Guardia International Airport. A black Chevy Suburban was waiting for him as usual. Twenty-five minutes after that, he was deposited on the corner of 42nd Street and Lexington Avenue.

Stepping out of the SUV and onto the sidewalk, Alexander Pontia inhaled long and deep, and with a slow turn took in the city. The air quality wasn't on par with the mountain air of Wyoming, but nevertheless, there was something intoxicating, addictive even, about the sights and smells of New York City. A thousand people, easily within eyeshot, all moving toward some unseen goal, thousands more beyond what he could see all doing the same. Taxis and buses honking and jockeying for position. Scaffolding and workmen – there was always some sort of renovation going on. A street project a hundred yards down Lexington.

A dozen different smells wafting past. Pigeons pecking about for some morsel. All of it and more made up the most exciting city on planet Earth.

Looking up, Alexander noticed for the first time that the sky was clear blue. The same as in Wyoming but different. Instead of the Tetons, the spire of the Chrysler Building found his gaze. Wasting no more time, he headed straight into the lobby of the art deco building. Making his way instinctively to the bank of elevators, he punched the up button and was rewarded with the chime of an immediately available lift. Three others joined him, all hitting buttons for different floors. The button Alexander hit had a 20 on it. The doors closed and after depositing two of the riders on other floors, the doors opened for Alexander. He stepped out of the elevator, rounded a corner, and was greeted by the large backlit golden letters declaring the international headquarters of Pilate Enterprises.

This was home base for Alexander Pontia. His pride and joy. What he had worked so hard for, for so many years. He had started with nothing. Literally. And now this.

Pilate Enterprises was officially the controlling entity for three separate businesses. Chief among the three was Token Exchange, an auction house specializing in the authentication, sale, and transfer of ancient art and relics. While Token Exchange was open to handling and had handled all sorts of auctions – they once moved to sell an original collection of Joe Shuster's drawings of Superman before Action Comic #1 ever featured the now iconic superhero – they focused primarily on the *old*. Sometimes the very old, as in thousands of years old. Other times, old simply meant hundreds of years.

Such was the case the previous week. Token Exchange signed a contract to auction off a golden dragon from the Yuan Dynasty of the early 1300s. Alexander authenticated the piece personally, although he had little doubt going in. The provider was a friend, Marcus Cabrera, an Argentinian who had done business with Token Exchange for more than a dozen years and had never brought anything less than authentic merchandise to Alexander.

The dragon would likely go for $200,000 or a bit more when it auctioned in two weeks. Token Exchange would get twenty percent. Not big money, but then again, Marcus Cabrera was a friend. And he would be back with bigger prizes.

Notable compared in size to other well-known auction houses such as Sotheby's and their eighty locations in forty countries, Token Exchange did well and had branch offices in twelve countries. This was just fine for Alexander Pontia. He had no interest in being the biggest and dealing with the public attention that would come with such success. Alexander defined success in other ways and his real interests demanded a certain amount of discretion.

The second company under the banner of Pilate Enterprises was Dominion Safe, a corporate security firm providing elite protection services for companies and their leadership. Because of the security demands of Token Exchange, Alexander had decided a decade prior to stop paying for said security and simply start providing it himself. It was a short step from that point to marketing security services to his business partners in the antiquities acquisition industry. And thus, Dominion Safe was born. Even before an item was identified for auction, Alexander Pontia was already involved in its protection via Dominion Safe. The security arm of Pilate Enterprises grew rapidly after that as Alexander's partners began to talk up Dominion Safe with their own business associates. Using a combination of retired military and police from around the world, along with the DNA of Alexander Pontia that required nothing less than perfection, Dominion Safe had grown to elite status in the security world. *Stay Safe with Dominion Safe* was the company's well-known tag line.

The final leg of the Pilate Enterprise's tirade of companies was a nondescript shipping company simply named Straight Line. Rather than rely on third party shippers and carriers, Alexander, once again, decided it would be better – and more lucrative – to provide premium shipping services for items coming to auction. Plus, there was the need to safely ship the items to their new owners after the sales were made final. *We are, after all, talking about ancient and priceless artifacts*, he reasoned. And that was the selling point to his partners. The idea gained fast traction and in short order led to a small fleet of planes, armored trucks, helicopters, etc. All designed to ferry valuable auction items to and from their intended destinations quickly and efficiently on, yes, a straight line.

All of this together carved a unique spot for Alexander Pontia in the world of antiquities. If you had an item that needed to make the auction market, Alexander Pontia under the banner of Pilate Enterprises could guard it, transport it, and sell it for you. It was a one-stop-shop kind of experience working with Alexander Pontia. Those doing business with Pontia liked it that way and so did he. All in all, it proved to be a lucrative arrangement. It also gave Alexander Pontia the perfect system in which to conduct, let's say, more private sorts of dealings. The kind of transactions that one would not necessarily want advertised or documented on "the books." The world of ancient artifacts and antiquities can sometimes produce the need for, what some would term as, illegal exchanges.

Alexander breezed past the beautiful blonde receptionist stationed behind an imposing oak station. Tess Greenway may have had the look of a Fox News personality, but she was a killing machine. Literally. The Joplin, Missouri, native had served a stint in the Air Force choosing not to go to college. After the Air Force, she was trolling around on Ancestory.com and discovered that she had, of all things, a Jewish bloodline. This led her on a personal journey of self-discovery that eventually landed her in Israel serving in the Israeli Defense Force. The IDF schooled her in the art of Karv Maga, a combination of martial arts techniques derived from aikido, boxing, wrestling, judo, and karate.

Tess excelled in the art of Karv Maga, and after righting the wrongs of the world for the Jewish Nation, she decided to take her skills to the private sector. The pay was much better, and her skirmishes along the borders of the Palestinian/Israeli conflict combined with the terrorist elements of the PLO and Hezbollah had jaded her morals. Alexander stumbled upon her in one of his market trips to the Middle East and knew immediately she would be a perfect fit for Dominion Safe. Her combination of skill and beauty eventually pulled her to the larger Pilate Enterprises side. Yes, Tess Greenway was both disarming and lethal.

"Good morning, Mr. Pontia," she called out as he swept by. "Dimitri is waiting for you in your office," she finished as Alexander acknowledged her in turn with only the wave of a hand. She was not offended. She understood that when Alexander was in go-mode this was how he was. Focused.

Pontia's twentieth floor corner office had a spectacular view of the New York skyline. But none of this caught the self-made millionaire's attention. He was consumed instead by the shoebox-sized old oak box sitting on the small table between two leather highbacked chairs.

Dimitri Bezrukov sat in one of the chairs.

"You've got it!" Alexander exclaimed. "Was there any trouble with the operation?"

The large Russian laughed. "I believe the saying is, *like taking candy from a baby.* It was no problem, Comrade."

Alexander knew very little about the background of Dimitri Bezrukov other than the fact that he was Russian, born and bred, and that he was former GRU, Russian military intelligence. Like most people that worked for Pontia, money had replaced nationalism as the primary motivator. The six foot five, two-hundred-and-fifty pound Russian war machine had been with Alexander since the beginning. He was Alexander's first hire, in fact, and the man had remained fiercely loyal for many years now.

As always, Dimitri sported a bald head, with a perpetual two-day look of stubble covering his dome, and was found dressed impeccably in an expensive suit from Armani, Brioni, or some other fine clothier. In this way he mimicked his employer. He was also the head of Dominion Safe and thus handled every aspect of security for Pilate Enterprises as a whole, as well as for Alexander personally.

"And they have no idea it is gone?"

"No idea. The forgery you had commissioned was laid perfectly in its place," he replied with a satisfied grin. "The cloth is never removed as a point of order. It could be a decade or longer before they realize the real artifact has been taken. And honestly, they may never know."

Alexander was salivating. "Perfect," he whispered. His eyes bulged as he took the box in hand and moved to the larger meeting table set against the south-facing window. "Did you have to...handle anyone in order to get it?" Not that he cared but Alexander felt compelled to ask.

"You mean did we kill anyone, Comrade?" The Russian laughed again. "Sadly, no."

Alexander looked from the box to Dimitri. It was impossible to tell if he was joking or serious. He raised an eyebrow.

"It was simple really. The security in Spain as a whole is weak. And at the Cathedral of San Salvador itself, it is weaker still. The city of Oviedo is not overly large. Something like two hundred thousand people is all. The policia there are amateurs compared to the team I sent. As I said, it was a simple operation."

"Good, good." Alexander was most pleased. "Then let us see the fruit of your labor."

He gently lifted the lid of the box. Not that the box itself was anything special, but the gravity of the moment caused him to move with reverence. Almost forgetting himself, he rushed to his desk and withdrew a pair of white cotton gloves, donning them as he made his way back to the now-opened box. Carefully, as if handling the most delicate of objects, he removed the stained cloth from the silk-lined container. He set it on the table and began the process of unfolding it. Not until all thirty-three inches of the cloth were stretched out did he step back to actually look at the piece.

He felt his breath catch. It was his. He now "owned" it. The blotchy brown image on the cloth sent chills up his spine. He was staring at the Sudarium of Oviedo. The bloodstained face cloth of Jesus Christ.

Chapter 4

"Happy birthday!!"

The small crowd shouted as cardboard horns blew and confetti was thrown into the air. Phineas Crook blushed and worked to stifle a grin as he gave his wife Autumn a raised eyebrow.

"You got me," he admitted.

She was clinging to his arm and beaming with a smile that lit up the already festive room. They were actually gathered in the reception area of the Hobbs College of Theology and Ministry located on the second floor of Montgomery Hall on the campus of Oklahoma Baptist University.

The couple had just stepped off of the elevator in a ruse devised by Phin's wife. Something about wanting to borrow a giraffe carving from Africa that he kept in his office. They had dozens of animal carvings around their home from

Phin's numerous trips overseas, but Autumn had insisted she needed this specific trinket. She didn't, of course. And Phin, always in the posture of doing whatever it took to please his bride, had stepped right into her little surprise birthday party for him.

Phin found himself staring at his closest friends, most of them colleagues in the Hobbs College or other departments around the university. Dr. Vance Mildrot, Dr. Leslie Wang, Dr. John R.L. Smitherton, all caught his eye and were beaming.

"So many doctors in one room," he called out, "yet if I were to suffer a heart attack in this moment due to shock, I would be in severe trouble." The group laughed at Phin's well-placed jab at the academic prowess in the room. "Thank you all, sincerely. It means so much that you would come and wish me happy birthday."

And with that the gathering broke out in a chorus of *Happy Birthday to You*. A cake with a flaming 3 and 6 appeared, prompting Phin to make a wish and blow the candles out. Another round of clapping and well wishes and everyone broke into small groups of conversation as Phin worked his way around the reception area. Even Carol, the receptionist and assistant to the dean, had come. Phin apologized for the mess in what was essentially her space. Gracious as ever, she gave him a hug and told him not to worry.

"Did you enjoy your dinner?" An arm grabbed Phin and pulled him around.

"Max! I didn't see you. I thought maybe you'd skipped out."

"Uh uh. No way I'm missing the birthday of my best friend. Somebody had to pick up the cake while you and Autumn were eating dinner. I barely made it before you guys arrived, though. You were early getting here, my friend. You almost blew your own surprise."

"Gee, I'm sorry, Max. This coming from the man who is almost always late to everything," Phin ribbed him back.

Dr. Max Allred truly was Phin's best friend. The two had been close since their days in college at the same university where they now both served, Max as the associate dean of the Hobbs College and Phin as the esteemed associate professor of the Sam and Martha Goldman Chair of Preaching and Pastoral Ministry.

"Look, I've got to go take care of a few things...and then we all chipped in and got you a gift we want you to open."

"Max, you shouldn't have - "

"Nonsense, ol' buddy! Just hold tight and I'll be back in a few, but first, I think someone would like to say hello."

Max shoved a phone into Phin's hand and hurried away. Phin looked at the screen and saw what looked like a video cued up and ready for him to press play. Trying to block out the noise around him, Phin turned the volume to max and hit the little triangle in the middle of the screen. There was some jostling and erratic movement, and then the face of a square-jawed soldier with a crew cut filled up the screen. As if talking to someone else, the gruff voice began to bark, "This gadget on?...What do I do now?... Oh... okay, 10-4.... You there, Doc? They're giving me the thumbs up so I'm just gonna talk.... So, uh, it's me. Ol' Sarge. But I guess you know that by now. So... yeah... so... happy

birthday, Doc. Hope it's a good one... yeah... Sarge out."
More jostling of the camera. "Is that it? What do I do
now? Oh..." And then the playback stopped. Sergeant
Billy Warren. Phin smiled. Maybe one of the best birthday
greetings he'd ever received given who the sender was.

"Excuse me, Phin. Just wanted to shake your hand and
wish you a happy birthday as well."

Phin lifted his head and the look of surprise must have
been evident. Dr. Clayton Reynolds was smiling and took
Phin's hand in a warm embrace. Phin had not expected the
dean of the Hobbs College to be here as well, but here he
was nevertheless. Phin was genuinely touched.

"Dean Reynolds, how good of you to come." And
Phin meant it. He and Clayton Reynolds had not always
been on the best of terms. Phin had a penchant for what
the dean deemed erratic and unpredictable behavior, and
Phin's personal interests and pursuits did not always align
with the vision and mission of the university. But the
tension between the two had cooled considerably in the last
year with the return of Phin's wife, Autumn, the couple
becoming new parents of their adopted son, Patrick, and
Phin's promise to pursue a quieter pace of life.

"I wouldn't have missed it, really." Even in a social
setting Dean Reynolds was imposing. His six foot plus
frame capped with a head of salt and pepper hair gave the
man an ever-present air of authority, even without his
normal uniform of a suit and tie. "Listen, Phin, I won't be
staying long."

"Yes, of course, I understand. You must have had a
busy day, I know." Phin didn't mean to cut the dean off,

but for some reason his nerves had kicked in. Maybe it was the look on the dean's face or something in his eye.

Dean Reynolds smiled and continued, "Oh, all days are the same this time of year and we are all busy, aren't we? As I was saying, I can't stay long, but I wonder if I might have a quick word." He nodded toward the open door to his office. "I don't want to take you from your party and it won't take long. I promise."

The dean began to move toward his office and it was clear Phin had no choice in the matter. Not that he minded. His interest was peaked. Very rarely did Dean Clayton Reynolds go out of his way to engage Phin one-on-one, so it must be a matter of some importance. Phin moved to follow and just happened to look back over his shoulder. Autumn was looking at him from across the room, a look of concern on her face. She'd seen the exchange. Phin mouthed the words, *don't worry*. He followed with a wink and ducked into the dean's office.

Dean Reynolds was already seated at his personal conference table holding a manilla folder. "Have a seat, Phin. We've got a small problem and we think you might be just the person to help us with it."

Chapter 5

*W*e, thought Phin. *Who is we?*

And the idea of being pulled into a problem of any sort was not the kind of birthday he had been aiming for. A day of teaching classes, a few advising appointments, a nice dinner with his wife - that had been the plan. The surprise party was a nice touch, and while unnecessary for a man turning thirty-six, he knew it meant a lot to Autumn and so he was happy to go along. She'd missed so much the last few years and was working to make up for lost time. But sitting in the dean's office about to be presented a problem had not been on the radar when the day began.

"Go ahead and have a seat, Phin." Dean Reynolds likely sensed Phin's hesitancy. "I promise this won't take long. I need to bring you in the loop and to get your opinion."

Not that he had a choice at this point, he was the dean after all, but Phin was a sucker for a good mystery and the cryptic nature of how Reynolds was speaking to him was beginning to draw him. And who doesn't want to be "in the loop" and to give their "opinion" when someone higher up the food chain comes asking for help? Phin inwardly chided himself for his earlier attitude and took a seat across from Dean Reynolds.

"Absolutely, Clayton. What can I do to help? You mentioned a problem?" Since Dean Reynolds called Phin by his first name, he typically returned the gesture in private settings. It always felt a bit unnatural to do so – Reynolds was such an imposing figure – but Phin forced himself to do so anyway. Reynolds – Clayton – didn't seem to mind.

"What I'm about to share with you is sensitive and you will understand what I mean once I begin. It goes without saying that I need your confidentiality on this matter."

"Absolutely. No need to worry. I'll follow your lead in however you direct on this."

Reynolds smiled and continued. "As you know, the university has just gone through another round of budget cuts." Phin's heart sank. Any optimism he had mustered up began to fade. "The school is going through a season, Phin. Nothing to be too concerned about and nothing any other institution similar to ours isn't facing. The climbing cost of education makes it harder for parents to afford and thus makes the competition for new students that much more fierce. What we need at OBU is a competitive advantage. Something that sets us apart from all others. Are you following me, Phin?"

Phin nodded. He was following, he just had no clue where Reynolds was going.

"So there have been discussions. President MacDonald himself has been spearheading the talks. They were actually his idea. I was hesitant at first but it really does all make sense."

Phin was no longer following. He wrinkled his brow, trying to make sense of what Reynolds was talking about and how it could possibly have anything to do with him.

"Make sense?" Phin interrupted. "What makes sense?"

"The Garden of Eden."

Reynolds uttered the name cautiously and then sat back to see how Phin would respond. Phin was stunned. Shocked. He thought his heart would rupture as his blood pressure soared.

"I'm sorry...the Garden of Eden?" he was able to stammer. "What about the Garden of Eden?"

"Well..." Reynolds began, clearing his throat into his fist. "We know, obviously, where it's located. Or I suppose I should say, you know where it's located. The president would like to establish a Center for Modern Biblical Exploration. Not formal archaeology per se, but something a bit more novel. This new center would lean heavily on the biblical text, something that our Baptist tradition is convinced is the inspired Word of God. That means it is true and trustworthy. That means we can read it and when it talks about matters of geography, those places...those locations are accessible to us today. They can be explored in their modern context and written about. This is all still a loose concept as of right now, but President MacDonald believes that the Center for Modern Biblical Exploration, if promoted correctly, would be something wholly unique in the world of private Christian academia and would bring national and international attention to the school. That would do nothing but help with institutional development - aka *giving* - and enrollment."

Dean Reynolds paused to allow Phin time to consider what he was saying and hopefully catch the vision.

His head was still spinning and he unceremoniously blurted out, "So what does this have to do with the Garden of Eden?"

Reynolds nodded. "We would like to make the Garden of Eden the first project of the new center. There is so much that could be written about it-"

"Absolutely not." Phin raised his voice louder than he intended, cutting off his boss. "There's no way, Clayton. You and MacDonald both know this. The legal team from LaPhage was crystal clear and we are bound by confidentiality. Nobody is allowed to talk about the garden. Can't write about it. Can't say anything at all about my and Max's trip there. Period. The whole subject is off limits."

Phin's exploration of the Garden of Eden had been the most harrowing experience of his life. And it had almost taken his life, and the life of his best friend Max Allred, and also a former student of his, Jason Morris. It actually *did* take the life of Ruth LaPhage, the CEO of LaPhage Industries, the entity that had financed the whole operation to find the garden. Ruth's body had never even been recovered and neither had Tony Chen's body, another casualty of the garden whose life ended in a brutal fashion. The Garden of Eden was forbidden in more than one sense.

By LaPhage Industries. And by God. It was a dangerous place.

"Yes, we understand that LaPhage Industries has locked out all discussion, publications, etc. of everything that happened at the garden. You can't even talk about ever going there. But, listen Phin, our own attorneys have examined the documents that were signed." Dean Reynolds's excitement was growing and the pit in Phin's stomach was sinking even further. "It's complicated, of course, but the short answer is this: You and us...the school...we are all prevented from acknowledging what happened in the past with the Garden of Eden. But there is no language that says we cannot go back. Obviously, you are the key to this, Phin. You're the only one that truly knows where it is. You and Max, of course, but you are the one who found it. You did all the research on it. There is nothing in the LaPhage legalese that prohibits *future* exploration. So, we go back, Phin. You lead the way. You write it all up. You get the publishing credit. And OBU benefits. We say nothing at all about your previous trip. LaPhage Industries is never mentioned. It will be as if that trip never happened, which is what LaPhage wants. It's a win-win. President MacDonald is convinced that he has a donor who would pay for the whole operation if you agree. What do you say, Phin? Are you ready to go back?"

Phin ran his hand though his floppy brown hair, a habit when he was stressed or thinking. Clayton Reynolds was not an easy man to spar with. "This can't happen," he began slowly. He looked Reynolds in the eye, matching his gaze. "Clayton, people died in the garden. It's a forbidden place. I never understood that before. Until I went. We can't...I can't do this."

Dean Reynolds looked sympathetic. He was surely disappointed with Phin's response, and for a moment Phin thought he'd succeeded in dissuading the man.

"I understand this is hard, Phin. Everything you've said I anticipated." *Of course you have,* Phin mentally barked to himself. *You're Clayton Reynolds. You anticipate everything.* "You are a vital part of our OBU family, Phin. We don't want you doing anything that would jeopardize life or limb. The LaPhage exploration was haphazard and sloppy. You would be in charge this time, Phin. You would call the shots. Go, but only go as close as is safe and no closer. Photograph and video what you can but take no chances. Fly drones over the garden and capture what you are able to on video. Anything is better than nothing. It will be completely different than before."

Clearly nothing Phin could say would stop this train from moving down the tracks. The whole scenario was nearly laughable to Phin. It wasn't but a year ago that he sat in this very office, chided for even believing the Garden of Eden still existed. His very job was on the line, he was told, if he continued to pursue his interests in finding the garden. An embarrassment to the institution, he was. And now that same institution was counting on him to steer it through a rough season. He was no longer an embarrassment. He was valuable. And the same man who once questioned him was now pleading with him.

"I don't know, Clayton. I need to think about it. Talk to Autumn. You understand." What he really needed was to get out of this office and buy himself some time to figure a way out of this mess. He needed to talk to Max. Max would understand. He'd been there too, seen the beauty and horror of it all.

"Yes, of course. Take some time. No rush. I've already taken more of your birthday than I intended."

Phin shook hands with the dean and left the office to rejoin his party. A few people had left but most were still mingling. Phin noticed a confused looking FedEx delivery man standing by the elevator. He had just exited and was looking around the crowd for someone in charge. Phin made his way to the young man.

"Can I help you?"

"Yeah, I've got a package for a Dr. Phineas Crook. Had a full route today so I'm running late. I normally deliver packages to the student center but this one had specific instructions to deliver to Montgomery Hall. Saw the lights so thought I'd give it a shot."

"Well, you're in luck. Or I suppose I'm in luck. I'm Dr. Crook."

The FedEx employee seemed relieved to hand the package over and hustle on his way.

"What have you got there, Hon?" Autumn arrived at his side, taking his arm.

"Oh, looks like a package intent on finding its way directly to my office. I'm sure it's some vendor peddling software or the next great piece of media technology. It can wait."

But Phin failed to put the package aside. Instead, he turned the shoebox-sized parcel over in his hands, looking for some clue as to the sender. It was wrapped in plain brown paper and had no markings of any kind except for the standard FedEx stickers and postage label. He found himself popping loose the tape on one end and removing the wrapping. Max Allred joined the pair, a look of curiosity on his face.

The paper cast aside revealed a shiny hunter green box made of a light material that felt like basal wood. A lid included delicate gold hinges and a latch that clicked open with the slide of Phin's thumb. He set the box on a small table that had an assortment of pamphlets featuring the college's degree programs and an upcoming mission trip.

Perhaps this was not the time or the place to open the box but Phin felt he'd come too far to turn back. The presence of his wife and friend served to urge him on. With only a slight tremor in his hand, Phin lifted the lid and was met with a curious sight. The interior was layered in cotton and sitting on top, as if supported by a cloud, was a sliver of some sort of hardwood. Phin stared at the gnarled sliver the size of an overly large spike.

A gasp and Autumn was pointing at the underside of the box's lid. "Phin look."

A message painted in black script read:

Happy Birthday, Little Brother. Are you ready to play a game?
                                                    -Remus

Chapter 6

Phin scratched his head. He picked up the shard of wood for the hundredth time and turned it over in his hands. It was about six inches long, pointed one end, and perhaps two inches wide on the other. It truly did resemble a large nail, but the overall shape looked more accidental rather than something fashioned on purpose. It was obviously very old, ancient even, and was pitted and rutted all over, though it had clearly been handled extensively. The whole thing had a dull smoothness to it.

"What do you think it is?" asked Autumn.

"I haven't the faintest clue," Phin answered without taking his eyes off the piece.

The couple was sitting on the couch in the living room of their cozy little home on Broadway Avenue in Shawnee, Oklahoma. After the shock of the gift - both the sender and the shard itself - Phin had quickly closed the lid to the box and shuffled it to his office. He'd rejoined the remainder of the party — his own birthday party — and did his best to enjoy the occasion. Autumn had put a lot of effort into the surprise and his closest friends and colleagues were all there. As difficult as it was to push thoughts of the box and its contents out of his mind, he had succeeded. Many stories were told, light snacks, cake, and punch were shared, and then the whole thing eventually broke up with the guests headed home for the evening.

Phin couldn't wait to gather the box and rush home with it, as if it were some treasure that wasn't "safe" out in the public domain. It was a silly notion, he knew, but there was a security about being in the privacy of his own house with something like this, whatever *this* was. Given that the gift was from his brother, Remus, was indication enough that this was no benign sliver of wood. No, whatever this was and wherever it came from, there was a meaning to it all.

"Let me get this straight," Max interrupted Phin's interlude of contemplation. Having seen the shard and the note, he asked if he could join Phin and Autumn at their house, and Phin couldn't refuse him. He'd been pacing around the small living room, contemplating the strange gift himself. "You've not heard from Remus at all in the last six months? And then you get...this?" He pointed at the object in Phin's hands.

"More like ten months, Max. That's the last time I saw Remus. When I visited him at the Big Mac. That's when we were having that strange dream connection. But once that ended, I've heard nothing from him. All I got six months ago was the note from the prison saying that he'd escaped. But nothing from Remus directly. The state police paid me a visit, questioned me, and all that. They were pretty sure he'd reach out to me at some point, but so far nothing."

"Until today."

"Yeah, until today."

The dream connection he referred to was a phenomenon that Phin still could not explain. There was a supernatural element to it all, he was convinced. He and Remus had been tied together for a period of months, sharing the same dream. A nightmare, really, of both men being tortured and hung on crosses. Phin bristled every time he recalled those months of horror and restless nights and the physical pain that followed him into his waking hours. Setting the shard of wood back in its box, Phin rubbed the palms of his hands as if massaging away the memory.

"Max, there's something I need to confide in you. About the dreams and about me and Remus. Something I've not shared with anyone except Autumn. But you deserve to know and...I don't know, maybe it all has something to do with this...game Remus wants to play."

Max Allred had known for many years that Phineas Crook came from a family of literal thieves – crooks. Phin had confided this family secret to his friend a long time ago. It took some convincing, but Phin's father had passed on a record that traced the family heritage back to the founding of the United States. What Max did not know, and what Phin only discovered in the last year, was that the family heritage went back further than the founding of the nation. Much further.

Phin's nightmares and a visit with his brother, Remus, who was still locked up at the time, spurred Phin on to do something he'd sworn he would never do: visit the Crook family archives located in the city of Jerusalem. Phin had sworn off his family's thieving ways, and had disappointed his brother in the process. He wanted nothing to do with the family archives. But the nightmares compelled him to seek them out. And it was there, in an ancient chamber below the city streets of the Holy City, that the truth finally came out. The records were meticulous. Volumes of bound registries tracing the Crook family lineage back - all the way back - to its point of origin. It was a stunning discovery. One that Phin himself had not fully come to terms with.

Phin's family – the Crook family – began with two brothers, both thieves. Both convicted and both sentenced to death. On crosses. It was just by chance, or more likely Divine providence, Phin knew, that the two brothers were scheduled to be executed by the Roman government on the same day as another convicted criminal. That man's crime: claiming to be a king in a world where everyone knew that only Caesar was king. Insurrection, that's what this other man was convicted of. His name: Jesus of Nazareth.

Max Allred sat in stunned silence as Phin recounted the tale. Staring at the floor, his mouth gaped open, the college professor finally found his tongue. "This...this is all true you are telling me? You and Remus are the actual descendants of the two thieves crucified with Christ?"

Phin nodded.

"Holy...wow...wow. It's so hard to believe. I mean...I

don't believe it, but I do. Only because it's you, Phin. And you've got proof of this?"

"Yes, well I know where the proof is. As I said, in Jerusalem."

"I can't believe this, my best friend is a walking piece of history."

Phin laughed. "We all are descended from someone, Max. I'm not any more special than anyone else. My family just happens to be...I don't know...."

"Infamous, Phin. That's what your family is."

"There's more though," Autumn broke in. "You need to tell him the rest, Hon. How this all ties into Remus and you."

"Of course," Max replied. "There's more. What was I thinking? We're talking about Phineas Crook. There's always more, isn't there?"

Phin smiled. "Well...yes, and here's what Autumn's talking about. So, the archives," he began.

"The archives that show you are related to the thieves on the cross." Max was still incredulous.

"Yes, the archives are very detailed, Max. They clearly record that in every generation of Crooks, from the two brothers who were crucified all the way until today, there are always two brothers who are born." Phin let this revelation sink in. He could tell Max was struggling to put it all together. "Two, Max," Phin repeated. "There is never just one. Sometimes twin boys are born. Sometimes the brothers are separated by a few years in age."

"Like you and Remus."

"That's right. Sometimes there's a girl mixed in. But there is never just one boy and never three. Always and only...two. And get this, each and every one of these generations of Crooks were active thieves, involved all over the world in all manner of indiscretions. But I found something really curious."

Max raised his eyebrows as if to say, *go on.*

Phin did. "Every once in a while - there's no rhyme or reason I could find - but now and then, there would be one of the two boys who would choose to not participate in the family business, so to speak. Who chose to do something honest and more honorable."

"Like you."

Phin shrugged his shoulders. "In each of these instances, the archives stopped recording that branch of the family. As if that individual wasn't worth noting any longer."

"Just. Like. You." Max repeated more loudly, each word with emphasis.

"And Remus," Autumn added. "History is repeating itself with Phin and Remus. My husband is the good thief and Remus is...well."

"And just like the thieves on the cross railed at each other...well, you and Remus haven't always gotten along." Max was putting it all together.

"We've had our scrapes like most brothers, that's true. But Remus *is* my brother, and I love him. Something happened to me while I was in the Crook family archives. At the moment that it all came together, I passed out. It's hard to explain. I had a vision of sorts. That's the best way to say it, I guess. But Remus was there too. I think he must have experienced the same thing I did from his cell down at the prison. After that, I've heard nothing from him."

"Until today," Max stated.

"Yes...until today." Phin's attention drifted back to the strange box that had arrived by courier.

"What does he mean by: Are you ready to play a game?" Autumn asked.

"I have no idea." By instinct, Phin picked up the shard of wood and set it aside. A tickling in the back if his mind drew his attention to the mound of white fluffy cotton on which the shard had rested. He reached down and began to carefully peel the cotton away, layer by layer, setting it on the coffee table along with the shard. When he reached the bottom of the box his eyes grew wide, taking hold of an old photograph - two school aged boys standing in front of a modest brick house.

"What is it, Phin? What's it a picture of?" Max's voice was urgent.

"It's a picture of our house in Moore, Oklahoma. The place where Remus and I grew up." Phin lifted his head to look at his wife and best friend. "Remus wants me to go home."

Chapter 7

Dimitri Bezrukov stood at the front of the auction hall, his eyes not leaving the gentleman sitting on the back row. The head of Dominion Safe would normally not involve himself in the supervision of the weekly auction held by Token Exchange, but Alexander Pontia had requested his involvement on this day.

The featured attraction was a complete scroll of the Old Testament Book of Esther, which was being advertised as a previously unknown portion of the Dead Sea Scrolls. The Dead Sea Scrolls had been discovered in 1947 when three Bedouin shepherd boys were scurrying around the caves of Qumran, located some distance from the city of Jerusalem in what the Bible would have called the Judean wilderness. It was more like a desert. The young men were bored and, boys being boys, started tossing rocks up into the caves. That is until one of them heard the sound of breaking pottery. The boys clamored up the cliff face to the cave, only to find some worn out looking rolls of parchment inside a broken pottery jar which they promptly gathered and eventually sold for $28 at a market in Bethlehem. One of those scrolls ended up being the oldest complete copy of the Old Testament Book of Isaiah ever discovered, over one thousand years older than any previously discovered copy of the prophetic book.

What came next was a scramble among archaeologists and the government, of what at the time was Palestine, to secure the site from looters and to uncover what exactly it was the earth had been hiding for two thousand years. As it turned out, a chain of multiple caves contained a treasure trove of scrolls and scroll fragments that had been copied and preserved by an ancient Jewish sect known as the Essenes.

This collection of scrolls became known as the Dead Sea Scrolls, the greatest single collection of biblical material ever discovered. The Dead Sea Scrolls collectively contained copies of every book of the Old Testament except for one. The Book of Esther. Most scholars felt this made sense since the Book of Esther is the only Old Testament book to not contain the name of God. Some biblical linguists have even argued that the Book of Esther should not be included in the canon of Scripture at all because of this. Nevertheless, the idea of its inspiration has endured these criticisms.

A few scholars, however, wondered if the Book of Esther was indeed part of the original Dead Sea Scroll collection, having been pilfered off by looters or some unsavory opportunist during the early days of the Qumran cave exploration. It was widely known that other scroll fragments had found their way to the black market, only to slowly be reacquired since 1947. Perhaps the Book of Esther fit into this category.

Dimitri Bezrukov didn't know anything about any of this and he didn't really care. All he knew was that the Book of Esther was up for auction with the purported origin of it being one of the Dead Sea Scrolls. It had survived initial scrutiny after it was brought to Token Exchange by the known Egyptian antiquities dealer, Tyrell Lapis. Additional verification of the scroll's authenticity would be a subject of much debate in the months ahead. Tyrell Lapis was a man with shady underworld connections, which didn't help matters much. But he was a friend of Alexander Pontia, and the furor around the scroll's appearance indicated a likely selling price of more than ten million dollars. An extraordinary amount for such an item.

The auction had drawn a cadre of characters for the bidding, some of them unsavory and some of them not. The head of New York's MET had made the short trip across town for the auction, but so had members of many of the leading museums around the world: the Louvre, the National Gallery, the Padro, the Rijksmuseum, and even the Vatican.

There were also black market dealers in the room. Most of them were known players to Dimitri, but a few he had never seen before. The man sitting on the back row held his attention in particular. He was dressed in a black wool peacoat, which was unusual being that it was May. His head was covered in a scraggly mane of black hair and his face sported a pair of oversized Ray Bans that he'd not once removed. This was not necessarily out of the ordinary in and of itself, a lot of people wore sunglasses indoors. It seemed like the trend had begun with Bono of U2, thought Dimitri. And there were a few others in the room with sunglasses as well. But there was something about this individual in particular that bothered Dimitri Bezrukov.

The man in the black coat had arrived just as the first item of the day went up for auction. It was some vase from Tibet. Again, Dimitri didn't care, but he noticed the man immediately as he settled into a back row chair. His years in the Russian intelligence agency, GRU, had trained him to spot that which didn't belong. And in Dimitri's estimation, the man in the black coat did not belong. Using his in-ear headpiece, Dimitri called for the name of the man. He had registered as James T. Kirk. Dimitri scowled at the revelation. Again, it was not unusual for clients of Token Exchange to register with false names, especially if items were bound for the underground after purchase, but to be so flippant as to use the name of the famous science fiction captain from Star Trek, well, Dimitri viewed it as a bold move. A thumbing of the nose.

The bidding through the minor items progressed as did the morning. Captain Kirk did not attempt a bid on a single item. This only added to Dimitri's suspicions. The high profile bidders trickled into the auction hall of Token Exchange as the morning moved along and time grew closer for bidding on the Esther scroll.

The moment arrived.

"And now, ladies and gentlemen," boomed the heavily accented voice of auctioneer Fredrich Imka. The native South African was an international figure in the world of antiquities. He'd been hired by Token Exchange specifically for this event. "Our final item up for bid today is a complete scroll of the biblical Book of Esther. Its origins are the Dead Sea Scroll collection, which was discovered in 1947. This particular item has been dated at circa 200 B.C., making it one of the oldest copies of this ancient book in existence today. I must say it is an impressive artifact sure to be the prize of any collector or institution. Your brief contains all the specifics of the scroll. Bidding will now begin at the $2 million mark."

Placards shot up around the packed room.

"Yes, number 14 has the bid." It was Jeremiah Shank, a lone collector who lived in Argentina. Dimitri knew him well. *Nice try, Jeremiah*, Dimitri smiled. He would not be taking home the prize, the security chief knew. He'd be easily outbid in short order and not be able to keep up.

Within five minutes the bid on the Esther scroll hit the $6 million mark and Jeremiah Shank excused himself from the hall. He was not alone, as a number of others, seeing the futility of their effort – and bank account – followed suit. Others were no longer in the running but stayed to see who *would* land the prized scroll.

Bidding accelerated to $9 million, driven by representatives from the Vatican, the Louvre, and two private individuals registered under faux names. The Vatican bidder was the most animated of the bunch, Dimitri observed. He also noted that the man in the black wool coat on the back row had not bid once. *Why are you here?* the Russian questioned as he squinted at the man.

The price moved past $10.5 million and came to a halt. The representative from the Louvre, a stern-looking French woman that Dimitri did not know, held the high position. The man from the Vatican was on his cell phone, getting instructions from someone close to the pope in Italy, no doubt.

"Ten-five is the current bid," Fredrich Imka called out. "Do I have ten-seven-five?"

Silence. The French woman wore a thin smile. The Italian wiped his forehead, phone still pressed to his ear, waiting. Everyone was waiting. The tension in the air was thick. This was the moment. Dimitri knew it. He'd seen it a hundred times before. It was almost over.

"Number 25!" shouted the South African auctioneer. "We have $10.75 million."

Heads whipped to the back row.

Captain Kirk was holding up his placard.

Dimitri Bezrukov felt the heat in his face rise. *Why do I care?* He scolded himself. *He's here to bid just like anyone else.* But the man in the Ray Bans wasn't just like anyone else and the thick Russian knew it. He could feel it. Like a sixth sense.

The French woman scrambled, punching speed dial on her own phone.

The Italian representative from the Vatican looked defeated. The Catholics had hit their limit apparently.

"I have a standing bid from Number 25 for ten-seven-five. That's $10.75 million. Do I hear -"

"Eleven million!" the French woman called out, not even attempting to raise her placard. She seemed to have lost her previous sense of decorum, likely nervous that her prize was slipping away.

"Number 42 has called the raise. The current bid is eleven. Do I have eleven-one?"

Silence once again.

The French woman stared back at the man in the black coat.

"*Come on*, Captain Kirk. What's your next move?" muttered Dimitri under his breath.

The figure sat stoically.

"I have $11 million. Going once. Going twice." A long pause as the room collectively inhaled. "SOLD! The Esther scroll goes to the lady from the Louvre. Congratulations, Madame."

The room broke out in applause. The representative from the Lourve looked both relieved and proud. People began to gather their belongings and move toward the exit.

The man on the back row rose, moved to the side aisle, and began a casual walk toward the front of the hall. Toward the Book of Esther scroll.

"What is this?" Dimitri said aloud, instinctively patting his concealed sidearm.

"*Come again, boss. What is that you said?*" The security chief's in-ear piece crackled. He'd apparently been holding the talk switch without realizing it.

"Everyone hold your positions," he replied back. "We may have a situation."

But the man in the black coat wasn't moving toward the scroll after all. He was moving instead toward...Dimitri Bezrukov. He walked boldly up to the beefy Russian, removed his Ray-Bans, and stuck out his hand.

"Nice to see you again, Dimitri. Why don't we go somewhere more private."

Chapter 8

"Remus Crook!" Dimitri Bezrukov stammered. "What on earth...what are you doing here? This is much too public a place for you. Come, we must leave at once."

The Russian grabbed the arm of the smiling Remus, ushering him quickly behind the black curtain that ran the length of the front of the auction hall. It was a bustle of activity backstage and Dominion Safe security personnel were plentifully scattered, overseeing the packaging of items won from the auction. Straight Line shipping vans were waiting outside to immediately begin the process of ferrying the day's bounty to all parts of the world.

Dimitri, with Remus Crook in tow, pushed through the organized scramble, made his way to a back hallway, and then ducked into a video surveillance room occupied by a bank of monitors and two Dominion Safe employees.

"Out. Now," the security chief demanded.

"But..." one of the men said, standing, a look of confusion on his face.

"OUT."

The two men complied in short order, leaving Remus and Dimitri alone. The Russian slammed the door and whipped around.

"Remus, what is the meaning of this? You cannot be here, Comrade. You are a known thief!"

"Relax, *Comrade*. I'm not here. James T. Kirk is." It was a flippant reply.

"I am serious, my friend. You are wanted as well. All of law enforcement is looking for you."

"I said relax, will you? I'm here because there are no cops at Token Exchange, only you guys. *Dominion Safe*. And besides, no one will recognize me. Heck, even you didn't recognize me, did you? Come on, you can admit it." Remus stepped back, holding his hands out to his side in a proud pose.

It was true. It had never crossed Dimitri Bezrukov's mind that he had been staring at Remus Crook for nearly two hours. The man looked wholly different. The Remus Crook he'd known was bald with a stark goatee, muscles and tattoos covering his arms, always in a short-sleeved shirt so as to show off both. This version of Remus Crook had lost weight, grown his hair out, and shaved. The out-of-place wool coat served to cover his distinct markings, although a long-sleeved shirt would have done the job as effectively, he thought.

Dimitri relaxed, realizing that Remus was right. He still didn't like the unannounced appearance. "Why today, of all days, have you come to us, Comrade? You could have reached out using the phone we gave you and we could have made arrangements."

"It's been six months. Today. That was the plan, remember? And I knew you and Alexander would both be here...today. So, I came. I'll admit, too, I wanted to test you. See if you'd recognize me, which clearly, you did not."

"That is true." Dimitri nodded his thick, stubbled head. "But you *did* stick out. I knew immediately...the moment you walked in, that you did not belong. We had surveillance on you the whole time. It is not wise, my friend. You must be more careful."

"Okay, noted. Next time, I'll dress for the weather. No more wool coat. So, let's get down to business. Where's Pontia? It's time we officially meet and prepare for our next move."

Dimitri nodded and the two exited the monitoring room, much to the relief of the two security personnel who quickly ducked back in and resumed their duties. The head of Dominion Safe ushered Remus down an extended hallway to a private elevator, which deposited the two men two floors up at the offices of Token Exchange. Alexander Pontia was present, along with a gaggle of businessmen, all of different ethnicities, most of them being winning bidders on one of the catalogue of items for the day. He looked up at the arrival of his chief of security, eyed Remus, and frowned ever so slightly. Recovering quickly, he resumed his charismatic smile and excused himself from the group. A quick jerk of his head indicated, "In my office, now."

Once the three were behind closed doors, Dimitri spoke first. "I am sorry for taking you away, Alexander, but...allow me to introduce you to Remus Crook."

Remus cocked his head and gave a sly smile at the introduction.   Alexander Pontia stared at the escaped convict, measuring the man up.

"Amazing," he finally muttered. "So, you are *the* Remus Crook.   I would never have recognized you.   Dimitri Bezrekov speaks very highly of you. It is a pleasure to make your acquaintance, Mr. Crook.   Finally."   He extended his hand, taking Remus's in a warm embrace. He didn't seem bothered at all that Remus had appeared unannounced in such a public fashion.

"The pleasure is all mine, I assure you. I've waited six long months to formally thank you for all your efforts in springing me from the fine care of the State of Oklahoma. It was a big risk, I know, and I promise you won't be disappointed."

The plot had been hatched nearly ten months prior. Alexander Pontia had confided in his head of security about an ambitious plan, the likes of which he had never attempted before. One that would require specialized skill, in particular the skill of a master thief. Dimitri knew of just such a man.

Dimitri Bezrukov and Remus Crook had a history that predated Dimitri's association with Alexander Pontia. When both were young men, they had crossed paths in a most dramatic fashion. Dimitri had been newly recruited by the GRU, and Remus had been hired by a wealthy Russian dissident named Boris Ivanov to infiltrate Vladimir Putin's personal residence to steal a dossier of financial information that would supposedly be very embarrassing to the Russian president if it was to be made public. Remus didn't know exactly what was in the dossier and he didn't care. It was a job, plain and simple. And it paid well.

But the whole operation was a setup. Putin wanted Boris Ivanov's head. He had planted the whole story about a damaging dossier knowing Ivanov would come for it. The plan was to catch the thief in the act and then turn him in order to deliver Ivanov's head on a platter.

Dimitri Bezrukov had been chosen to lead the operation. It was his first opportunity to prove his loyalty and worth to the Motherland.

Remus Crook had indeed been caught in the act of stealing the dossier. It had been in a secure safe, behind a portrait of Lenin in Putin's personal study in his home. Just like in the movies. Dimitri Bezrukov was waiting for him, watching the whole time, waiting until the safe had been breached and the fake dossier was in hand.

After working Remus Crook over in a most brutal fashion and then tying him to a chair, the young Russian GRU agent explained the *new* plan. Dimitri Bezrukov and his team would follow Remus Crook to the delivery location where he was to meet Boris Ivanov. That's when the arrest would be made. Remus inquired about how much they were willing to pay for this betrayal. The answer: his life. He thought that was a reasonable offer and accepted.

But then the new plan didn't go according to plan. At least not for Dimitri Bezrukov. Remus Crook led the strike team to the rendezvous location for Ivanov, a warehouse in a seedy part of Moscow. But there was no Boris Ivanov. And then, inexplicably, there was no Remus Crook. It was as if he had vanished. The warehouse had been surrounded on all sides. A thorough search ensued, but no Remus Crook ever turned up.

For his part, Remus delivered the dossier to Boris Ivanov at the real rendezvous point and received his generous payment. He didn't care that it was fake. He'd done the job he was paid to do and Ivanov would find out soon enough that the information was useless. Sure, he'd be angry, but not at Remus.

But Remus wasn't done yet. Two days later, Dimitri Bezrukov received in the mail a manila folder with pictures. Compromising pictures of the Russian president with women who were not his wife. Remus Crook, it appeared, had been more active while he was robbing the Putin household than anyone would ever have suspected. Remus was asked what his price was to keep the pictures a secret. His life, came the reply. And $1 million. Remus thought it was a bargain for the Russian government and they agreed.

From that day forward, Dimitri Bezrukov had the utmost respect for Remus Crook. And when he discovered the thief was incarcerated in the Oklahoma State Penitentiary, along with the knowledge of what Alexander Pontia had planned, he knew the two were a match made in heaven.

Chapter 9

"Well, now that we are all together for the first time, let us sit down and discuss the future, shall we?" Alexander Pontia led his security chief and his hired thief to a small table in the corner of the office ringed by four comfortable chairs.

"Let me say again, thank you for springing me from the Big Mac. And for the money and resources while I've stayed off the grid."

"You are most welcome, Mr. Crook. But I simply supplied the conditions for your escape. I believe that some measure of skill was still required by you in order to make your exit from the care of the people of Oklahoma a reality." Alexander smiled.

"Well, as I said, you've been very generous and I am grateful."

"Yes, and to that point, my generosity is not without certain expectations. Expectations we are now in a position to discuss."

Remus Crook nodded. It was time to get down to business.

The whole series of events that led to their current meeting in New York began just over six months ago when Dimitri Bezrukov parked his Land Rover in the parking lot of the Oklahoma State Penitentiary. He checked in as one, Daniel Parker of Muskogee, there to visit prisoner Remus Crook.

Remus accepted the request from the unknown Daniel Parker because he was bored that day and no one ever visited, except his brother Phineas, twice a year. Maybe.

When Remus took his seat and stared across the table at Dimitri Bezrukov, his eyes grew wide. It was the first time he'd seen the Russian since he'd played him for a fool years earlier.

The Russians had lived up to their end of the bargain, leaving Remus alone. And he'd lived up to his end as well. The compromising pictures of the Russian president never surfaced.

But had something changed?

Remus was instantly on edge.

If Dimitri had come to finish what had been started all those years ago, if this was the end for Remus, then he'd been perfectly played. He wondered for a brief moment how Dimitri would do it. He knew the Russians were fond of poisoning people they didn't like.

Is that how he was to die this day?

Some exotic powder blown in his face?

There was nowhere for him to run, and he had no way of retrieving and releasing the photographs.

But Dimitri Bezrukov had not come to relive old grudges or to settle the matter in a final sort of manner. No. Dimitri was there to help Remus Crook escape. The Russian no longer worked for the GRU. He was now a mercenary for a man named Alexander Pontia. A great man with many resources and a grand idea for which he needed a man of Remus's particular skill set. If Remus was willing to play along, then a plan would be put into motion.

Dimitri Bezrukov had already planted two security guards in the penitentiary who were really Dominion Safe employees.

It was a very simple plan.

On a given day, the two guards would come to escort Remus to the infirmary for what would appear to be food poisoning. Once in the infirmary, Remus would "need" to go to the bathroom in order to be sick. A sack containing a guard's uniform would be waiting for him in the bathroom.

After a few minutes, one of the guards would go into the bathroom to check on Remus. Then the guard would exit, except it wouldn't be the guard. It would be Remus, dressed as a guard.

Remus would then leave the infirmary and move to the hallway to wait for exactly five minutes. That's when the guard in the bathroom would emerge, still in uniform. He would then join Remus in the hallway, leaving one guard to continue to supervise the now empty bathroom.

Of course, the whole operation would be monitored on video and they knew it. But they also knew that all the going in and out of the bathroom would look like the game kids play where a ball is under one of three cups. The cup is lifted, showing the ball, then the cups are shuffled while everyone watching tries to track which cup conceals the ball. The video would look "off," but the threesome would count on the hope that whoever was watching the monitors that day wouldn't be paying too close attention.

If the guard viewing the video feed did sense something was off, he would need to rewind the video and re-watch it a number of times before he figured it all out. In the meantime, Remus and the guard would simply clock out for the day and leave the prison.

The guard left behind would actually be the one who would go back into the bathroom in order to retrieve Remus's prison clothes and then sound the alarm. This would sufficiently divert the attention from him until he could also vanish while the prison was being searched, top to bottom, for the missing prisoner. By the time the whole puzzle was solved, all three would be long gone.

The designated day came and the escape went off without a hitch. Remus was given a car and a bag with clothes, money, and instructions. A safe house had been prearranged for him in Georgia. He was to live a quiet life there for six months. Pay for everything he needed in cash.

And he was given a list.

Alexander Pontia wanted to see what his effort had purchased, and if Remus Crook would be capable of the ultimate task for which he was being tapped. The list was a test. Five items that Alexander wanted to add to his collection. If Remus could acquire these items successfully, then in six months' time, after the furor around his escape had died down, Pontia and Remus Crook would meet face-to-face.

"And so, Mr. Crook, let us get down to business, shall we?" Alexander Pontia moved into a more formal posture.

"Please, just call me Remus, okay?"

"As you wish. So, Remus. The list. Let me say I am very pleased. Yes, pleased indeed. I had my doubts when Dimitri suggested we," Pontia paused, looking for the right word, "involve you," he finally continued. "But he was insistent that you were the man. And for what I would like to do, I need someone completely unrelated to myself or any of my ventures that are a part of Pilate Enterprises. You obviously are the perfect candidate."

Remus smiled and leaned back in his chair. "I am glad I can offer my services to someone who can truly appreciate them."

"Yes, well, as I said, I was skeptical. Which was the point of the list. I needed to see if you truly were as skilled as I had hoped."

"And are you pleased?"

"Oh, I am indeed. Exceedingly. When the Holy Sponge arrived four months ago, well let's just say, I was impressed. The Basilica di Giovanni in Rome is not an easy target."

Alexander was speaking of the two-thousand-year-old sponge that was purported to have been the very one lifted to the mouth of Christ while he hung on the cross.

"It was not a problem. Only took a week of planning to acquire it."

"And only a few weeks later the Reliquary of the Holy Crib arrived. As you can imagine, I was elated."

73

"That was a bit more challenging. The Basilica of Saint Mary Major housed the sticks of wood in a crypt the Catholics call the Confessio. They've got it right in front of the main altar. Lots of people in the day and cameras at night."

"Those sticks of wood, as you call them, are what is left of the manger where Christ, himself, lay as a baby."

"Sure, whatever." Remus's irreverence was evident.

"You moved so quickly on the first two items I began to think my little challenge wasn't challenging enough. But we received nothing more until three weeks later."

"The theft of the first two items created quite a stir. I figured I needed to let things cool down."

"This is true," Dimitri inserted. "You were wise, Comrade. The Catholic Church in Rome sought to keep the thefts as quiet as possible, but journalists were leaked word anyway. And my sources tell me the Church is frantic to recover the holy relics. They've engaged their full network, which has many ears and eyes, I can assure you. They are obviously scrambling to find them, but also hoping to be contacted at some point with an opportunity to purchase the items back."

Alexander laughed, his arrogance on display as he puffed his chest. "They can hope all they want. I can promise you, no such offer will come. I will never surrender the holy relics."

"So anyway," Remus continued his account, letting the Italian gloat, "I had to back off. Plus, I made up my mind that I needed to approach the remaining items differently. I didn't like the heat so I needed a way to turn it down. I've got...let's just call them...friends. I was able to lean on a few of them to produce copies."

"Forgeries!" Alexander blurted out. "I knew it. When the Holy Coat arrived, followed by the Holy Lance, I waited for the uproar, but there was none."

"That's because my copies are good. Very good. I've got very talented friends." Remus went on to brag about how he had handled the next two operations. He was as prideful of his trade as Alexander Pontia was of his own. The Holy Coat, claimed to be the seamless robe of Jesus Christ that was gambled over as he was led to the cross, had been housed in the Cathedral of Trier in Germany. The caretakers had been on alert because of the other thefts, but Germany was a long way from Rome and Bethlehem where the other thefts had occurred. And the robe itself was on clear display in an annex chapel. Taking the Holy Lance from Saint Peter's Basilica in Rome was a whole other ordeal altogether. The theft required a good deal of planning, engaging some more of Remus's friends, and even the payment of a few bribes on the inside. But he'd done it. He'd captured the relic that is said to have pierced the side of Christ while he hung on the cross.

"You and I think much alike, Remus." Alexander congratulated the master thief. "We have also relied on forgeries for other items that Dimitri has worked to obtain for my collection." He was thinking of the most recent acquisition of the Sudarium of Oviedo, the face cloth of Christ. "So, I find myself a bit puzzled."

"Puzzled?" Remus questioned.

"I assumed you would use a forgery as well when you stole the last item on the list, the most famous one, the

Shroud of Turin. But when I saw in the news that the Shroud had been taken, I thought perhaps you wanted to go out with a bang. It makes no matter at this point, but discretion might have been wiser."

"I didn't take the Shroud of Turin," Remus said flatly. Alexander stared at the thief, deadpanned. "Oh, I intended to. Had everything worked out, people paid off, etc. The forgery was excellent. But then," Remus wrinkled his own brow, confused, "I assumed you went ahead and took it without me, not that I was too happy about it. I'd put in a lot of work and expense. But that's why I came on in today. The last item on the list was marked off. But you're saying..."

"No, you're saying, Mr. Crook..." Alexander looked like a volcano about to erupt. "You're saying you didn't come here today to deliver the Shroud in person?"

"This is no time for games, Comrade." Dimitri Bezrukov leaned forward, the veins on his neck bulging.

"Easy boys." Remus held up his hands to deflect the sudden change in the room temperature. "No games. No Shroud. Sorry. I thought you took it without me. Look, if that blows the deal we had arranged I'm sorry. I can just be on my way."

"No, no. Of course not," Alexander said as he quelled his rage. "I just thought the whole time that it was you. But obviously...."

"There is another player in the game." Dimitri finished his boss's sentence for him.

Chapter 10

Remus Crook spent the remainder of the day learning about his new employer and the fantastic scheme for which he was specifically needed. It didn't matter that he'd arrived at Token Exchange unannounced; Alexander Pontia was delighted and had cancelled everything on his schedule. This was all Remus needed in order to be convinced that the matters for which he'd been sprung from prison were of the highest priority for the auction/security/shipping mogul.

Lunch had been ordered via a quick text. Thirty minutes later a cart arrived with steamed lobster tail, sauteed vegetables, and an assortment of warm breads. Water and tea were on tap. No alcohol before sundown, Alexander proclaimed. He needed to think clearly and he needed Remus and Dimitri thinking clearly with him.

Remus still wasn't sure what to think of his new boss. He clearly had resources and was willing to use them for any reason he deemed necessary. That part Remus didn't mind. He was much of the same mindset. But as lunch wore on, he couldn't shake the thought that there was more to Alexander Pontia than he let on, much more. Then again, Remus couldn't fault the man for that either. Remus Crook had his own agenda. Oh, yes, now that he was finally out of prison, there was a score that needed to be settled.

And then there was Dimitri Bezrukov. Remus remembered the Russian well. He'd suffered one of the worst beatings of his life under the meaty paws of the intelligence officer. Then Remus had embarrassed the man profoundly upon his escape all those many years ago. But it was more than an embarrassment for Dimitri Bezrukov. Remus discovered over lunch that the botched operation and near embarrassment of President Putin had cost Dimitri his career with the GRU. That began a long path of lonely depression for the proud Russian. He would go on to question his commitment to communism and eventually even his beloved Motherland, both of which had turned their back on him. Dimitri Bezrukov came to believe that the only person he could count on was Dimitri Bezrukov, a very western notion indeed. And then he met Alexander Pontia. What began as a relationship of simple monetary exchange – you pay me X and I will do Y – grew into one of mutual loyalty.

And now these two men were cracking lobster together, about to bring Remus Crook into a scheme that, ironically, would serve Remus's interests as well.

The newly freed convict threw his cloth napkin on the table and leaned back. "Let me ask you a question about this list of items you had me gather for you."

"Yes of course, what do you want to know?" Alexander seemed as if he expected what was coming.

"They're all items related to Jesus Christ."

"That much is obvious." Alexander's lips curled into a cool smile.

"Yeah, so there's that. But also, these aren't just any items. These are like the crown jewels of Christianity."

"Yes, they are indeed. That is the point."

"Well, that's what I'm curious about. What exactly is the point? The manger that Jesus laid in, his robe, the sponge that touched his lips, and the spear that pierced his side."

"Oh, and I have more than that as well. I also have the blood-stained cloth that covered Christ's face as he lay in the tomb. The Sudarium of Oviedo. You probably noticed that the tip of the Holy Lance was missing when you took it from Saint Peter's in Rome. Well, I've had the iron tip for some time now. It had been held at the Cathedral in Notre Dame. There are also two other Holy Lances, one is in Vienna, and the other in Armenia. They can't all be real, of course, and I am certain the one you acquired is the authentic one, but nevertheless, they are all now in my possession. There are a number of other minor artifacts related to the Christ I've collected as well."

"What's the deal? Why the fixation?"

"Excuse me?"

"With Jesus. All of these artifacts are a part of his legend. I'm just wondering why you're doing all of this."

"Ah yes, you've hit on the key word, I think. Legend." Remus cocked his head. He was trying to follow his host as Alexander reached for another slice of tomato basil bread from the basket and began to butter it. "Who exactly do you think Jesus was? If I may ask."

Remus responded almost too quickly. "He was a charlatan. Nothing more. Nothing less. Probably good with words, which is how he got people to listen to him. Some even sold out and followed him. But most of those were losers with nothing to lose anyway. He might have been a magician. Like the David Copperfield of his day. You know, did tricks and things to fool people. But he mixed it all with enough common sense talk that people actually drank the Kool Aid he was pouring. That's what I think, anyway."

"So, in other words, you're not sold...on his divinity. That he was God."

"Heck no!" Remus replied with a bit too much force, but Alexander liked what he saw. Yes, this was working out very nicely.

"Exactly." Alexander matched his volume. "I can tell we are two of the same kind, Remus Crook. You and I." He paused half a second. He wanted the compliment to sink in. "You are correct when you use the word legend when talking about Jesus Christ. Yes, I believe there was a man named Jesus. The history on that is irrefutable. But the Christ part is where the legend comes in. The idea that he was some sort of god come to earth in a body. That he performed miracles, healed people of blindness and leprosy and such. I'm sure you've heard the stories." Remus nodded and Dimitri cracked open another lobster tail. The

Russian had heard this speech more than once. "The Christian New Testament even purports that he controlled the weather at times. But the biggest chapter in the Christ legend involves his death. Or I suppose I should say, his resurrection. The idea that a man came back to life after three days. It's a fantastic claim for sure. One that would never survive the scrutiny of today. Yet, for some reason, because it supposedly happened two millennia ago, that makes it all of a sudden believable for people now. How is this possible, I ask you?"

"Well, I don't believe it. I already told you. None of it. He was a scam artist as far as I'm concerned. I've seen a lot of men get Jesus in prison, but as soon as they're back on the street, they shake him off as easily as changing out of their prison robes. It ain't real, none of it."

"Yes, I know you don't believe, but millions do. And that's my question. Why? Why do they believe? If Jesus were alive today, he'd be exposed. Social media would roast him. He'd never survive. No pun intended. But because he lived a long, long time ago, somehow, he gets a pass from people today. Well, part of the problem is that there exists all of these items, or relics, if you will. They are physical items tied to the legend. The Church guards them and holds them up as proof that Jesus was more than a man. They claim he was also the Christ. And just like that, the legend comes to life. But here's what you and I know. These are just mere objects. Wood and cloth and metal. My word, sometimes you have more than one of the same item. Like the Holy Lance. But they each claim to be the *real* lance. And for some reason that doesn't bother people. And what makes one of these items *holy*, anyway? Is it that it touched Jesus's physical body at some point and so now it becomes special or, as I said, holy? But what does that even mean? Does it have divine power? Can it be used like a magic wand? No, I tell you!" Alexander Pontia's hand slammed onto the table, causing the mostly empty dishes to shudder.

Remus Crook was captivated by Alexander's logic. He'd found himself swept along in the moment until the spell had been broken by the pounding of the table. Yes, Dimitri had heard this all before, a version of it anyway. But he'd never seen his friend this intense.

"I'm right there with you, buddy," Remus managed to croak out slowly.

"My apologies for my...enthusiasm."

"No need to apologize to me. We've all got something that flips our switch."

"What I'm saying is this. I've got many of these items now. These holy relics. I've held them in my hands, touched them, treated them with reverence. And do you want to know what I've discovered?" The Russian and the thief looked on, waiting for Alexander to continue. "Nothing. That's what I discovered. Absolutely nothing. No tingle. No vision. No magic of any kind. They are all completely...normal." Alexander sat back in his chair, finally calming himself. He laid his cloth napkin on the table in front of him, smoothing it out with his hands as if to signify that his monologue was finished.

"Well, none of that surprises me." Remus finally found his voice. "So, what are you planning on doing with all of these Jesus relics? And let me just say this. It's not going to go unnoticed forever that someone has stolen all of this stuff. There's an international hunt already for the items that weren't replaced with forgeries. But once those are discovered as well -" Remus let out a high-pitched whistle. "Let me just say, you better have really good security and a really good hiding place." He looked at the Russian security chief.

"Oh, you don't need to worry about that. Yes, they will come. The Catholic Church, INTERPOL, the FBI, all of them. The forgeries have bought us some time in terms of the intensity of the hunt. I understand all of that, and rest assured, I am more than prepared." Remus had only known Alexander Pontia for a short time but somehow he believed him. "But I'm not quite done yet. I have a few more minor artifacts to collect, and then..." He rubbed his hands together as if relishing what he was about to say. "Then I will be ready for the main event, as they say. Which is why I need you, Mr. Remus Crook. And once everything is in place, then I plan to erase the Jesus legend from the earth once and for all. And trust me, everyone will see...and they will believe. Or maybe I should say...stop believing."

Alexander Pontia released a sinister laugh.

Remus Crook found himself joining in.

Chapter 11

Phin pulled into the driveway of the two-story brick and vinyl siding home on Baxter Circle in Moore, Oklahoma. He had waited until Saturday morning to come home. Autumn sat silently by his side in the couple's new Toyota Highlander, a flood of images and emotions cascading over Phin.

There was nothing spectacular about the 2,500 square foot structure. It was a home like all of the other homes in the neighborhood, not sticking out from the houses on either side, except that every window blind on both the top and bottom floors was drawn shut. The grass had been freshly cut and the landscaping manicured. Phin noticed that a fresh layer of mulch had been recently laid down. It appeared that Calvin had been faithful to the tasks for which he was hired.

Calvin Bates. He was the family.... Phin didn't even know what to call him. Butler sounded too British or bourgeois. Calvin didn't wear a tuxedo and there was no staff to manage. It really was an ordinary home, but one that his mother was completely unable of taking care of.

Caretaker.

Yes, that would be the closet label to apply to Calvin. Faithful caretaker. Faithful because he'd operated in the role since Phin's father had died when the boys were teenagers. Caretake because that's pretty much what he did. He took care of the house, and he made sure that Dara Crook had her needs met. Phin and Remus's mother was simply in no shape to handle...well, anything. Calvin Bates had some sort of connection with Adonis Crook that went way back. It was professional for sure, but so much more than that. There was an obligation that he felt he owed to the family. Again, Phin didn't understand it and he had never probed to know more. Calvin had always been a presence in his life, and so he was trusted to take care of matters when Adonis had so suddenly and violently died.

"Well," Phin placed his hand on Autumn's, "let's go." She nodded and the two stepped out of the vehicle.

It was a beautiful day, the sun edging brightly toward the noon sky. Phin caught the unmistakable whiff of pine bark as he walked up the sidewalk to the front porch. Yep, fresh mulch indeed. Put down only in the last couple of days.

Phin knocked lightly on the door and then inserted his key into the lock. It never ceased to amaze him that the contents of this house were secured by such a simple lock and key. Not even a deadbolt. But then again, he knew that the basement wasn't so easily accessible. And that's what no one would ever guess by looking at the very ordinary Crook home from the street - that under its two stories lay a massive basement that had been command central for Adonis Crook's vast exploits as a master thief.

"Hello," Phin called as he stepped into the entryway. The house was dark and musty, only a few lamps glowing from the living room illuminated the whole downstairs. Phin noticed the same white floral couch that had been in the house since his youth. Not a stich of furniture had been updated. No surprise there.

A figure appeared in the opening of the hallway, on the opposite side of the living area. Autumn tensed and grabbed Phin's upper arm.

"Mr. Phineas, oh my, I heard something but did not know it was you."

"Hello, Calvin." Phin assured the old man with his voice. "How are you doing?" It had been just over a year since Phin had come home. A year since he'd last seen Calvin Bates, but by the looks of the man, Phin would have guessed it had been much longer. He looked ancient. Yes, he was in his late seventies by now – Phin did the quick calculation in his head – but he appeared much older than that today. His white wispy hair was uncombed and looked to have thinned, and he was unshaven. He squinted through his thick glasses with even thicker brown plastic frames. And his buttoned collared shirt was untucked.

Phin was slightly shocked.

Calvin had always been so sharp and put together. He worried that something had happened to the man. A stroke maybe? But then again, if he had to live in this house for any length of time, he doubted that his own motivation to bathe, dress, tuck, and comb would survive.

"I'm doing well, sir. I apologize, I did not know you were coming or I would have..." The old man looked nervously around the house and began to work his hair down with the palms of his hands.

"You don't need to worry about us, Calvin." Autumn's chipper voice brightened the room by a hundred lumens. "We were just in the area and thought we'd pop over." She winked back at Phin and moved across the room, giving Calvin a big hug. She'd always been fond of the family caretaker. "Are you really doing well, Calvin? You seem to be tired."

"Yes, yes. I am fine. I had just closed my eyes for a bit. Wasn't expecting anyone. Mr. Phineas, I am so glad you are here. Please come in, you mother will be happy to see you."

Mother.

The reason he had come home. Or one of the reasons. The other was to find out why Remus had sent him the gift and the note. And the picture. Of the house. This house. Remus had wanted Phin to come home. But why? And what kind of game was his older brother inviting him to play?

Well, he'd come home and now it was time to talk to his mother.

Chapter 12

To say that Phin's relationship with his mother was complicated would be an understatement. For all of his life, as long as he could remember going back to his childhood, Phin's mother had been...unwell. Not in a physical sense. Oh, no, Dara Crook's body was the picture of health. She ate well, was active, more so when she was younger than these days, and her annual doctor's visit indicated perfect ratios for cholesterol and all the other enzymes and levels measured by her blood profile. But it was in her mind where the sickness that plagued her lay.

As a small boy, Phin had always known that his mother was not like the other mothers. He noticed that other moms distanced themselves from her. She had no friends. None. As Phin and Remus grew and became more active, she would take the boys to their various sporting events and activities, but rather than cheering and participating like most parents, she would tend to wander off and do her own thing, as if she were escaping into a private world. Phin and Remus had always just thought the detachment was "mom being mom," but as they grew toward their teenage years, her aloofness became more exaggerated and it was clear that their mother was not only not like other moms, she was barely able to mother at all.

Adonis Crook took the lead in covering for and taking care of his wife. She increasingly became more reclusive, preferring to spend most of her time in her room or sitting in the backyard.

On Phin's thirteenth birthday, his mother left the house to buy him a present and never came back home. She was found the next day, wandering down Riverside Drive along the banks of the Arkansas River in Tulsa. Two hours from home. The car was never found and she claimed to still be on a shopping expedition for a birthday present for her son. Adonis finally sat the boys down and told them the hard truth of what they had already known in their hearts. It was the first time Phin had heard the word *dementia* before. A cruel form of mental illness. Detached from reality as she was, Dara Crook could no longer be left at home alone. Adonis hired various caretakers to stay with the Crooks during the weeks he would be traveling, practicing the family trade, so to speak. The boys came to rely upon each other, and their mother became less and less an active part of their lives.

After Adonis's death, Calvin Bates appeared on the scene full time. Remus had already picked up the family business and was gone from the home, and Phin quickly left for college. The boys would each make trips back home periodically, to check on their mother and make sure all was well, mostly out of a sense of duty. Any heart connection to their mother had died a long time ago. Yes, it was a sad situation, indeed. One that Phin preferred to not think about. To do so very often made him feel guilty.

He felt guilty right now. It had been too long since his last visit. He could make excuses about the extraordinary year he'd endured, but really that's all they were, excuses. His childhood home in Moore was only a forty-minute drive from his driveway in Shawnee, after all.

"Hello, Mother." Phin eased the door to her room open with a gentle peck of his knuckles on the doorframe.

"Come in sweetheart, I've been expecting you. Did you bring the chocolate milk?"

Dara Crook was sitting at a small table in her large master bedroom, facing a window that was open to the backyard. A breeze carried fresh air into the room, pushing back the staleness of the living space. Phin was grateful. Depression could descend quickly in this kind of environment, but there was something healthy about letting the outside in.

In her mid-60s, Dara Crook's thin shoulders slumped forward inside the flower-dotted dress she was wearing. Her hair was short but still held its deep brown color, and Phin wondered if it would ever gray. She was busy working on something. *Ah yes, a puzzle.* Phin eased up behind her.

"Sorry Mom, I forgot the milk. How are you doing?"

"Such a pity. Ah well, perhaps your father will bring some home later tonight. His plane lands right before dinner time. I do so love chocolate milk."

"Mom, you know Dad passed away a long time ago." Dara Crook's hand froze as it was about to place a puzzle piece. She turned her head and looked at Phin for the first time. He didn't know why he was trying to bring her back to reality. As soon as he was gone, she'd form whatever world she wanted anyway. One where his father was alive and well and they would carry on endless conversations together.

"That's right," she said. "He was shot. An accident. He is dead." Sadness pulled on the edges of her face and Phin was sorry he'd said anything at all.

"It's okay, Mother. I'm here though. And look, I brought Autumn with me as well." Autumn stepped forward and laid a gentle hand on her shoulder.

"Autumn." She was trying to work something out by repeating the name. "You are beautiful dear. How long have you and Remus been married?"

"Not Remus, Mom," Phin corrected. "It's me, Phin. Your other son."

"But I don't have...oh, yes I do. Phin?" She was struggling.

"Yes, it's me." Phin had always felt like he played second fiddle to his big brother, Remus. Remus was clearly the more gifted of the two in every sport and anything that involved physical activity or performance. Phin struggled all through school with feelings of inferiority. He also believed that his parents, both Adonis and Dara, favored Remus over him. He tried to reason that it wasn't true, but then there were always little reminders.

"But Remus...he was here you know. Just the other day. He was planning a big party! One for all of us. A family reunion, I think. There will be cake and lots of chocolate milk. Your father will be here and everything.

And he said...yes, he said you would come and try to stop the party." His mother had grown excited and then a dark expression passed over her, her voice becoming stern. "Why are you here, Phineas? And why did you bring this Jezebel into my house?"

"Mother." Phin straightened up. "Please don't do this. This is Autumn, she's my wife. We're not here to stop anything."

"Get out. Get out, now! And take your little whore with you. Don't come back. You're not invited to the party. Remus said so. You must leave now." She had risen to her feet and was pointing to the door.

Tears had formed in Autumn's eyes and Phin was frozen, not knowing how to respond. He eased toward the door, taking Autumn's hand. Normally he'd push through and try to calm his mother, to re-center her in reality. But the attack on Autumn. What was going on? His mother was easily agitated and thrown into fits, but this was different. Somebody had gotten to her.

Remus.

It had to be Remus.

She said he'd been here. Normally it would be impossible to know if he had really been here or whether it was part of her active imagination. But Phin believed that Remus had indeed been to the house.

The box.

The note.

The picture.

Remus had been here. Oh, yes. And he'd left behind a poison in his mother's mind, knowing Phin would come.

Why am I here, Remus? What do you want me to find?

The answer could only be in one place.

The basement.

Chapter 13

Phin keyed in the secret family code and held his breath. It had been many years since he'd descended into the family basement and he hoped the code had not been changed.

The light on the top of the keypad switched from red to green, followed by a soft click. Phin exhaled, turned the handle, and pulled the door open. Gently, he eased the switch on the wall to the up position using his thumb and index finger. Lights came on and he could see clearly to the bottom of the carpeted staircase.

Why am I being so careful? Phin questioned himself. *Because this is what Remus wants,* he concluded.

Remus wanted him to come home. Remus wanted Phin to go to the family basement. It was the only thing that made sense. Nothing else about their childhood home was remarkable. From the outside and even the inside, it appeared as an average middle class home in an average middle class neighborhood. And for the most part, it was. Phin and Remus had been raised by their parents, Adonis and Dara, and they functioned like any other family. They shared meals around the dining room table and watched TV in the living room.

The boys did their homework at the kitchen counter and Dara would bake cookies on Saturdays when the boys were very young and she still had the majority of her faculties. A basketball goal – long gone now – had sat just off the driveway where the boys would gang up on their dad in games of two-on-one, or they'd all three play HORSE until the sun set and it was too dark to continue. Adonis would go away for one to two weeks at a time on business trips, not unlike other fathers of the boys' friends.

But what was unique and different about the Crook household was Adonis Crook's "business." While other dads might be on sales trips around the region, or perhaps fly to Dallas for corporate level meetings of whatever company they worked for, Adonis Crook would be somewhere in the world, stealing a piece of artwork from a museum or private collection. The next week he might be a continent over, lifting gemstones from a bank vault. Most of these items were jobs for which he was hired.

The elder Crook had a strong reputation in the underworld of antiquities theft and thus was always busy. And paid well. Very well. However, the Crooks lived well *under* their means. Adonis's way of staying off the radar.

There would be times, however, where the deal would go bad and payment would not be made. Adonis would be stuck with the "merchandise" with no quick way of turning it back to the black market. And sometimes, a job presented him the opportunity to take something a little extra...for himself.

Some people are paranoid and bury cash in their backyard. Adonis Crook wasn't paranoid, but he wasn't trusting either. Much of his wealth was buried literally under his house. A bank could be too easily robbed. Adonis knew this all too well. Plus, there were limits on what a bank could hold for an individual. Trying to secure a stolen Rembrandt might raise a few eyebrows.

A self-storage unit was totally out of the question. Adonis viewed that on the same level as parking a car on the street with the keys in the ignition and the windows rolled down.

No, the safest place for his stash was at home, right under his own nose. And when he was traveling, under the noses of his wife and boys.

No one would ever suspect, driving through Baxter Circle, that over a million dollars in stolen antiques, jewelry, and various other items rested peacefully ten feet underground.

Over the years these extra items accumulated into quite a collection. Items were always coming and going as Adonis was able to move them, but more than anything the collection was growing.

Upon his death, the brothers had met in the basement to decide what to do with it all. The decision had been made to leave it alone. Phin wanted to return as many of the items as possible to their rightful owners, but had no clue where to even begin. Remus wanted to put the items on the black market and liquidate everything, then split what was made. But he too didn't know where to begin.

Neither of the boys had the network and connections their father had accumulated over a lifetime of thievery. An impasse was reached and the decision was made to leave it all alone. Untouched. Perhaps they'd revisit it all one day when their mother passed.

That was the last time Phin had been in the basement with Remus. And he'd visited it only a hand full of times since, the last time being years ago.

Phin grabbed Autumn's hand, gave her a look that said, *Let's do this*, and descended the stairs.

At the bottom of the stairs, a short hallway turned left and ended in a second secured door. More tapping of numbers into a keypad. A click. And Phin turned the handle while holding his breath.

The door opened into a massive expanse. The basement was one giant open area, larger than the footprint of the house itself. Maybe 2,000 square feet. A bank of safes lined the wood-paneled wall on the right. Some of them presented with doors wide open, and others were opened only a crack. But they'd all been unlocked. Industrial shelving and cabinetry lined the wall on the left. There were twenty or more work tables in the middle of the room. All of it together was used to hold the family fortune.

"Oh my gosh, tell me he didn't." Phin gasped at what lay in front of him.

Nothing. Absolutely nothing.

"Where is everything?" Autumn asked as she squeezed past him into the room.

There was a gray stillness in room. The only sound the buzzing of an overhead fluorescent light that needed a new ballast.

"I can't believe it. He took it all."

"Remus?"

"It has to be. Who else would?" He looked at Autumn, his face wrinkled in confusion. "Certainly not Mother."

"Calvin maybe?"

"I don't...no, I don't think he would do something like this."

Phin rushed to the safes. The ones with the doors open wide had clearly been cleaned out. He pulled open the unlocked doors of the rest. Empty. Unbelievable.

"There was a fortune in these safes, Autumn. Cash, bonds, raw gemstones and jewelry. He took it all."

Autumn had moved to the cabinets and was opening them. Phin joined her and it was all the same. Every door. Every drawer. Cleaned out.

No more paintings. No more sculptures. Gone were all the works of art, original compositions of music, even furniture belonging to famous world leaders – all dead, of course, which is what gave the pieces their value.

"Where would he have taken it all, Phin? And what does he plan on doing with it?"

Phin stood in the middle of the empty room, massaging his forehead with the fingers of his right hand.

"And how did he get it all out of here? You don't understand, Autumn. There was *so* much stuff down here. This room was packed. Not the kind of volume you just throw in the trunk of your car and drive away with. He would have needed a truck. A big one. And help."

Phin turned in a circle. Slowly. Taking in the whole of the room.

You wanted me to come home. You wanted me to come to the basement. Why?

"He's sending me a message."

"What kind of message?" Autumn was continuing to open doors, searching shelving. A futile effort, Phin knew.

"He's out of prison and needs money. So he has that now. In abundance," Phin said out loud, but talking to himself. "But he wanted me to *know*. Know what?"

"And what about the game he wants to play? What is that about?" She pulled open the door on another cabinet.

"He's in control. He wants me to know he's in control." But there was more, Phin thought. There had to be.

"Phin, I found something!" Autumn was at the far end of the basement room, bent over. "It's another safe. But this one is locked."

That was strange. All the other safes were on the opposite wall. Phin hurried over. Sure enough. A small safe, only three foot tall and cubed-shaped. Remus must have pulled it from the other side of the room. Clearly out of place. Trying to get Phin's attention. This is why he had come. Why he was supposed to be here. He could feel it.

"Can you open it?"

Phin looked at his wife as if offended. "Please," he said, voice dripping with sarcasm.

He knelt down and studied the safe. It read on the front: J. Baum Safe & Lock Co. Cincinnati, O.

An antique in and of itself from the early 1900s. It featured an old-school knob with numbers and internal tumblers as the locking mechanism. Piece of cake. Phin pressed his ear to the door and began to turn the number wheel. It took less than ten seconds. He pulled down on the lever and the door opened freely.

Phin stared into the black opening.

There were three items in the safe. An old piece of wood that Phin drew out carefully. It was roughly two feet long and the girth of a 2x4. The remnant was rough and pitted and it was easy to see where the shard Remus had sent him on his birthday had been sheared from this larger piece. He had no idea what he was holding but it must be important. He walked the chunk of wood to one of the work tables and carefully laid it down.

Returning to the safe, he extracted the last two items. A manila folder and a note. Yes, another note.

Dear Dismas,

Welcome home. I hope you like what I've done to the place. But knowing you, probably not. This was the easy part. Just a warmup. Now it gets much harder. Are you ready to keep playing my game? Two more clues to see if you are smart enough to keep up with me. Something from the past. Let's just call it a family heirloom. And if you're stuck, I've included some reading material to help you along. Now that you've got yours, it's time to go get mine. Why don't you try to stop me? It could be fun!

-Your beloved, Gestas

Phin stared at the note, his mind spinning.

"Why does he call you Dismas and sign it Gestas?" Autumn asked.

Another voice spoke at the entrance to the basement room, causing Phin and Autumn to startle. They both whipped around.

"He just opened the safe, sir. Yes, he found it." Calvin Bates was standing at the doorway, cell phone pressed to his ear, the old flip kind. He pulled the phone from his ear and snapped it shut with a trembling hand. "I'm so sorry, Mr. Phineas. He made me do it."

Chapter 14

"Calvin, how could you allow this to happen? Why didn't you contact me?"

Calvin Bates sat in a folding metal chair in the stark basement. He was a mess. His hair was still disheveled and the poor old man continued to uselessly try to tame it with his hands. Phin had ordered the caretaker to explain himself and the situation at the home.

"Be easy, Phin, he's obviously been through a lot." Autumn tried to calm her husband who was pacing back and forth.

"He wouldn't allow me to call you, not until you came. He said you would come, sometime this week. I don't know how he knew, but he said you would come to the house and that you would open the safe. He said that as soon as you had the door opened to call and let him know. And then he gave me instructions."

"Instructions?" Phin's head was spinning. He had a piece of wood, a note from Remus, and a folder he had yet to open. And now instructions?

What are you up to, Remus?

"I'm so sorry, Mr. Phineas." And then the old man broke down. His head collapsed onto the table as he wrapped his arms around himself. He began to sob. Autumn sat in a second chair and laid an arm across his shaking shoulders.

"Shhh...," she comforted. "What did he do to you, Calvin? What did Remus do? It's okay, we aren't upset. We just need to know what happened."

But Phin was upset. He continued to pace.

What kind of game is this? What is all the stuff you left behind, Remus? What do you want from me? And Calvin...why make Calvin a part of this?

Yes, he was angry, but not at the old man. Not really. It was all about his older brother. He was goading Phin, trying to pull him into something that he would likely not want to be a part of. But Phin was beginning to wonder if he even had a choice.

Calvin recovered somewhat with the help of Autumn's gentle care. He pulled an old stained handkerchief from his back pocket and blew hard into the cloth. Autumn cringed and pulled away a bit. "Mr. Remus came to the house last month. I didn't even know he was out of prison, so I was quite surprised at his appearance. It was a Monday morning. Your mother was delighted to see him, of course. She never understood why he was in the penitentiary to begin with. He stayed for ten days. Ten awful days, Mr. Phineas. He spent all his time here in the basement with

Mrs. Crook. She seemed to come to life down here. She knew the story behind most of the items, especially the jewelry. You know how your mother always loved expensive jewelry."

It was true, Dara Crook submitted to a simple, ordinary life for the purpose of outside appearances, but she had one indulgence - fine jewelry - which her husband was able to readily feed given his profession.

Calvin went on. "It was quite remarkable really. She seemed to be almost...her old self. She and Mr. Remus spent days together sharing stories and reliving the past. But Mr. Remus had his own plans. He was recording everything your mother told him. In a book. About all the items, that is. And then on Sunday, a truck arrived."

"A truck?" Phin asked. "What kind of truck, Calvin?"

"A moving truck," he answered with bulging eyes. "The do-it-yourself kind. Big and yellow. Very long. It was loaded with all kinds of packing materials. Boxes, pads, crates, a dolly. And then he went to work. I tried to stop him, I did. Please believe me. I knew that this was not the way. I suppose the collection belongs to him....in a way. But it also belongs to you, Mr. Phineas. To both of you. It wasn't right, what he was doing. But then...there was something evil about your brother." Calvin's voice began to shake.

"It's okay, Calvin. I don't blame you. Go on. What do you mean there was something evil about Remus?" Phin was now even more concerned than before.

"It's so hard to explain. But you could feel it. In the house. Whenever he was close, a darkness emanated from him. I told him we should call you and that's when he became irate. He locked me in my room. Barred the door so I could not get out. Two days, Mr. Phineas. Two days I was in there. I was so hungry. There was no food. I only had the water from the sink in my bathroom and I'm too old and weak to climb out a window. I thought I might starve. I thought perhaps he would finish what he was doing in the basement and just leave me in there to die."

If Phin was angry before, he was boiling now. This was not the Remus he knew. Remus had never been one to be cruel. Arrogant? Yes. Selfish? Yes. But never mean or vindictive. Not like this. Something had changed.

Calvin's voice grew a bit stronger and he went on. "But then, after two days, the door opened. I was lying on my bed because I had grown so weak. Two days with nothing to eat will do that. Mr. Remus stood over me and that is when he gave me my orders."

"Orders? What did he have you do, Calvin?"

"Nothing. He ordered me to do nothing. He said he was done and leaving and that I would never see him again unless I failed to follow his orders. That's when he told me you would come. On this particular week. He said you would come for a visit. I was not to contact you ahead of time. He said he would know if I did and that he would come back. I am so sorry, Mr. Phineas." He began to cry again. "I wanted to call and tell you about the house and the basement. He took it all, you see. It's all gone. All of it. I knew you would want to know. But I didn't want him to come back. I'm scared of him, Mr. Phineas. I don't ever want him to return. So I waited, because he said you were coming anyway."

"You did the right thing, Calvin," Autumn reassured the old caretaker. "Are you sure he didn't harm you in any other way?"

"No, he never laid a hand on me. But...I think he could," he answered with a raspy voice of urgency.

That was unlike Remus as well. He had never been prone to violence of any kind. In fact, it was part of the Crook family code. No violence. In spite of Adonis Crook's profession as a master thief, he had passed on a moral code of sorts to his two boys as he mentored them in the craft. That code included two points of non-violence.

Number one: never take or use a gun or weapon of any kind when doing a job. It was always about the theft and the merchandise. It was never about life and death. No item was more valuable than a human life.

Period.

Which led to number two: if you were ever caught, you would surrender and take whatever punishment the law divvied out. You didn't fight back and you certainly didn't take a life in order to escape with your own.

Number two also had the additional effect of making sure you did not even attempt a job unless you had done your homework, honed your skills, and made absolutely certain you would be successful. The goal was to come home after all, not go to prison.

Phin, of course, had sworn off the family business and gone and *found religion*, as his brother called it. But Remus had readily embraced life as a thief. And in doing so, he had also embraced the code. Which was exactly how he had landed himself a ten-year sentence in the Big Mac.

He had not been careful enough in the heist of five million dollars in gemstones from a high-end jewelry broker in Oklahoma City called McPhearsen's and he'd been caught.

That was four years ago. Remus was out now.

Somehow.

He had escaped and clearly something had changed.

Would you really harm Calvin, Remus? Is that who you've become now?

A thought.

"Calvin, you said just now that Remus gave you more instructions...when you called him a moment ago on your cell phone. What did you mean by that?"

"Oh yes, I'm sorry I almost forgot. I don't understand the message but he said you would. He said to tell you: *Tell Dismas that the clock starts right now.*"

Chapter 15

They left the house on Baxter Circle in the rearview mirror. Phin would come back at some point, just to visit his mother, but he had no idea when. Dara Crook had refused to open her door to let her son say goodbye. Whatever evil seed Remus had planted in her mind about Phin, the thing had sprouted and taken root.

Calvin Bates was a mess. They'd left the old caretaker sitting on the sofa in the living room, still in a fog. Autumn had comforted the poor thing, assuring him that he only did what he had to do. Nothing that had happened - the emptying of the family basement - was his fault.

There was nothing more for Phin and Autumn to do at the house so they simply left.

Calvin had been horribly abused by Remus and for that Phin was both infuriated and puzzled. This was not like his big brother at all. Something had changed with Remus, going back to the last dream they shared together, so many months ago now. Or maybe it was a vision. Whatever it was, Remus had been there too. Both he and Remus had been beaten and nailed to crosses. Just like the two thieves that hung on two crosses nearly two thousand years ago.

Two brothers.

Just like he and Remus. Two brothers whose lineage could be drawn forward in time in a dark red line of blood to Remus and Phineas Crook.

"What are you thinking?" Autumn asked, breaking the silence.

"I'm thinking I need to find Remus."

"How are you going to do that? I don't like this, Phin, any of it."

"I don't know. Let's just get to the house. I need to go through all this stuff and see if I can figure out Remus's little game." He jerked his head toward the back seat. The piece of wood, along with the folder of material, sat in the back seat. Phin reached for the center console and picked up the handwritten note Remus had left and read it again, careful to keep one eye on the road.

The silence drew out for another five minutes before Autumn spoke again. "We should talk about this Phin."

"I don't want to talk, Autumn. I just need to think."

Phin didn't often snap like that. It wasn't in his makeup. Autumn felt bruised by the verbal rejection but decided to let it be. She was concerned though.

Phin's family had always been a trigger for him. He'd endured rejection from his older brother when Phin had made the decision to not pursue the family trade. He could not reconcile the lack of morality inherent in the act of stealing. Even back when his father was alive, Phin had battled with these questions of right and wrong. But with his father now dead, his brother shunning him, and his mother's disconnection from reality, Phin felt like a ship with no harbor. This was why he had clung so tightly to Autumn once she entered his life. It was a chance at a brand-new beginning.

A new family.

A new legacy.

But the old family and the old legacy had come calling. Phin was sucked back in. Like being spun in a whirlpool, not knowing when the spinning would stop or when he would hit bottom.

"I'm sorry, E." He reached over and took her hand. The letter E was his special term of endearment for his wife. From her middle name: Autumn Eden Rose. Like the Garden of Eden, as Phin liked to tease. But it was exactly how he felt. She was his own private garden. A place of safety and refuge. His special E.

She smiled at him in return and placed her other hand on top of his.

They arrived at their home on Broadway Avenue. The drive back to Shawnee had seemed twice as long as normal. Phin's mind was tormented with all sorts of possibilities. He had some large chunks of the puzzle already placed, but he needed to look at everything Remus had left him.

He and Autumn shuttled the items from the back seat into the kitchen of their house and locked the door behind them just because it felt safer to do that. Already on the table were the green box, splinter of wood, and the picture of the house in Moore that they had just left only forty-five minutes ago. All delivered on his birthday.

Phin began by taking the sliver of wood that so much resembled a spike, and matched it up to the larger beam of wood from the safe. It was a perfect fit. The two belonged together.

What is this, Remus? What makes this piece of wood special?

He picked up the note left in the safe and eyed it yet again. One line stuck out to him: *"Now that you've got yours, it's time to go get mine."*

Now that I've got mine? What does that mean?

Phin began to mentally sort the additional puzzle pieces in his mind.

The sliver was delivered on his birthday.

A gift for Phin.

It matched up with the larger piece of wood.

He picked up the larger stick with both hands and muttered. "So, this one is mine."

"What did you say, Hon?" Autumn asked.

"Shhh...I'm trying to work this all out."

She was not offended, instead she turned her attention to the manila folder. Opening the cover, she found an assortment of newspaper articles.

"I'm Dismas and this is mine," Phin said to himself. The fog was thinning.

"Who's Dismas?" Autumn asked as she thumbed through the articles. They all were dated in the last six months from newspapers, mostly in Europe. "And why does he call you that?"

"Dismas is the name of the good thief who hung on the cross next to Christ."

She stopped with the newspaper clippings and looked at Phin, eyebrow raised. "Let me guess, that means that Gestas is the name of - "

"The impenitent thief."

"I was going to say bad thief."

"All thieves are bad, Autumn," he poked sarcastically. "The good thief was given that moniker because he was sorry for the life he lived and he asked for Christ to remember him in eternity. The other thief...well, not only was he not sorry for his life of thievery and sin, but he taunted Christ, attempting to provoke him into saving the both of them if possible. That's why he's called the impenitent thief."

A pause.

"Remus," Autumn finally said.

"Yes, Remus."

"What is your brother up to?"

"I'm not one hundred percent sure, but it has something to do with this." Phin continued to turn the large beam of wood over in his hands, looking for clues as to its origin.

"Phin, look at these articles. They all have to do with ancient artifacts, stolen from churches around the world."

Phin put down the wood and eased his chair next to Autumn's so he could see the contents of the folder.

"Here let me look at those." They carefully began to lay them out on the table, side-by-side, so they could be seen all at once. There were five articles in all.

The story that captured Phin first was a computer printout of an article from *The Local*, a website featuring

Italian news. The story was dated back in January and the headline simply read:

"Holy Sponge Stolen from Basilica di Gionvanni"

A quick scan of the text went on to describe a bold and professional operation which breached the security of the Church sometime in the early morning hours of January 3. Nothing else had been harmed, only the sponge itself was taken. The very sponge claimed to have touched the lips of Jesus Christ as he hung on the cross. Officials of the Church lamented the theft and expressed anxiety that such a thing could occur. The Polizia Stato were working diligently to investigate and recover the artifact. A Chief Inspector Antonio Rossi pledged to find those responsible and bring them to justice.

Phin's eyes landed next on another printout of an article, this one from the UK's *The Guardian*:

"Holy Crib Victim of Unholy Act"

The January 28th article chronicled a break-in of the Crypt of the Nativity housed in the Basilica of Saint Mary Major, again in Rome. This time, wood fragments said to be the manger that baby Jesus lay in after his birth were stolen. Phin stole a glance at the stick of wood sitting on his kitchen table and wondered. Chief Inspector Antonio Rossi was once again quoted along with officials from the Vatican. References to the earlier theft of the Holy Sponge were mentioned and there was conjecture that the two were linked.

A third headline from *Euronews* was even more perplexing:

"Suspected Forgery Found in Saint Peter's"

Another artifact, the Holy Lance, had apparently been stolen and replaced with an impressive copy. The article was dated April 1st, just last month, but this was no April Fools Day joke. Again, Chief Inspector Rossi was quoted, and again, the Vatican expressed deep concern and resolve to recover the holy relics. The full force of the Catholic Church was promised. There was no indication of when the theft occurred, but an overhaul in the security of all the Church's basilicas, abbeys, cathedrals, and churches that housed relics of any value had been ordered, and that was what led to the discovery of the forgery. Phin's eyes drifted again to the wood fragment and the broken-off splinter.

"Oh my...Phin, look at this one." The urgency in his wife's voice broke Phin's concentration. She had reached for an article laying on the far end of the table. Phin stood to get a better look, but the headline instantly made him sit back down:

"Bad Thief Targets Good Thief: Cross Stolen from Church"

Chapter 16

Chief Inspector Antonio Rossi ground the butt of his cigarette into the porcelain black ashtray that sat on the corner of his desk. It was against policy to smoke indoors, but Rossi didn't care. His title afforded him a small private office on the second floor of the Polizia Stato building (the State Police) that included a small window. The thing had been sealed shut with multiple coats of paint applied over time, but when Rossi took over the office five years ago upon achieving his current rank, he'd made it a priority to break the bond that held it shut. This allowed him to close his door, open the window, and smoke to his heart's content while he toiled away on his caseload. It's the small things that matter.

Two knocks and the door opened. "Antonio, the head of the Gendarmerie of the Vatican is here to see you. And you really should quit smoking. I know you're fit on the outside, but those cancer sticks are surely rotting your insides."

The chief inspector rolled his eyes and ignored the comment of assistant Dominic Bianchi. He stood and straightened his uniform, checking himself in the small mirror on his wall. He pulled a small comb from his coat pocket and ran it through his dark hair, a habit of his anytime he stepped out of his office.

Antonio Rossi was the quintessential Italian man with the good looks to grace the cover of a fashion magazine. At age 42, he not only looked fit but felt as fit as he ever had. Yes, he smoked and not in any small amount, but he also swam an hour each morning at five-thirty and was careful with his diet. It was a paradoxical lifestyle, he knew, but thoughts of the evils of tobacco were far from his mind. He'd smoked since he was 16 as had his father who was 72 and still alive and, by all accounts, healthy as well.

Chief Inspector Antonio Rossi greeted the head of the Vatican security force in the small lobby of police headquarters and ushered him back to his humble office.

Giovanni Lombardi was also titled Chief Inspector, although his title carried more weight than did Antonio Rossi's.

As chief inspector of the Gendarmerie Corps of Vatican City State, Giovanni Lombardi was the leader of the Vatican police, or security force.

He was at the top of the food chain.

Chief Inspector Antonio Rossi's title, while not insignificant, only meant that he had several more levels of rank above him. If this meeting with his Vatican counterpart went well and he could bring about a successful conclusion to the current mystery at hand, then he was in line for a promotion to senior chief inspector and a bigger office with a bigger window.

Normally, Rossi would have traveled to the Vatican for the meeting they were about to conduct, but Giovanni Lombardi had insisted on coming to the Polizia Stato headquarters to meet with Antonio Rossi.

Away from the Vatican.

The two had a big problem on their hands. Much bigger than anyone in the public knew. The Vatican would certainly be involved. It was simply unthinkable for it not to be. But it was also imperative that the scope of the crimes committed against the Church not erupt in the media more than it already had.

And there were eyes all over Vatican City.

Too many eyes. It was simply safer for Lombardi to come to Rossi than the other way around.

"My good Giovanni," Antonio quipped with more enthusiasm than he felt. He embraced the Vatican man's hand, and the two retreated back to his office.

Settling into a surprisingly comfortable chair while Antonio took his own behind the desk, Giovanni Lombardi gave the simple office a quick once over, wrinkling his nose in the process. Probably a reaction to the smell of stale tobacco.

Antonio didn't care. He was used to it.

"Thank you for coming, Giovanni. I would certainly have come to you had you only asked."

"It is better this way, Antonio."

The two men were on a first name basis. Friends might be too strong a description, but they had both had numerous interactions throughout the years, being close to the same age, having come up through their respective ranks at the same pace. There was never a shortage of activity surrounding the city of Rome and the Vatican, mostly protestors who didn't like some new fiscal policy of the government or papal decree from the Church. The two men were always involved when tempers in the city flared.

The matter they had gathered to discuss today dwarfed such common annoyances.

"It's much worse than we thought, Antonio," Giovanni began with a deep exhale from his chest. "Are you familiar with the name Alexander Pontia?" he asked. The Vatican police inspector removed his navy blue kepi and placed it on Antonio's desk. He leaned back, smoothing the front of his matching navy uniform.

"Of course. An American with Italian roots but most notable for his auction houses around the world. Ten or twelve, I think. One of them is here in Rome. Token Exchange is the name. You don't mean to suggest - "

"He's our man." The Vatican inspector cut him off.

Antonio Rossi had trouble believing that a man of Alexander Pontia's reputation could be involved in something so bold. "Are you certain? It seems almost too obvious. Too risky. An antiquities dealer operating right here in Rome, stealing artifacts from the same city? He would be insane to try to move them onto the black market from here."

"Insane, maybe. But he has no intention of moving the items to market."

"Then what?"

"We are not sure. Perhaps a vanity collection for himself. Perhaps something else."

"Incredible. And you are sure it is him? Alexander Pontia?"

"There is no doubt. We had people in New York just this week. He was hosting the auction of an ancient copy of the Book of Esther. We sent someone to bid for it, but he failed. Yes, the Church would have liked to have had it for our own study and to perhaps display in one of our many chapels, but that was not the real reason we were in New York. We wanted to get close to Pontia. To verify what we had been told."

Antonio Rossi held up his hand. "Please slow down, Giovanni. You're going too fast. To verify what you were told? What does that mean? Who told you what?" The chief inspector flicked open a gold-plated case and drew out a cigarette that he lit and inhaled, all in one practiced motion.

Giovanni wrinkled his brow but continued. "My apologies. Yes, much has happened since we last debriefed two weeks ago. We have identified the theft of ten holy relics from churches and basilicas around Europe but mostly from right here in Rome."

"Ten! I don't believe it. I thought we were talking about five thefts at the most. And a questionable sixth."

"As did I, but it is indeed much worse than we thought. And it was already bad. Antonio, we are talking about the greatest crime against the Church, against Western civilization itself, since the Muslim invasion of the Holy Land that led to the Crusades. Churches were burned and the holy sites desecrated. And numerous holy relics were carried off, most never to be seen again. It was a tragedy unrivaled. Until now."

The chief inspector thought his peer from the Vatican was perhaps overselling the situation in his description, but he let it slide without comment. Staying on task, he continued his questioning. "And again, you are sure that it is Alexander Pontia who is at the center of it all?"

It seemed too incredible to believe. Antonio Rossi had met the American auctioneer on numerous occasions. As chief inspector of the Polizia Stato, he had worked security for state dinners and gatherings throughout the years. Alexander Pontia was an invitee to many of these. The man came across as warm and sincere. A businessman from America but with interest in the welfare of Italy. *"An adopted second home,"* he remembered the man telling him once.

"We received a letter," Giovanni Lombardi replied in a somber tone. "It was from an unknown source, delivered directly to me personally by courier. It, in no uncertain terms, named Alexander Pontia as the man behind this scandal of thievery. We were skeptical, of course. But there was proof."

"Proof? Of what nature?"

"Of the most incriminating. A photo. Taken from a distance but very clear."

Gionvanni Lombardi reached into the inner pocket of his navy jacket and extracted a postcard-sized photo that he handed to Antonio Rossi. The chief inspector took the photo and examined it, smoke curling from the cigarette smashed between his lips.

It was Alexander Pontia. There was no doubt.

And what was it that he was holding? Antonnio Rossi leaned closer, lifting a magnifying glass from his desk.

"It's the Holy Lance," Giovanni helped him. Antonio looked up at his peer in law enforcement. "The Holy Lance that pierced the side of Christ. Stolen from Saint Peter's Basilica right here in Rome."

Antonio Rossi didn't know what to say.

"This is why we sent our people to New York last week. The bidding on the Esther scroll was a cover. We had multiple people all over the Token Exchange building that day. You must be careful around Pontia. He has his own security personnel, you know."

Yes, Antonio did know.

Dominion Safe.

They were well known in Rome, providing personal security not only for Token Exchange, but for numerous other private antiquities dealers and other business people. Anyone willing to pay the price, really. The Polizia Stato had had more than one encounter with Dominion Safe throughout the years. It's not that private security was all that unusual, but Dominion Safe had a reputation. For being aggressive. And for employing people with questionable histories.

"And did you discover...anything?"

"We did indeed. And as I keep saying, it is much worse than we thought."

Chapter 17

All Max Allred knew was that his best friend had said to come and to come quickly. With Phineas Crook, that could mean anything. Usually not good.

Max parked behind the Mabee Center and quickly thumbed the lock button on his car's fob as he hustled into the university's library. It was late, nearly nine o'clock, and darkness was quickly descending, the sun having set about a half hour earlier. Max noticed students huddled around the main floor in groups, studying for finals, finishing papers and projects. Summer break was nearly here but there was still the end of semester crunch to navigate.

Phin was waiting for him by the stairwell leading to the basement.

"What took you so long?"

"You called me ten minutes ago, Phin."

"It's only a five-minute drive from your house."

"I have a wife and two kids, buddy. It's called a life. You should try it sometime."

"Whatever. Let's go."

Phin took off down the flight of stairs at a rapid pace. Max struggled to keep up for the first few steps and finally gave up. He knew where his friend was headed and decided to not risk killing himself getting there. He arrived at the landing and Phin was gone - through the fire door, down a short musty hall, and standing at another door fumbling with a set of keys. By the time Max caught up to him the door was open and the two stepped in together.

"We need to talk."

"Obviously. And since we're down here, I assume that means you've got some kind of big secret that no one else can be allowed to listen in on. *Again.*"

"This isn't funny, Max. I need you focused."

Max was already dreading where this was going. Phin kept a private study carrel in the basement of the library. It was really an old storage closet that he had commandeered a couple of years earlier. Just moved in and made it his own. There were more formal carrels on the upper floors of the library, but Phin preferred to be out of the way. As in way out of the way. Max doubted anyone in charge of the library even knew about the secret study space. And to provide an extra layer of security, Phin had added an additional lock that only he had the key to.

"Look, I'm here, aren't I? At nine on a Saturday night. Just tell me what's going on."

"I went home today, Max. To see my mother. To see what it was that Remus wanted me to see." Max took a seat in an old wooden chair and Phin joined him, leaning toward his friend, elbows poised on an ancient-looking worktable in the middle of the room. Max noticed a folder and a stick of wood in the middle.

"How's your mother?" Max began by asking. But what he really wanted to know about was Remus. Why had the older sibling directed Phin there? He eyed the wooden beam and began to wonder where this would go.

"She's...not well. Remus had been there before us. Me and Autumn. She went with me. Mother's not really all there anyway, you know, but something had changed. Remus got to her. Into her mind, I mean. She turned on me, Max. My own mother practically kicked me out of the house."

"She's sick, Phin. You can't take that personally."

"I know, I know. Autumn told me the same thing. It's just hard. And it makes me angry too, Max. Remus had been there for over a week and a half." Phin pulled himself almost halfway across the table. "He cleaned out the basement, Max. He took everything."

Max knew about the Crook family legacy, of course. One of the few outside the family who did. Years ago, when all Phin knew was that his family was a clan of thieves, he had taken Max to his childhood home to prove it to him. By showing him the contents of the basement.

"You're kidding," Max let out. "Phin, that basement was full. Packed end to end with - "

"I know, Max. And that's what I'm telling you. He took it all."

"You're talking about a fortune. What's he planning to do with it?"

"I'm not sure he's planning to do anything with it. I think he's sending me a message. The game, Max. Remember the game he taunted me with on the birthday note? It's all about that."

"I just can't believe he took everything." Max was imagining what he had seen in his one visit. The paintings, the jewels, the furniture and sculptures and banknotes and on and on. Like a modern-day King Tut's tomb, he thought.

"Well, he did...but then he left me something in its place." Phin patted the wooden stick on the table.

"What exactly is that?" Max asked. "It looks really old." He eyed the smaller splinter of wood that Remus had sent to Phin on his birthday. He could instantly see that the two pieces belonged together, the smaller one shaved or cut from the larger.

"Let me start by showing you these." Phin opened the folder that contained the various articles Remus had left him in the safe. He spread them out, one by one, for Max to absorb.

It was incredible.

A chronicling of theft on a massive scale. The scale being magnified because each item was related to Jesus Christ.

Max saw the connection immediately.

The crib Jesus had lain in, the lance that pierced his side, and the sponge that touched his lips. The face cloth laid across Jesus's head after he died, still darkened with the stains of his blood, and the Holy Coat, the seamless robe worn by Jesus for which the Roman soldiers had cast lots.

The revelation of it all was stunning.

"Oh my..." Max whispered in disbelief. "I remember seeing a couple of news flashes on some of this. The crib and the lance maybe. But I had no idea. Phin," he looked up at his friend, "are you telling me Remus has stolen all of these items?"

Without a word, Phin slid one final article across the table to his best friend. The headline:

"Bad Thief Targets Good Thief: Cross Stolen from Church"

Max read the copy, unsuccessfully attempting to calm his quivering hands.

The article described a recent break in at the Basilica di Santa Croce in Gerusalemme. The Church was famous for being one of the seven pilgrimage churches in the city of Rome, so its security was above average.

A thief had breached the security net, however, and stolen one of its prized artifacts – the Cross of the Good Thief. This small beam of wood was said to be what was left of the crossbeam that one of the two thieves crucified with Christ hung on, the good thief, a man known traditionally as Dismas.

A forgery had been left in its place, but because of a string of other thefts in and around Rome in recent months, an inventory of the artifacts housed by the Church had led to a discovery of the forgery.

The Roman Catholic Church was up in arms, and a massive worldwide search was said to be underway for the relic, along with the other items taken from the various other churches. INTERPOL working with the investigative agencies of countries throughout the European Union were all engaged.

Max licked his dry lips and sat back in his chair. He crossed his arms and then flipped his hand toward the wooden beam on the table. "Tell me that's not what I think it is. There's no way. It can't be."

Phin only raised his right eyebrow.

"I don't believe it. I can't believe it. The Cross of the Good Thief? Not here in Shawnee, Oklahoma. It's a game, Phin. Isn't that what Remus said? A game? It's not the real thing. He's up to something else. He has to be."

"Oh, he's up to something alright," Phin finally replied. "But there's more."

"More. Of course, there's always more where Crooks are involved."

Phin handed over the handwritten note that Remus had also left him in the safe. "Now read this, and tell me what you think."

Max took his time dissecting the note, reading it three times before handing it back. "So clearly you are Dismas and your brother is Gestas."

"You are perceptive, my friend."

"And you've got yours, meaning your cross, the Cross of the Good Thief." Max pointed at the piece of wood on the table a second time. There was something churning his insides that made him not want to touch it.

He took up the note again and read from it aloud, "*Now that you've got yours, it's time to go get mine. Why don't you try to stop me? It could be fun!* So now he wants you to stop him from stealing the cross of what, the bad thief?"

"It appears so."

"Okay, you're not going along with this, are you? I mean, to my knowledge no one even knows where the Cross of the Impenitent Thief is. Probably lost to time or destroyed. I doubt it still exists. This can't be serious."

"Oh, I think it's very serious. You see, at the same time that Autumn and I found this, a call was placed. To Remus."

Phin explained how Calvin Bates had been coerced into contacting Remus the moment the Cross of the Good Thief had been retrieved from the safe. And then the additional message to Phin from his older brother: *Tell Dismas that the clock starts now.*

"What *is* it with you and your family, Phin? You and I have been involved in some crazy stuff...but this -" He spread his arms wide over the array of articles, notes, and again, the wooden beam that he was now being told was what was left of the two-thousand-year-old crossbeam of the good thief that hung next to Jesus. He still didn't want to touch it. "This is just beyond...beyond anything rational or sane. I mean, I have no idea what you plan to do with all of this, but why are you showing me? What do you want me to do with any of it? Because I'm telling you, friend, no way am I playing along with Remus's fun little game of catch-me-if-you-can."

"I'm showing you this, Max, because you're my best friend." Phin's tone was deathly serious. He allowed that statement to hang in silence for just a moment before continuing. "I'm showing you all of this because there's one piece more. And you're the only person I can trust. Even Autumn doesn't know about this."

More. Always more.

Max didn't like the sound of the word *more* when it came from the lips of Phineas Crook.

Phin stood and walked to the file cabinet in the corner of the room. He pulled his ring of keys from his pocket and found a small key that he inserted into the round lock of the old black metal box. He pulled open the top drawer and extracted a large brown cloth bundle, returning with it to the table. He gently moved the crossbeam of wood aside and gathered the news articles back into the folder before turning his attention again to the bundle. Max watched all of this with anxious curiosity.

"Max, please promise you aren't going to be mad at me."

He undid the brown bundle revealing a burlap type of cloth that he carefully began to fold across the top of the table. The staining on the cloth was evident but Max could not make out any particular form to it.

"What is this, Phin?" Max asked in reverence. "What have you done?"

Phin looked at his friend, deadpanned in his expression. "This, Max, is the Shroud of Turin."

Chapter 13

"You're insane, Phin. You're out of your mind!"

Max Allred was yelling at his best friend.

"Will you please quiet down and stop shouting? I don't want anyone to know we're down here."

"You've stolen the Shroud of Turin, Phin! And you've...you've brought it to campus to hide it? What do you expect me to do? Buy a ticket? Oh, how wonderful, the Shroud of Turin. The very cloth used to wrap the body of Christ in after his death on the cross. The cloth he left behind in the empty tomb after he rose from the dead. How nice. I've always wanted to see it, but a trip to Italy was always *too expensive*. I'm so glad you made it easy for me by stealing it and bringing it to the OBU library!" Max shouted the last phrase.

"I said hold it down, will you?!" Phin had already tried to explain to Max why the Shroud of Turin was in his private study carrel rather than its home in the Cathedral of San Giovanni Battista in Turin, Italy. He would try again. "Look, just sit back down, drink some water and let me talk you through this." He rolled a bottle of Ozarka over to his friend.

Max broke the seal and took a long drink, wiping his mouth with his sleeve. "This better be good. And I mean, real good."

"Okay, look, it all goes back to Remus, right? First, he escapes from prison. That's a very un-Crook thing to do by the way. Our father may have been a thief, but he also operated under his own set of moral codes, one of them being, if we were ever caught, we took the punishment coming to us. And under no circumstances were we to ever harm anyone. So, Remus gets caught trying to steal gemstones in Oklahoma City about four years ago. He gets locked away in the Big Mac and becomes a model prisoner. You follow?"

Max nodded and took another drink.

"But then he and I have this weird dream connection last year and after that he won't return any of my messages. Cuts off all contact with me. Then, all of a sudden, he breaks out of prison? It doesn't make any sense. He's due for parole in another eighteen months or so. So why the rush? And now I've got the Oklahoma State Police checking with me every week or two because they're certain he's going to make contact with me, his brother. Clearly, my mother is mentally deficient so they check with Calvin also, just in case. Which is interesting, because Remus just happens to hit a window between visits from the police to pay a visit to the old homestead. But I'm getting ahead of myself.

"So, I went and talked with the warden of the prison, and get this, Max. Remus had help. They got it all on video surveillance. At least two others were in on it, working as guards. And these guys were good. Professionals. And I keep asking myself, why? Why is Remus doing this? What has changed? And who's helping him? He's up to something and I just don't know what it is.

"So, I keep my eyes open. Especially the news. And that's when I see a story about a theft in Italy. The Holy Sponge it's called. Said to be the very one dipped in vinegar and lifted to the lips of Christ while he hung on the cross. It was a bold theft taken from its home in a church in the city of Rome itself. That raised an eyebrow, but I continued to watch.

"Then came a second theft, also from Rome, but in another church. The Basilica of Saint Mary Major. This time it was the remnants of the manger Christ lay in as a baby. Rome is now on fire. The Church is beside itself and the police have no clues as to who is behind the thefts. But I can read the fingerprints and I'm starting to wonder.

"Then a third story. The Holy Lance. Taken probably in March but replaced with a forgery that was discovered in April. And that's when I knew. Or maybe that's when I accepted it - something inside of me knew when the sponge was taken, but I just didn't want to believe it. It's Remus. He's behind it all."

"Wait, wait, wait," Max interrupted. "Remus escapes from prison and then relics in Rome go missing. And just like that it has to be Remus? That makes zero sense, Phin.

If your brother just escaped from prison, the last thing he's gonna to do is run off and start an international stealing spree. No way. He'd lay low. Maybe head to Mexico and lay up on some beach somewhere and drink margaritas all day long."

"You don't know Remus, Max. I'm telling you, something is going on. Clearly, he's not on a beach in Mexico. Just a few weeks ago he was here in Oklahoma cleaning out my father's collection. And again, why?" Phin reached down and picked up the folder that had all the news articles left for him by his brother. "These articles, Max. I'd already seen them, at least most of them. I read about all of these thefts *as they were happening*. Remus leaving these for me just confirms it all, but I knew. Don't you see? *I knew*. That's why I had to go...to Rome...and steal the Shroud."

Max slapped his hands against the tops of his legs. "Okay! So let's talk about the Shroud since you've finally gotten around to it. I've already declared you insane and I'm sticking to my diagnosis. Phin, this is like the Holy Grail of relics to the Catholic Church. I don't even want to ask how you stole it. I mean I know you're good, but that good? Geez. But what I just don't get is *why* you've done this. This puts your whole career on the line. Think about Autumn and Patrick. You could be the one headed to prison, and I don't mean one of the nice cushy ones like we have in the States, we're talking about a prison in Italy. You'd never see the light of day again."

"I had to, Max. I know you don't understand it but you just have to trust me. I knew Remus was behind the thefts and I knew he was going somewhere with it all. Somewhere big. I still don't know what this is all about but I knew I had to stop him. But in order to do that, I needed a wild card. Something in my pocket that I could play. Leverage. That's why I stole the Shroud of Turin. Two reasons really. First to protect it, and second to use it to lure Remus out into the open."

Max sat in silence, trying to absorb the mind of Phineas Crook. He couldn't help but think about himself too. And his own wife, Shelly, and their kids, Phoebe and Junior. He was sitting in the basement of the university library in Shawnee, Oklahoma, twenty-four inches from the Shroud of Turin, one of the most important holy relics to the Catholic Church. To the world, really.

He began to sweat.

He knew.

And now that he knew, he was responsible. At least that's how the authorities would see it when they came. And they would come. He was sure of it. How could they not? A massive search was on for the missing relics of the Church, all on a global scale. It was just a matter of time. Max began to boil inside.

"How could you do this to me?" he asked through clenched teeth.

Phin was taken off guard. He could see his friend was angry. He had been certain that once he explained everything, Max would understand. He'd always been able to convince his old college roommate to see his side of things.

"I'm sorry, Max. Look, let me try to explain it again."

"No! I don't want any more explanations. I don't want to hear about your messed up family or how you just had to fly to Italy and steal one of the most important relics to the

Catholic Church and bring it all the way to my front door." He looked up at his friend, a new, never before seen fierceness in his eyes. "I don't want to hear any of it anymore. I'm angry, Phin. And I'm tired. Angry that you would do this for one, but also angry that you would pull me into whatever scheme you are working without my knowledge. You've done this kind of crap our whole lives and I've just always gone along. But not this time, Phin. This time, I'm out. Because, like I said, I'm tired. Tired of the drama and the crazy that seems to follow you like the plague. But this time is different. This time you *chose* to do this. This time you've gone too far. No one made you steal this Shroud. So, I don't know what your plan is and I don't want to know. I'm tired and I'm out."

Phin didn't know how to respond. He stared at Max who returned the look with a hardness Phin had never seen before. Phin was the one who finally broke eye contact and looked down at the dusty floor of the tiny basement room.

"I have to stop him, Max," he whispered. "I'm the only one who can. I need your help."

"I'm sorry, Phin. This time you're on your own." And with that, Max Allred stood up and walked out of the basement closet.

Chapter 19

The plane rattled as it began its initial descent into Tel Aviv. Phin pulled off his sleeping mask and popped the silicone plugs out of his ears. He'd tried to catch at least a few hours of sleep, but had been wholly unsuccessful. Autumn had wanted to go with him, but he'd been resolute that he needed to do this alone. Plus, they now had a child, Patrick.

Phin had spent the long thirteen plus hours in the air replaying the events of his exit from his little home in Shawnee, Oklahoma.

"I'm going after him, Autumn. I have to."

She, of course, didn't understand this and had pushed back.

"Why do *you* have to be the one to save the world, Phin? Why does it have to be you? And for the record, the world is not at stake, but your wellbeing might be. I'm worried about you, Phin. I've never seen you let your brother have this kind of control over you."

"I know the world's not at stake, E. But Remus is planning something. I can feel it. It's almost like I can feel *him*. Inside of me. Goading me."

"Don't let him do this to you." She had become adamant, her volume rising. "Your brother is his own person. He will have to answer for his own actions. Whatever he's doing or planning to do has nothing to do with you...with us."

"It's not that simple. I'm telling you, whatever he's up to has everything to do with me. I don't have a choice here, Autumn. One way or another he's going to pull me in. I can either be led along with him pulling the strings, or I can go on the offensive. I can accept his little challenge, but on my terms. I can take the fight to him."

"You sound like a teenager getting ready to wrestle his big brother over who gets to ask a girl to prom. That's not what this is...whatever *this* is. It's serious, Phin, and I don't want you to be a part of it."

Phin motioned to the remnant of the Cross of the Good Thief that was now sitting on his kitchen table. "Don't you get it, Autumn?" he snapped at her. "I'm already involved. This cross was stolen from a museum. It's sitting in our house now. Special delivery from one Remus Crook. He's committed me. One phone call from him to the authorities and our little home is descended on by the police, the FBI, probably Homeland Security. Whether or not I'm a part of his little game is no longer the issue. I'm behind the eight ball here, Autumn. And I don't like it. But I can turn the tables on him. I can take the cross away from here, our home, and I can go to him."

Autumn threw her arms in the air in frustration. She walked to the refrigerator and started taking leftovers out as if intending to begin working on dinner. Phin just stared. It was not like them to argue at all. Patrick was upstairs in his bedroom but surely had been listening.

"You don't even know where he is," she finally said. "He basically just said come and get me. You don't even know where to start, Phin. What does taking control of the situation even look like?"

She was right, of course. Remus had thrown down the challenge. *"Now that you've got yours, it's time to go get mine. Why don't you try to stop me? It could be fun!"* He recalled the words of Remus's note. Not his idea of fun for sure. None of it was.

All Phin wanted to do was finish the semester and spend the long summer break relaxing with his wife and son. Maybe take two weeks to drive West. Show little Patrick the Grand Canyon. He was finally a father and he was ready to play the part.

Except he was also a brother.

And Remus had apparently gone off the deep end. But there was something more to the whole thing. And Phin knew...he *knew*...that it had to be him - that he alone could stop whatever Remus had started. But where to start? Phin could only think of one place.

The clock starts now.

"I'm going to Jerusalem," he finally declared to his wife.

"Jerusalem," she repeated with a chuckle. "Because

that's where Remus is? Come on, Phin, you don't know that. You're flying blind here."

"Because that's where the archives are."

The Crook family archives. Phin had told his wife all about them. He himself had only been there once. He'd made a pledge to himself that he would never go. They represented a path he had chosen not to travel. The path of the family business, of thievery. The archives held no purpose for him. Until they did. His one visit had revealed more than he could ever have imagined. And now...they seemed to be calling again.

The clock starts now.

The Crook family archives were hidden away in the bowels of...a clock shop. The House of Reuben.

Remus had left him a clue. *The clock starts now.* Remus wanted him to go...to the clock shop...to the archives. And so, yes, he would go. What choice did he have?

Or maybe it was because Phin had no better idea where to go or how to start his "offensive" strike against Remus. Whatever the reason, the archives seemed as good a place to start as any. The entire record of the Crook family was contained in its depths. Tracing their lineage all the way back. To its beginning.

To two brothers.

Gestas and Dismas.

And now two other brothers.

Remus and Phineas.

Yes, he would go to the archives to see what other mysteries they held. And perhaps he would find something that would either point the way to Remus or reveal what it was he was up to.

It had been a cold dinner. Not because of the temperature of the food but rather that of the dining room. Autumn was not happy. Little Patrick may have only been seven years old, but he was smart. He could tell something wasn't right with his parents, his father mostly. He tried to liven up the mood over supper with some funny story about a substitute teacher and another student who got stuck in the bathroom. Phin and Autumn played along for his sake but after the meal was done and the two were alone again while cleaning up, Autumn threw out an olive branch.

"If you're going to do this, at least take me with you." She didn't like the idea of Phin going after Remus by himself.

Sensing that she had cooled from her earlier fury, he took her in his arms and held her close. She relaxed and let him take her. He liked it very much when the two of them came together like that. They were both fiercely strong, each in their own way, but when they came together...well, it really was as if they were one flesh.

"I'd love nothing more than for you to go, E. But this time it just needs to be me. Plus, we have a son now. Patrick needs you right now more than I do." She didn't argue with his reasoning but he read the concern as her shoulders tensed slightly in his embrace. "Don't worry about me. I'm a big boy. I can take care of myself. I just need to see if the archives have any information at all about what Remus might be planning. I'll keep you in the loop on anything I find. Promise." He kissed her gently and the conversation was over.

Phin spent the evening playing with Patrick and watching the first half of an Avengers movie on Netflix

140

before tucking the boy in bed. He told his son he was going on a trip and pledged to bring him home a surprise. Something "really cool." This brought a smile and a hug.

He packed a bag, made arrangements via email with Max to be away for the week from campus, and tried to get some sleep. He was unsuccessful.

Early the next morning, he kissed Autumn goodbye and drove to the Oklahoma City airport to catch the first flight to Atlanta. After a two-hour layover he boarded the American Airlines direct flight to Tel Aviv.

He left behind a wife who was still worried. Very worried. And struggling with what to do with that worry.

The plane touched down with a thud, jarring Phin from his thoughts of home and family. It was time to focus. Autumn and Patrick would be fine. It would be but another ordinary week in Oklahoma for them. His classes were covered with no need for him to dwell on them. He needed to turn his full attention now to his brother. Remus Crook.

Phin said a quick prayer that the archives would shed some light on what he should do next.

And then he stepped off the plane.

Chapter 20

Phin loved the smells of the Jewish Quarter. The scents of fresh breads being baked mixed with the wares of various vendors setting up for the day ahead – nuts, dates, olives, watermelon, and of course, honey.

This was the land flowing with milk and honey, after all.

Phin felt remarkably fresh and his dour attitude had seemed to improve some. He'd made the one-hour drive from Ben Gurion Airport to the King David hotel in Jerusalem the evening before. He was exhausted after a fitful flight where his mind never seemed to settle. This actually worked to his benefit. The eight-hour time shift normally meant two to three days of jet lag until his body could adjust. But Phin had collapsed into the plush king size bed and slept solidly until the sun came peeking through the cracks in the curtain, serving as his alarm clock.

He roused himself feeling fresh and alive.

It was half past nine o'clock when he set out from the hotel after a hearty Kosher breakfast. He carried over his shoulder the Cross of the Good Thief nestled in a protective backpack. Phin had decided he wanted to walk the twenty minutes or so to the Jewish Quarter.

It was a beautiful day.

The sun's rays were beaming across a baby blue sky with only a few fluffy clouds here and there. A slight breeze coming from the direction of the Mediterranean made for a mild chill, but even that was burning off quickly in what was promising to be a perfect morning.

He was here because of Remus. But Remus seemed very far away at the moment.

His thoughts, instead, drifted to his father. Oh, how he found himself missing his father more than usual as he walked the streets of the holiest city on planet Earth. Ironic, he thought, because Adonis Crook had been anything but religious. He was a Crook, a thief, after all. But he had been a wonderful father, doting on both his boys with love, affection, and gifts from his travels around the world.

He used to play ball with the boys in the front yard. All kinds of ball – baseball, football, basketball. He never missed any of Phin's league games when he was home, and even though Remus was the better athlete, and not by a small margin, he was never critical of his youngest son, who in truth, preferred to read a book as opposed to playing sports.

It is never easy for a son to lose his father, but to lose him at the tender age of eighteen, and in such a violent way, had left a certain kind of scar that Phin found itching the corners of his soul from time to time.

The family dynamic had instantly changed.

Remus was already on his own and the death served as an excuse to stay away. The boys' mother had accelerated in her mental decline, refusing to admit that her dearly beloved was really gone.

What would Dad think if he could see me now? Phin asked as he was walking the final blocks toward the Crook family archives. *He would probably be proud of me,* he concluded.

The thought made Phin smile.

His decision to not pursue the life of a thief would surely have disappointed his father, but what kid doesn't want to know that his father is truly proud of him? And here he was, for the second time in a year, making a pilgrimage to the family archives.

Misgav Ladach Street was a small cut-through between two more prominent roads. And off of this little out-of-the-way street was an even more out-of-the-way alley. Phin remembered it well as he retraced his steps to the door of the House of Reuben.

A small wooden shingle written only in Hebrew identified the little shop that sold clocks and other timepieces. At least that is what any passerby were to believe.

The clock starts now.

Yes it does, Phin thought.

Phin knocked twice and let himself in.

There she was, just as before. A middle-aged Jewish woman stood behind the counter, just as portly as Phin remembered, looking exactly the same as his previous visit, black hair still in a bun. Phin wondered if anyone else ever relieved her or if her lot in life was to stand in this little shop day after day.

"Hello Mary," Phin greeted the shopkeeper.

"Ah, the prodigal son returns yet again," she replied with a genuine warmth in her voice. Did she remember him?

The clocks in the shop struck ten o'clock, setting off a cacophony of bells and chimes that lasted nearly a minute as timepieces scattered around the shop announced the top of the hour.

Phin could only smile.

"It is time," he said, playing their little game. It was the secret phrase his father had instructed him to present to the keeper of the archives.

"It is time for what, my friend?" came the expected question.

"It is *my* time."

Mary raised an eyebrow and glanced at Phin's arm.

"Oh, I almost forgot. Sorry." He quickly rolled up the sleeve of his right arm to reveal the Crook birthmark located on his inner biceps. Remus had the same birthmark, as had their father. As had every Crook male in the genealogy. A small red spike with a red dot at its tip. It was an unexplainable phenomenon.

Mary eased from behind the counter and moved to the back room as Phin followed. Just as before, Phin found himself stepping over musty old boxes and broken clocks littering the floor and the flat spaces of every shelf and table. The keeper of the archive stopped at one such large shelf and, taking hold of one side, gave a heave.

"The archives have been busy as of late," Mary said, not looking at him.

A wave of adrenaline shot through Phin at the passing statement. Yes, it was right to come here. Keeping his thoughts to himself, he watched as Mary punched the code into the digital keypad next to the security door that had previously been concealed. A click and another pull by Mary and the hallway to the archives lay before Phin.

"You have knocked and the door has been opened. What you seek, may you find." She stepped out of the way, allowing Phin access. He thought her choice of words curious. Very close, maybe too close to those of Jesus in the book of Matthew.

"Thank you, Mary." He paused and looked into her kind brown eyes. And then he gave her a hug. Why? He didn't know. It just felt like the right thing to do. She gave a chuckle and patted him on the back.

"Go now. What you seek awaits." It was almost as if she knew something. Something more than what she was letting on. Phin gave her a sly smile and stepped into the hallway.

It was a straight shot down a dank cinderblock hallway lit only by incandescent bulbs every thirty feet or so. Then came the stairs leading down.

Next the ladder.

And then another tunnel. This one was rock-hewn.

Ancient.

Phin knew this corridor went for a long distance, winding this way and that on a slight downward slope. It felt very much like walking backward in time. And it was easy to lose track of time. But eventually the tunnel ended, not at a door, but at a doorway...that opened into the chamber of the archives.

Phin stepped into the massive chamber and simply stood, allowing himself to take in the expanse of the room. It looked unchanged from his previous visit. But what had he expected? There were other Crooks in the world – all over the world really. How many of them made this same journey? Mary had said the archives had been busy lately. Was she talking about other members of the "family"? Or was she talking about....

The chamber had a high ceiling, very high. The rock from which it had been formed gave the effect that the ceiling went up until it was swallowed by the night.

Torch light burning in scones around the chamber added to the medieval atmosphere of the chamber.

And then there were the shelves.

Shelves upon shelves spanning the chamber floor, all packed with books. More books set stacked on ancient-looking tables spread around the room.

In the middle of the room was the biggest table. The one Phin knew. The one he'd sat at the last time he was here. He knew what was at that table. He knew what was contained in the volumes stacked on its surface. But that was not why he was here this time.

Phin looked around the room, overwhelmed. He could only imagine what the contents of the rest of this library held. One could spend a lifetime exploring. But he didn't have a lifetime.

"Hello, little brother. I was beginning to wonder what was taking you so long."

A shadow stepped out from behind one of the bookshelves on the opposite side of the chamber. The dim lighting made it impossible to make out any features, but that didn't matter. Phin knew exactly who it was.

"Remus," he echoed in reply.

Chapter 21

The two brothers allowed the silence of the chamber to engulf them.

Remus made the first move.

He stepped forward from the shadows so that Phin could see him...see his face. He had changed his appearance from the last time Phin had seen him, sitting across a table from his brother in the visiting room of the Oklahoma state penitentiary. His brother now had a head full of hair and a clean-shaven face. He looked good, Phin thought. It would take a bit of getting used to, but in some ways, he reminded Phin of a teenage Remus, when the boys were young and before his brother could even grow facial hair.

"What are we doing here, Remus?"

"You tell me, little brother. Why are *you* here?" Remus walked a few more steps from the shadows.

"I'm here to stop you, Remus."

Remus laughed. "Stop me? What are you going to stop me from, Phin? What is it you think I'm doing?"

"I know you're the one...the one who's been stealing the Jesus artifacts from the churches around Rome and Europe. The only thing I don't understand is why."

"Yes, why?" Remus asked as he thoughtfully sauntered forward. "Why do any of us do what we do, Phin? Why have you chosen to forsake your own flesh and blood? Why have you chosen to follow a myth? Why have you sided with fantasy over family? The little question of why can take you down a rabbit hole I'm not sure you want to go down, little brother." The bitterness came oozing out with every word Remus spoke.

This was a side of his brother Phin had never seen. Yes, the two fought as brothers do when growing up. And there were times that Remus exerted the "big brother knows all" bullying tactics onto Phin. But this...this felt different. Like something had changed. And that's because something *had* changed and Phin knew it. Going back a year ago to their shared dream-link, or whatever one wanted to call it. They had each emerged from that connection...changed.

Phin for the better, and Remus clearly not so much.

"Don't talk to me like I'm still thirteen, Remus." Phin pushed back hard. "Don't lecture me on family honor and betrayal. We're here right now because *you've* broken the code, not me. You broke out of prison. Isn't that against the Crook code of conduct? You got caught, fair and square. You weren't good enough. So, the code says you must accept your punishment. We should be having this conversation at The Big Mac, but we're not. We're in Jerusalem. And once again, I wonder why."

Remus lifted his head to the rock-domed ceiling and raised his voice. "Big Phin is all grown up! Did you hear that, world?!" He laughed. "Touché, little bro. You've caught me now, haven't you? And so what is your next move? You gonna call the cops and send me back to Oklahoma? What exactly do you mean when you come in here and say you're going to stop me?"

Phin had no answer. He truly didn't know what he was going to do, or even what he was supposed to do. His goal had been to find Remus.

And he had.

Now what?

"Why don't we both have a seat, Phin. And let me tell you a little story." Remus walked to the large table in the center of the chamber and took a seat, motioning with his hands for Phin to join him.

Phin closed the distance to his brother with caution. He doubted there were any tricks in play, that wasn't like Remus. But nevertheless, he felt uneasy, not knowing where this was going. Phin sat across from his brother and lay his satchel with the wooden crossbeam inside of it on the table next to him.

Remus eyed the package with a smile.

"Do you know what this place is, Phin?" Remus began. He leaned back, arms spread, taking in the whole of the chamber.

"The one place I swore I'd never go, but now here I am...for the second time. And it's because of you." Phin made no attempt to hide his resentment.

Remus powered on. "This place is more than an archive, little brother. This place is a testimony to the truth.

I've spent a lot of time in this place over the years, mining its secrets. And oh, let me tell you...this place contains one of the biggest secrets in the world." Remus could tell by the look on Phin's face that he had hooked him. "I said I wanted to tell you a story, so why don't you sit back and relax and just listen to what I have to say."

"Go ahead, I'm all ears."

Phin really did want to know why Remus had drawn him along, all the way apparently, to here. His big brother had been waiting for him after all, knowing he'd come. Something about that bothered Phin more than he wanted to admit.

It seemed that no matter how hard he tried to flip the script on Remus, that his brother was one step ahead, that he knew exactly what buttons to push to get Phin to do what he wanted.

"A long time ago, let's say *two thousand years*." Remus winked at Phin and smiled. "Rome ruled the world and peace reigned. They called it the *pax Romana*, the peace of Rome. But that peace came at a cost. Caesar commanded with an iron fist and the price of peace was the fear of the people. And also taxes. We gripe and complain about high taxes in the U.S., well what we pay is nothing compared to what Caesar demanded. If you had to make a choice to pay Caesar or buy milk for your kids...well, let's just say you'd be drinking water for dinner.

"Poverty among the lower classes was rampant. And throughout the whole empire, no class was lower than the Jews. The Romans treated them like dogs. Worse really. But the Jewish people fought back. There was the

Maccabean revolt. It was a good try, but no army could match the might of the Romans.

"The Zealots were another group. They began a guerilla war and that was a bit more effective. The Jews became a thorn in the side of Rome. Not leading to any sort of real change but at least there was the satisfaction of irritation.

"And then there was this one family. We will call them the Crook family, although that's not what they were known as at that time.

"In this family were two brothers. Two very close brothers who decided that they had had enough. Or I supposed I should say they decided that Rome had enough, more than enough. And so they decided to simply take it back.

"Let me ask you this question, and you don't have to answer: Is it really stealing if you're only taking back something that was stolen from you in the first place?

"Well, that's the way these brothers viewed it. Rome had stolen from them, so they would just steal it back. And they did. And they became very good at their craft.

"This became a different kind of irritation, or thorn, in the side of the Romans. And the best part was this...the brothers got rich. Oh, they couldn't flaunt it. That would attract too much attention. But they could spread it around and everyone could benefit. So that's what they did.

"And everything was going beautifully...until this one man entered the picture. A preacher of sorts. And he came bearing a dangerous message. He talked about loving your enemy. He rattled off verbal junk like, 'If a Roman soldier takes your cloak from you, go ahead and give him your shirt too.' And here's the crazy thing about this nutjob's message: people actually listened to him. This wasn't fighting back against Rome, this was rolling over and letting them have *everything*. It was crazy.

"But let me tell you what was crazier. One of the brothers, the younger of the two, he started attending gatherings where this preacher was spewing out what he called 'good news.' Can you imagine? 'Hey look, I come bearing *good news*. The Romans want all your money...so let them have it. Have a nice day while you die of starvation.' What kind of good news is that? This younger brother got brainwashed by the preacher and this led to, let's just call it a family dispute.

"Now what happened next you're not gonna believe," Remus said with sarcasm.

Phin knew exactly where his brother's story was headed but let him continue uninterrupted.

"The Romans finally had enough. Of both the thefts of property from their soldiers and magistrates and of the preacher and his good news. Too many people were listening and following and the Romans don't like crowds of common people gathering.

"The brothers were caught red-handed and arrested and the preacher was arrested too. The brothers were tried for stealing from Caesar and the preacher was tried for being an insurrectionist. And on a Friday morning all three of them found themselves hanging on Roman crosses. I'm sure you know how the story ends, don't you little brother?"

"What is your point, Remus? Why are you telling me all of this?"

Remus leaned half way across the table as he said

through clenched teeth, "Because you've bought into a lie, Phin. Don't you see? Jesus was no different than any other Jew trying to stick it to the Romans. He thought he could sidle up next to them by telling the people to just go along to get along. Love, peace, joy, a bunch of 1970s hippie crap is what it was. And the whole time, all he was doing was building his own personal following.

"He was a headcase. But look where it ended him. On a cross, the same as the two thieves. At least the thieves were able to enjoy some of the finer things this life has to offer before it all came to an end. But what gets me is the younger brother. Do you hear me, Phin? The *younger* brother. He got suckered by Jesus, just like the masses. There he was, hanging on a cross about to die. Hanging next to Jesus, who was also about to die. And he still drinks the Kool Aid."

"That's because there is more to this world than...this world. More to life than this life!" Phin shot back at Remus. He had finally heard enough.

"And that's where you are wrong, little brother!" Remus yelled, slapping the table with the flats of both hands. "Paradise, heaven...dang, the whole concept of eternity. It's all a lie, Phin. Don't you see? One giant bucket of red cherry Kool Aid. And you've been drinking one glass after another."

"You're the one that's deluded in your thinking, Remus. Self-deluded. It's real. All of it. Jesus is the Christ. Eternity is real. And Jesus is coming back one day...in the flesh."

"Nope." Remus began shaking his head vigorously. "You're wrong, little brother. And I'm going to prove it to you."

Chapter 22

Phin laughed.

"You're going to prove to me that Jesus isn't real, that eternity is an invented idea? That's a pretty tall order for anyone, especially you, Remus."

Remus didn't like being laughed at. "Oh, Jesus *was* real. A real *man*. And as for eternity, what exactly do you think happens when we die, Phin? Oh, let me guess: you think we go to heaven, right? Or at least our spirit goes. And we all just float around in the bye-and-bye for forever and ever, amen. But, oh I forgot, not everybody, though, right? Because all the Jesus people don't think it's fair for us non-Jesus people to get to be a part of the heavenly party. So, wouldn't you know it, ZIP BANG, you've got a place for the rest of us called hell. Real hot, no clouds, lots of fire. And all the non-Jesus people, which is pretty much the majority of everyone who's ever lived, by the way, get sent packing to burn and burn but never really burn all the way up. Sort of like a divine torture chamber. That's the Sunday service. Time to pass the plate. Have I pretty much got it, little bro?"

A profound sadness swept over Phin. His brother was lost. As lost as anyone could be. And consumed with a rage that was new for Phin. He was scared for his big brother. Yes, for his eternal destiny, but also because a man cannot live with that much pent-up anger and be happy.

"Remus," Phin began very evenly and very slowly. "I don't know where all of this anger is coming from, and I don't know if it will do any good to argue theology with you, but you've chosen to see Jesus and the whole issue of heaven and hell through a tainted lens. Like looking through a shattered piece of glass. You see bits and pieces but it's all distorted. You're not seeing clearly. Eternity isn't just about heaven, it's also about Earth. A new Earth. And a new body to replace the one we have now that is wearing out. And hell? Well, that is simply God giving people what they ask for. They want an existence with no God and so he says, okay, and hell is what's left. But Jesus is the key, don't you see? You were there with me, Remus. Last year, when we were sharing the same dreams, night after night. Don't you remember how it ended? We were hanging on crosses, both of us...and *he* was there."

"Oh yeah, I was there all right. I still have nightmares about that nightmare." Remus began rubbing the palms of his hands. "Do you know I still feel the pain in my hands from that drill? You remember the drill from the dream...don't you, Phin? The one those guys used to run holes through our hands. What kind of dream does that?"

"That's my point, Remus! It *was* real. I mean not physically real, but like a vision. It was God...Jesus, the son of God, he was speaking to us. Isn't that proof enough that he was more than just a man?"

"Let me tell you what I saw and experienced, little brother. I felt pain. Real pain. And I still feel it today." Remus continued to massage the palms of his hands. "A devilish nightmare, and for what purpose? Because God loves to punish us little peons down here on planet Earth?" He used air quotes when he spoke the name of God.

"And I begged him to stop. Do you remember that, Phin? I challenged him to prove he was God and to end it all right then and there. And you know what happened? Zero, zilch. It went on and on and on. And then let me tell you what else I saw. Nothing. That's right. Jesus, or whoever he was, just vanished. And you along with him. I was left all alone, Phin. All alone, in agony, hanging on that cursed cross. I willed myself to wake up because I knew in my heart it was a dream. But I couldn't make myself do it. I hung there for what seemed like days. Days, Phin. Hanging and bleeding and in the most horrible pain of my life. And then...finally...it was over. I don't even know how it happened, but I was back in my cell, laying in my bed, soaked with sweat. Two guards were leaning over me trying to wake me up because I guess I had been crying out. As soon as I saw them, I freaked. They were guards, remember. I wasn't myself after the nightmare so I freaked. They drug my butt to solitary and I spent two more weeks there, Phin. Alone. All alone."

Phin had no idea what had happened to his brother after the vision ended. This was the first time he'd heard

Remus's account. "I'm so sorry, Remus." It was all Phin could think to say, but he truly meant it. He pitied his brother.

"Don't be sorry for me, Phin. But I need you to open your eyes. I think you're the one who's looking through shattered glass. Yours is the lens that is dirty. But I intend to clean it for you."

Phin looked at his brother with a puzzled expression on his face.

Remus pointed to the ceiling. "Up there, Phin. That's where the journey takes us next."

Phin looked at the ceiling of the domed rock cavern. The lighting was dim so he had to strain his eyes, but he saw what Remus was pointing to.

A hole, right in the center, about thirty feet up.

He recalled seeing the hole upon his first visit to the archives last year but had really paid it no attention. A breathing hole for fresh air, he assumed.

"What's up there?" Phin asked.

Remus laughed this time. "For a bookworm, you really should read more, you know it? The answer is right here in this room, Phin. Like I asked before, do you know what this place really is?"

"You said it was a testimony to the truth. Yes, I was paying attention."

"You get a gold star in class today, little bro. Yes, the truth. Up there is one more piece of the puzzle of truth. And oh, baby, it's a big one. That's why you're here. I need your help."

"My help?"

"Look how high it is, Phin. Can't do it by myself. Plus, I wanted you here to see it for yourself. Trust me. This sort of thing is right up your alley."

Phin couldn't resist. "What's up there, Remus?"

Remus looked at the bundle that Phin had set on the table. "You brought it, didn't you? The little gift I left for you in the safe at Mom's place." Remus was smiling big from ear to ear.

Phin reached over and put his hand on the bag. "The cross. Of the good thief. Yes, I brought it."

"I knew you would. You're nothing but predicable, little bro. You need to work on that, by the way."

"It needs to go back to its home, Remus."

"Oh no! It's not going back. It's going forward. But first...it needs its mate." Remus continued to smile, knowing it would only be but a moment before Phin figured it all out. He was correct.

"Nooo...it isn't...here?" Phin looked back to the hole in the ceiling.

Remus just smiled.

"I don't believe it."

"Well then, why don't we go take a look? You know what they say, seeing is believing.

Chapter 23

The two brothers went to work in earnest. Remus produced a duffle with rope, headlamps, harnesses, and hard hats. He rolled a Pelican case to the table in the middle, hoisting it on top as Phin carefully stacked the books on it to the side.

"Be my guest," he said, stepping back and motioning to Phin. Phin unlatched the case and opened the lid. A Bridger line-throwing gun lay nestled in the foam cutout insert, along with a series of loaded cartridges.

"Well this will certainly do the trick," Phin replied, looking from the case to the hole in the ceiling.

"Yeah, it's overkill for sure. This baby can shoot a hook five hundred feet with the proper cartridges. I brought the small loads but they can still reach nearly a hundred feet."

"Looks like we only need thirty." Phin was judging the distance to the hole.

Remus assembled and loaded the Bridger, carefully fastening the brass projectile into the barrel.

"Phin, grab the big flashlight in the bag. And be careful when you turn it on, that sucker is supposed to be the most powerful flashlight in the world. Puts out one hundred thousand lumens."

Phin curiously extracted a large black light labeled the Imalent MS18 on the side. He pointed it at the ceiling, flipped the switch, and could have sworn he felt it kick back on him. The entire cavernous room exploded in bright light.

"That's what I'm talking about!" Remus exclaimed with delight. "Like being outside in the sun, huh, little bro?" He lifted the line gun to his shoulder and, standing directly under the hole in the ceiling, pulled the trigger. A loud *THWUNK* sounded. The brass projectile shot through the hole, pulling the line of rope with it. The muffled sound of a *CRACK* could be heard as the projectile embedded itself in rock somewhere in the black distance beyond the hole.

"Bingo! The eagle has landed. Not bad for a first shot if I do say so myself."

Phin turned off the powerful light, plunging the cavern into something that seemed much darker than before. He grabbed hold of the rope and gave a firm tug. It held fast.

"Go ahead - put your whole weight on it," Remus encouraged. "Let's see what we have to work with."

Phin complied, hoisting himself a foot off the ground, the result was the same.

Remus went next, declaring he was heavier, which was true.

The line was secure.

"Well, which one of us is going first?" Phin asked.

"Let's arm wrestle for it," Remus replied. It was a tease.

Phin had never been able to best his brother in any kind of physical challenge. They both knew what the outcome would be.

Remus moved on quickly. "Look, I went to all this trouble to get you over here, so why don't you go first. I'll let you have the honors."

"Thanks." A pause. "I think." Phin eyed him with a suspicious grin. "Or maybe you aren't so certain this rope will hold after all. Maybe I'm your guinea pig."

"You hurt my feelings, little bro," Remus feigned, sagging his shoulders. "Haven't I always taken care of you?"

"Yeah, like the time we were gonna steal the new Air Jordan's from the Foot Locker in the mall? Remember that one, Remus?" Phin decided to bring up the famous basketball shoe caper that never was.

Remus had been fifteen at the time and Phin thirteen. Remus had also enlisted the help of his then girlfriend, Nancy, to help. The whole operation was a miserable failure.

Phin had never forgotten about it and he brought it up often just to remind his brother.

"You sent me into the back of the store to find our sizes. Said all I had to do was grab the boxes and walk out the back fire door into the parking lot. Super easy. You'd stand guard and make a racket if an employee started heading my way. Except you didn't. In fact, you disappeared altogether. I wasn't back there fifteen seconds before the manager grabbed me and hauled me to mall security. And you were nowhere to be found."

"That's because *you* didn't wait until I told you it was all clear. Nancy was gonna distract the manager - get him to answer a bunch of questions about running shoes. I can't even believe you're holding that against me after all these years."

"Nancy asked to try on a pair of shoes, Remus. That's why the manager came to the back and how he caught me. *You* were the one who didn't tell Nancy exactly what to do. She was supposed to ask *about* the shoes, not ask to try any on. And what about the warning so I could slip out the back? That never came, either."

"Whatever, little bro. We obviously remember it differently."

"All I remember is getting the third degree from Dad when I got home about how I have to be better if I'm going to be a real Crook."

It was just another example of how Phin's family was different than all others. Phin's father wasn't mad that his son had tried to steal a hundred-dollar pair of basketball shoes, he was mad that his son had been caught.

Crooks were better than that.

Crooks didn't get caught.

It was experiences like that that began to plant the seeds of doubt in Phin's mind about the morality of the family "business." Doubts that would eventually lead Phin down a whole other path. To become a pastor and now a college professor in a Christian university.

And now it appeared he had come full circle because here he was with his brother, Remus, involved in something very big and very international in scope. Phin still didn't know what all he had gotten himself into by playing Remus's little game, but the answer appeared to lie thirty feet above him.

Phin shook off the conversation with his brother. The past was the past. He gave the rope another tug to satisfy any misgivings. Shouldering a small pack with some additional gear, he returned to the rope, got a big grin from Remus along with a thumbs up, and began to climb.

Phin's ropework skills quickly returned. He was in good shape, plus he'd had a much more rigorous challenge when he'd stolen the Shroud of Turin only a few months before.

The thought flashed through his mind, once again angering him. He'd stolen it to protect it. From Remus.

But the reminder that the Shroud was sitting in the basement of the Mabee Learning Center on the OBU campus in Shawnee, Oklahoma, only served to raise Phin's anxiety level. The Shroud would have to go back to its home when this was all over.

Yes, he needed to see this through to the end. There was no turning back at this point. He climbed on, arriving at the hole in the ceiling in short order.

He pulled himself over the lip of the opening and quickly flipped around. Laying on his belly, he stuck his head over the edge and yelled to his brother below, "All good, come on up!"

It was impossible to tell what lay in the darkness around him or how big of a space he was even in, plus his concentration was on making sure Remus made the climb safely. His big brother may have been stronger than Phin, but his added weight also made for a more strenuous and slower climb.

Phin couldn't help finding some measure of satisfaction watching his brother strain. But make it he did. Phin grabbed Remus under the armpit and hauled his brother over the edge of the opening and into the darkness.

Remus laid on his back for a moment, panting. "Dang, that was harder than it looked."

"Only for one of us," Phin jabbed back.

"Ha, ha, little brother. I guess I had that coming." Remus sat up and began adjusting his headlamp. "No need to waste any more time. We've come a long way. Ready to see what all the fuss was about?"

He flipped on the switch.

A beam of light shot into the darkness.

Nothing.

Confusion wrinkled the brow of Remus Crook.

Phin inhaled sharply. "Remus...this way." Phin was facing the opposite direction, his own headlamp shining. Remus turned in the direction of his brother's voice.

And he saw it.

Chapter 24

A dark mass leaned upright against a wall.

Phin judged that it was maybe ten feet away on the other side of the hole that now lay in the floor of the room they were standing in.

"Hand me the Imalent," Remus commanded, not daring to take his eyes off of the dark object.

"Uh...I left it back down...in the main room."

Remus diverted his eyes to look at Phin. "You're telling me that we climbed all the way up here into a dark hole and you left the world's most powerful flashlight behind? Unbelievable."

"Hey, this is your little operation, remember? I'm just along for the ride."

Remus shook his head and made a move toward the object, careful to step around the hole. Phin eased past the opening on the opposite side and joined his brother, the two creeping closer to their goal.

It didn't take long for their headlamps to sufficiently bring the object into focus.

"And there it is." Remus let out a whistle.

Phin stared in awe.

"The Cross of Gestas. What once was lost has now been found," Remus whispered, as if he were afraid someone might hear. It stood a good five feet tall, by Phin's estimation. This crossbeam, unlike the remnant that Phin had wrapped down below, was fully intact.

The Cross of the Impenitent Thief, Phin thought. "How in the world did it end up here?"

A chuckle. "Like I said, little brother, you really need to bone up on your history. Everything's recorded down there." Remus's head cocked toward the hole behind them. "Helena, the mother of Constantine, came here to Jerusalem in the 300s. Dug around and found this very place where you and I are standing. Only back then it contained three crosses and a wooden plaque, a sign really, the one that hung above Jesus's head. And of course, the Church being the Church decided to take the cross of Jesus, the plaque, and the Cross of the Good Thief and spirit them away, to show them off around the Roman Empire. Sort of Constantine's way of bragging that God was on his side. But they had no use for this one."

Remus stepped closer to the crossbeam, leaning over as if in reverence, to get a better look.

"So, they left it here." He looked to Phin. "Right, here, Phin. That's when the guild came in and took over. They enclosed this space we are standing in now and excavated the cavern below to make it larger. It became the archive, Phin. The family archive. The city and time added layer upon layer on top of us, sufficiently burying the archive...and the cross...until both were lost to time." And then his tone suddenly lightened up. "Except to us Crooks, of course."

"Amazing," Phin replied.

"Yes it is, little brother."

"It's amazing you read enough books to figure all this out."

"Hey...what...did you just insult me?" Remus stammered.

Phin smiled. He truly was impressed with the scope of what Remus had discovered, but couldn't resist the poke. "Can you blame me? I've never known you to read a book in your entire life."

"Well, it's been a long time since we were kids. There's a lot about me you don't know anymore." Remus's voice returned to a somber tone. His attention was back on the cross. He couldn't resist any longer. He reached out with both hands. They stopped only inches from the rutted and splintered beam, as if a forcefield was preventing him from going any closer.

And then Remus broke the barrier, grabbing the cross full on. He closed his eyes in the process.

Phin held his breath. Why? He was not sure.

Silence.

A moment passed.

"Yep, just what I thought." Remus broke the spell as he broke his release on the cross. "Nothing. A big fat nothing." He let out a big belly laugh, no longer afraid of who might hear, although, clearly no one could.

Phin wasn't sure where to go with Remus's revelation.

Remus thought the look of confusion on Phin's face was funny.

"Ah, come on little bro, don't look so disappointed. Did you really expect the sky to split open and for God to speak, 'Congratulations, you've found the golden egg'? Can't you see, Phin? It's just a plain old piece of wood. And by old, I mean *very* old. Like two thousand years old."

Phin had to admit, he didn't know what he had expected. Did he really believe that some sort of aura would emanate from the relic? Why would he? He had possessed and held the remnant of the Cross of the Good Thief and there didn't seem to be anything special about it either.

Still there was something about the legend of the crosses that tickled the back of his mind; but try as he might, he couldn't bring it forward. And dominating the mist of his cloudy thoughts was the biggest question of all: Why? Why was Remus orchestrating this elaborate relic hunt?

"So, what do we do now, Remus?" he dared to ask.

"Yes, what do we do now? That's the question, isn't it? Well, let me tell you what I'm going to do now and you can decide if you want to be a part of things or not."

Remus sat down on the rock floor in front of the Cross of Gestas. Phin took this as an invitation and sat as well while Remus continued. "The next step is to take this cross out of here and deliver it to my employer."

"Employer?" Phin asked.

"Hey, I didn't get out of prison on my own. But, of course, you know that. Haven't you been just a little curious, Phin, as to who sprung me and why?"

"Now that you mention it, yes. Eighteen months, Remus. That's all you had left and then you'd been out anyway. Why in the world would you do this? What's so important that it couldn't wait eighteen months? Now you've got all of law enforcement in the U.S. looking for you. Heck, you've got the whole world looking for you now with all these stolen relics. They just don't know it's you."

"I was given an offer I couldn't refuse. A man, a very wealthy and powerful man, sent a proposal to me while I was in prison. It seems that his interests and mine align. We both want to see the truth about Jesus exposed."

"Truth about Jesus? What are you talking about, Remus?"

"That he was just a man, Phin! Haven't you been listening to anything I've said today? All of these...relics," Remus motioned at the cross, "that are supposed to be holy and contain some sort of supernatural aura or power. I'm telling you, Phin, they are nothing. Do you hear me? *Nothing.* Just a bunch of wood and cloth and bits of metal, whatever. There's nothing any more special about them than what could be found in the local dump. One man's trash is another man's treasure, huh, little bro? Well, it's time someone took the trash out."

Phin was stunned. At the hatred. The rage. Remus was consumed.

"So, who is this mystery man who's behind all of this, Remus? Who are you working for?"

"Oh, nice try Phin. But not so fast. If you're not on

board, and I'm pretty sure you're not, there's no way I'm giving up his name. I'm willing to bet you won't spill the beans on me to the authorities. Cuz you love me so much." He winked at Phin. "But I doubt you'd have such gushy feelings about him. And we don't need any more heat than we already have on us. But all I can say is this: his interests and mine align. Call it a stroke of luck or divine intervention," Remus mocked, "but he is after the same thing I am. And I *had* to take the deal to bust out of the Big Mac. He made it clear he was going ahead with the whole operation with or without me. No way I was gonna sit in the slammer and miss the whole party."

"But why pull me into this, Remus? Why send me what's left of the other cross and lead me all the way here?"

Remus laughed again. "Because I wanted you to know, Phin! I wanted you to know, beyond any shadow of doubt, that it was me, your dear ol' brother, who was going to expose the whole Jesus lie and bring your little religious world crumbling down. I wanted to look at you face-to-face and tell you. I wanted you to see and hold the relics yourself and know that you were that close...that close, Phin, to stopping me, but that you couldn't."

Rage boiled again. But this time inside of Phin.

Remus always knew which buttons to push to get Phin going. He'd promised himself he would not take the bait. He'd done so well at controlling himself.

But in that moment, something snapped inside.

Phin launched himself at his brother.

His shoulder landed with full force in the chest of Remus, threatening to knock the breath out of the bigger man.

The two brothers grabbed on and rolled into the Cross of Gestas, causing the wood beam to land crossways on top of the pair. Phin threw a punch into the gut of Remus while the older brother had Phin in a headlock and was pounding his face with his knuckles. Their scuffling threw the cross to the side and toward the opening in the floor where it landed halfway across the hole and began to teeter.

Phin tasted an explosion of blood in his mouth, as his brother released his grip.

"No, the cross!" Remus yelled as he threw Phin to the side, scrambling toward the relic.

It was pure instinct that took hold of Phin in the next few seconds.

Seeing the cross precariously situated over the hole, Phin gathered himself and bounded over his brother toward the wooden beam.

But not without tripping over Remus.

He fell headlong into the hole and instantly knew he'd made a huge mistake.

Phin scrambled wildly as he fell, arms flailing... grasping...entangling with the rope.

His fall did more harm than good as his legs caught the crossbeam, pulling it over the edge with his body. Somehow Phin managed to grab the cross with one arm while the other wrapped around the rope. But his effort was all for naught.

The Cross of Gestas was too heavy. Phin slid down the rope, his left arm enduring the burn. The cross slid from his grasp and tumbled to the floor below with a crash. Phin heard his brother cry out from above.

That's when the brass crampon holding the rope fast in the rock ceiling above gave way. There was nothing left to slow Phin's fall.

And so he fell.

And he fell.

And as Phin fell, he found himself focusing on the black hole above.

Until his whole world went black.

Chapter 25

The black turned to gray.

And the gray turned to a fog.

Phin's head was working to clear itself. He could tell that he was laying on his back, but lumps of something were under him, pressing and poking. He decided that the discomfort was a good sign.

He wasn't dead.

At least not yet. His next thought was of his wife, Autumn. She might just kill him for being so careless.

Phin worked his head back and forth and finally forced his eyes to open. He could still taste the blood in his mouth from Remus's relentless round of punches. Another good sign, he reasoned.

Without getting in too big of a hurry, he methodically worked his left arm, and next his right. He turned his attention to his legs, pulling them up, bending each at the knee.

So, he wasn't paralyzed.

Autumn would be happy.

His eyes tried to focus on something dangling in front of him. A rope. But hadn't the rope pulled free from its anchor? This was a different rope, he realized. The first was green and this new rope was orange. Remus must have had it in his backpack.

Remus!

Phin pulled himself into a sitting position and took in his surroundings.

He lay on atop a duffle which explained the poking in his back. The green rope that had pulled loose was piled in a tangled mess around him. He was mildly amazed that he was not broken and bleeding. He must have slowed his descent and shortened the distance of the fall more than he realized based on the condition of the palm of his left hand and forearm. Both bore the marks of rope-burn, his palm having lost a nice layer of skin. The pain from both was setting in.

But where was Remus?

And for that matter, where was the Cross of Gestas?

Phin pulled himself to his feet and slowly turned in a circle, taking in the whole of the archive chamber. The cross was nowhere to be found. And neither his brother. But the gear remained. The Pelican case with the air rifle still sat on the large table, the duffle with lights, rope, and other gear on the floor next to it. But something was out of place.

Phin's head was still clouded from the fall. He ran his hand over the back of his head and felt the rise of a lump already forming. *Ouch!* It was tender to the touch.

The satchel...the one Phin had brought with him that contained the....

Phin moved quickly to the table and searched for it.

Gone.

Remus had taken both the Cross of Gestas and the remnant of the Cross of the Good Thief.

What had Remus said when they were in the chamber above their heads? He is going to deliver the cross to his employer. Well not just one cross but two. Clearly, he has plans for both crosses.

But who is this mysterious employer that Remus is working for?

Someone smart enough, powerful enough, resourceful enough, to pull off an escape from a state penitentiary. And to orchestrate the theft of some of the most holy and well-guarded relics of the Christian faith.

But why? That was the big unanswered question. Why?

Remus had said it was all being done in order to expose Jesus as a liar. Phin still struggled to understand how all of that was supposed to work. What was this unnamed employer going to actually do with all of these stolen relics that was going to prove Jesus was a liar?

More questions.

No answers.

Phin had no idea what to do next. Remus was the only lead he had and now he had vanished. If Remus didn't want to be found, it would be next to impossible to locate him. The only reason Phin had been able to track his brother here was because he'd left him clues. But now...his brother had bested him once again.

Phin slammed both fists onto the top of the table in a fit of fury.

A lone piece of paper on the opposite side of the table bounced and flitted to the floor.

Phin stared at it.

He walked cautiously around the table, bent and scooped it up.

Phin,

Don't worry, I didn't leave you for dead, little brother. I checked and all seemed in order. No broken bones or lacerations. I think you'll be sore tomorrow, though. And you might want to put something on that left hand of yours. Looks like a pretty bad rope-burn. Sorry if I sound overprotective, just playing the big brother role. Haha. So, part one of our little game is finished. You wanna keep playing? Part two will blow your mind. I understand, though, if you wanna run on home to that pretty little lady of yours. Say "Hi" to Autumn for me. First, we got yours. Then we got mine. Now, it's time to go get his. See you soon....maybe...

-Remus

Phin read the note a second and then a third time.

Now it's time to go get his.

What in the world? What was he supposed to do with this?

He had a splitting headache, maybe even a mild concussion. What time was it anyway? He looked at his watch.   4:15 p.m.   He must have lain unconscious for several hours. The day was almost over.

What he needed now more than anything was some food and a shower. Then he'd call Autumn and fill her in and then he'd get some rest.

Now it's time to go get his.

He needed time to process and to think.

To go get his.

His? Who is...?

Lightning struck. Phin's mind was crystal clear in that moment.

"No, Remus...you're not...you can't...."

Phin quickly looked to gather his belongings but there was nothing to gather. The only thing he'd brought with him, the satchel with the Cross of the Good Thief, Remus had taken. Phin exited the archive chamber without looking back. If he never returned again to this place it would be too soon. Two visits were twice too many as far as he was concerned.

He walked the long passageway back to the ladder. Then more walking and stairs. He had a slight limp to his gait. His right knee was also sore. He had no doubt that Remus was right about one thing. He'd really feel the effects of his fall come morning.

Phin arrived at the exit of the hidden passage leading back to the archive. He pushed open the door, swung it back into place, and heard a series of clicks as the automatic lock engaged.

"Stop right there!" A voice barked.

Phin whipped around. A lone figure stood ten feet away, a flashlight shining in Phin's face.

"Identify yourself! What's your name?" The voice commanded.

"Phineas Crook. Dr. Phineas Crook."

"Crook? You're Crook?"

Before Phin could answer in the affirmative he heard, "We got him!" The figure lowered his flashlight and drew a weapon.

A handgun.

Phin noticed for the first time that this was a police officer. Israeli police. Phin recognized the navy slacks and light blue shirt adorned with red epaulettes. He held his hands up in a show of non-resistance.

Two more police officers appeared in the back room to assist. "He identified himself as Crook," the officer with the drawn gun confirmed.

"You're Phineas Crook?" a second officer asked.

"Yes, that's right. What is all this about? What's going on?"

"You're under arrest, Dr. Crook." The officer spun Phin around and yanked his arms behind his back. With trained proficiency, he found himself in cuffs in a matter of seconds.

"Please, what's going on?"

"This way, Dr. Crook."

With one officer on either side, Phineas Crook was escorted from the back room out into the main lobby of the clock shop.

Phin squinted as they emerged from the darkness of the storage area into the brightly lit shop. The first thing he noticed was the presence of more officers and what looked like a forensics team.

Everyone was wearing latex gloves; feet were adorned in surgical blue footies.

A woman was taking pictures.

Yellow crime scene tape was strung across the shop's doorway.

And then Phin saw and his heart sank.

Mary.

The kind shopkeeper lay behind the counter. Her eyes were wide open. Staring. As was her neck. Wide open. Staring back at Phin. A massive pool of blood surrounded her body, having gushed from the violent wound.

Phin began to slide into a state of shock.

In what seemed like a great distance away, he heard a voice echoing, "Dr. Phineas Crook, you're being placed under arrest for murder.

Chapter 26

Chief Inspector Antonio Rossi leaned back in the dark green vinyl chair and took a long drag on the cigarette between his lips. It was a cheap chair, much too cheap for someone of his rank. He was a chief inspector of the Polizia Stato, the State Police in Rome. But he wasn't in a position to complain. This was not Rome and thus not even technically his jurisdiction. He was here in Jerusalem by invitation only. At least that was the formal arrangement.

In reality was it was a tip that had brought him to the Holy City. A note really.

Chief Inspector Rossi eyed the folded piece of paper sitting on the metal desk in front of him.

What had started as a search for missing relics and the one who had stolen them had turned into a murder investigation. Something felt off to the seasoned Italian police official.

"Please, Inspector, no smoking. This is not Rome and we don't have the tolerances for such vices as you Italians."

Rossi blew a long line of smoke, emptying his lungs of the toxic chemicals mixed with nicotine. He licked the tips of his fingers, pinched off the end of the cigarette, and casually flicked it into the waste bin. The Jews didn't tolerate much of what Rossi, or for that matter most of the Western world, turned to for comfort.

He found the Kosher laws by themselves to be much too restrictive for his pallet. No pork (he loved his sausages and salami as any good Italian would). And the restriction on cheese - that made no sense to him at all. He was told cheese could only be eaten at breakfast with fish, not at any other meal. Lasagna or fettuccini was nowhere to be found in this country, either. He had to admit, however, that he was mightily impressed with the array of fruits and vegetables available at any time.

He was also grateful for the reception he'd been granted by the Jerusalem police upon his arrival. Of course, the way had been paved by phone calls from the Vatican. It seems that Jews and Christians can find common ground after all...if the right individuals are involved.

Marcus Hadadd seemed to be one of those individuals. His scolding had not been laced with malice or contempt; he stated his request more as a matter of fact.

"My apologies, my friend. I am addicted, I will admit it. The nicotine focuses my mind. But I will abide, of course."

The matter was quickly forgotten by both. The pair

had much more important matters to discuss and could not afford to get bogged down in trivialities.

"The suspect is secure and waiting to be questioned. We have agreed to follow your lead. You have friends in high places, it seems. When it comes to matters of security in Israel, but especially in Jerusalem, we are not used to capitulating to outsiders." Once again, no trace of bitterness or frustration. Only stating the facts.

Antonio Rossi liked this Marcus Hadadd. The man was a Tat Nitzav, an assistant commissioner in the Jerusalem police force, one of the higher-ranking individuals. He had all the features of a typical Jew - olive skin, black curly hair (he kept his cut short), and deep brown eyes. And he had a kind face but Rossi could tell that the fifty-ish something man had seen his share of human depravity.

Security in the Holy City was a daily grind. The normal tensions between Jews and Palestinians would be more than enough to keep most departments busy.

Add in flares to those tensions, along with Muslims and Christians from around the world making pilgrimages to the city, and you had a daily Molotov cocktail just waiting to be lit.

But what he was dealing with now was certainly out of the ordinary. It wasn't because a murder was involved. No, it was because of the circumstances leading up to this murder that made the current situation unusual. In fact, they had not anticipated a murder at all.

A tip is what had led Chief Inspector Antonio Rossi to Jerusalem. Specifically, a detailed letter addressed to him and delivered by courier to his office in Rome just two days prior.

That same letter was what sat on the desk between the two police officers now. The contents of the letter laid out in precise detail a listing of the thefts of each of the holy relics from the churches of Rome and Europe, in order, by date. Some of the thefts were not even known to the public. The only item not listed was the Shroud of Turin, perhaps the most famous, which Rossi found curious. He filed that little tidbit away for later consideration.

The most startling aspect of the letter was the naming of the one responsible: Dr. Phineas Crook, religion professor at a little Baptist college in Oklahoma. Not someone anyone on the task force in Rome or the Vatican had anticipated.

A quick search of Phineas Crook had revealed nothing spectacular about the college professor. By all accounts he led a quiet life. A mugging four years previous had led to the near death of his wife, a one Autumn Eden Rose. An experimental technology had preserved her life and she'd recovered only within the last year. They apparently were infertile but had adopted a young boy from a small village in Ireland. That seemed very atypical but not the kind of red flag that would indicate something more sinister.

A red flag that *did* catch Rossi's attention was the brother. Remus Crook. This man was a *known* thief. He was supposed to be in prison for the attempted theft of a cache of gemstones, but had escaped about six months prior.

Authorities in the United States had assumed the two brothers would connect, that perhaps Phineas Crook was behind the prison break, but so far nothing had turned up to implicate the professor, and Remus Crook was solidly off the radar.

None of it added up to an international scheme to steal holy relics though.

Yet Dr. Phineas Crook had been named in the letter.

And furthermore, the letter indicated that Dr. Crook would be in Jerusalem on this particular day and gave the address of the clock shop where he could be apprehended.

That was enough to engage the powers that be.

Calls were made.

The cooperation of the Jerusalem police was secured, and Rossi was placed on a plane the previous night in order to be here in case Dr. Crook actually showed.

Well, the good doctor did show, and that's when matters took an unexpected turn.

"We don't know with certainty that Crook is responsible for the murder of this shop clerk." Chief Inspector Rossi stated his own fact as he reasoned.

"This is true. But no one else was present. We must start somewhere and since he's all we have, we must start with him. And there is the knife. The murder weapon."

"Yes...the knife. That does seem to point to the doctor, doesn't it?"

The knife in question had been found in the back storeroom where Phineas Crook had been apprehended. A dusting of the handle had confirmed the doctor's fingerprints. That would likely be all the evidence needed to convict the man.

They had a body. They had a weapon. They had an assailant. But what they didn't have, and what bothered Chief Inspector Rossi the most, was a motive.

"But why, Commissioner? Why kill a defenseless old woman who works in a clock shop? What's the threat? And your team searched the premises, even those old tunnels and the chamber buried down low. No relics, right? Nothing stolen or illegal."

"Please, my friend, call me Marcus. We are brothers, are we not? Maybe I am a Jew and you a Christian, but we are both of the brotherhood of law enforcement. And may I call you Antonio?"

"Yes, of course...Marcus, and thank you." Rossi was genuinely touched by the man's warm turn.

"So motive is the great mystery. That is what I sense in you." The assistant commissioner was perceptive. "But let me tell you from experience, a lifetime of living in one of the most contested and volatile parcels of land on planet Earth. Motive takes on many forms. And when it comes to religion, that by itself is enough motive for some. I have seen the radical face of religion rear its head over and over. If you live in Jerusalem, you will see it on nearly a daily basis. A kind-looking Palestinian woman will walk into a market to buy bread and blow herself up. This is why the security in Israel is so tight. It is why we are the best in the world at what we do. We can't afford not to be. Everyone who surrounds us wants to see our destruction. And that is motive enough for some."

The Jewish officer paused to pick up his coffee mug from the table and take a sip.

"You have your vices and I have mine," he said smiling. "Now these crimes you are investigating, that have brought you to my city...they are clearly religious in nature. Artifacts related to Jesus have been stolen, and at great risk to the one stealing them, I think. These are bold and brazen thefts. That alone indicates a radical nature to the perpetrator. In my experience, such a man is capable of anything. Even murder."

Rossi had to admit that his Israeli colleague made sense. But nothing about the scene at the clock shop pointed toward violence. Especially not the kind that would lead to the viciousness of the attack on the pitiful shop clerk. She had nearly been decapitated in the assault.

But Rossi and Hadadd had what they had to work with and that was all. And what they had to work with was sitting down the hall chained to a table and chair.

Rossi rose from his chair. "I suppose, then, it's time we have a conversation with Dr. Phineas Crook."

Chapter 27

Phin sat in the hard metal chair and leaned over with his forehead resting on the equally hard metal table.

How can this be happening to me?

He knew they would be watching him. There were cameras in each corner, tucked up next to the ceiling. One wall of the tiny room was a glass mirror, likely the kind on TV where they can see you but you can't see them.

Phin could not get the image of Mary out of his mind.

Poor Mary.

Laying in a pool of her own blood.

Dead.

In the most horrible and undeserving way possible.

She didn't deserve what happened to her. And somehow the finger was pointed at him? What was he supposed to do? He couldn't tell them the truth, at least not the whole truth.

He'd been sitting in the room for what felt like hours. There was no clock on the wall. He'd seen something on the serial crime dramas about that too. They want you to lose track of time.

He had to pee.

What was he supposed to do about that if they kept him in here much longer?

The door clicked and two men entered.

Phin sat up straight, eyeing the two men as they casually walked to the table and took seats opposite him. The older of the two was clearly part of the Jerusalem police, as evidenced by his uniform. The other he was unsure of. Very sharp, dressed in a nice light gray suit and white shirt but no tie. The police officer was carrying two Styrofoam cups, one of which he slid toward Phin.

"Something for you to drink, Dr. Crook. It may be a long evening for us."

Coffee. Phin's bladder spasmed.

"Can I please call someone? I need some counsel."

"This is not the United States, Dr. Crook. Different country, different laws. No, you cannot make a call right now. Perhaps later, though. By the way, my name is Marcus Hadadd. I am the assistant commissioner assigned to this case."

"Look, I understand what you're thinking, but it's not true. It wasn't me."

"And what exactly are we thinking, Dr. Crook? Enlighten us, please."

"You think I killed her, don't you? But I didn't. I had fallen, you see. Hit my head and was out cold. When I woke up, I was just going to leave, go back to my hotel and call my wife. I didn't even know she'd been killed until after I was in handcuffs."

The officer eyed Phin with suspicion. "Okay, let's talk about the murder then. The one you know nothing about. How exactly did you know Mary Gannab?"

"Mary Gannab," Phin repeated in a whispered tone. "So that was her name." He thought about the face of the kind woman, the warmth she had exuded.

"You didn't even know her name?" the Israeli officer asked. The man in the suit still had not spoken since entering the room and that unnerved Phin for some reason.

"I knew her first name...Mary. But not her last. We'd met only twice."

"Yes, Gannab. That was her surname. An unusual last name for a Jew. It's Hebrew, of course, but would be translated in English as *thief*."

This little revelation startled Phin, but he tried not to let it show. He noticed that the man in the suit gave his partner a quick glance as if this was news to him as well.

"Don't you think that is an interesting, how shall we say it...coincidence? That here you sit, Dr. *Crook*, being questioned in the murder of a woman that you claim you hardly know, but whose last name is *Thief*? So, what we have here is a Crook accused of murdering a Thief. What do you make of that, Dr. *Crook*?"

Phin had to laugh.

The logic was absurd. Clearly, generational family connections were at play. Mary Gannab was the guardian of the Crook family archive and obviously part of the larger "family" of Crooks or Thieves or whatever the archive sought to chronicle and preserve. But how in the world was he supposed to go about explaining any of that in a way that would make sense to the two accusers sitting in front of him? And did it really matter? Mary was still dead and Phin didn't do it.

And then Phin thought about his brother.

Remus.

Why would Remus kill Mary?

What purpose would it serve?

Did she try to stop him from leaving with the Cross of Gestas?

Had things turned violent?

But she was an old woman, no match for the brawn of Remus. Plus, violence was completely out of character for his older brother. And it was against the family code. No violence. The Crooks didn't even carry weapons when they conducted their operations of thievery.

But something Remus had said to him down in the archive chamber came rushing back to the front of Phin's thoughts.

"It's been a long time since we were kids. There's a lot about me you don't know anymore."

Was it possible that Remus was capable of murder? Of an old woman? If so there really were a lot of things he didn't know about his brother. And he had already broken the Crook code once when he broke out of prison. *Crooks take their punishment if they're caught*, that's what their father had taught them. But breaking out of prison is far removed from murder. Then again, if Remus didn't kill Mary, who did? Phin's thoughts were going round and round in his head.

"Dr. Crook!" A hand slammed down on the metal table. "This is no laughing matter. I asked you a question."

"Excuse me? I'm sorry. I was just thinking."

"Less thinking and more talking, Dr. Crook. Now why don't you tell us about how you knew Mary Gannab. Are you related somehow? Is this a family dispute gone wrong? You said you'd only met her twice. Maybe we should begin there."

Phin gathered himself and began, not really sure where his words would take him. "Look, all I can say is this. I met Mary Gannab two times in my life. Once was about a year ago, on another visit to the clock shop. The second time was today. Just a visit."

The Israeli officer wrote a few notes down on a piece of paper. "Was anyone else with you?"

Phin thought carefully before answering. "I came alone."

Not a lie.

More jotting of notes.

"Let's go back to this fall you said you had. The one that knocked you out. How exactly did that happen?"

"I was climbing. And I slipped."

"Climbing." The officer repeated as if he wasn't buying it.

"That's right. I was...looking for something."

"What exactly were you looking for, Dr. Crook?" The man in the suit spoke for the first time.

Phin was surprised. He was not Jewish. His accent made Phin think of an Italian.

The man in the suit saw the look of surprise on Phin's face.

"Let me introduce myself, Dr. Crook. My name is Chief Inspector Antonio Rossi, of the Polizia Stato in Rome. I am in Israel by invitation of the Jerusalem police. I am conducting an investigation into the theft of holy relics belonging to the Catholic Church. To get to the point, my investigation has led me to here, to the Holy City. And to get even more to the point, my investigation has led me very specifically to you. Dr. Phineas Crook. So let me ask again, Dr. Crook, what exactly were you looking for?"

Chapter 28

"I need to go to the bathroom."

Phin's bladder was about to explode. Plus, he needed to buy some time. Time to think. He also felt like he might get sick.

In one moment, he was being questioned about a murder. In the next, the finger of blame for a string of thefts from churches around Rome and Europe was being pointed right at him. By name. An Italian inspector had come all the way from Rome looking specifically for him.

How is this possible?

Phin thought about his best friend back in Oklahoma, Max Allred. He'd tried to warn Phin. *Don't go down this road. It won't end well.* That was the whole reason Max had refused to come with him. *You've gone too far this time, Phin.* Those were some of Max's last words to him. It appeared Phin should have heeded his friend's advice. He really had gone too far this time.

Chief Inspector Rossi leaned back in his chair and looked at his Israeli colleague. Assistant Commissioner Hadadd seemed resigned to the inescapable call of nature.

"Yes, of course, you need to use *ha sherutim*, the restroom. Let's take a short break, shall we?"

The Israeli rose and rapped twice on the door to the interview room. A short officer dressed in military fashion, fatigues and all, entered, took Phin by the underarm, and lifting him to his feet, escorted him down a long hallway. They passed two more rooms similar to the one he had been in.

The doors were open.

Empty.

A larger, more open area was dotted with numerous desks, most occupied by other officers, male and female. They all stopped what they were doing as Phin was led past, looking at the American who'd been arrested for murder.

The door to the bathroom was within an easy line of sight from this open area, Phin noticed. He made it a point to notice all the details of his surroundings, from the time he'd been driven away from the clock shop and the body of Mary, right up to where he now stood.

He was on the second floor of a four-story building. The first floor was occupied by a small lobby and a heavy metal security door.

Behind that door was a beehive of activity. Lots of police, phones, radios, computers.

An elevator had deposited him on the second floor and into the room where he'd sat for several hours alone. That same elevator was behind him now, at the end of a long hallway.

He had not been photographed, fingerprinted, or undergone any other type of processing. Phin assumed that was because once his information was entered into the "system," it would accelerate the widespread knowledge that an American had been arrested in Jerusalem, and that, in turn, would alert and engage the U.S. Embassy.

For some reason, the police didn't seem to want that to happen just yet. That must mean, Phin thought, that more was going on than just a murder.

Phin chided himself for thinking of Mary Gannab's killing as "just" a murder. A kind woman had her life ended in a violent and cruel act today. Phin didn't do it, but someone had - maybe his brother - and Phin was connected on some level. He just didn't know how.

The officer nudged Phin toward the bathroom door. He turned and lifted his shackled hands. "Help me out here?"

"Sorry, no can do. You've got enough slack to take care of business."

"Ah, well. It was worth a try."

Phin knew they wouldn't remove the cuffs and chain. That wasn't really the purpose of him asking anyway. He could remove the chains on his own in less than ten seconds if he wished. The very thing he needed was in the heel of his shoe.

Phin was an expert at locks. One of the advantages of his DNA.

His real intention was to deflect. By asking the officer to remove the chains properly, the man would never suspect that Phin could release himself should that time come.

Opportunity.

That's what Phin was looking for as he took in all the details.

He noticed an exit sign on the far end of the room where the officers sat. Having taken their attention off of him, they were busy back at work.

Phin entered the bathroom alone, which mildly surprised him. He understood once inside. A one-seater. No room for a second person. Phin made a quick look of the small bathroom. A counter and sink he could stand on. A drop-down ceiling with tiles that could be lifted. It was possible. If given enough time. Phin didn't have that luxury right now. He began taking care of business.

What would escape accomplish right now, anyway? They already knew his name, and likely more. Where he lived, his employer, his family. If he ran now, Autumn would get a visit shortly.

Unless.

Yes, there was a reason they had not processed him into the system. Something bigger was indeed going on. The key was the Italian. He knew enough about Israeli security to know that they would not easily just open themselves to outside influence. The one named Rossi was here because of the thefts. The missing holy relics of Christ. They were the key. Phin had to think and think quickly about how to answer the inspector's questions.

He finished, flushed, and washed his hands. Exiting the small restroom, the officer again took him by the arm and led him back to the interview room.

Empty.

The two officials had left the room.

He took a seat, the door closed, and he was alone again. But not for long.

The door opened and his questioners were back. This time the Italian was carrying a folder and the Israeli was caring...a knife.

It was inside a plastic Ziplock bag. He set the knife on the table halfway between himself and Phin. Blood was still on the weapon and had smeared the inside of the clear plastic bag. Phin thought he might need to rush back to the toilet but knew he'd never make it in time. He swallowed hard and looked away. The men were watching all of this — his eyes, his reaction — with great interest.

"Let's talk about what has brought me to Jerusalem, Dr. Crook."

Chief Inspector Rossi opened the folder and began to lay out on the desk a series of photographs. Phin recognized them all: the holy lance, the Reliquary of the Holy Crib, the Sudarium of Oviedo, the Shroud of Turin, and more. They were all there, the thefts Phin had read about on the newswire and one (and only one) he'd been responsible for. He swallowed hard a second time but for a different reason.

"You look disturbed, Dr. Crook. Perhaps, you can explain."

"Explain?"

"Yes, explain. All of these items have been stolen from Rome's great churches and basilicas in the last six months. Most of them are public knowledge but a few of them are not, because the thief left behind a forgery and covered his tracks well. But not so well that my investigators did not notice. This is a major crime, Dr. Crook. Perhaps the crime of the millennium. Never before has such a thing been attempted and the reason I am here is to make sure that the thief does not succeed." Chief Inspector Rossi's accusatory eyes bore into Phin's. "So, that is why I am here, Dr. Crook. Now, let's talk about why you are here."

"Me?" Phin stuttered in spite of his best efforts to remain calm.

"Yes, you said you were at Ms. Gannab's shop because you were looking for something. Perhaps something you had left in her care, Dr. Crook? Something or some things that perhaps she sold for profit? And then when you came to collect them, you were enraged and...well, rage can lead the best of us to do the...unthinkable. I've seen it many times. You may not believe me but I suppose I could say that I understand, in a manner of speaking."

Rossi slipped a gold case from his coat pocket, thumbed it open and extracted a cigarette. He ran it under his nose, inhaling the fragrance of the tobacco, but did not light it. He began to finger it instead, turning it over and over.

"As I said," Phin began with his best effort to sound sincere. He knew everything he was about to say would be recorded. "I've been to Mary's shop twice and met her both times. I was here today because I was interested in a specific timepiece. Something very old. I thought, perhaps, that Mary could help me. She allowed me to rummage through her back room, and as I told you, I was climbing up to reach something when I fell. Hit my head and was out cold. When I came to, well...you know the rest."

Not exactly the whole truth but enough of it that Phin comforted himself with not having just lied to the police.

Rossi continued to eye him carefully, turning the cigarette over and over in his fingers.

"Let me show you something else, Dr. Crook." He opened the folder once again and extracted a single piece of paper. "Please take a look at this. I think you will find it very interesting. Especially the part that includes your name."

Chapter 29

Chief Inspector Antonio Rossi and Assistant Commissioner Marcus Hadadd observed as Dr. Phineas Crook picked up the letter and read. They both, of course, knew the contents of the note, but were keen to see what sort of reaction the American college professor might betray.

> *To Chief Inspector Antonio Rossi,*
> *Who I am is of no consequence to you. Please do not attempt to identify me or investigate the origins of this letter. I can assure you that both will be met with futility and will result only in a waste of time. Precious time that you do not have, Inspector. Holy relics belonging to the Church have been stolen over the last six months. Attached is a detailed list of each theft - we both know some of these thefts are publicly known and others are not. What you are most interested in is catching the one who so*

skillfully avoided detection and stole these items, and then securing the return of the holy relics of Christ. The thefts by themselves have created a massive embarrassment for the Church. I can help you with your first goal - catching the thief. I cannot, or I should say, will not help you with the second. But if you are successful in catching the thief, he will surely be the clue to helping you accomplish your second goal of seeing the items safely returned.

I offer you two pieces of information. The first is a name: Dr. Phineas Crook. The second is a location and date: Dr. Crook can be found at the House of Reuben, a small antique clock shop located in the Jewish Quarter of the Holy City of Jerusalem. You will find Dr. Crook at the House of Reuben two days from now sometime after the noon hour.

Sincerely,
A friend

Phineas Crook held the letter in his hands for quite a bit longer than a single reading would warrant. Chief Inspector Rossi surmised that he was reviewing the contents a second, perhaps a third time. At last the doctor set the paper back onto the table and slid it to the mid-point, next to the bagged knife.

"A most interesting letter, is it not, Dr. Crook?" Rossi asked.

"It is indeed. So, you received this two days ago?"

"That is correct. And where, may I ask, were you two days ago, Dr. Crook?"

"I was home, in Oklahoma, with my family."

Rossi leaned forward, and in one swift motion pointed the cigarette at Phin. "At last, the truth! Yes, you were indeed home two days ago. And it was on that day, the same day this letter came to me, that you booked your flight to Jerusalem."

Rossi paused. He wanted the man across from him to weigh what he'd carefully revealed. The Italian police had been watching him. For two days. They knew he'd booked a ticket. They would have been here, in Jerusalem, before he arrived. Would have followed him from the airport to his hotel. Would have observed him as he left this morning for the House of Reuben. Yes, he could see the college professor working all of this out in his mind.

"Well then, you know that I wasn't the only one in the clock shop, don't you? You obviously had the placed cased. Am I correct?" Phin's questions were good. The American was thinking with him.

"We were watching, yes."

"Then tell me, what else did you see? *Who* else did you see? Because I'm telling you, I didn't kill Mary Gannab."

And that was part of the problem for the two police officers. Yes, they had personnel positioned to watch the alley where the House of Reuben was located. But Misgav Ladach Street was small and narrow, more of a cut-through between two larger streets. It had been impossible to place anyone too close to the little clock shop without raising suspicion, so they had been relegated to the ends of the alley, still a good distance from the centrally located shop which had been Phineas Crook's destination.

The doctor had arrived late morning. Much earlier than had been expected in light of the arrival information in the mysterious letter: *sometime after the noon hour.* The decision had been made to wait until sometime after noon before closing in and detaining Phineas Crook.

What had they seen?

Plenty.

Plenty of locals and plenty of tourists using the alley as a shortcut, or to even stop in to do some shopping at the House of Reuben or one of the other few shops that resided along the passage.

Dozens of people had crossed down the street in the hours they observed. Yes, they took pictures of them all.

It had been solely Antonio Rossi's investigation at that point. If Dr. Phineas Crook was using the House of Reuben to house and hide the stolen holy relics of Christ, perhaps there was also a plan to sell them on the black market, a very shady and very real underground of unscrupulous antiquities dealers. Men and women who collected historically unique works for their vanity collections.

So, Rossi had ordered anyone coming or going to be photographed. Nothing unusual had occurred at all save one man who had exited the street carrying what looked to be an old piece of lumber. But nothing resembling any of the stolen relics of the Church. They would obviously go back and run all the faces through the various crime databases to see if anyone got a hit.

"The problem, Dr. Crook, is not who else was or wasn't present at the House of Reuben." Assistant Commissioner Marcus Haddad responded to Phin's question before Rossi could. "The problem is the knife." He put his hand on the bagged weapon and slid it a few inches closer to Phin.

"Let me be clear, Dr. Crook. Your fingerprints are on this knife. As is Mary Gannab's blood. What I'm saying is that we have the murder weapon and it has your prints on it."

This was the first news that truly seemed to stun the American, who, up until now, had been pretty calm and collected in his mannerisms. Rossi was a bit perturbed with his Israeli colleague, though. Yes, it was true, what had started off as an investigation into stolen holy relics had turned into a murder investigation. And the murder in question was not within his jurisdiction. But he was beginning to feel like the two of them, Rossi the Italian and Hadadd the Israeli, were stumbling over each other with opposing agendas.

It wasn't that Rossi was unconcerned about the murder. In fact, he was very concerned about it. But only in light of what it had to do with his primary objective: find the one who stole the relics and secure the return of those relics.

Something didn't feel right to Antonio Rossi. He'd spent a career in law enforcement and he'd never experienced anything like the web that was being woven in front of him.

The letter he had received bothered him immensely.

Who had sent it?

What agenda was at play?

Because there absolutely was an agenda.

This was not a simple case of someone trying to do good by informing on a thief. It was all too neat and convenient, that he could just show up in Jerusalem and arrest Phineas Crook and find the relics.

And now a murder.

Something was very much out of place with this whole scheme.

And then there was the issue of Phineas Crook the man. Rossi had been around a lot of bad men in his career. He had interviewed liars, terrorists, thieves, murderers, rapists, you name it. He could smell evil a mile away. Dr. Phineas Crook had no smell about him. He struck Rossi as sincere and decent. He sensed no outright deception. Oh yes, there was more that the good doctor knew than he was telling, but he had serious doubts that he had murdered Mary Gannab.

Phineas Crook was, by all accounts, who he presented himself to be: a humble college professor, a family man. Crook's passport indicated he was well traveled though. But lots of Americans travel. That doesn't make a man a murderer. So, Rossi had more work to do. Was Crook the thief he was looking for? He had his doubts about that as well. For now, Antonio Rossi would keep all his thoughts on this case to himself while he continued to work it out.

"Well, here is what I am going to say," Phineas Crook began his response to the facts being presented to him. "I don't care if my prints are on that knife or not. I did *not* kill Mary Gannab. I told you, I was out cold. Doesn't it seem possible...likely even, that whoever did kill Mary would want to cast the light on someone else? In order to cover their tracks? It would have been no trouble at all for the real killer to wipe the weapon and then use my hand to put my prints on it while I was unconscious."

"Spoken like a man who is guilty and desperate to build a case for the courts." Commissioner Hadadd was unconvinced.

"Unbelievable. You people are impossible. You've already made up your minds, haven't you?"

"In my experience, Dr. Crook, the answer to any puzzling question is always the one that is simplest and makes the most sense."

"Makes the most sense, huh? Well, explain to me please, what kind of sense it makes for me to kill someone and then hang around until you guys show up? Wouldn't it make more *sense* for me to run?"

"Except we have this matter of the missing holy relics of Christ. The reason my colleague from Rome is here. If you indeed are the thief, you'd be desperate to find what you believe Ms. Gannab had stolen from *you*, what you had placed in her safekeeping. But then she betrayed you. And, of course, you had no idea that Chief Inspector Rossi was closing in. You only just now saw the contents of the letter. So, you would have been in no hurry to search the House of Reuben for your precious stolen relics. Only you didn't count on your unfortunate fall, did you? But it doesn't matter, because either way, we were there. The whole time. Watching and waiting. You were never going to escape, Dr. Crook. You need to face the truth - you have been betrayed and now you have been caught. You are a thief, and yes, you are a killer."

Phineas Crook threw up his hands, clearly exacerbated.

Chief Antonio Rossi took in the whole exchange with great interest. He was more convinced than ever by what he had just seen. He still wasn't sure who Phineas Crook was, and there were many questions still to be answered, but he was certain that the man was no murderer.

Chapter 30

Phineas Crook sat in an isolated cell. He was alone. And he was exhausted. The long day had more than caught up to him. All he wanted to do was curl up into a fetal position and fall asleep. Perhaps he would wake up to discover that all of this was one bad dream.

No, that wasn't going to happen.

Instead, Phin stood and walked to the entrance of his cell. A solid metal door with a thick glass window. He was grateful for at least that. There was no other window in his new home.

How long will I be here?

No idea.

He had once again paid attention to details as he'd been led to his cell. Back to the elevator, down two levels. That meant he was in a basement below ground level. He had passed a lobby with chairs, larger than the lobby on the first floor. Most likely a place for family to wait when coming to visit someone in the jail. Behind a security door was a processing area. They skipped that. He had still not been photographed, printed, or gone through any kind of formal booking. He was even in his street clothes. They were keeping his arrest quiet for some reason.

They had taken him down a long hallway with white tile, white walls and a white ceiling, past a number of cells just like his. Several of them occupied. A few empty. They eventually came to the one he was currently in. They deposited him, removed his wrist and leg irons, and left him alone. Phin walked back to his bed – a cot was more like it – and laid down, staring at the ceiling.

The letter...sent to the one named Rossi...is why he was laying in this cell. His mind had reeled when he read the message and saw his name in print.

Someone had known he was coming to Jerusalem – to the House of Reuben. Two days ago, they had known and they had sent a letter by courier to Chief Inspector Antonino Rossi in Rome. A letter naming him as the mastermind of a string of thefts against the Church. And "they" could only be...Remus. His brother. But why would his own brother do such a thing? His encounter with Remus in the archives had disturbed him greatly. His brother was consumed by some brand of anger unfamiliar to Phin. Was this Remus's way of punishing him? For not falling in line with the family business? For what Remus had endured during the final dream or vision they had experienced together? It felt like Remus was holding all of this against him.

And then the murder.

The killing of Mary Gannab was inexplicable to Phin. She was a helpless old lady. Remus was ten times stronger than her. She was no threat to him in any way. He could have walked out of the shop with the Cross of Gestas and she could have done nothing to stop him. Why did Remus have to kill her? And in such a brutal fashion. Phin closed his eyes and shook his head, trying uselessly to erase from his mind the image of Mary in a pool of her own blood.

And then Remus had committed one more unthinkable act of betrayal. He had taken the knife he used to slit Mary's throat, walked it all the way back down to the archives where Phin lay unconscious from his fall, and planted Phin's fingerprints on the knife. Then he walked the weapon all the way back up and deposited it in the back storeroom of the shop.

That took thought.

That took premeditation.

It painted the picture not of a man who had a moment of bad judgment and had made a mistake. No, it painted, instead, a picture of evil. Remus had not killed Mary and then panicked and run away. No, he had slowly, methodically, framed his own brother for the killing, and then calmly walked away from the scene.

Is this who Remus Crook had become? Remus had always resented Phin for walking away from his destiny, his calling to follow in their father's footsteps.

But what about Remus?

Nothing in his brother's actions the last six months, since breaking out of prison back in Oklahoma, resembled anything like what Adonis Crook had taught his boys. His father was a thief, yes, but a thief with a sense of honor, a code of ethics as it were. And Remus had seemingly thrown all of that to the wind.

Phin didn't like thinking of his own brother in this way, but what choice did he have? It appeared that this was who Remus had now become. Phin could think of no other explanation for all that had happened to himself. It truly did look like this was Remus's plan all along. To steal the holy relics of Christ from the Church of Rome, to pin the whole thing on Phin, and to top it off, throw in a murder to boot. Remus clearly didn't want Phin wiggling his way out of this one.

And Phin could see no way out. His interrogators were good. The Israeli, the one named Haddad, a commissioner of some sort, had already made up his mind. Guilty. Of murder.

The other one, Rossi, the inspector from Rome, was more focused on the thefts, as he should have been. That's the whole reason he came to Jerusalem in the first place. He had but one task at hand: find the thief and find the relics. And from his perspective, it looked like he may have caught his thief. Phin knew otherwise, of course.

But then a thought. A rush of adrenaline.

Phin sat up and swung his legs over onto the floor.

Rossi would send people to the U.S.

To Oklahoma.

To his home.

There was probably a team on their way now. They would interrogate Autumn. She was his wife. She would know about her husband's side hustle, right? That he was traipsing around Europe stealing religious artifacts. Except he wasn't, and she wouldn't know anything. Because there was nothing to know. But if they searched his office at OBU, and then made their way to his study carrel in the library...they would find...*the Shroud of Turin.*

"Oh, no...." Phin whispered through clenched teeth. "Stupid, stupid, stupid." he said louder. "You're an idiot, Phin." They would eventually interview Max. What would his best friend tell them? If he admitted to knowing about the Shroud, then he would be in a lot of trouble. Not as much as Phin, but enough to lose his job and career. Phin had not only messed up his own life, but he had put in jeopardy another man's good name and life.

Phin's mind began to spin out of control. Max. Autumn. Poor Autumn. What would she think when they came? Would they tell her where he was?

He had to warn her. Tell her what was about to happen. Maybe she could take Patrick and leave for a while. Go to her parents. But he couldn't even make a phone call. Heck, he wasn't really, technically, even here...in jail. But he was. He just wasn't in the system. To anyone looking for him...well, it would be just like he had slipped off the grid.

Blank.

Zero.

Nowhere to be found.

He thought of his son. Patrick. The boy had been through so much in the six months before the adoption. The trauma of losing both his birth parents. And now he was facing losing another father. He couldn't let that happen. He had to do something. But he was helpless. Utterly helpless.

Phin rose and went to the door of his cell. He examined it. There was no locking mechanism on his side.

Only the outside.   No doorknob either.   Just a thin
rectangular crack all the way around where the door fit into
the jam.   The lockpick in his shoe would do him no good.

But he had to get out.

He had to fix this.

All of this.

He had to find Remus and confront him.   Not only to
clear his own name; Remus would have to face justice for
his crimes.   The thefts...the murder.

The kind face of Mary flashed through his memory yet
again.   Such a warm person.   He'd given her a hug just
before descending into the archives and she had responded
with an infectious laugh.   Remus would be held responsible
for what he had done.   Phin would see to it.

The key to the whole thing was the relics.   The ones
Remus had already stolen.   And if Phin was right, then...a
new thought.

Phin dug his hands into his pockets.   His left one
smarted terribly from the rope burn.   Which one was it in?
He felt it in the right pocket.   The note.   The one Remus
had left for him when he woke up in the archive.   He
unfolded it and read it again.   This time certain lines stood
out from the page.

> *You might want to put something on that left hand of yours.*
> *Sorry if I sound overprotective, just playing the big brother role.*
> *Part one of our little game is finished.   You wanna keep playing?*
> *First, we got yours.   Then we got mine.   Now, it's time to go get*
> *his.*
> *See you soon....maybe...*

Phin scratched his head. These were not the words of a man who was finished with Phin. No, there was more to come. *So why the setup, Remus? Why am I here in jail?*

It didn't make sense. But there was one thing Phin knew for certain, he had to get out of this cell. But how?

Just then a guard appeared at the door. Phin's stomach rumbled, reminding him that it was probably mealtime. Phin didn't know how this would work, whether he would take his meal in the cell or, was there a cafeteria?

The door lock clicked and the guard stepped in. He wasn't carrying a tray so Phin guessed they'd be headed down to the...

"What's up, Doc?!" came a gruff voice. Phin slowly rose, unsure of the man in front of him. "Hey, don't look so surprised, will ya? You didn't think we'd just leave you in here to rot did you? Now hurry up and move fast. This is a jailbreak after all!"

Phin couldn't believe his eyes.

He was staring at Sergeant Billy Warren.

Chapter 31

"Billy! What...how...?"

"No time for chitchat, Doc. We gotta move."

"Sure...yeah, whatever you say. Let's go!"

Sergeant Warren threw an arm into Phin's chest before he could step into the hall. "Hold up." A pair of cuffs appeared and the sergeant secured Phin's hands with quick precision. A hand went to his ear and Phin saw the in-ear security speaker, a white coil coming off it and down his shirt. "Oz, we ready? Coast is clear?"

"Oz?! You got Oz on there with us?" Phin had not seen Oz Jenks, the computer whiz who worked for LaPhage Industries, in nearly a year.

Warren put a finger to his lips as if to hush Phin. "Ten-four, got it." He was talking to Oz. Back to Phin. "Okay, let's go, Doc. Walk slow and calm now, just like I'm escorting you."

Phin nodded and moved out into the hallway led by Sergeant Warren. He closed and re-locked the cell door behind them. A foul odor emanating from the retired Marine caught Phin off guard and caused him to wrinkle his nose and slip to the side. Warren seized Phin firmly by the arm and pulled him back close.

Phin had no idea what the plan was. Would the sergeant attempt to simply walk him out the front door? Billy was in a guard's uniform, but Phin would surely be recognized.

This isn't going to work.

Panic began to set in. Phin had participated in his share of clandestine activity when he was a teenager – he and Remus together. He knew enough to listen to his gut and his gut was telling him this was not going to end well. The Israelis were the best in the world at security. When every country around you wants to wipe you off the face of the earth, you sort of get good at things like that.

Sergeant Warren had them only halfway down the hall before he darted into an open cell. He jerked Phin in with him. It was unoccupied. Good thing, Phin thought. Then his confusion cleared when he saw the rope hanging from the ceiling. He looked up. A hole. Cut with some kind of torch by the look of the burnt edges against the white paint.

"Okay Doc, up you go. I'll be right behind you."

Phin nodded. He obediently grabbed the rope and hoisted, only to drop back to the floor in pain.

"Ahhh, my hand!" He shook his left hand, the rope burn firing back at being abused once again.

"Let me see." Sergeant Warren grabbed his arm and examined the wound. "Second degree. Nasty. Bet it hurts like a mother. Hold on a sec." Warren dug in a small black canvas duffle in the corner of the cell. Out came a pair of gloves and a small canister. "Here take these and let me see that hand again." He shook the canister and sprayed its contents on Phin's left palm. An instant sensation of cold overwhelmed his nerves, almost to the point of a different kind of pain. Then it settled into a soothing feel and finally more of a numbing effect. "There, that should take care of things in the short term. Now get going."

Phin moved back to the rope.

"Doc!" Phin stopped and looked at the sergeant. "The gloves, Doc. Put the gloves *on*. Sheesh, you're a crappy patient." Sergeant Warren smiled and winked.

Phin donned the gloves and grasped the rope a second time.

Much better.

In fact, he felt no pain at all. He shimmied up the rope with decent skill.

Thinking back to the climb in the archives, it struck Phin as ironic that this was his second climb of the day, albeit this one was much shorter. But more was at stake with this climb. He had to get out of here and figure out what to do next. He had no idea where Sergeant Billy Warren had come from or how he even knew Phin was locked away, but there would be time for questions and answers later. He was grateful and, knowing Billy, had risked a lot to come get him, he didn't want to be the one that screwed things up on the way out.

He crested the cutaway in the ceiling and, pulling himself through, rolled over and gave Warren a thumbs up. The sergeant had gathered his bag and was waiting. He too made short work of the climb, and in only a moment was through the hole and alongside Phin.

"Now sit tight while I take care of this." Sergeant Warren pulled the rope into the crawl space. He then lifted a large plate. It was the portion of the ceiling that he had cut away. He went to work securing it back into place.

Phin took the opportunity to look around.

The two of them were hunkered down in a tight space between the basement and first floor of the police precinct center. It was pitch black except for the tiny worklight Warren had set off to the side. Conduit, ducting, and utility pipes snaked around them. There was maybe three feet of headroom.

It was good that the holding cells were in the basement, Phin suddenly realized. If they had been on one of the main floors, there would have been virtually no space for what they were doing now.

Phin imagined that when the design of the building was approved, the thought of placing the holding cells in the basement added to the security of those being held. They were underground after all. But that one design feature had seemingly provided for his escape.

Which shifted his thoughts.

"How exactly are we getting out of here, Billy?" Phin whispered.

"Hold on a sec," the ex-Marine grunted. "There, okay. That should be good enough." He wiped his hands on his pants and turned to Phin. "They won't know what happened to you. You'll be gone from your cell. Poof! Oz hacked the security video and created a short loop. Bought us time to duck in here without being seen on the cameras.

Once they come to check on you and see you're gone, the last place they will look is another cell. And if they do happen to look through the window, all they will see is empty. They'd have to walk all the way in and look up to figure it all out. But they'll be too panicked to take time to do that at first. By the time they get around to a thorough search, we'll be history."

"But how? How'd you get in and how are we getting out?"

Warren only smiled. "You may not like it, Doc. But follow me."

The sergeant flipped around, grabbed his light, and began to duckwalk into the darkness. "Be sure and position your feet on these support beams. Don't want you falling back through the ceiling into an actual locked cell. And the steel beams will mask our movement. We need to be as quiet as possible."

Phin waddled after Billy Warren. He led them through what began to feel like a maze. A few turns and he was completely disoriented. They scrambled through a mishmash of pipes. One of them hot, carrying steam likely. Phin had to take care to not add to his burns. It was also muggy and he began to sweat. Soon his shirt was soaked. He was again amazed that his friend had actually come for him. He had so many questions.

As he crawled on, the stench he had smelled on Warren began to grow.

What is that?!

Phin wanted to recoil.

They came to a cinderblock wall that had been breached. By Warren, he assumed. It looked to be an external wall of the police facility. The hole was just big enough for a body to wriggle through. A four-inch PVC pipe that ran through the wall had been broken off just on the outside of the wall. Gunk and water looked to be leaking from it in irregular spurts.

No. Not gunk and water.

Warren turned to Phin. A look of *I'm sorry* on his face. "Came through the city drainage system to breach the building. Broke a sewage pipe from the building on the way in."

Now Phin understood the odor that had been emanating from Warren. "No..." His voice trailed off.

"Yeah, it ain't pleasant that's for sure. I'm sorry for what I'm about to ask you to do, Doc. But there's no other way."

An alarm went off.

It could be heard blaring above and below them. Phin's heart shot into his throat. They both immediately knew what it meant.

"Well, looks like the jig is up. Hold your nose, Doc. We gotta go. Now!"

Chapter 32

Chief Inspector Antonio Rossi was back in the borrowed office the Jerusalem Police had lent him. He inhaled deeply on the Marlboro Red, an American cigarette but very popular in Italy - one of Rossi's favorites. He'd brought a carton with him to the Holy City, unsure if he'd be able to feed his habit locally.

He blew the smoke out the open window next to where he was sitting - a compromise that his Israeli colleague had agreed to. Not unlike the arrangement in his office back home.

"What do you make of our man?" Assistant Commissioner Marcus Hadadd asked.

"I think he is guilty of less than we think but knows more than he is letting on," Rossi concluded.

"So, you trust his word, Antonio? You believe him when he says he did not kill the woman?"

"I don't know that I trust his word, my friend. But I think I trust his soul. And no, I do not think he is the one who killed the shop clerk."

"What does that mean...you trust his soul?"

"It means I think he is a good man. It means that I think he has given us a layer of truth, but there is more going on with Dr. Phineas Crook. Much more."

"And you don't think he killed the woman?"

"No."

"Interesting." Commissioner Hadadd dwelled on this for a moment. "I am not sure I do either."

Antonio Rossi was surprised by the admission. "But you seemed so certain when you questioned him. Accused him is more like it."

Marcus Hadadd smiled. "There is a saying the Americans have when questioning suspects. Good cop, bad cop, I believe it is. I let you be the good cop, Antonio. And I chose to be the bad cop. I wanted to see if I could get him to crack. To give up what he knows."

Now it was Antonio Rossi's turn to smile. The chief inspector from Rome had been bested by his new Jewish friend. He had already liked Marcus Hadadd, but now he liked him even more. The Israeli officer had good instincts, something that he himself took pride in having. Rossi decided he could confide in Hadadd about the additional layer to this whole mystery that he was struggling with.

"Marcus, let me, as you say, give up more of what I know...about what has brought me to your Holy City." This piqued the interest of the Israeli and he leaned forward. Antonio Rossi ground his cigarette into a mug that his new friend had provided, a makeshift ashtray of sorts. "Have you heard the name Pontia before? Alexander Pontia."

"Pontia. Pontia." Hadadd repeated the name, his thoughts grinding. "Yes, somewhere in my mind...isn't he some sort of antiquities dealer?"

"Yes, exactly. He's the one. Owns an auction house called Token Exchange. He's also into security and international shipping. I believe he has some sort of presence here in Jerusalem."

"It's all coming back to me now. Dominion Safe. That's the name of his private security firm. We take security very seriously here in Israel, of course. Outside security firms are heavily scrutinized by our government. There have been some tensions between our own police and Dominion Safe at times. But nothing we haven't been able to work out. Certain wealthy individuals prefer and can afford their own security. We try to accommodate."

"The letter I received two days ago is not the only letter that has been received about the thefts I am investigating."

"Not the only letter?" the assistant commissioner questioned. A look of concern wrinkled his brow.

"The letter sent to me, naming Dr. Crook, was actually the second letter. Another letter, along with a photograph, was delivered to the Vatican. Understand, I am sharing this with you in the strictest confidence."

"Of course. You can trust me, my friend. Please continue."

"This first letter named Alexander Pontia as the architect of the theft of the Church's holy relics."

"And there was a picture you say?"

"Yes, of Pontia. He was holding the Holy Lance. The

very instrument that the Bible claims pierced the side of Christ as he was hanging on the cross."

"Fascinating. And there is no doubt? As to the identity of Pontia?"

"It is him. So clearly, he is involved. But he would not be so foolish, or have the skill I don't think, to pull off the actual heists. I was hoping that the letter I received, the one pointing to Dr. Phineas Crook, would be the other piece of the puzzle. If we could capture him here in Jerusalem, *with* artifacts in his possession, then we could perhaps squeeze him for details: Why did he do it? How much is he being paid by Pontia? And most importantly, where are the relics?"

"And you don't want to simply walk into Alexander Pontia's office and arrest him, do you?"

"Certainly not. A man with as much power and resources as Pontia-"

"Would immediately insulate himself." Assistant commissioner Marcus Hadadd finished Rossi's sentence for him.

"That's one way to put it. He'd likely disappear. Along with the relics. We would never see Pontia or the Church's property ever again."

"And you have another problem, my friend. A glaring one."

"And what would that be?"

"Who is this mysterious sender of letters and photographs? And why is he helping you?"

Antonio Rossi couldn't agree more. Perhaps, more than the theft of the holy relics themselves, this was what bothered him the most. He'd never encountered anything like this in his entire career. A string of thefts so bold and brazen. An attack on the Holy Roman Catholic Church - on Christianity itself. And someone close enough to the whole thing that they were naming names and informing the authorities of both the Vatican and the Roman Polizia Stato.

"I'm not sure he is helping me." Antonio Rossi unpacked his candid thoughts for his Israeli colleague, for whom he was developing an unusual trust. But this mystery was bigger than himself, he needed another mind on this. "I feel like I am being pulled along. Led as it were by some puppet master. I don't like this feeling. And now after meeting and talking with the good Dr. Crook, I am more convinced than ever that something is not right. There is a game being played here, Marcus. And I don't want to play, but I may have to in order to get to the bottom of what all is happening."

"I see your point. The murder of the old shop clerk does indeed feel like a distraction, doesn't it? I am thinking...yes, I am thinking that the whole matter goes back to the stolen holy relics. They are all connected to Jesus, you say? That is the common thread?"

"It is."

"So therein lies the answer to what all is going on." Seeing that Antonino Rossi was struggling but intrigued, Marcus Hadadd continued. "Jesus is no stranger to us here in Israel," he laughed.

"So, I've noticed. He's literally everywhere around this country it seems."

"He is indeed. You see, Christians from around the world pilgrimage here each year, throughout the year. It never stops. They come to see the holy sites: the Mount of the Beatitudes, the Sea of Galilee, the ruins of Capernaum, some even get baptized in the Jordan River. And then there is Jerusalem... Zion. They come to walk the streets of Bethlehem, just a stone's throw from the Holy City. They ascend the Mount of Olives, descend into the Garden of Gethsemane, and then rise to the Temple Mount itself. They take what they call the Lord's Supper in the Garden Tomb area, and I could go on and on. We Jews have a special relationship with Jesus. We were, you see, the ones that demanded Jesus be put to death – at least the religious leaders of the day. The idea was to get rid of the troublemaker. Crucify him and he would be done away with once and for all." Marcus Hadadd laughed yet again. "Well, that didn't work out very well, did it? There is more of Jesus around Israel and in Jerusalem than there has ever been. The death of Jesus, it seems, was only like planting a seed in the ground. What sprouted has spread out of control."

Antonio Rossi listened in fascination to his friend's perspective on Jesus Christ. Despite the crude analogy of a weed spreading without regard, there was no bitterness in his tone.

Rossi thought of his own faith. He had been raised Catholic. Haven't all Italians? But his was a domestic faith more than a devoted one. Yes, he believed in Jesus. The son of God? Sure. But did such a belief have any impact on his daily life? Not really. He rarely attended mass. In fact, this case of the missing relics had turned his attention to Jesus more in the last six months than his combined church attendance over the last ten years.

"You are a Jew, are you not, Marcus?" Antonio Rossi finally asked.

"Yes, I am, my friend. An observant one too. I keep Shabbat and follow all the Kosher dietary laws. I read the Torah each day and I pray to God. There are many who are Jewish only by birth but, yes, I am a religious Jew as well, I suppose you could say."

"It sounds like you are a better Jew than I am a Christian. I hardly attend church at all and I never read my Bible."

Marcus Hadadd laughed again. This time with a bit more gusto.

"What's so funny?" Rossi fired back.

"Look at us. A devoted Jew and a rogue Catholic, brought together around the man, Jesus. Both of us running from the man, yet neither of us can escape him! Now tell me you don't find that humorous."

Rossi had to agree. He found his shoulders shaking as he laughed as well at the absurdity of it all.

Hadadd gathered himself and turned serious again. "So, it's about Jesus, my friend. Not about Pontia and not about Crook. Find out *why* the Jesus relics have been stolen and you will find out what is truly going on here."

Assistant Commissioner Marcus Hadadd of the Jerusalem police was correct. The holy relics of Christ had been stolen for a reason. Discover why and the case would solve itself.

"So, I think you are right, Marcus. With that in mind, let me explore with you an idea about all of this."

Before Rossi could explain himself, he was interrupted

by the blaring of an alarm. "What's that?!" he yelled over the blaring.

"Quick, we must hurry, someone is attempting to break out of the holding cells in the basement."

Chapter 33

Phin stepped out of the shower, having washed the filth from his body. He could still smell the odor of raw sewage in his nostrils. Most likely a mental thing.

He'd summarily discarded his soiled clothes upon arrival at the safehouse. Sergeant Warren seemed to have thought of everything. He hoped in time, and a short time at that, the memory of crawling through the drainage from the broken sewer pipe would fade.

Billy Warren had apologized in advance for what they had to do, but that made the visceral nature of the act no less real.

Phin searched the medicine cabinet in the small bathroom and found a bottle of Old Spice. He popped the top and generously applied the classic sent all over his chest and face. Hopefully that would do the trick.

In the bedroom attached to the bathroom, he found a dresser with a wide range of clothing. He found some boxers in his size along with some jeans and a plain light blue t-shirt. The closet contained six pairs of the same style of New Balance running shoes sizes 6 through 12. He tried on the size 10 and they were a perfect fit.

He joined Billy Warren, who was on a laptop in the living room, already showered and changed himself.

"You look like a new man, Doc," Sergeant Warren called over his shoulder without fully looking at Phin. "Smell like one too!"

"That may have been one of the worst experiences of my life."

"Trust me, Doc, it can get a lot worse." Warren held up his left arm and kicked out his left leg. The left arm was clearly a prosthetic. The sergeant was clad in his signature tight-fitting black t-shirt. Phin knew that under the khaki cargo pants was a prosthetic leg as well. But not just any old prosthetics. Billy Warren sported LaPhage Limbs, advanced limb technology that connected a robotic prosthetic directly to the brain, allowing near lifelike control and even nerve sensation. It was literally like having one's severed limb back. Very expensive, of course, but Billy worked for LaPhage Industries, having been recruited personally by the company's late CEO, Ruth LaPhage.

Phin couldn't help but think of the beautiful heiress to her father's kingdom every time he was around Billy. Her death was a tragic one, the pinnacle of an ill-fated adventure to the center of creation itself, the Garden of Eden.

Sergeant Billy Warren and Phin had not gotten off to the best start relationally, but since Ruth's death, they had grown...close would be one way to describe their relationship, but even that did not mine the depths of their friendship and mutual understanding.

Billy had somehow inserted himself as a presence in Phin's life, always seeming to pop up just when he was needed. Something Phin felt inadequate to return on his part. The relationship felt very one-sided because of that.

Phin sat down on a loveseat in the sparsely decorated living room. "Okay, it's time we talk. How in the world did you know I was in trouble, not to mention have any sort of clue as to where I was?"

Sergeant Warren rotated away from the laptop and desk to face Phin. "Your wife called me."

"Autumn? But why?"

"Max was with her. They Zoomed with me. Told me you were in over your head. Max mentioned something about some blanket that covered Jesus. Had a fancy name I can't remember."

"Shroud. He's talking about the Shroud of Turin."

"Yeah, that's it. Anyway, he said you really stepped in it this time, Doc. I looked up this, what'd you call the blanket thing again?"

"Shroud." Phin buried his head in his hands.

"Yep, Shroud. I looked up this Shroud and I gotta tell you, you're in a heap of doo-doo, Doc. Lots of folks buzzin' about that deal. I knew you were a sneaky sucker, underneath all that tweed and smartness you sport yourself in, but dang, Doc, that was a pretty impressive job you pulled off swiping the Jesus blanket thing."

"So Autumn knows. I can't believe Max told her."

"Well, it's a good thing he did and a good thing they called me. Your little lady said she had a bad feeling about what you were up to and asked me to join in your little treasure hunt for your brother, but it didn't take long for me to figure out you'd really fallen down a hole on this one."

"And how exactly did you find me, Billy? They didn't process me at all, no mug shot, no paperwork - it was like they were trying to keep me off the grid on purpose."

Sergeant Warren smiled, reached back and grabbed his laptop. He showed the screen to Phin. "Say hey to Oz. He's the boy genius that found you."

Phin couldn't believe it. Oz Jenks, sandy-colored moppy hair and all, was smiling big behind brown plastic round-rimmed glasses, his brown eyes sparkling. It looked like the Incredible Hulk was his t-shirt of choice for the day. From the looks of the computers and various other gadgets behind him, he was in The Lair, his personal and very secure lab in the basement of LaPhage Industries back in Fort Worth, Texas.

"Oz! How are you? I'm speechless. I don't even know how you did it, but thank you."

"Hey Dr. Crook. Don't just thank me. Israeli cybersecurity is the best in the world. I had a little help hacking into their system to get a lead on where you were. Say hello to my new partner." A second face came into view and the blood drained from Phin's face.

He was staring at a ghost.

Oz Jenks could see that Phin was struggling and quickly helped him out. "Dr. Crook, meet Ronald Chen. Tony's *brother*. Yeah, I know, they look a lot alike."

That was an understatement.

Ronald was the spitting image of Tony.

A wave of sadness and joy swept over Phin all at once. The Asian tech superstar had lost his life at the Garden of Eden, along with Ruth LaPhage. It was a tragedy that impacted all involved, but mostly Oz Jenks. The two worked side-by-side in The Lair and were as close as two people can be. Blood brothers. At times, they were so in sync that it seemed as if they shared one brain. Oz had been devastated at Tony's death.

"I called Ronald, he goes by RC...I called RC last year to see if he wanted to come and take Tony's place...to work, you know, with me. We both thought it would be a good idea. To help us both move on. I gotta tell you though," Oz's somewhat somber tone picked up, "he's every bit as sharp as Tony. I think it must run in the Chen genes."

"It is so nice to meet you, RC," Phin replied. "You have no idea what an honor it was to work with your brother. I am so sorry for your loss."

"Thanks, Dr. Crook," the spike-haired young man replied. "It's super great to meet you as well. And I'm glad we could find you so Sergeant Warren could break you out."

Phin sat back, taking it all in. It was like his past was repeating itself. The gang from LaPhage Industries was all back together again: Billy Warren, Oz Jenks, and now Ronald (RC) Chen. And they'd all come together to help him. Overwhelming.

"I don't know what to say."

"How 'bout thank you," Warren butted in. "Took a heck of a lot of work and chicanery to find you and get you out of that jail. And now we've really kicked the hornet's nest. I don't know what your plan was in coming here and if you found what you were looking for, but my plan says we get out of this country a-SAP. The police are buzzin' and I'm pretty sure the whole military's gonna be looking for you shortly."

Phin couldn't agree more. He'd found what he'd come for: Remus. And now Remus was gone, who knows where. But he'd left behind his one clue: *First, we got yours. Then we got mine. Now, it's time to go get his.*

Phin knew what he had to do.

But Sergeant Warren was right, they had to get out of Israel as quickly as possible. He couldn't risk being caught again. If he were, the Israelis would make certain he'd not escape a second time.

"So, what's the plan?"

"The plan?" Warren echoed the question. "Easy...we're goin' swimming with the tourists."

Chapter 34

"He's on the run."

Dimitri Bezrukov stood outside the Jerusalem precinct building, watching as police scrambled on foot and by automobile. The Russian relayed the message by phone to his boss in New York City.

"He must have had some help. I don't believe he could escape this quickly on his own. I'm surprised he escaped at all, really." Alexander Pontia was contemplating the news from Dimitri.

"I can pursue him, or them, if you like. Find them both. Dispose of the help, and ensure Crook is recaptured."

"No need for that. We've already accomplished my goal with Dr. Crook. All the attention is on him now. He cannot go home. He must run and run he will. We'll come back to him later. It's not ideal but we can work with this minor change of plans. I want you to turn your focus back to the older brother. Are you still scheduled to meet with Remus tomorrow?"

"That is correct."

"And he has no idea his brother is in trouble?"

"None."

"Perfect. So go ahead and meet with Remus and follow the instructions just as we planned."

"Your wish is my command, Comrade." Dimitri Bezrukov ended the connection and disappeared into the bustling streets of Jerusalem.

Alexander Pontia laid his cell phone down and turned his attention back to Tess Greenway.

"The Jews have mishandled Crook. Somehow, through their incompetence I am sure, he has escaped." Alexander paused a moment, considering who he was talking to. "My apologies, Tess. I did not mean to offend your heritage."

It was easy to forget that Tess Greenway had Jewish roots by her physical appearance, particularly her blonde hair. Alexander wondered for a moment if it was her natural color or if she dyed it for some reason. Whichever the case, she was stunningly beautiful and one certainly did not think of her as a Jew, her last name the only outward clue.

"You do not need to apologize, Alex. I served my time in the IDF. Gave two years of my life to the nation of Israel. But there are too many religious zealots in the country for my tastes. If you ask me, they will be the ruin of Israel one day." She spoke with firmness and held his gaze with an intensity of her own.

The truth was that Alexander Pontia was thoroughly anti-Semitic. He hated the Jews and viewed them as a scourge upon the earth. He did his best to hide the depth of his disdain and succeeded for the most part. His distaste for Jews was perhaps only exceeded by his distaste for religion as a whole, particularly Christianity, which he viewed as a religion born from Judaism. He had no love for Islam either, but the Judeo/Christian tradition was where his true energies were focused. Which was what his current project was all about. Yes, even with Phineas Crook's escape, his overall plan was still on track.

"Maybe I should send you to join Dimitri and his team," he mused out loud.

He may have hated the Jews, but Tess Greenway fit in a different category for Alexander. He was drawn to her beauty, yes. But he was also attracted to her strength of personality and her killer nature. She reminded him of himself. Not more than a few times did he imagine himself beginning a romantic relationship with her. But he was more disciplined than that. Plus, he truly did love his wife, Jillian. She was a woman of strength as well and had helped him build the empire they both now enjoyed, although she'd slipped into the background in recent years.

Most of the men who ran in the social circles of Alexander Pontia had at least one mistress on the side. But as much as he was attracted to Tess Greenway, he did not need the complication that an affair would bring. Her value to him was in her deceptive skill. She didn't necessarily look it on the outside, but he could send her anywhere to do pretty much anything and she was resourceful and skilled enough to get it done. No matter what the task.

"If you need me to go, I will go. But I don't think the focus will be in Israel after today, will it?"

Tess didn't know the whole of Alexander's scheming, but she had been brought along on enough of the plan that they could converse about it.

She adjusted herself in the seat directly across from Alexander, uncrossing her legs and recrossing them from one side to the other. Her knee length skirt rode up just a bit until she adjusted it.

No, Alexander didn't need that kind of distraction.

Stay focused.

"No, it will not. The brother, Remus, will be headed back to Rome. I need him to retrieve one more artifact. He already has his instructions. This will be the most difficult theft yet, I think."

"Because he's already robbed from that church once before?"

"Absolutely. The Basilica di Santa Croce in Gerusalemme is where he stole the Cross of the Good Thief. I had hoped the forgery he left in its place would conceal the theft and allow him to more easily return, but it was not so. I imagine security will be elevated. It will not be easy."

"I don't understand why you didn't just have him steal both pieces the first time. Why go to the trouble and the risk of a second break-in?"

"Because, my dear Tess, that wouldn't have been as much fun." Alexander Pontia's demeanor took on a more sinister tone. This appeared to excite Tess Greenway. She smiled, the tip of her tongue brushing her upper lip. "I need everything into fall in place, one controlled step at a time. I needed the Cross of the Good Thief first because I needed Remus to pull his brother into my little game."

Alexander Pontia recalled how easily it had been to manipulate the hapless Remus Crook. He was so drunk on his own vengeance that he'd followed Alexander's suggestions like a starved dog pouncing on a meat bone.

"Don't you have a younger brother, Remus?"

Of course, Alexander already knew this. He was never unprepared.

"Maybe he could help us?"

The disgust Remus had for his own flesh and blood had been obvious.

"Oh, he's just a college professor. I see."

And it had only taken the slightest of nudges to convince Remus to pull Phineas Crook into the web of the spider. Alexander had even succeeded in making Remus believe that sending the birthday gift along with the note and splinter of wood from the Cross of the Good Thief had been his own idea. Remus Crook may be an extraordinarily skilled thief, but he was an extraordinarily stupid man - more easily manipulated than Alexander would ever have imagined.

For his grand spectacle to play out as he had dreamed, Alexander needed two brothers from the Crook lineage – this had been the plan the whole time. That two brothers had so easily come to him after Dimitri Bezrukov had brought Remus Crook to his attention – well, what a stroke of luck it was. No, it was something more...

Destiny.

Vengeance.

The wrongs of history made right.

Alexander Pontia could see it all falling into place.

"I won't be sending you to Israel or anywhere just yet,

Tess. I want you focused on the logistics with the Egyptians. It won't be long before we are all ready to leave for the mountain," he continued speaking to his assistant. "And let's see how well Remus does with this next theft."

"And the brother? Dr. Crook? What about him?"

"Let him run. For now. If he's good enough to escape a Jewish jail cell, he's likely good enough to evade capture. He can't go home so he'll pursue his brother, Remus. He has no other options. And the police will continue to pursue him - especially that one officer from Rome. Antonio Rossi."

"That's the one part about this that makes me the most uncomfortable. Why, Alex? Why have you been so brazen about revealing yourself? Why the letters and the picture?"

Alexander Pontia laughed out loud at the question. Yes, Tess Greenway was a Jew after all. Shallow and unseeing.

"Because, dear Tess, I *want* them to know. All of them. I wanted that fool at the Vatican to see me - Alexander Pontia - holding his precious relic...his *Holy Lance*. I wanted all of them to know that I have all the relics of Christ, well almost all. Remus is still headed back to Rome. And I want the Polizia Stato to come. That is why I sent the letter to Rossi naming the younger Crook brother. Did you see how quickly he jumped at my beckoning call? That's because I *want* him to come. INTERPOL. The FBI. The Vatican. All of them. Let them chase the brothers in order to find me. But I will only show them *what* I want to show them, *when* I want to show them. And when they see...oh, when they see, they will know exactly how wrong they have been.

Not just about Alexander Pontia, but about Jesus...about everything!"

When Alexander finished his rant, he found himself breaking out in just a hint of sweat. Even when Alexander Pontia was out of control, he was still in control.

Tess Greenway was enthralled by the charisma of her employer.

She stood up, walked over to Alexander, and to his great surprise, sat down on his lap and began to kiss him deeply.

Chapter 25

Phin and Sergeant Warren found themselves sitting in the back of a tour bus, cruising across the Judean wilderness on Road 90. Desert was a more accurate term.

The Jewish tour guide was ever-present on the bus's loudspeaker, explaining in great detail how the surrounding geographic features fit with the biblical text that the rest of the occupants had read about their whole lives.

"We are driving right now through the area known as the Valley of the Shadow of Death. This is where King David was camping when he wrote his most famous Psalm, Psalm 23. You know it, do you not? *Yea, though I walk through the valley of the shadow of death, I will fear no evil.* This is the area, my friends. Take a moment to look around as we drive and think on those words of David."

The guide, whose name was Avi, took a break and refreshed himself with a drink of water.

243

It was early in the morning but the day was growing increasingly hot as they had descended from the heights of Jerusalem into the scorched desert wilderness area of Israel. Their destination – The Dead Sea.

It had been a fitful night waiting for morning to come. Phin didn't get any sleep, even though Sergeant Warren had told him to try. The sergeant had promised to keep vigil all night and make sure their safehouse was not discovered by the authorities, who were surely crawling the city by now.

Sirens wailed and lights flashed outside the windows periodically, but they never came. The commotion, however, was enough to keep both men awake and alert. Plus, the spray Warren had used on Phin's hand had worn off and the raw sting had returned.

The tour bus had stopped at a small shop selling olive wood products just one block from the safehouse at 8:30 that morning. Oz Jenks had made arrangements for them to join the church group. As it turned out, Oz's own grandmother was on board and it was her church from Georgia that was on a ten-day tour of the Holy Land. This was the same grandmother that had taken Oz to church when he was a little boy and had planted the tiny seeds of an unrealized faith in him.

Phin was amazed at the timing. That a tour bus with Oz's grandmother from Georgia just happened to be stopped one block from their safehouse on just the day that they needed help getting out of the city was almost too much to believe.

"Sometimes it's better to be lucky than good," Sergeant Warren had commented with raised shoulders.

The men had shuffled quickly to the bus as soon as Oz gave the word. It was as if he was their "eye-in-the-sky." Who knew what kind of satellite system he'd hacked into, but he gave them the coast-is-clear sign in Sergeant Warren's earpiece and off they went.

The maroon bus was immediately visible at the end of the block. In short order they had joined thirty-five American tourists as they were exiting the olive wood shop, small plastic sacks in hand with their purchased treasures.

Oz's grandmother was delighted to meet them. She'd been on the lookout for her grandson's friends who, according to Oz, were in the city for business but had the day off and wanted to take a dip in the Dead Sea. Mae Geer was her name and she was a wiry old woman with a charming smile and a stronger than expected hug.

"You must be Billy and Phin!" she had exclaimed, grabbing each of them in turn in a powerful embrace. "Ozzie says you are a doctor," she said, looking at Phin. "I've got this pain in my shoulder, maybe you could look at it?"

"Whoa, whoa, whoa, Grandma!" Sergeant Warren inserted himself. "He ain't that kind of doc." Mae Geer looked at the sergeant, trying to understand what he was saying. "You know...he's not a doctor, doctor. He's like a book doctor. All brains, no hands."

"What he's trying to say, Mrs. Geer, is that I'm a college professor. Oklahoma Baptist University. I teach Bible classes." She was a dyed-in-the-wool Baptist herself and before long was introducing Phin to the rest of the group, bragging that her grandson's good friend was a college professor at the prestigious Baptist university of Oklahoma. And she *insisted* that the men call her Mae.

Things eventually settled down and Billy Warren and Phin found themselves near the back of the fifty-passenger bus as they motored toward the Dead Sea.

"So, what's the plan, Sergeant?" Phin finally asked when they could speak without being overheard. "How exactly are we getting out of the country?"

"You'll see, Doc." And with that, Billy Warren leaned over and closed his eyes for the first time since breaking Phin out of jail.

It was a quick nap.

The ride from Jerusalem was only forty minutes until Avi announced over the loudspeaker that they had arrived at Kalia Beach. He informed the group that they would stay here for only ninety minutes. That was enough time for those who wanted to float in the Dead Sea to do so. Avi was very strict: do not open your eyes in the water. The high magnesium chloride and potassium chloride contents would cause severe pain and burning. These same sediments made it impossible to drown in the Dead Sea.

"If you can't swim, no worries. You will automatically just float," he reassured the group.

Those who did not want to float could enjoy ice cream in the shade of the cabanas on the boardwalk.

The group filed off the bus, chattering with great excitement about the opportunity to touch the famous sea, which sat 1,300 feet below sea level.

Sergeant Warren grabbed Phin by the arm and quickly led him from the group to the gift shop.

"Pick out a set of trunks and let's get changed."

Phin obeyed as ordered. He found a coral pair with a red floral pattern. Warren was waiting at the counter with his selection already paid for and in a plastic sack. He paid for Phin's and the two exited, Warren walking quickly. Phin worked to keep up.

Kalia Beach was crowded with tourists, which was the case most days.

"Perfect," Warren declared.

IDF personnel could be seen scattered throughout the area in their olive fatigues. Phin could only imagine how stifling hot it must be for them. He had already soaked his t-shirt.

The men found an empty changing booth supplied by the beach staff for tourists. Phin went first and then waited for Warren.

When the sergeant emerged, Phin let out a howl. "You've got to be kidding me!"

The ex-Marine presented himself in a neon blue Speedo, very tight, with one very white leg and one mechanical prosthetic a more natural color.

"What?! Don't laugh, Doc. Prevents chafing. You'll be crying before long and beggin' for a pair of these babies. Let's go."

Warren hustled on down to the beach, blue Speedo and all. The only other item he carried was a type of fanny pack. He headed toward the portion of the beach where the kayaks were moored. He spoke with an attendant, exchanged money, and began dragging two of the floats into the water.

"Here, take this." He shoved a two-sided paddle into Phin's hand, all business. "You ever done this before?"

Phin nodded, "Yep, floated the Buffalo River in Arkansas a couple of times."

"Good, let's go, but act natural. We'll take our time paddling to the edge of the swimmers and then kick it into gear. Just follow my lead."

Phin obeyed.

The two men made their way through the menagerie of men and women, all ages, floating on the Dead Sea. Several had scooped handfuls of mud from the bottom and smeared it all over their bodies. Supposedly the chemical makeup of the sediment held therapeutic value for the skin.

Lifeguards were stationed on the beach, making sure everyone stayed safe, even though drowning was theoretically impossible. Several other kayakers paddled around as well.

The two men reached the edge of the swimming area.

"Okay Doc, let's just take our time and row down a ways from the swimmers. Try and look normal, just like a couple of tourists out for a paddle. Doesn't look like anyone's paying too close attention. That's good."

"I still don't understand what we're doing. What's the plan?"

"The plan is to paddle across this sucker, Doc. It's nine miles to the Jordanian shoreline. We can do that in two hours if we hump it. But the border is technically only halfway across. Once we're there, we've made it."

Made sense, but Phin wondered about what came next. Two men in swimsuits in the desert of Jordan with no supplies. He chose not to ask. Billy Warren always seemed to have a plan.

Another twenty minutes and the two were at least two hundred yards from the swimming area and still had not attracted any extra attention. Warren gave the nod and the two began to head straight across the Dead Sea.

"Row hard, Doc," he grunted. "Let's get some speed and momentum if we can."

It was hot and there was no breeze. Phin wished he had brought some water and he wished desperately for more of the cooling spray the sergeant had used on his raw hand the day before. The paddle dug in and any time the tepid water splashed on the wound it burned like wildfire. But the college professor pushed all that aside. He did not want to be re-captured and find himself back in an Israeli jail cell.

His thoughts began to drift to Remus. His brother. *Where are you now, Remus? And where are you headed?*

Phin was trying to formulate a strategy on how to stop Remus from what he was now certain he was going to attempt to do.

The men rowed for half an hour before the wail of a siren could be heard from the shore.

"Dang! That ain't good, Doc! Let's go...row, *row*, ROW!"

The men dug in.

How far had they come?

The sergeant had said two hours to cross from shore to shore. That meant halfway would be one hour. They'd been rowing for...nope...not enough.

Phin pushed even harder.

It was only another five minutes before the whine of engines could be heard. Had they been recognized? Had someone from the tour group been questioned and had they been identified that way? Or had some drone spotted them from above and noticed they were running for the Jordanian border? But is that even illegal?

"Heave-Ho!"   Warren shouted.   "Go, Doc, GO!" Warren's muscles of his natural arm bulged.

Phin chanced a look back and saw three black dots but they were still a distance away.

Hope flared.

Would the IDF violate a sovereign border in order to bring them back? And how would they know if they had made it to the Jordanian side of the sea?

The boats were more than dots now. Phin could see armed soldiers inside. Someone on a loudspeaker was yelling at them in Hebrew.

He rowed on.

Left side. Right side.

Left side. Right side.

Left.

Right.

Flares shot from the stern of one of the boats and popped overhead. Some kind of warning, Phin knew.

He didn't stop, keeping pace with Sergeant Warren, the two nearly side by side.

They weren't going to make it. It was obvious.

Phin thought about Autumn and Patrick. Hope began to fade. Sergeant Warren was good, but not that good, and their luck had apparently run out.

Then Sergeant Billy Warren stopped paddling. "Okay, Doc. Do you trust me?"

Phin stared.

"DO. YOU. TRUST. ME?"

Phin nodded.

Sergeant Warren reached over, grabbed Phin by the shoulders and plunged the both of them into the depths of the Dead Sea.

Chapter 36

Forty minutes earlier...

"We've got a hit and a location!"

The Israeli technician burst into the office where Chief Inspector Antonio Rossi was finishing his coffee and a raisin bagel with cream cheese. Assistant Commissioner Marcus Hadadd was typing away at his computer. Both men bolted to their feet.

"Let me see," ordered Hadadd. He snatched the paper from the hands of the underling.

It had been a long night after Phineas Crook's escape from the basement jail facility. A long and embarrassing night for the Jerusalem police. If the Israelis prided themselves on anything, it was their security. The best in the world. No one just breaks out of an Israeli jail cell. In fact, such a thing had never happened. Yes, the holding area in the building's basement was not meant to be a permanent solution for someone facing long-term incarceration. It didn't have the features of a dedicated facility. Nonetheless, it was still an *Israeli* security center and that meant something. Heads would roll over the breakout.

It was a controlled chaos in the aftermath. Both Hadadd and Rossi knew that Phineas Crook could not have gotten far, yet it seemed he had vanished into thin air. That he had been assisted from an unknown outside person or persons was without question. This had the feel of a professional operation. And while the two colleagues in law enforcement had both agreed that Dr. Crook was not the likely murderer of the clock shop owner, clearly there was more to him than met the eye, much more.

The entire Jerusalem police department had been mobilized to find the missing American college professor. The IDF had also been engaged. Checkpoints were enhanced. Within minutes, the face of Dr. Phineas Crook appeared on the handheld devices of every law enforcement officer in the country:

WANTED: Considered Unarmed. High Priority Target. Accomplices Likely Involved. Engage With Caution.

All border crossings and ports of entry (water and air) were on alert. The Israelis employed the most sophisticated surveillance system in the world. Their advancements in technology rivaled the Japanese, Chinese, and even the Americans.

"It's definitely him," declared Hadadd, looking at the printout with the image of two men. He handed it to Rossi, who nodded and confirmed the face of Dr. Phineas Crook.

"Who's that with him?" Rossi asked.

"Eighty percent likelihood that it's a man named William Barfield Warren. American. Former military. Marine. He currently works as a consultant for an American conglomerate called LaPhage Industries. Not much else came up. Unmarried, no family." The tech specialist had come prepared to be questioned.

"How long ago was this taken?" Hadadd asked this time.

"We got the hit just five minutes ago."

Rossi was impressed. Five minutes and the Israelis already had a profile on the unknown accomplice, William Warren. *These people are good*, he thought.

"And?"

"Sir?"

"Where are they, man? Spit it out!" Hadadd's mind was churning with ferocious speed. The prey was cornered and he was impatient to spring into action.

"Yes, sorry sir. Kalia Beach. They're at the Dead Sea with a bunch of tourists. This image was captured from a camera in the gift shop there."

Antonio Rossi looked confused. "What does that mean, Marcus? Why are they at a beach? That doesn't make any sense."

"Yes it does, my friend." The commissioner looked at the technician who knew as well. The young man nodded. "Jordan. They're gonna make a run across the Dead Sea for the Jordanian border. Makes perfect sense. They would know that we would be watching the airports and the roads.

But the Dead Sea...it's the most unguarded portion of our border, only nine miles to get across."

"Only four and a half miles to the Jordanian side of the Sea," the technician corrected.

"Only four and a half miles." Hadadd repeated.

"They can cover that distance in only ten minutes in a fast boat." Rossi was alarmed. Had they found their target only to lose him?

"They won't have access to a boat. No boats at Kalia Beach."

"Then..."

"Yes, they'll have to swim or paddle more likely."

"We've got IDF on site," the technician reminded the assistant commissioner. "It's standard at all tourist locations," he explained for the benefit of their Italian guest. "But they've blended into the crowd. They're looking, but it's very difficult with so many people. It's the high season for tourists."

"They'll show themselves when they break across the Dead Sea." Hadadd looked at his watch. "We've got time! Mobilize the IDF water patrol. Order some boats to Kalia as quickly as possible. Come on Antonio, we can be at the beach in thirty minutes."

The two men tore out of the second-floor office and down the stairwell. No time to wait for the elevator. They left the technical specialist to follow the assistant commissioner's mobilization orders. Hadadd would follow up on the phone while in route.

The men tore through the streets of Jerusalem, the lead vehicle in a three-vehicle entourage of black SUVs.

Lights and sirens blared. Shooting out of the city they made quick time headed east, then south.

Twenty-eight minutes and they arrived at Kalia Beach. No doubt a record.

Four boats manned with IDF personnel were waiting on the shoreline. Metal Sharks. Defiant Class 27, Rossi observed. Again, he was impressed.

"You Commissioner Hadadd?" A beefy man in olive fatigues and a black beret was waiting on them.

"That's right." Marcus Hadadd clasped the hand of the soldier.

"I'm Lieutenant Colonel Levi Rubin. We got 'em spotted. About two and a half miles out. They're on kayaks."

Two and a half miles. Antonio Rossi did a quick calculation in his head. Yes, they still had time.

"Thanks for your quick response, Colonel," Hadadd replied.

"You're welcome. Been waiting on you for about ten minutes, though. Could've had 'em rounded up by now but was told to wait."

"Well, let's wait no longer. Let's go get them."

The Jerusalem and Italian officers waded into the shallow water and climbed into the waiting Defiant. It shot out from the shore and joined three others. Very quickly all four boats were jetting across the Dead Sea.

Colonel Rubin handed a pair of binoculars to Hadadd and pointed. He could see them. They were paddling hard, one of the men looking over his shoulder at the approaching boats.

"That's right Crook, we're coming to get you," he muttered under his breath. He handed the binoculars over to Antonio Rossi. "This will all be over within a few minutes, my friend."

Rossi took the eyeglasses and held them to his eyes, although they had closed the distance enough to where one could see the pair of fugitives without the enhancements. Rossi found his heart racing as the boats closed the gap.

The men stopped paddling.

Rossi turned the dial on the binoculars to get a closer look. Were they giving up? It looked so. They could clearly see the futility of their efforts. The men were talking to each other..

And then they fell over into the sea.

Chapter 37

Phin's head popped out of the water.

Sergeant Warren had dragged him to the opposite side of the kayaks, positioning the flotations between them and the approaching speedboats. Phin worked hard to shake the water from his face. He remembered what Avi the tour guide had warned about not getting the water from the Dead Sea in your eyes. He wasn't joking, just the little bit that invaded the corners of his eyes was causing them to burn. But nothing matched the screaming fire in the palm of his raw, rope burned hand. He worked to ignore both.

"Okay, listen to me carefully, Doc. We're gonna make it out of here if you follow my instructions and most of all if you trust me."

"Yeah sure, Billy. Whatever you say." What other choice did he have? No way was he going to just turn himself over to the Israelis. They thought he was a murderer.

Warren went to work, fishing around his waist area, which was underwater. Phin remembered the fanny pack he'd been wearing. Out popped a pair of goggles. "Here, put these on. Non-negotiable for what we're about to do."

About to do?

Phin obeyed.

Next came a Ziplock bag full of gray and black gunk. Warren held it at head level, just out of the water, and broke the seal. He grabbed a handful and began smearing it on Phin's face. "Mud from the bottom of the Dead Sea. Scooped some up before we rowed out. This stuff sticks like glue. It'll hide our white boy skin when we surface."

When we surface?

Phin submitted to the smearing of the mud. The sergeant then applied a generous helping to his own face.

Finally, out came a small cylinder with a mouthpiece. Small, as in the size of couple of rolls of quarters stacked end-to-end. The name *LaPhage, Ind.* was printed on the side.

"Okay, Doc. This is the big magic trick for the day. Shove this baby in your mouth. When we dive, press this little red button on the side. Breathe in nice and easy. Not too deep or too fast, and you'll get a lung full of nice clean oxygen. Got it?"

When we dive?

"Billy, what exactly are we about to do? I can swim maybe a mile, no way I'm gonna make it."

"Easy, Doc. Ol' Sarge is gonna take care of everything. Remember, I said you're gonna have to trust me." The boats were almost on top of them. Time had run out. "Ready? Just link your arm with mine like this." Sergeant Warren ran his own left arm, his LaPhage Limb, through the underside of Phin's right arm, linking them together like a chain. Phin's adrenaline surged. What were they about to do? "Get your breathing cylinder ready and on three. One. Two. THREE!" Warren wrapped his lips around the mouthpiece and slid underwater, pulling Phin down with him.

The dark water swallowed Phin for a second time, but this time he could open his protected eyes. He had instinctively taken a deep breath before going under and held it as long as he could before letting it out. He pressed the red button and hoped Warren had been right, that the small contraption would actually work.

It did.

Clean cool air filled his lungs as he sucked in. He remembered what the sergeant had said about taking it easy.

WHOOSH!

One of the speedboats zipped past overhead. Phin could tell they were maybe six feet under the surface. Only six feet from those looking to take them into custody. He held tight to Warren's arm, wondering what technique the ex-Marine was using to stay just below the surface. He didn't seem to be struggling at all, he was simply floating...suspended under the water, completely at ease. Phin knew that if he let go of the sergeant's arm he'd pop to the surface.

Another boat came roaring in above their heads. Then another. He had counted four pursuing watercraft when he'd been paddling so he knew that was the number circling above them.

How long can we stay under like this? Phin wondered. The air in the tiny cylinders would surely not last long. It had to have been an emergency device only. The men above them weren't going anywhere soon.

Phin discerned that Sergeant Warren was wiggling, like he was adjusting something.

And then a sensation.

A small tug from Warren's arm and the feeling of being pulled. Yes! Phin could feel the flow of water peeling past his face and an odd sense of moving kicked in. They gained speed. Not much, but they were definitely moving away from the boats circling above.

Five minutes.

The dark water turned to gray, then lightened another shade, and Phin's head broke into the open.

"Keep your arms below the surface, Doc." Sergeant Warren's voice was urgent. "And your head...keep it low. Only your eyes and nose exposed."

Once again, Phin obeyed. Sergeant Warren had asked if Phin trusted him and the answer was yes. He turned his head around and saw the search team. They were a good two to three hundred yards away now. Two men on each boat had binoculars out and were scanning the surrounding ocean for the two of them who, from their vantage point, had simply disappeared into the Dead Sea.

Phin was amazed at the distance they'd covered in such a short amount of time, and so effortlessly while suspended just under the surface. How was Warren making this happen? He could tell they were still moving away from their pursuers - how was he doing this? But they were a long way from free. If they were spotted, the boats would be on top of them in mere seconds.

"The mud on our faces will help camouflage us," Warren explained, as if reading Phin's mind. "We've got exactly eighteen minutes of air in the cylinders. No more, no less. They're rated·for fifteen minutes but believe me, there's an extra three to spare, in case of an emergency." Their situation definitely qualified. "We've expended five so far. Get ready, cuz we're about to do another dive. Just needed to check and see where they were at and how far we'd gotten from 'em. They won't stay there for long, though. They'll spread out and start searching a wider perimeter. Okay, let's go." And with that, the pair was back underwater again.

Three minutes later they popped to the surface.

They'd increased their distance by what looked like double. Good. And they had still not been spotted.

Sergeant Warren grinned. "Right about now they're starting to think we've drowned. No way we could stay underwater this long and not come up. They can't imagine we are this far away. I love it when a plan comes together!"

Phin began to calm down and finally asked the question that had been nagging at him while being drug underwater. "Billy, how are you doing this? You're not kicking or moving your arms or anything. How have you pulled this off?"

"Oh! Right, yeah. Sorry, forgot to fill you in on that part, Doc. Okay, so it's all about these fake limbs I've got." He was referring to his left arm and leg prosthetics, his LaPhage Limbs. "Pretty advanced stuff, right? Well, I had an idea awhile back and Oz, in his little Lair, was able to make it all happen. You see, these limbs are heavy suckers, lots of metal and electronics and stuff I don't know about. Forget what the Jewish tour guide said on the bus about not drowning in the Dead Sea. Doesn't apply to me. You throw me in a pool of water, or any kind of water, I'd sink to the bottom like a rock. So, I had Oz add a buoyancy feature to the arm and leg. I can control it just by thinking about it. Remember, this stuff is all connected to my brain. I can make us float at whatever depth I want. Then he added a small motor and fan blade thing to the bottom of my foot. I flip a little switch on my thigh and out it pops and presto, we've got us a little trolley motor and can move through the water, submarine style, or on the surface."

Which is exactly what they were still doing at the moment. The distance was growing.

"Let's take another dive, Doc. I want to get further away." One of the boats was headed in their direction and he wasn't sure if they'd been spotted.

Down again they went. This time for even longer. Phin had no way of keeping track of time but it felt like close to ten minutes. They'd be nearly out of air. He hoped when they surfaced that they would be far enough away from the search team that no more dives would be necessary. And then he began to wonder what they would do when they made it to the other side. They'd be two men in swimsuits with no supplies, not even any shoes, stuck in the Jordanian desert, who knows how far from the nearest city.

Turns out Phin's worries were all for naught.

The men popped to the surface and a mere ten feet from them was a boat with two soldiers pointing rifles at their heads.

Chapter 38

"We've lost them...or worse, they're dead." Colonel Rubin's grim assessment was met with nodding heads by his men.

Chief Inspector Antonio Rossi couldn't believe it. Why had they done it? Gone overboard in the middle of the Dead Sea. Surely they knew they'd never make it swimming. They were simply too far from the border and they were outmanned with the four boats and IDF personnel in hot pursuit.

And *how* exactly had they drowned? No one drowns in the Dead Sea. Everyone just floats. The only way to drown would be to do it on purpose. To submerge yourself and inhale the putrid water deeply into your lungs. Who would do that? And why would two men agree to do that together? Nothing about the whole situation made sense. There was no way that Phineas Crook and this Sergeant

Warren would commit suicide in order to avoid capture. No crime was worth that.

Assistant Commissioner Marcus Hadadd had equal misgivings. "If they drowned themselves, then their bodies would have floated to the surface. Why have we not found their bodies?"

It was the question of the moment. Colonel Rubin accepted the implication. He keyed up the mic on the radio. "Attention. This is Shark One. Expand the search area. Shark Two. Shark Three. Shark Four. Expand the perimeter half a mile in the designated direction. No bodies means we keep looking. Activate sonar and monitor for underwater craft that might be providing assistance. Report any anomalies. Repeat, report any anomalies." He hung up the mic and looked back at the Jerusalem police commissioner. "You mind telling me now about what this is all about? Who exactly are we looking for and what have they done?"

"If he is indeed still alive, then he's a man proving to be more resourceful than we would first have thought," Rossi replied. He wasn't sure how much else he should say. This wasn't his jurisdiction.

"He's wanted for murder and he may be the most brazen thief of the modern era. Capturing him is essential." Assistant Commissioner Hadadd's frank assessment caused the seasoned colonel to lift his eyebrows. "If you've followed the news, Colonel Rubin, and the thefts of relics related to Jesus across Rome," he swept his arm out across the sea, "our man in the water is linked...somehow."

"We'll find him, Commissioner. Even if it becomes a recovery effort, we won't leave 'til we have them both."

The boat accelerated due east across the Dead Sea at ten knots. The other three boats were doing the same in ninety degree increments to create a full perimeter search pattern. Lieutenant Colonel Levi Rubin had supreme confidence in his team; they were extremely well trained and competent. Just for good measure, he called for ariel support as well.

"We've got a helicopter firing up now. They'll be here in less than fifteen minutes," he explained to the two police officers.

"I think I see something!" Chief Inspector Rossi had a pair of binoculars and was scanning the area in front of the boat. "It's so hard to tell with the sun and waves, but..."

"Here, let me see." Colonel Rubin snatched the binoculars and Rossi pointed.

"Out there, maybe half a mile or so."

"Half a mile." Colonel Rubin sounded mystified. "How's that possible? Nobody can swim that fast. And then he saw what Rossi had seen. Sure enough, two heads bobbing in the water. "You've got a good eye, Inspector. A real good eye." He slapped the driver hard on the arm then pointed. "Punch it, soldier! Full speed 'til I say stop."

The boat lunged forward. Rossi and Hadadd were knocked off balance by the sudden jump in speed, and chose to sit down. Neither wanted to endure the embarrassment of going overboard.

Colonel Rubin kept his eyes on the pair of floating heads until... "They went back under!" he yelled. "Go, go, GO!"

The boat flew across the water.

After only another moment, "FULL STOP!" he commanded. Just like that the boat decelerated and came to a standstill. The colonel scrambled around the edge of the boat, scanning the water. Rossi and Hadadd joined him.

"Colonel!" cried the driver/radio man. "We got chatter on the comms. Looks like the Jordanians are joining the party."

"Ah! I was afraid this might happen." Colonel Rubin pounded the canopy of the boat in frustration. "How far are we from the border?"

"Less than a mile."

Rossi looked at Hadadd for an explanation. "Jordanians, what does he mean?"

"He means it's about to get crowded out here," the colonel replied. He whipped up his binoculars once again, scanning the horizon. "Yep, here they come. I've got four watercraft headed in our direction."

"That doesn't sound good," said Rossi.

"It's only not good if we cross the border into Jordanian waters or if they cross into our waters. We play these games of chicken all the time. Good news is, they don't have a clue what we're doing out here – that we're looking for a man down. Probably assume we're doing some sort of tactical maneuvering, so they're coming out just to flex their own muscle. Keep us honest. Happens all the time, on both sides."

The last thing Rossi wanted to do was see his investigation accelerate into an international conflict between Israel and Jordan. That would be a hard one to explain to his bosses back in Rome.

"Let's just focus on finding these two men who are clearly out here somewhere," Colonel Rubin continued. "Not sure how they've made it this far, but now that we know…" He paused to jump on the mic and order the other three boats to his position.

Rossi could see it all playing out around him. Three more Israeli boats were plowing their way toward their position from behind. And in front of him he could now see with the naked eye the four Jordanian boats headed their direction with equal swiftness.

He reached down, taking hold of the binoculars once again. He wanted to get a better look.

The four Jordanian watercraft let up on the throttle maybe only three quarters of a mile away. They must've stopped just on the water border between the two nations, Rossi surmised. He could see that each boat carried two men, both armed.

These boys aren't playing.

Four hundred meters.

That was the distance that separated the two armed forces.

What Chief Antonio Rossi saw next through his binoculars stunned him, causing his heart to sink.

Two heads popped to the surface, only feet from one of the boats. The two Jordanian soldiers saw the pair immediately. Rossi could do nothing but watch. He was too shocked to even speak. He watched helplessly as Dr. Phineas Crook and the mysterious Sergeant Warren were pulled out of the water and hauled into the boat.

"You've gotta be kidding me…" Colonel Rubin had finally seen it as well.

269

Then the soldiers fired up their engines and headed back toward the shoreline of Jordan.

Chapter 39

Remus Crook walked through the streets of Jerusalem carrying the Cross of Gestas. He'd wrapped it, of course, in a leather covering, yet it was still heavy and cumbersome. He had pre-arranged a storage compartment to keep the cross in overnight after retrieving it from the Crook family archive the day before. It was only a short distance from the House of Reuben where he'd exited onto a public street with the cross in hand.

His plan had been to secure the relic quickly, return the next morning to prep it with the leather covering, and then deliver it to the Russian as planned.

And everything had gone as planned...until Phin fell and almost killed himself. Stupid idiot. But Remus had been relieved to find that Phin had not killed himself. It was a scary moment for sure. He had been fairly certain his younger brother had not broken any bones and would wake up with only a splitting headache. He was likely recovering right now back in his hotel room. Remus smiled, thinking about how frustrated Phin must have been to wake up only to find that both crosses were gone and so was he. Big brother had won again. And that would only drive Phin to continue the chase.

The chase. Yes.

He was the puppet master and Phin was the puppet. After that, it was a toss up as to whether Remus was leading Alexander Pontia or Alexander Pontia was leading Remus. Either way, it was a stroke of luck...good karma...the aligning of the stars, whatever one wanted to call it, but it certainly wasn't God. No sir, God had nothing to do with it. Remus Crook was in charge of his own destiny, and maybe that's what it was...destiny that brought Alexander Pontia and Remus Crook together.

Pontia.

A man who hated God and religion almost as much as Remus.

A man whose goal dovetailed perfectly with that of Remus's.

The only thing that mildly perturbed Remus was that he'd not thought of the scheme first. Steal the most precious artifacts related to Jesus from the safekeeping of the Roman Catholic Church. Then take those artifacts to what Jews believe to be the holiest place on earth and destroy them. Crush two religions at the same time. Like a BOGO – buy one get one free. Remus laughed. Of course, the world would have to see it all in real time and that was more than Remus by himself could pull off, but Pontia seemed to be a man of infinite resources and equal determination. He had a plan, Remus had been reassured.

And Remus was only too glad to help. For him, though, it was personal. He had to show — had to prove — to his naïve brother that he was wrong about it all. God, Jesus, and mostly, the family.

There was nothing wrong with being a crook.

There was nothing wrong with being a *Crook*.

He adjusted the cross from one side to the other. *Man, this thing is heavy.*

He imagined his ancestor, Gestas, being forced to carry the beam of wood through the city on his shoulders. People shouting and cursing and throwing things. The indignity of it all.

And then to be lumped in with The Charlatan. Gestas may have stolen from Rome to give to the poor, but The Charlatan stole people's souls. He truly *was* guilty. Guilty of being a fake. Yet history had exalted Jesus and had labeled Gestas as *impenitent.* Impenitent of what? Of bettering the life of the less fortunate? Of taking back from Rome what they had stolen from his own people?

The truth caused Remus to burn with anger. A truth that nobody knew. Well, his was a quest to prove to Phin that he'd been wrong. That his younger brother had chosen the wrong path. And if he joined along in Pontia's grander scheme of showing off to the whole world, well that was fine too.

Crossing into the Muslim Quarter of the Old City, he traveled down the Via Dolorosa until it became Shaar Ha-Ariot Road, which ran alongside Saint Anne's Church. Remus found it ironic that he was walking the exact same path with the Cross of Gestas as Jesus had carried his own cross to Golgotha. This time the story would end differently, he thought to himself.

Parked on the street outside of Saint Anne's was a Straight Line delivery van. Remus was right on schedule. It was eleven o'clock in the morning and Pontia's shipping vehicle was right where it was supposed to be.

Remus walked up to the rear and rapped hard on the door. He looked around out of instinct before pulling on the latch. The famous Lion's Gate was just up ahead and tourists were pouring in, ready to complete their various pilgrimages. Fools.

He flung the door open and set the wrapped cross inside along with the backpack he'd been carrying that held the remnant of the Cross of the Good Thief. He closed the door and moved quickly along the side, sliding into the passenger's seat of the van.

"It is good to see you, Comrade," bellowed Dimitri Bezrukov. "You were not followed?"

"Please, *Comrade*, give me some credit, will ya?"

"Remember where I found you, my friend. You were in prison because you were careless. I mean no offense, but wisdom dictates I ask."

"Point taken. Let's just say all is well and you can consider the package delivered." He cocked his head to the rear.

"Most excellent. So the cross, both crosses, are in the back?"

"That's what I said, isn't it?" Remus was still growing used to working *with* the Russian as opposed to against him. It felt strange.

"Mr. Pontia will be most pleased. You have performed well. But your brother, it is a shame the trouble he is involved in."

Remus stopped his scanning of the area through the windshield. His senses kicked into high gear. "How did you know about my brother, Dimitri?"

The Russian cursed himself. How had he been so careless? As far as Pontia and company were *supposed* to know, Remus was working purely alone. The hired thief had no idea that, while he had pulled his own brother into the game, Alexander Pontia had also been pulling strings to entrap Phineas Crook. Remus had no clue that Pontia had sent a letter to the Roman police implicating Phin in the theft of Rome's prized relics — that he had in effect generated an international manhunt for his brother that was currently in full swing.

Dimitri Bezrukov had to think fast. "You do have a brother, do you not?" Turning the question back to Remus was all he could come up with.

"Yes..." Remus replied cautiously, "but...he's just a college professor. In Oklahoma."

Checkmate.

The ex-Russian intelligence officer was cornered. He could see no way out but forward.

"But he's not in Oklahoma right now, is he?" Another question. Perhaps he could flip the script. Maybe he could rig a trap for Remus, make him believe that *he* was the one that had been found out by Pontia and not the other way around. "We never agreed on anyone else being brought into the operation." *Yes*, Dimitri thought, *this could work.* He plowed on. "We are not as careless as...as you have been in the past, Comrade. We have eyes that see and we have ears that hear. You invited your brother to join you. For what reason, I do not know. Money, I assume. We know he was with you yesterday when you retrieved the Cross of Gestas." He stopped to see if he had succeeded.

Remus stared at the Russian. How much was fact and how much was fiction? The tension in the van grew. "If your eyes were so sharp and your ears so keen, then you would have known there was no trouble, Dimitri. So why did you apologize? What did you mean when you mentioned trouble?"

"I was only...what is it you Americans say? Chit-chat, isn't that the phrase? I was only making chit-chat. Conversation between friends." Dimitri Bezrukov's tactic had not worked. Remus Crook was too suspicious. "Let's talk about the next operation. The last one and the most important."

New strategy. Divert to a new topic.

"What else do you know about my brother, Dimitri?"

"You are to travel immediately to Rome and proceed with the final theft. You will break in once again to the Basilica di Santa Croce in Gerusalemme."

"My brother, Dimitri. Dr. Phineas Crook. That's his name. Tell me about my brother. What kind of trouble would he be in?" Remus's voice grew more firm.

"You must take extra caution as it will be the second time you have broken into the basilica in the last six months. They will have enhanced security. They might even be waiting on you."

"What have you done, Dimitri?! What have you done with my brother?" Remus yelled.

The Russian was frozen. He'd run out of things to say to cover for his blunder. The only thing he had left: fall back on instinct.

Dimitri Bezrukov reached inside his jacket for his Makarov pistol. His training as a Russian GRU agent meant he was fast.

But he wasn't fast enough.

Remus Crook jumped out of the van and disappeared into the crowded streets of Jerusalem.

Chapter 40

Phin and Sergeant Warren sat in a small - and hot - cinderblock room. One window with bars was set high next to the ceiling and it provided absolutely no relief from the sun that beat down on the roof of the structure.

Phin imagined they looked the sight. He in his floral swim trunks and Warren in a blue Speedo. Their virgin white skin had been replaced, though, by a nice first-degree sunburn. The result of time spent rowing and swimming halfway across the Dead Sea. It never crossed either of their minds to secure and apply sunscreen.

Somewhere next door or down the hall of the small security building, in which they'd been unceremoniously deposited, decisions were being made about what to do with them.

The two men had been plucked out of the water, apparently having made it to the Jordanian side of the sea.

That meant they'd been successful, in a manner of speaking. They'd escaped the clutches of the Israeli government, but in doing so, they'd illegally crossed into a country that was, let's just say, a tad bit on the paranoid side.

Jordan wasn't exactly hostile to Westerners, but they were very serious about the security of their borders, especially from anything or anyone coming from Israel. The 1994 peace treaty between the two nations signed by Israeli Prime Minister Yitzhak Rabin and Jordan's King Hussein, with American President Bill Clinton along for the ride, had outlived either of the two men who signed it. Tensions in the Middle East are always ebbing and flowing and such has been the case with Israel-Jordan relations. Phin hoped their little swim across the Dead Sea wouldn't be interpreted wrongly.

"Do you think that *they* think we're spies?" he asked the sergeant, breaking the silence they'd been sitting in.

"Oh, that's definitely a possibility, Doc. Would not be a stretch for them to see us as a highly trained special forces unit, dumped into the water while the Israelis were conducting aquatorial maneuvers. A real nice distraction while we just slip into their country in order to conduct clandestine operations."

Phin couldn't tell if Warren was being serious or not, so he just let the matter drop.

"Since we've got the time, Doc, why don't we have a little discussion about why exactly I've had to come to your rescue. Again, I might add. Gotta say, for a book-boy, you sure find trouble easier than most."

"I'd say the rescue part is still in question." Phin had no problem trusting Billy Warren, but he couldn't resist poking a little fun. They'd been through a lot together in the short time they'd known each other. More adventure than most two men in a lifetime.

"Easy there now. Ol' Sarge is working on a plan as we speak."

What did that mean?

"So, here's the scoop, Sergeant. I've got an older brother. Remus is his name. He's a thief by trade. Long story, but sort of a family trait that runs in the DNA of us Crooks." Sergeant Warren nodded as if he understood perfectly what Phin was talking about. "So, Remus has been doing time the last four years at the Oklahoma State Penitentiary. Got caught stealing some gemstones."

"Uh," Warren grunted. "The Big Mac. Nasty place."

Phin furrowed his brow. What did Billy Warren know about the Big Mac? Ah well, he kept going. "Anyway, he was scheduled for parole in just eighteen months. But someone, I don't know who yet, broke him out of prison."

"Yep, saw that one on the news. Your brother, huh? Looks like trouble runs in your whole family, Doc."

Phin ignored the comment and carried on. "So, several months go by and I start seeing stories from Rome about artifacts being stolen from churches around the city. And here's the thing: all the relics are related to Jesus Christ. The manger he was laid in when he was born, the robe he wore when the soldiers flogged him, the lance the Roman soldiers used to pierce his side, and others."

"That ain't cool, Doc. I don't like people messin' with Jesus."

And that was the strange thing about Sergeant Billy Warren – or at least one of the strange things. He had no use for religion and wasn't even sure about where he stood when it came to God. But he had an unusual reverence for Jesus Christ. Phin had never explored that aspect of his friend's life. Perhaps he'd have the opportunity while waiting to see what the Jordanians did next.

"Me either. So that's why I did it. The Shroud of Turin."

"The Jesus blanket that you stole. Yep, I'm tracking, Doc. Keep going, a little faster if you don't mind."

What's the hurry? Phin thought. "Yes...the uh, the Jesus blanket. So, the Shroud of Turin - its technical name - is one of the most prized relics related to the Christ in existence. I could see the writing on the wall. Whoever was going after the relics of Jesus would be coming for the Shroud. And I had this feeling. I can't explain how, but I knew it was Remus. You see, he and I... how do I explain it? We have a very complicated relationship."

"Oh yeah, I get complicated relationships, Doc. There was this girl in Manila one time. Hold up...scratch that...it was New Guinea...nope, nope...Taiwan. Yep, it was Taiwan. Tell you what, let's forget what I just said...it's complicated. I get it. Keep going."

"Yeah...right...okay. What I was saying is that I'm a college professor, right? A *Christian* college professor. And I teach Bible classes. My faith is very important to me. And Jesus is more than a topic of study or a historical figure to me. He's alive and real and active and... well, I have a personal relationship with him. Not sure if that makes any sense to you or not."

"I think I follow you, Doc. You know me, got no use for church or religion or any of that stuff. But Jesus. Now he's the man. Something special about that dude. This is real interesting to me. Keep going."

"Well, my brother, Remus, doesn't feel the same way as you or me – about Jesus. He's got this, I don't know...hatred toward religion and especially Jesus. He doesn't think that Jesus is anything special. Believes he was just a man who fooled a lot of people into thinking he was God and that he died and that was it. And so he's driven by this intense rage to prove me wrong."

"Yep...sibling rivalry stuff. That's what I was thinkin' the whole time."

"Well, yes, but it's more than that. So, I stole the Shroud of Turin, to protect it. I'm kind of second guessing the wisdom of that move now, but what's done is done. Shortly afterward, on my birthday in fact, I got a package delivered to my office from Remus."

"The video! How'd I do, Doc? Did you like my little birthday video I sent you? Not super professional, I know. But hey...you know, it's me."

Phin laughed at how Billy Warren's brain processed information. "Yes, Billy, I did. Great video and I really appreciate it."

"Sorry I didn't send a gift. Looks like your brother had one up on me on that end."

"Well, not really. The *gift* was actually what was left of what's known as the Cross of the Good Thief. Not sure if you know the story or not-"

"Two other dudes. One on the left, one on the right. Crooks." A pause. "Hey Doc! Two crooks. Like you and your brother. Haha. That's pretty ironic, ain't it?"

"You have no idea." Phin didn't want to go into the whole family legacy connection between he and Remus and the two thieves that hung next to Jesus on the cross. "So, Remus had stolen this cross and sent it to me along with a note. He basically admitted to being the thief behind the stolen relics and he dared me to come find him and stop him. And that led me to Jerusalem."

"To Jerusalem. Because?" Sergeant Warren's brow tweaked upward.

"I wasn't sure where to start...looking for Remus, I mean. But there's a... how do I say it? A family archive in Jerusalem."

"You've got family in Jerusalem? Is that what you're sayin', Doc? Like you're Jewish?"

"Yes, sort of. I've got a Jewish heritage." It was no use. Phin couldn't explain it in part without explaining it in whole. So, he took the next few minutes to unpack the whole Crook family legacy all the way back to the two thieves who hung next to Jesus on crosses two thousand years ago. He explained how Remus had been waiting on him in the archive, knowing that he'd come. And the retrieval of the Cross of Gestas, Phin's fall, and then the murder of Mary Gannab, the shop clerk and keeper of the archive.

"And that's how I ended up arrested and in jail. Which is where you entered the picture."

Sergeant Warren let out a whistle. "Holy ding dang dong, Doc. Wow, wow. The longer I hang with you the weirder it gets, that's all I gotta say."

"I'm sorry, Billy. I really am." Phin leaned over with his elbows on his knees and hung his head.

"Hey, no sweat, Doc. I'm cool with weird. And if I can help you and help Jesus, then I'm all in. Listen, Doc... you're my friend." Warren reached over and put his mechanical arm around Phin's shoulder. "Okay, enough of the sappy stuff." He jerked his arm back. "Let's see if I got this straight. You're trying to protect Jesus. Your brother's trying to destroy him. Clearly, I'm on your side on this one. He's stolen a bunch of stuff from churches but the stuff really belongs to Jesus. He's gonna do who-knows-what with all this stuff, but somehow, it's gonna make Jesus look bad. So, we can't let that happen. Problem number one: you've got the whole world looking for you. And the murder of this lady who guards the big family secret ain't helping matters. To the law, you are one bad mother. A thief and a murderer. Problem two: your big bro ain't in this alone. Somebody big, way big, is the real kahuna that we've gotta find and ultimately stop. Does that about sum it up?"

Sergeant Billy Warren truly had a gift of making the complex simple. "I believe that covers it. But we have one more problem. Problem number three."

"And what's that?"

"We're stuck in a Jordanian holding cell."

"Ah, come on. Didn't you just say you were a man of faith, Doc? How 'bout using a little of that faith now."

A bang and the door to the room opened.

A tall soldier entered. He was older than the men who'd locked them up and by the appearance of his uniform looked to be in charge. He spoke in accented English. "Gentlemen, I hope my men treated you well. Now, if you will follow me, it is time to go."

Chapter 41

Dimitri Bezrukov returned to the Straight Line shipping van and banged both fists on the dashboard. He wasn't sure if he was more angry with himself or with Remus Crook. Either way, Alexander Pontia would not be happy.

He had chased the career thief as far as he could but that wasn't very far. The crowd was too big and Remus Crook was too good. A professional. The cat and mouse game was back and it reminded him of the origins of their relationship. Remus was on the run and Dimitri would have to find him. His boss had invested too much in breaking the man out of prison and housing and supporting him for six months. Pontia would not just let him slip away. Plus, Remus knew about Pontia's plan. He could go to the authorities and blow the whole thing wide open.

But where to begin?

Finding Remus Crook would be harder than finding a needle in a haystack. And then there was the task of convincing Remus to trust him once again as his handler and Pontia as his employer. The more Dimitri thought about it the more hopeless the situation seemed. It was impossible. Remus Crook was gone and he would have to let Pontia know.

He drove the van to the Straight Line shipping facility and parked it in the main warehouse. The first order of business was to hand the crosses off to the manager of the Straight Line Israel operations who would secure them and make sure they were delivered to their pre-arranged location. There they would wait until the time came that they were needed by Alexander Pontia.

Lionel Meadors exited the office and met Dimitri as he exited the van. He shoved the keys into the manager's hand. "You know what to do. Secure it, crate it, and ship it. I'll be in your office. Do not disturb me."

Meadors nodded without a word and went to work, whistling for three men to join him at the back of the van. Dimitri had no need to supervise. The men knew that failure to comply would not end well for them...or their families. Meadors would also avoid the office as instructed by the head of Dominion Safe. He understood that the beefy Russian was a man to be obeyed.

Dimitri Bezrukov plopped down in the manager's chair and pulled out his phone.

May as well get this over with.

He texted Alexander Pontia on his private secured cell: *We have a problem with Crook. Need to discuss.*

Exactly ten seconds later the reply: *Video chat. Now.*

That was fast. He'd gotten his boss's attention.

Dimitri walked to the corner of the office to a safe that had the Dominion Safe logo on it. Every Straight Line office around the world had one. A benefit of being a part of one big happy family: Pilate Enterprises.

He punched in the code. A green light. Then he placed his thumb over the sensor, verifying his identity. The safe clicked and was unlocked. He pulled it open. Inside was an array of handguns and ammunition. Money in various currencies and denominations, cell phones, and a laptop. He took the laptop out and sat down at Meadors's desk. He powered on the machine and hit the video chat icon, a custom piece of software called P-Link. P for Pontia. A secure network for Alexander Pontia to communicate anywhere around the world using the Straight Line/Dominion Safe network for distribution.

A window opened and Pontia's face appeared. He was sitting at his desk in New York. Tess Greenway was standing behind and to the side.

"What kind of problem has the good Dr. Crook caused for us now? Nothing you can't handle, I'm sure."

Of course. Dimitri Bezrukov had not been specific in his text. Alexander assumed he was talking about fugitive Crook and not employee Crook. Well, actually, they were technically both fugitives from the law.

"My apologies, Comrade," Dimitri began nervously. "I was referring to Remus, not the brother, Phineas Crook."

Pontia's face darkened. "What has happened, Dimitri?"

"He discovered that we have become...involved with his brother. He knows that Dr. Crook is in trouble."

Pontia was silent. Thinking. "And how has he come to this knowledge?"

No need to run from the truth at this point. Alexander would find out. He always finds out.

"It is my fault, Comrade. I...made a mistake. I mentioned his brother in our last conversation...when he delivered the crosses earlier today. I might have said something about him being in trouble after Remus retrieved the Cross of Gestas." Pontia leaned forward. It looked as if Tess Greenway was shaking her head. "I know. It was an...unfortunate slip on my part. He was not supposed to know that we had knowledge of his brother's visit to Jerusalem to join him. I take full responsibility."

Pontia began to massage his temples. "And what did Remus do with his newfound knowledge for which you are taking responsibility?"

"He bolted. Ran."

"He ran? As in you no longer control him as an asset?"

"That would be correct. I tried to subdue him but he escaped."

"Subdue? Oh, I'm sure that went well. Well then, he's gone. Never to return. This is unfortunate, indeed, Dimitri. And yes, you are responsible. I am most disappointed, I must admit."

"I will find him, Comrade. I will make this right, if you allow me. I will hunt him down and I will dispose of him...permanently. Of this I promise you."

"Nonsense, Dimitri. Don't be ridiculous. Remus Crook is not some meaningless store clerk like the woman whose throat you slit yesterday."

"But if he goes public...and informs the authorities on our plans. You must let me find him and silence him."

"Dimitri, listen to me. This is not the Russian GRU. We don't just go around eliminating our enemies at will. We are more...subtle than that. And I'm not worried about Remus Crook going to the police and exposing our plans, or INTERPOL, or anybody for that matter. You must remember that no matter what he knows or does not know about Alexander Pontia or Dimitri Bezrukov, or any of us, he's still a fugitive of the law and more than anything he wants to remain free. No, he will remain silent and it won't require you to help him along."

Alexander Pontia was right. Remus would not be the threat he had initially feared. "But we are not done. The theft at the basilica in Rome. That was his job."

"Yes, and so now it is your job, Dimitri. And I am sending Tess to assist you. In fact, I want her to coordinate the theft. She leaves within the hour as will you. I want you both to connect at Dominion Safe headquarters in Rome at noon tomorrow to begin final preparations. As for Remus Crook, he may still be useful to me. Does he still have the cell phone we gave him?"

"He does, or at least he did. He may ditch it if he thinks we will use it to track him."

"Oh, he may turn it off, but he won't separate himself from it just yet. I know his type. Remus Crook is an arrogant man. He's angry that we know about his brother. He knows more is going on than he first thought. No, he will want to keep a line of communication with us available. I can use that to my advantage. I'm not anywhere close to being done with Remus Crook, or his brother. I've got a special message for Remus Crook that I will send at just the right time. That is all."

And just like that, Alexander Pontia ended the transmission.

Dimitri Bezrukov breathed a sigh of relief. Perhaps matters were not as bad as he had thought.

Chapter 42

The Via Flacca was a highway that periodically hugged the coast as it wound its way along the western edge of central Italy. Sergeant Billy Warren gripped the leather steering wheel of the silver Maserati MC20. It was a silver bullet as it rocketed around hairpin turns, and on straightaways the ex-Marine pushed the sportscar's 621 horsepower engine.

"Take it easy, Sarge," Phin exhorted as he squeezed the door handle. "We're not trying to break a world record here."

"This thing is unbelievable, Doc! It's like the tires are glued to the road. You gotta take a turn behind the wheel."

"No thanks, I'll leave the driving to you." What Phin was really thinking was that he didn't want to be responsible for a $250,000 car if something went wrong.

The pair was making their way toward the coastal city

of Terracina. Phin knew he had to get to Rome. He'd known it since reading Remus's last note.

First, we got yours. Then we got mine. Now, it's time to go get his.

Rome was the goal.

That's where Remus would be headed next, and if he had any hope of stopping whatever madness his brother was involved in, he had to beat him to Rome and execute the theft first.

They'd chosen on purpose to not fly directly into Rome. Mostly because the airport in the nation's capital would be crawling with police and they would certainly be looking for someone fitting Phin's description trying to enter the country.

Phin thought back to the Italian inspector that had questioned him in Jerusalem. Antonio Rossi had been his name. And Phin wasn't certain but he thought he had recognized the inspector as one of the men in the boats that were closing in on them while they were swimming across the Dead Sea.

Phin looked out his window at the lush Italian countryside, trying to block out the speeds that Sergeant Warren was pushing the Maserati toward.

It had been a whirlwind since leaving the custody of the Jordanians. Warren had teased him about his lack of faith. But the whole time, the sergeant knew the gears of LaPhage Industries's global influence were turning in their favor. Apparently, before leaving their safehouse in Jerusalem yesterday morning, Warren had worked out all the details with Oz Jenks back at LaPhage headquarters in Texas.

The two men would make the swim across the Dead Sea, land on a beach somewhere, and then they were *supposed* to be picked up by Jordanian security.

Apparently, the king of Jordan had been personal friends with Charles LaPhage, the late founder of LaPhage Industries. When the king visited Fort Worth to negotiate oil leases, he and Charles would ride Harley Davidson motorcycles out across west Texas. The king apparently kept his personal Harley at LaPhage Industries headquarters for safekeeping. After Charles's death, the king and his "people" kept close ties with LaPhage. *Who knew?* Phin had wondered at the revelation.

It didn't take more than a call from LaPhage's new CEO to the king's "people" to get the help they needed. The Jordanians were more than happy to assist anyone fleeing from Israel on less-than-good terms. No love lost between the two countries.

The Jordanian army had been put on alert and were patrolling the coastline waiting for Phin and Sergeant Warren to appear.

When they were alerted to increased aquatic activity on the Dead Sea by the Israeli army, they reasoned rightly that the pair was being pursued in the water. They launched their own watercraft and, well, having just crossed the border into Jordan, the two were aptly plucked from the water and to safety.

The soldier who had come to retrieve them from their holding cell turned out to be a general of the Jordanian military, General Omar Abdallah. He apologized for the rough treatment. They had to determine with certainty that they were, in fact, the two men they were expecting, and once that was done...well, the Jordanians essentially rolled out the red carpet.

First order of business was a shower and change of clothes. The general had eyed Sergeant Warren up and down in his blue Speedo with a disapproving look. All they had on hand were standard-issue fatigues but that was welcomed by both. Showers had been luxurious, washing the gunk of the Dead Sea off their bodies. Then came a hearty meal followed by quick transport to an airfield for the biggest surprise of all. One of the king's Learjets was waiting with instructions to take them anywhere in the world they wanted to go.

Before sending them on their way, General Abdallah shoved a packet into each of their hands. Each hefty envelope contained $5,000 American dollars and a Jordanian passport. Phin realized in that moment that his ID and all his belongings were still in his hotel room in Jerusalem.

He thumbed open the blue passport with gold embossing on the cover that read: The Hashemite Kingdom of Jordan. There was his picture along with his name: Quasi Ali. Sergeant Warren was now Ahmed Ibrahim. Clearly, Charles LaPhage and the king of Jordan had been *very* good friends.

Phin knew exactly where they needed to go. But instead of risking a landing in Rome, they opted for Bari on the eastern coast - still a good five-hour drive to Rome.

They landed and negotiated Passport Control with no issues. Phin breathed a sigh of relief and tucked his passport identifying him as Jordanian tourist Quasi Ali into his bag.

Oz had told Sergeant Warren that a LaPhage car would be waiting for them at the airport. Phin had no idea it would be one of the famed Italian sportscars. Sergeant Warren had beamed when he saw the silver bullet. "Hot dog. You are the man, Oz!" he had said aloud, even though the computer genius was not around to hear him.

Off they went to a very nice InterContinental hotel to crash for the night. They were exhausted. Nevertheless, they were up early this morning. They hit a store for some more traditional clothing (time to ditch the fatigues), and then they were off at breakneck speed.

But before Rome, a stop.

"I need to see an old friend," is all Phin had told the sergeant.

As they approached Terracina, they shifted onto Via Appia and Warren immediately decelerated the horses under the hood.

"Whoa, will you look at that? Now that is a postcard view right there, Doc."

The road snaked along a cliff overlooking the Tyrrhenian Sea. It was breathtaking. The vivid blue water swept in front of them as far as the eye could see. There were white fluffy clouds spaced around an equally vivid blue sky. A couple of miles ahead was a beach blanketed in tourists, and next to that was a small harbor. Tiny sailboats dotted the calm waters of the sea and seagulls soared overhead.

"This, my friend, is what people come to Italy to see." Phin pulled up the GPS on his phone. A new iPhone courtesy of the King of Jordan. "We are almost there."

Phin craned his neck, catching glimpses of homes nestled in the rocks above them. "Just up ahead is a driveway."

Sergeant Warren found the steep drive, flanked by stone columns and a black wrought iron gate, which was open. He gunned the engine, forcing the Maserati to make the climb which included one, two, then three sharp switchbacks. Higher they went before leveling out in front of a majestic stone manner overlooking the sea. Phin exited the car and the first thing he noticed was how utterly private this house was. He was not surprised at all.

"Some friend you've got," Warren said as he clicked shut the driver's door of the car. "Wouldn't mind a place like this when I retire."

"You'll have the chance to buy it in six months or so. He doesn't stay anywhere long. Moves around every year or so. We're extraordinarily lucky that he just happens to be in Italy right now. But I would've gone out of my way if I had needed to just to talk to him."

"Well, I hope the fridge is full." Warren glanced at his Ironman watch. It was half past noon. "I'm starving."

"That won't be a problem, I promise," Phin assured the sergeant as he walked toward the tan stone steps leading up to the front door. Phin's nose could just catch the whiff of something cooking in the air. He smiled. Looking back at Warren, "I hope you like pizza."

Phin knocked on the door as Sergeant Warren joined him by his side. There was no doorbell.

They waited.

Phin had sent a message to tell his friend they were coming. He was about to knock a second time when the sound of locks being disengaged could be heard.

The door flew open.

"My oh my, oh my! Phineas Crook! How are you my good friend?" A short man rushed forward and enveloped Phin in a bear hug.

Whatever Sergeant Warren had been expecting it was not this. A round little man, quintessentially Italian, released Phin from his grasp. He was maybe five feet tall but a full two hundred and fifty pounds. He was clean-shaven with slicked-back black hair — a little splatter of white on the sides — and an equally black mustache, the sides curled with wax.

"Sergeant, I'd like you to meet my old friend, Sergio Nardovino."

Chapter 43

A black-headed, beardless Santa Claus. That's what Sergio Nardovino reminded Sergeant Warren of. The jolly old man stepped back from the pair.

"Quickly, come in, come in!" he beckoned. "Lunch is almost ready."

The threesome moved through the doorway into the foyer of the coastal home. It was spectacularly decorated. Phin was not surprised. Sergio Nardovino was independently wealthy and that wealth had the appearance of being extreme. Because of the nature of Sergio's business - illegal antiquities - he moved around...a lot. A year in one place would be a long time for the rotund Italian. When Phin had last spent time with the man, Sergio had been living in Ireland where Phin had coincidentally found himself in a bit of trouble.

Phin's relationship with the man he affectionately called Nardo went back many years. His father had been friends and business partners with Sergio, using the Italian's many connections to move the items he stole through the black markets of the world. And while Phin himself did not have a professional need for Sergio Nardovino, he considered him a family friend. His warm and jolly personality was too much to resist.

The reason for the stopover before heading to Rome was simple: knowledge. Phin and Sergeant Warren needed to get some sense of who might be behind the theft of the Jesus relics from the Holy Roman Catholic Church, and who was also pulling the strings of his brother, Remus. It would be impossible for Sergio to not have heard something by way of information buzzing along the grapevine of fellow thieves. If Sergio knew anything at all, he would tell Phin.

"Nardo, it's so good to see you. Thanks for agreeing to host us," Phin said, his voice echoing through the entry chamber.

"Nonsense!" He bellowed with laughter. "My home is always your home...if you can find me. Haha!"

"I'm just grateful you replied to my message. And I gotta tell you, it's a stroke of luck that you are here in Italy. I'd have gone wherever to find you, but we're headed to Rome and well, here you are only two hours away."

"Rome. Yes, I know." His jovial demeanor faded for just a moment. Phin and Warren looked at each other. *He knows?* And just as quickly it was back. "But who do we have here? Who is your friend with the big muscles and the very short haircut?!" Sergio reached over and gave Sergeant

Warren's left arm a squeeze. "Oh my! Well would you look at that. A LaPhage Limb. I thought it might be. Very impressive. And very expensive." He winked at the sergeant, who only grunted in reply.

"This is a very good friend of mine. Nardo, I'd like you to meet Sergeant Billy Warren. He's ex-military. No need to worry though, he's not on the government payroll anymore. You can trust him."

"Yes, yes of course! Any friend of Phineas Crook is a friend of Nardo. Now I know you have come to talk, but first...we must eat!" He laughed big and long, the echo carrying up to the rafters. "Tell me, Mr. Sergeant Man. Do you like *pizza*?" He said the word almost reverently.

Phin had not told Warren anything at all about Sergio Nardovino before their arrival. Among the man's many talents, he was also an accomplished chef with an eccentric fetish for pizza. He handmade his pies from start to finish. He fashioned the dough with only organic ingredients. The toppings tended toward the exotic – various meats such as elk, buffalo, musk ox, salmon, as well as all the traditional ones you might imagine. Sauces and vegetables of all sorts offered another layer of various mixings. The result was anything but what you might ever call a normal "pizza."

"Pizza. Yeah, boy. I love me some pizza," replied Warren with a new hunger in his eye. "And a beer too if you have one."

"You are both in for a treat today, I think. Yes, yes." Sergio rubbed his meaty hands together. "I've been working on a new creation just...for...you." He pounded on Phin's chest. "It has a cauliflower crust. The primary meat is crocodile, straight from the Nile in Egypt. I am using a mustard-based sauce with a secret ingredient to give it a pop. Mixed in are caramelized onions, apples, and goat cheese. Oh my, I can taste it as I talk. The best part...I am calling this one...*The Crooked Road.*" He let out the biggest bellow of a laugh yet. "You see, don't you? The Crooked Road. Named after-"

"Yes, I see, Nardo. Named after me. Very nice. Very funny, indeed." Phin was shaking his head.

"No, not funny. Serious, very serious. A serious pie for a serious man and his even more serious friend." He looked over at Warren, who was scowling. "What is wrong, my new friend? You do not approve?"

"Goat cheese? Apples? Mustard? What the heck kinda pizza is that?"

Phin covered his face with a hand and shook his head.

Sergio Nardovino wrinkled his brow. He gave the sergeant a deadpan expression. "I am sorry," he began slowly. "You obviously do not approve of the...exotic. So please tell me. Tell Nardo what you would prefer. I can make any pizza you like."

"Hmmm...how 'bout a good 'ol pepperoni pizza? And that beer I mentioned."

Sergio Nardovino stared at the ex-Marine.

Phin hung his head lower. Pepperoni.

Suddenly Sergio's eyes grew wide. "Yes! Pepperoni! That is what you like. Of course. I have just the pizza for you, my grumpy friend. I will make the best pizza you have ever tasted and we will turn your grumpy into lumpy!" He grabbed his fat belly and gave it a shake and offered another laugh.

"Nardo, I need to ask you some questions. It's very important. I'm in trouble." Phin broke the mood of food talk.

"You are always in some sort of trouble, my little professor friend. It is the way of the Crooks it seems. I am not surprised and neither should you be. But there will be enough time to speak of your trouble...after we eat! Come, follow Nardo through the kitchen while I make Sergeant Grumpy his special-order pizza." Sergio turned and began to waddle down the hallway, his huge white cotton linen shirt, untucked, swaying behind him as he went.

"That man is weird, Doc. You have strange friends."

"Don't forget you're my friend too, Sarge."

A grunt. "Point taken. I think I ticked him off but no way I'm eatin' apples and goat cheese. Uh, uh. Not me."

"You didn't make him mad. He was just measuring you up. Trust me, whatever he's about to make for you, you're gonna love."

"Come my friends!" He called back to them as he pushed through a swinging door and disappeared into the kitchen.

"How exactly is he gonna help us, Doc?"

"I know he doesn't look like it, but you are standing in the home of one of the most well-connected thieves in the world. Actually, he himself is not a thief, he just traffics in stolen goods, mostly ancient relics. Moves the stuff around the world from seller to buyer. He knows people and he knows...things. Information. That's what I'm after. Remember problem number two? Somebody is behind what my brother has been up to. That's who we need to find if we're going to stop whatever is going on and clear my name."

The two men moved down the hall toward the kitchen. As they approached the swinging door, they could hear talking. Two voices. One was Sergio's and the other...

Phin froze.

No. It couldn't be.

Had Nardo betrayed him?

Phin pushed through the door. And there he was, standing next to the kitchen island holding a large knife.

His brother Remus.

Chapter 44

"Well, it's about time you showed up, little brother. What took you so long?"

Phin stood frozen. Eyes shifting back and forth from Remus to the knife in his hand. Sergio seemed relaxed. Even pleased with himself.

What kind of treachery is this?

Staring at the knife, another image flashed through Phin's mind. Mary Gannab, lying on the floor behind the counter of her shop, throat slit open.

By a knife.

"Aaaahhhhh!"

Phin heard a yell coming from behind just before he was shoved to the side. Sergeant Warren launched himself at Remus. The knife came up and Warren blocked it with the power of his LaPhage Limb. He squeezed Remus's wrist with impossible strength, causing the man to yell. The knife dropped to the floor. With trained precision, the ex-Marine flipped Remus around and put him in a chokehold.

"I got him, Doc! Threat defused. You want me to keep holding him while you punch him?"

It happened so fast Phin's mind spun to keep up.

Remus was struggling to say something but the force to his windpipe made it impossible.

"Please, friends. This is not necessary!" Sergio was yelling.

Phin stared at his brother, secured in the grip of Sergeant Warren, and he began to see red. Phin had fallen through the hole in the chamber of the archive. Remus had let him fall. Remus had left him, unconscious, and taken both the Cross of the Good Thief and the Cross of Gestas. Remus had...Mary Gannab. She was dead. And Phin had been framed for her murder. His own fingerprints planted on the murder weapon while he laid unconscious.

He walked up to his brother, stared into his bulging eyes. He was having trouble breathing.

"You," he said through clinched teeth. "YOU!" And then he punched his brother in the stomach with all the built-up fury inside of him.

Remus expelled a gut full of air and struggled to inhale again.

BOOM!

The gunshot caused all three men to flinch.

Sergeant Warren released the grip on Remus. The trio stared at Sergio Nardovino holding what looked to be a Walther PPK, the same kind of gun used by James Bond, Phin noted. He was a fan. The small firearm was still raised over the man's head, bits of plaster and dust trickling down in front of him.

"Now that is much better!" he laughed. "I will not have lunch - LUNCH of all things - disrupted by foolish banter. We eat. Then we talk. Remus, finish slicing the pepperoni." Like an obedient child, Remus shrugged away from Sergeant Warren, picked up the knife from off the floor, glared at Phin while making a show of the knife, and returned to the large sleeve of meat on the butcher block island. "Wait, you clumsy thief! Not *that* knife. Not from the floor. Use a new one from the block." Remus shrugged sheepishly and pulled a fresh instrument from the butcher block and went back to slicing the meat.

Pepperoni, Phin realized.

Remus had been preparing toppings for the pizza at Sergio's direction. He had overreacted. Instantly he felt the fool. But no, there were so many questions flooding his mind. What was Remus doing here anyway? His thoughts were cut off.

"And you, good Phineas. Instead of throwing punches, why don't you start throwing this dough." Sergio picked up a large mound of dough and plopped it down next to the workspace where Remus was slicing.

"Me? Toss dough? I've never-"

"Tsk, tsk. It is easy. Nardo will show you."

"And you. Mr. Sergeant Grumpy. Why don't you look inside that cabinet and retrieve the utensils and placemats we will need. There are napkins in there as well. Take them all outside to the veranda and set the table. Once you are done you can help yourself to a beverage of your choice. No beer in Nardo's house, but you will find something to your liking, I am sure." He bellowed again. "Now, let us get to work!"

Like a stern father, the billowy Italian had a strange command over the three men. They fell in line and dutifully began to execute their assigned tasks.

Sergio Nardovino supervised all, from the exact thickness of each cut of meat, to the finer points of rolling and tossing dough into a pizza crust. He even waddled his way to the veranda to correct the placement of the dinnerware, whipping Sergeant Warren into shape. The man worked all three of them with amazing efficiency. And per their host's orders, no one spoke of the matters for which they all had come to his house.

Thirty minutes later, the group sat at the outside table. It overlooked the Tyrrhenian Sea, a picture of extraordinary beauty. Sergio appeared with two pizza pies straight out of his outside wood-fired oven – it was the only way he would ever cook one of his treasured delicacies.

The Crooked Road was laid between Remus and Phin, who sat across from each other. Next came a pizza only for Sergeant Warren that the chef deemed Death by Pepperoni. There were five varieties of the famed meat stacked high with three kinds of cheese layered between the carne. A special red sauce was used that Sergio described but Warren failed to comprehend. The beefy ex-Marine drooled over the steaming feast in front of him until Sergio finally gave the word to dive in.

The group ate and the mood lightened, carried mostly by their jovial attendant. Phin began to feel better about his whole situation. Good food and good company has a way of doing that. It didn't hurt that it was a stunning day. And

Sergio's presence served to mediate the tensions that had been brewing between the brothers.

Finally, Sergio sat back and tossed his white napkin on the table. "Now my friends, let us talk about why you have really come to visit Nardo. Remus arrived first so I will let him go first."

Phin bristled at playing second to his older brother. Again. But whatever.

"Thanks, Nardo," Remus began. "Thanks for everything - the food, the hospitality, and just for being here. First, let me say it is good to see you, brother. I am glad you are okay."

"I fell, Remus. A long way. I was knocked unconscious and you left me," Phin blurted out. His brother's talk of being glad he was okay had washed away any goodwill created over lunch.

"I didn't just leave you, Phin. I checked and made sure you were okay. I promise. If you had been really hurt, I would have taken you to the hospital. Surely you don't think I'd leave you for dead. You're still my brother after all." Remus was firm with his response.

"Me being your brother didn't stop you from framing me for murder."

Remus was silent at the accusation.

Finally, he said, "What are you talking about?"

"I'm talking about Mary. The shop owner. The House of Reuben. She's dead, Remus. Her throat was slit. My fingerprints were on the knife that killed her. As soon as I woke up in the archive and came back up to the shop, the police were waiting for me. I was arrested, Remus. Arrested."

"But..." Remus was working to keep up. "How did you...you know...escape...get here, to Nardo's?"

Phin pointed at Sergeant Warren. Then a round of introductions.

Warren lifted his glass filled with some sort of fruited drink he found in Sergio's refrigerator. "You boys, keep talking. I'm just sittin' here enjoying the show."

Remus sat back, his mind filling in gaps. "Okay, it's all starting to make sense."

"Perhaps you can enlighten me then. Cause none of it makes sense to me. All I know is I am a wanted man. Same as you, by the way, which is stupidly ironic."

"Except you're wanted for murder, Doc." Warren couldn't help but butt in. "That puts you one up here on your ol' bro."

Phin glared at Warren.

"Okay, for starters," Remus continued, "I didn't kill Mary Gannab and I know you didn't either. But I am about 99% sure I know who did kill her. It's a Russian named Dimitri Bezrukov, former GRU. And he for sure is behind framing you for the killing."

"Russians!" Warren shouted. "I knew it. There's always gonna be Russians involved when the crap hits the fan."

"Billy, *pleeaassee!*" Phin pleaded.

"Oh, sorry."

Remus smiled, amused. "So let me tell you how it all went down on my end. I made sure you were okay after the fall. As far as I was concerned, I had what I came for. The Cross of Gestas. And you had brought back to me the Cross of the Good Thief. It was time for me to make my delivery. To my employer. So, I said good-bye to Mary, exited the shop, and was on my way. She was very much alive when I left her. Next day, I met up with Bezrukov."

"The Russian," Warren grunted.

"Yes...the Russian." Remus rolled his eyes. "We work for the same man. But the meeting didn't go as planned. He ended up asking me about you, Phin. He knew you and I had met, and he asked about *trouble*. That's when I knew something was up. I hadn't told him or anyone else about our little game."

"Your little game, Remus. *Your* game. I was just minding my own business, taking care of my family until you decided to do what you do best. Start messing around with things you have no business messing with."

Remus let it go. "The point is, I knew they had been following me. And following you. That more was going on than they were letting on. Look bro, you gotta believe me. I can be a real horse's you-know-what sometimes. You and me have our...issues. I'm not gonna lie. But you are still and always will be my brother. Nobody messes with my brother. Well, except me, I guess."

Phin didn't know whether to be touched or offended at his brother's sentiments. But he did feel his heart softening. His and Remus's relationship was complicated to say the least.

"Next thing I know, Bezrukov pulls a gun on me."

"RUSSIANS!" Warren shouted again.

"Will you please be quiet!" The brothers both yelled in response. Warren sheepishly took another drink.

"So, I took off, man. Like I was out of there. Relationship severed. I knew that whatever was going down with you happened after I left you. So, I went back to the House of Reuben. That's when I found out Mary had been killed. But I had no idea they had framed you. I promise. Not until now. Something's going on, Phin. Something big."

"It was already big, Remus. You've stolen I don't know how many relics from the Catholic church. The whole world is looking for them. Oh, and by the way, that's all being pinned on me as well. I was paid a visit in jail by an Italian inspector. A man named Antonio Rossi. He's assigned to find the relics and the one who took them. And they've decided I'm the one. There's a letter, Remus. A letter was sent to this Rossi fellow from an informant. Someone who names me specifically as the thief. And then the letter told him the day and time I would be in Jerusalem at the House of Reuben. So, they showed up to arrest me and low and behold not only did they find me, but they found a dead body as well."

Remus took all this in. More new information. "I had no idea," he began. "This was not what I had planned. What I wanted. It was just a game, between you and me is all. To show you that, well, you know how I feel about religion and all. I was going to show you that it was all fake. Not real."

"Remus, why can't we just agree to disagree? Why does there always have to be a game or some stupid peeing contest to see which one of us is better or right? I am so sick of it." Phin let that set for a moment. "I guess at this point all that matters is who is behind all of this. I've got to clear my name, Remus. On all of this. The thefts. The murder. I have to get my life back."

"Alexander Pontia."

"Excuse me?"

"That's the name. He's the one who broke me out of jail and hired me to steal the stuff. Alexander Pontia. I thought it was just a job. You know, to pay back the favor for springing me. But...it looks like Pontia is playing his own game. One I didn't know about until now."

"Alexander Pontia." Sergio Nardovino spoke for the first time since releasing the brothers to have at it. He'd been sitting quietly, absorbing the whole exchange in silence. Until now. "I know this name. Alexander Pontia. And I have much, I think, I need to share with you."

Chapter 45

Phineas Crook had traveled to Terracina, Italy, in the hopes that Sergio Nardovino would have knowledge of the stolen Jesus artifacts circulating through the dark markets of the world. Perhaps even Sergio himself had moved one or two of the items. But mainly he was seeking to know what Nardo might know - namely, the person behind the whole scheme.

But Remus had now answered that question. Alexander Pontia.

Phin had never heard the name before, not that he would have a reason to know the man. An answer to one question seemed to only give birth to more questions.

Who exactly was Alexander Pontia?

Why had he engineered the theft of relics attached to the person of Jesus Christ?

Why had he broken Remus Crook out of prison? Surely there were other thieves up to the task.

And most important to Phin: Why had Pontia pointed the finger at him? And why have an innocent woman killed and hang that crime also on him? It seemed clear that Pontia must have been behind the note sent to Chief Inspector Antonio Rossi. But, once again, why? So many *why* questions.

"I have known Alexander Pontia for many years," Sergio Nardovino began. "Very resourceful and secretive. Of course, the business he is in requires both. He is, if I may, a pizza delivery man. Like the little Dominoes boy that comes to your house with his cookie cutter pizzas. But Alexander Pontia's pizza is not cookie cutter. It is extremely rare and valuable. He is very good at finding this pizza, guarding this pizza, and then making good on the delivery. He has a trio of companies that work together to accomplish his purposes. His legitimate work all flows through Token Exchange, an auction house with a presence around the world, even here in Italy. Dominion Safe is his security firm that keeps the pizza safe and hot!" The round man chuckled at his own wit. "And then there is Straight Line - they make the delivery. But underneath his legal work there are pizza markets that are very exclusive. If you know of a pizza or a topping you want and it is, say, already sitting in someone else's kitchen...well, as I said, he is very resourceful. For the right price he can acquire the item and bring it to you."

Phin absorbed Alexander Pontia's resumé. "But what about the artifacts stolen from the Catholic Church? The Holy Sponge and the Holy Lance. The Holy Crib and the

Thief's Revenge

Sudarium of Oviedo. And you don't know about this, but he now has the Cross of Gestas to go along with the Cross of the Good Thief."

"*Oddio!*" Sergio exclaimed. "The Cross of Gestas? The Impenitent Thief? I did not know it had even been discovered."

"You can thank my brother for that." Phin eyed Remus, who sheepishly raised a hand and waved.

"So, the big question is - what is he doing with all of these items? Who has he stolen them for? I was hoping you had heard talk among your...peers. Talk of whom the collector might be."

"Oh, there has been much talk among my network. It is buzzing like a hornet's nest. You ask the question everyone wants to know the answer to. But I am sorry to say I do not know. Even Nardo has his limits."

"I can answer that question." All heads turned to face Remus. "I know who Pontia has stolen the Jesus artifacts for and why."

"Of course. You have worked for this master chef yourself. Pray tell, good Remus. What is the answer to the question the world wants to know?" Sergio asked.

"Himself. Pontia has taken the items for himself."

"Interesting," mused Sergio. "He is not known to be a collector, only a mover for those who are."

"Oh, he doesn't want to collect the items. He wants to destroy them."

The stunning revelation shocked the group.

"What?!" Phin blurted out. "No way. You've got to be kidding." He laughed, not because it was funny but because it was so absurd. "There's no way, you've heard

315

him wrong. Why would he do such a thing? What's the point?"

"Because he hates Jesus and Christianity more than I do. Didn't think that was possible, but he does. That was the hook for me, why I pulled you into this, little bro. I was going along with the whole thing just to show you that...well, that you're wrong about this decision you've made to walk away from family and give your life to a man who lived two thousand years ago. But like I said, it was just supposed to be between you and me. The personal side of it. I never intended for it to go this far. Pontia's up to something more and I don't know what it is."

This was all coming at Phin faster than he could process. "I'm sorry, how exactly does destroying the relics of Christ accomplish anything at all?"

"Well, that's the thing. He's not just gonna destroy them. He says he's gonna take them to the holiest place on earth and destroy them in front of the whole world."

"That's absurd. Insane. What's the point?"

Sergio Nardovino had been listening, as was his nature, but finally spoke. "The point, good Phineas, and I am surprised you have not already put it together, but the point is to destroy Christianity itself. Or at least the faith of those who are a part of it. Yes, it is so clear to me now...these toppings...the relics of Jesus...they contain *power*." He whispered the last word with a fierce intensity. And then he sat back with a wave of the hand. "Or at least that is what the legend says."

Phin knew he was correct.

Sergio could see the tumblers falling into place in Phin's

mind. "Perhaps, Professor, you could give us all a history lesson."

Phin would do the best he could. "Well, Nardo," he looked at the Italian's lips curled broadly in a smile under his equally curled mustache, "You are correct, in a manner of speaking. It all goes back to the Crusades really. That time when Christianity and Islam were at war over the Holy Land. We're talking roughly a two-hundred-year period from 1090 to 1290. This is really an oversimplification, but essentially the Muslims pushed out the Christians and built mosques on top of holy sites. The crusaders came in and retook the land, destroyed the mosques and built churches. But in the process, part of the great campaign included locating and protecting the holy relics of the Church, mostly related to Christ. And Nardo is correct, there was a mystic belief that the relics contained special power to protect the crusaders as they fought. Power derived from Jesus Christ himself, since the holy items came in contact with his physical body."

"And this is why I went along with the whole thing," Remus interrupted. "You know, destroy the relics and prove that this whole idea that they have special power is just junk. That's what I wanted to show you, little bro. But I didn't sign up for anybody getting killed and certainly not you getting pulled into it by Pontia. I just wanted to embarrass the Church and you. Just a little innocent fun."

Phin shook his head. Remus still didn't get it. There is so much more to Jesus and being a follower of his than a bunch of relics from the past. It wouldn't do any good to argue with him right now.

"But let me tell you this," Remus continued. "He's not done. Pontia's not done."

"What do you mean?"

"I mean, he's got one more theft to pull off. And this one is the grand-daddy of them all. He is going to steal the cross that Jesus hung on. Something called the True Cross."

This confirmed what Phin had believed all along.

First, we got yours. Then we got mine. Now, it's time to go get his.

Of course.

It all made sense.

Why wouldn't he? If Pontia had come this far, why not go all the way? If his intent was to embarrass and inflame the Church by destroying its holiest relics, then he couldn't leave the most holy relic of all untouched.

Knock, knock, knock. "Excuse me." Sergeant Warren rapped on the table. "Playing a little catch up here. What's this True Cross business again? Cover that one for me one more time. You're saying this Pontia guy is gonna steal the actual cross that Jesus hung on?"

Phin took back over. "Well, not exactly, Billy. The whole legend of the True Cross goes back much further than the Crusades. Like back to the 300s. Constantine was the emperor of Rome and had converted to Christianity during a dramatic battle to unite the Roman empire called the Battle of Milvian Bridge. The night before the fighting began, he had a vision of the cross of Christ and claims to have heard a voice telling him to go forth under the sign of the cross and to conquer. So, the next morning he ordered all his soldiers to paint the Greek letters *Chi* and *Rho* on their shields – the first two letters for *Christ*. They rode, and history records a mighty victory. After that, Constantine converted to Christianity and became obsessed with *Christianizing* the empire. And he tapped his mother to help him. Her name was Helena. And she was quite a woman. Constantine bestowed on her the title of *Augusta Imperatrix*, making her the empress of Rome. He gave her complete access to the treasury of Rome, and he gave her a mission: Travel to Jerusalem and find the True Cross of Christ. At the impressive age of eighty, she traveled to what was then Palestine. She built churches in Bethlehem and on the Mount of Olives, the birthplace of Jesus and the location of his ascension to heaven. She also built a church on Mount Sinai to commemorate the burning bush in the Book of Exodus. But her most remarkable accomplishment was the discovery of the three crosses of Golgotha: the Cross of the Good Thief, the Cross of Gestas, and...the True Cross, the Cross of Christ."

"And where exactly is this True Cross?" Sergeant Warren asked. He was genuinely intrigued. "I've never even heard of it."

"Well, that's the thing. The actual cross is no longer in existence, at least that we know of. Helena left the bulk of the crossbeam in Jerusalem, along with the other two crosses. She took a small portion of the Cross of the Good Thief back to Rome. She also took several slivers of the True Cross with her, along with the three nails from Christ's cross, and then one other item...the actual sign that hung above Christ's head that read: King of the Jews. This wooden placard is called the *Titulus*. It is these fragments, very small I hear, along with the Titulus and one nail, that make up what we call the True Cross. And it's all housed...where else but Rome. Two hours north from where we sit."

"Wait a minute," Sergeant Warren broke in. "What about Jerusalem? You said this Helen chick left the biggest part of the cross in Jerusalem."

"Well, that's just it, the Crusades changed all that. According to church tradition, the Christian crusaders in 1187 rode out to fight the Muslim warrior, Saladin the Great, at the Battle of Hattin located in Israel. They decided to take with them the large crossbeam of Christ, the one Helena left behind. They thought it would give them the victory. But it didn't do any good.. The crusaders were defeated by Saladin, who in turn captured the cross. At that point the cross of Christ disappeared into history, supposedly burned."

"And that's what Pontia wants to do!" Sergio Nardovino joined the conversation once again. "He wants to be a modern-day Saladin! He wants to do what the Muslims were not able to do during the Crusades. He wants to totally wipe out what he sees as the mythology of Jesus. Yes, the dough is rising in my mind. The oven has been heated and the pizza is ready to cook. He is nearly ready. Pontia. He just needs the final ingredient – the final topping. The most important one of all. The True Cross. And remember, my good friends. It's all about the power. The legend of the True Cross is that it has immense power. Not just the power to protect, but the power to *heal.*"

"Okay, what is little man here talking about?" Warren had followed Phin but was puzzled again. "What does he mean the power to heal?"

"That goes back to the legend involving Constantine's mother," Phin answered.

"The Helen chick. Got it."

"*Helena*, Billy. The name is Helena. So yes, back to her. According to legend, because that's the category I think this fits in, when she found the three crosses, she didn't know which was which. So, she tested each cross...she tested its power to heal. The legend goes that a sick woman was brought to all three crosses. The first two did nothing to cure her ailment. But the third cross, well, as soon as she touched it, whatever it was that plagued her left. That is how she knew which was the True Cross. There is even another tale of the True Cross bringing someone back to life, but as I said, it's all very fantastical."

"The point is the power," Sergio said again. "Or the perception of power. Pontia wants to destroy it all."

Phin turned back to his brother. "Remus, you said that he wants to do this act...of destruction...he wants to do it at the holiest place on Earth and in front of the world. Where exactly is this place? And how exactly does he plan to show the world?"

"I'm a blank on both of those, little bro. I didn't hang long enough to get those details. The more I think about it sitting here, the whole thing sounds crazy."

"I wish you'd seen that before signing on with the guy."

"So, what's our next step?" Sergeant Warren asked. "How we gonna put an end to Mr. P's evil scheme?"

"First thing we're going to do is get to Rome and steal the True Cross before Pontia does. That's where Billy and I were headed anyway. We stopped here just to see if we could learn anything about who's behind it all. We've obviously done that."

"I'm going with you," Remus said. "In fact, that was my next job for Pontia before I bolted. I was gonna steal the True Cross and that was the last piece of the pie."

"The last piece of pizza!" Sergio inserted with gusto.

"Sure, Nardo. I get it, always pizza."

"Always, my friend." He shook his belly with his hands and laughed.

Phin was too bound up to find the humor.

"It will be like old times, Phin. Like when we were kids. You and me pulling off a caper. What do you say? We steal the True Cross, then use it to leverage against Pontia. Maybe find out where the rest of the stuff is but at a minimum, convince him to send some kind of message to this Inspector Rossi that you are innocent of murder and the thefts."

"Count me in, boys." Sergeant Warren rose to his feet. "LaPhage has an equipment warehouse in Rome. Give me a list of everything we need to pull this little heist off and I'll have it all waiting for us."

"This is good," Sergio Nardovino exclaimed. "To see the brothers working together again. Yes, your father would be proud."

The mention of his father sent an ache through Phin's gut. This is not how he ever pictured himself, working with his brother as part of the family business. Yes, his father would be proud. And that made Phin happy. At least for the moment.

Sergio kept going. "But first, there is much planning to do, I think. You will work here this afternoon. Then we will eat again tonight. Pizza for dinner! Then you will sleep in Nardo's house before leaving tomorrow to do what you must do. And I have my own work to do. I want to see what more I can find out about Alexander Pontia that might help you."

And so it was decided.

Phineas Crook was once again a thief.

Chapter 46

Phin reclined in the cushioned patio chair, taking in the setting sun as it eased toward the western horizon of the Tyrrhenian Sea.

Another postcard view.

A cool evening summer breeze was whipping up and Phin caught the scent of lilac. He thought of Autumn back home in Oklahoma. He wished she was here with him, in this place, looking at this view. He would put his arm around her and hold her close. They would sit and talk into the dark of the night and hold the moment as long as possible.

He closed his eyes, imagining the cool tones of her silken voice. He opened them again and was back to reality. The view was still stunning, but no Autumn. And he really didn't want her here, not with what he was facing. In fact, he wanted Autumn and his son, Patrick, as far from Alexander Pontia and his schemes as possible.

Sergeant Billy Warren was in the living room of the house on Sergio's secured internet connection working with Oz Jenks and Ronald Chen back at LaPhage Industries headquarters in Fort Worth, Texas. Phin and Remus had hammered out a list of supplies they would need to pull off a very tricky and bold heist in Rome.

Phin still could not believe he was going to do it: steal the True Cross of Christ. But then again, he had already stolen the Shroud of Turin, and for the same reason – to keep it out of the hands of the bad guys. In the case of the Shroud, that was Remus. And now he was working *with* Remus to steal the True Cross. But in reality, it was about Alexander Pontia. It had always been about Alexander Pontia, he just did not know it until this afternoon.

Banging and singing wafted onto the patio from the kitchen. Phin smiled. Sergio was making an audible show of cleaning up after dinner. Pizza, of course. But none like any Phin had ever had before. The featured topping of this evening's pie had been filet medallions, cut to an inch and a half in thickness. Essentially, the pizza had been an excuse to eat steak.

Maybe Phin would bring Autumn here for a vacation after this was all over with. That is, of course, if Sergio Nardovino was still living here. He'd likely pack up and move on to his next destination in a matter of months. It was Nardo's way. Never too long in one place. It was a wise way to live for a man that was wanted by the law.

Phin was also wanted by the law.

He was reminded of that hard truth. He had both

Israel and Italy looking for him. Probably by now the FBI as well. And here he was, sitting only two hours from Rome, about to head into the heart of the Italian center of power to pull off a heist that would no doubt shock the world. But it was necessary. The only way out, Phin knew, was to walk the road all the way through.

Soft footsteps padded behind him.

"Have a seat, Remus. Enjoy the view before it's gone."

"You still have good ears, little brother."

"I'm a Crook."

"Yes, you are. I'm glad you have remembered that."

Remus sat in another of the cushioned chairs catty-corner to Phin, drink of some sort in hand, and took in the scene. The bottom edge of the sun was about to kiss the watery horizon.

Silence.

"What do you think Dad would think?" Remus asked. Apparently he had been musing about their late father as well.

"Oh, I'm sure he would be very proud," Phin reluctantly admitted.

"Yeah, me too. But I think he would be concerned as well."

Phin puzzled over this. "How so?"

"Let's face it. We are both in a heap of trouble here. Me by my own doing, getting hooked up with this Pontia guy. But you got sucked in by me. Look," he shifted to face Phin, "I know I said it earlier, sort of, but I really am sorry to get you mixed up in this."

Phin was somewhat taken aback. Remus was never one

to be contrite. He was always too consumed with being right.

Phin's lack of reply seemed to beg for Remus to go on. So he did. "It's just that, you know...well, we are different, Phin. You and me."

Phin laughed and picked up the glass of water he'd been drinking to take a sip. "You can say that again."

"I've had a lot of time to think. Being locked up will do that for you. I suppose that as your older brother, I've sort of always felt responsible for you. Like when we were kids, just making sure you followed the family code, you know. Dad would teach me and Dad would teach you, but I felt like it was my job to teach you as well. And then when Dad was killed, well, you know how Mom is...so it was just you and me and I felt like it was my job to take Dad's place. To make sure you got off to a good start. But then you made your...*decision*."

Phin knew Remus was talking about the choice he had made to walk away from the family business – to not pursue life as a thief. But it was more than that.

Phin wanted to stay close to home after high school in order to be close to his mother and make sure she was taken care of. He'd chosen to go to a small private college just down the road from Moore, Oklahoma, in the town of Shawnee. That little college was Oklahoma Baptist University, the same college he worked for now. It was there, at OBU, that Phin met Max Allred, a man who had come to be his best friend.

Max had introduced Phin to a whole other world. A world where God not only existed, was not only real, but was also personal, through his son, Jesus. Oh, Phin pushed back on Max in every way possible. He studied all the arguments against God and particularly Jesus, but Max countered every one of them with common sense speech and reasoning. In the end, Phin was compelled. Compelled by Max's challenge to seek the truth, and compelled by a God who loved him more than he loved himself. Compelled by his son, Jesus, who died on a cross two thousand years ago to save Phin, who had not even been born yet. Phin became a Christian and then he became a minister, a defender and an advocate for the faith.

"I always looked up to you, Remus. When we were kids. Did you know that? But life happens, and death. And yes, I made my own choices with my life because, as much as I looked up to you...crud, I even wanted to be like you at one point when we were kids, but I'm not you. I'm me. And yes, I made my decision as you call it. But do you want to know something else? Something that I'm not sure you'll understand? I never really found myself until I found Jesus."

Remus scoffed. "I knew you'd bring him into the conversation."

"I can't not. If you haven't noticed, Remus, this whole operation we are involved in goes back to him. Like it or not, Jesus is inescapable. And for the record, and I'll just use your own words from a second ago, you're the one that got me *mixed up in this*. Didn't you say your whole plan was to prove to me that Jesus is a fake and that I've been wrong this whole time...to believe in him...to follow him? So, I think it is you, dear brother, that has brought Jesus into the conversation, not me."

"Touché. I'll give you that one, bro. I just don't understand how you can give your whole life away to a fable, a myth."

"Remus," Phin allowed the volume of his voice to rise, but he was far short of yelling, "didn't you and I experience the same vision last year? We were together...hanging on crosses next to him. I saw him and so did you. How can you say it's a fable?"

"I don't know what I saw, Phin. I just know what I experienced. Pain. Immense, unexplainable pain." Remus winced at the memory and began rubbing the palms of his hands. "I guess you were spared all that, but I wasn't."

"Maybe God was trying to get your attention."

"Oh, he got it all right! No doubt about that. But I didn't come away with warm fuzzies like you did. I came away with two weeks in solitary confinement to just think about how ticked I was at you and God."

"Me? Why were you mad at me?"

"Because you were out there and I was in prison. You've got a wife and now a kid, and I've got...what? Nobody. Forgive me for being a little human here, but maybe I was just a little bit jealous. There, I've said it. Big brother Remus is jealous of his little brother Phin."

Phin looked on his brother with compassion. "Don't you see, Remus? We all make choices in life. You've made yours and I've made mine. And your choices have led you to where you are in life. But let me tell you something. The choices we make today have consequences for today, yes that is true, but they also have consequences for all of eternity. This life is not all that there is, Remus. You need to trust your little brother on this one. This life is but a vapor, here today and gone tomorrow. And then comes eternity. This life is only the prologue for a much bigger story."

"And see, that's the thing I don't get. Yeah, maybe you believe that Jesus was more than a man and all that. Someone worth following who can *forgive* you and *save* you. If that makes you feel good so you can sleep better at night, then so be it. But this business about eternity, that's where I get stumped. Phin, how do you *know* there is life after death? Aren't we all just guessing?"

Phin thought about that for a moment. He measured his next words carefully. "Remus, everybody puts their faith in something or someone. None of us, no one, has the option of not living on faith. Up until now in your life, you've made your own decisions. Maybe quit focusing on my decision and focus on yours. You've made your choices and you've done so based on *faith*. Faith in yourself. Faith in Dad. Faith in the family code of honor, whatever. But you are as much a man of faith as me. You get up each morning believing that the day is going to turn out a certain way because of the choices you make. That's called faith. You believe *something* about how your life is going to end up. Maybe you believe in a type of heaven or hell or you don't. Maybe you believe in reincarnation - we all just die and then start the whole thing all over. Or maybe you believe that when we die that's it. Game over. But whatever you believe, Remus, that is called faith. Don't trick yourself into saying I'm a man of faith and you're a man of reason. No sir, you don't get that option. We are both the same, you and me. We are men of faith."

"I don't know, bro." It was Remus's turn to chuckle. "Sounds like you're playing mind games with me."

"Let me just finish by saying this: One of us is right and one of us is wrong. Or maybe we both are wrong. But let's just say for a moment that you're right and I'm wrong. So, you believe that when we die that that's all there is. We are finished and life ceases to exist."

"Yep, sounds about right to me," Remus replied. He took a drink of the dark brown liquid in his glass but Phin could tell he was getting to his brother.

"Okay good. So that's what you have faith in. So, if you're right and I'm wrong, about heaven and hell and eternity and all. Well, then what have I lost in the end, if you are right and I am wrong? I'm living a pretty good life. At least until this mess you pulled me into." Phin winked at Remus. "I don't really *lose* anything, do I? So, I was wrong about heaven and hell. So what? No harm, no foul. But listen to me, Remus. Let's flip it now. Let's say I'm right and you're wrong. Let's say there *is* a heaven and a hell and that eternity is real and it's forever. Let's say the only way to get to heaven is to follow Jesus, to put your faith in him. Let's say I am the right one this time. Well then, what do I lose? Nothing. I was right! But you, Remus, what do you lose? If I am right and you are wrong...you lose everything. You lose everything for eternity." It was a sobering notion.

Phin let his words rest for just a moment before finishing. "I know you love to gamble, Remus. Never miss an opportunity to hit the casinos in Oklahoma, do you? You're not stupid, brother. You'd never put money on a bad bet. Well, this is the biggest bet of your life. It's the bet of eternity. And it will cost you more than money, it will cost you your soul. Think about it. I don't lose the bet either way. I either get heaven or when life is over, it's just over. But you on the other hand. If I'm right and you're wrong, you've lost it all."

Remus rose and walked to the edge of the rock wall, looking out over the now sunless sky. The stars had crept out and the moon was half showing overhead.

"We've got a big day tomorrow, Phin. We better both get some rest." With that, Remus Crook turned and left Phin alone.

Chapter 47

This felt too easy. Per Remus's instructions, the team of three had booked a hotel room at the Domus Sessoriana, a hotel that literally adjoined the Basilica di Santa Croce in Gerusalemme – the Church of the Holy Cross in Jerusalem. The name could be misleading because the church sat squarely on the western side of the city of Rome, not in Jerusalem.

In just a matter of moments they would leave their room and steal the True Cross, which sat only yards from their makeshift workspace where Remus and Sergeant Warren were busy checking their gear.

Phin had a fitful night's sleep the night before, his thoughts flitting back and forth between what they were about to do today and his conversation with Remus. Of course, Autumn was never far from his mind. He had wanted to call her, to tell her he was okay, but he didn't want to risk putting her in danger. He was fearful that her phone was being monitored by the authorities.

The trio had risen early, enjoyed hot and delicious breakfast pizza courtesy of Sergio Nardovino, and then they were off. Just before Phin climbed into the Maserati MC20, Sergio had beckoned him aside.

"Be careful, my good boy. Something about this does not feel right to old Nardo." He placed a cell phone in Phin's hand, who tried to protest that he already had a phone, the one provided by the Jordanians. "This is a special phone. If it rings, it will only be me. I am looking into this Alexander Pontia. If I find out any information, this is how I will contact you."

Phin was grateful for the family friend. He tucked the phone into his messenger bag. "And one more thing. Watch out for this inspector from Rome, Antonio Rossi. I know this man. He is good at what he does. He has caused me to pack up and move more than once. But Nardo is better than him." He forced a laugh. Phin was not used to seeing the jovial Italian so somber. "If Rossi has his eyes set on you, he will keep coming, good Phin. At some point, I fear, you will have to deal with Rossi as well as Pontia. But I will do what I can to help. Now go and do what you must." Sergio gave Phin a crushing hug, spun the man around and guided him to the sportscar.

Sergeant Warren gave a wave and peeled out of the drive, kicking up gravel just for fun. Remus followed in a Toyota of some sort that he had acquired. They drove straight to Rome and to the warehouse where LaPhage Industries personnel were expecting them. They changed both vehicles for a blue Volkswagon Sharan with tinted windows. The Euro-styled minivan was more practical for the three of them and their gear, plus it would not attract attention.

They ate a quick meal and then drove straight to the Domus Sessoriana where they checked in without raising even an eyebrow. It was summer and a lot of tourists frequented the modest lodging.

That same feeling - *this is too easy* - hit Phin again. That they could just waltz into a room only yards from their goal.

Phin looked at his watch: 3:00 a.m.

The notion of easy swept away. Things were about to get much harder.

"It's time boys," Sergeant Warren announced. He zipped his backpack and swung it over his shoulder.

The sergeant would not actually descend into the chapel, it had been decided. Oh, he was capable of doing so. That was not the issue. It's just that Remus and Phin were much better at stealth. It was in their DNA. Plus, once inside, this was a two-man job at most.

Warren's role would be to help them breach the chapel from above, and then he would make his way back to the hotel portion of the complex, exit as normal, and make the short walk to the Volkswagen. He'd drive around the block to a street called Via Casilina and park opposite a grassy courtyard and an eight-foot-tall stone wall. This would be the route the brothers would use when it came time to exit with the True Cross. A bag with ropes and a hook for scaling the wall had been hidden in a tree earlier in the day.

Remus raised his hand toward Phin, who grasped it in return. Remus pulled his brother close with a jerk and gave him a slap on the back. "Let's do this, little brother. Once we have the True Cross, I'll contact Pontia and we can negotiate how to get you out of this mess."

"And you too, Remus. Not sure what our options are, but I'm not leaving you hanging either."

Remus gave a tentative nod. "Yeah, well, we'll cross that bridge when we come to it."

"If you boys are done making good, why don't you save the rest til Christmas dinner and let's get moving."

The three men left the room, all carrying backpacks. They were dressed in black, which would normally raise suspicions. But at this hour of the night, they walked undisturbed down the hall to the stairs that led to the rooftop patio.

It was a coolish summer night but somewhat sticky with the humidity that hung in the air. The three stepped over the patio barrier onto the roof of the hotel. Phin looked down into the courtyard and could make out the ruins of an old Roman chapel and palace, the very one that Helena herself had brought the True Cross to over a thousand years ago. The True Cross now resided just yards away in the 18th century building that had replaced it.

All that was required now were light footsteps in order to not wake the sleeping guests below them. The roof of the hotel literally touched the roof of the Basilica di Santa Croce, the two buildings side-by-side. Again, Phin marveled how absurdly easy it was to simply step across, their team of three now standing on top of the chapel itself.

Remus had broken into this same church four months previously to steal the Cross of the Good Thief, the one he'd sent to Phin on his birthday and that Pontia now had possession of. The big risk now was attempting a second theft from the same church. Last time Remus had posed as a security guard and had actually been able to take the cross during broad daylight while tourists mingled about. Because of that theft, the three of them knew that security had been enhanced, which likely involved closely monitored CCTV with guards nearby in case someone tried to do what they were attempting to do right now.

Phin stared up at the stone clocktower jutting out of the roof of the chapel.

This was their entrance.

Phin was hoisted up by Remus who then pulled Sergeant Warren up and over. They were now completely out of sight of anyone walking by on the street below who might happen to look up.

A small set of stairs descended to a door. Phin went to work. He was the expert on locks in the family. The door lock clicked and Phin put his tools away. He pulled the door open and looked back at Remus. Again, too easy, he thought. They had all assumed they would need to do some cutting to get inside the chapel. Seeing that this was no longer the case, they gave Sergeant Warren a thumbs up. He turned and disappeared back over the clocktower ledge and into the night. They'd see him next, hopefully, at the rendezvous point.

Remus and Phin carried on to the bottom of the stairs. Another door, this one locked as well. Two minutes later and that door too was ready to open.

Too easy.

Phin worked the old rugged door open just a bit and peered through the crack. They were at the back and side of the chapel. This was all expected based on the schematics of the chapel that Oz Jenks had sent them. There would be cameras everywhere. Plan A had been for Oz to hack into the chapel's system and loop the cameras so they could take their time and work freely. But he'd been unsuccessful. The only explanation was that the security of the chapel, under the oversight of the Vatican, had installed a closed system surveillance network that was independent of the Internet.

It was unhackable.

That led to the formation of Plan B. They would simply have to move fast. Rushing the altar, where the True Cross sat on public display, they would do a grab-and-go...but with a little help.

Remus had already unzipped his pack. He pulled out a black object the size of a small shoebox. It was very simple with a countdown display, a dial, and a button, all located on top. Remus set the countdown for sixty seconds and looked at Phin, who gave a silent thumbs-up, then he pressed the button.

The box would create a localized EMP – an electromagnetic pulse, the same type of device Phin had used when he stole the Shroud of Turin. Everything that ran on electricity in a two-block radius would be knocked out for five minutes. That plus reboot time would give Remus and Phin more minutes than they needed to snatch the True Cross and exit the way they'd entered.

It would be chaos for chapel security. They'd scramble personnel to the church, but by the time they arrived and assessed that the True Cross had been stolen, the brothers would be cruising away with Sergeant Warren behind the wheel.

That was the plan anyway.

Phin looked back through the crack in the door and his heart quit beating. Two security personnel appeared at the front of the chapel. He had not seen them before, probably because they were doing their rounds.

This was unexpected.

This was bad.

Phin looked back at the counter. Forty-five seconds. He motioned for Remus to come have a look. He rushed to the door and saw. Then he cursed under his breath. The brothers would have to think fast.

Bad turned to worse.

Two more security personnel entered the chapel from the back. They waved at the first two, who gestured in return. It looked like a shift change. Could they have picked a worse time?

The clock was now at thirty seconds. They'd have to wait until the shift change was over before setting off the EMP. Remus would have to stop the countdown.

He never got the chance.

The lights went out and they were suddenly shrouded in total darkness.

Chapter 48

The countdown clock showed twenty five seconds and still counting. So why had the power gone out?

Phin heard a grunt and a thud coming from the front of the chapel. More sounds of scuffling. It was hard to tell what was happening in the inky blackness of their enclosure. Phin decided to risk opening the door and easing his way into the chapel proper.

The emergency lights flickered and then powered on.

Phin ducked behind a wooden pew, struggling to take in the scene at the altar. One security guard lay on the ground, incapacitated. Another was in the clutches of... a woman. Blonde hair, in a bun - one of the relief guards who'd entered just before the lights went out. She had the man in a headlock from behind. Her partner, who'd entered with her, gave the guard a punch to the gut. *OOMMPH!* The man let out a lung full of air. The woman, though small in stature, pulled the man upright from behind, preventing him from doubling over. And then an act of unnecessary cruelty – she jerked the man's neck to the side. A sickening *crack* echoed throughout the chapel. It reminded Phin of twisting the parts of a chicken wing apart. The man slumped to the ground.

"Bezrukov!" Remus shouted from behind Phin. He was standing, in the open, glaring at the man and woman, both clearly not chapel security despite their uniforms.

"Ah, Remus Crook!" The man bellowed back. "How good of you to come, Comrade. To finish the job for which you were hired." Phin stood. "And I see that your brother has decided to join us as well."

"This is just between you and me, Dimitri."

"And Mr. Pontia, my friend. He wants you to know that he is very disappointed in you."

"Hello, Tess," Remus called to the blonde woman who said nothing in return. "I see Alexander sent his two bulldogs. You can tell Pontia that I am equally disappointed in him. This was supposed to be a business deal, that's all. He breaks me out of prison and I steal what he wants. He's decided to make this into something more. So, I'm out."

"*You* are the one that made it something more, Comrade. When you invited your brother to join you."

"No! You were the one that made it something more when you killed that innocent old lady, you Russian piece of trash."

Even at a distance, Phin could see the bald Russian's head turn red. Phin was internally calculating the passing minutes. Apparently, Pontia's people had shared the same idea as Remus and himself – they set off their own EMP.

They had donned guard uniforms to get into the chapel, but knowing this was not the scheduled time for a shift change, they used the darkness created by the electrical pulse to kill the real security guards.

Right about now the rest of chapel security would be assessing the power outage. They'd see it was affecting more than their systems, two blocks to be precise. They'd not suspect a theft in the chapel...yet. But time was ticking. The power would come back on, their systems would reboot, and they'd see the dead officers along with the four of them.

"Let's talk about this, but not take too much time, shall we?" Phin spoke up as he began walking toward the front of the chapel. "We have obviously both come here for the same thing, the True Cross."

He moved to the center of the narrow chamber, his feet crossing the elaborate marble mosaic floor. Behind Dimitri Bezrukov was the woman named Tess who stood in front of the altar, which was just up two stone steps.

Four black pillars framed an open structure and, in the middle, sat a large table with heavy square legs. As he grew closer, Phin could see, even in the dim emergency lighting, that the table was covered with a rich blue cloth upon which sat various gold objects. But to the right side lay the prize they'd all come for: the True Cross.

The *Titulus* was protected by a gold frame that looked to be roughly a foot long and half that much tall. Phin knew the glass was an inch thick. He also knew from his study of the object that it had only been removed from its frame four times in the last six hundred years. Latches on the side of the frame provided access to the sign that hung above the head of Christ as he, himself, hung on the cross.

A small gold box encrusted with jewels caught Phin's eye as well. Inside that box were three small slivers of wood and one nail. This was all that had survived of the cross itself. The *Titulus* and the contents of that little box – the True Cross.

"Yes, we have all come here for the same thing, brother of Remus Crook. It is nice to finally meet you," Dimitri Bezrukov said. "Comrade Pontia said you would be here with your brother and he was right. He seems to always be right about these things."

The main power snapped back on. Phin knew their time was running out. The security system would begin its reboot process.

"Ah, yes, the electricity is back." Dimitri declared the obvious. "I believe Comrade Pontia would like to speak with you himself, Remus. You should power on the phone he gave you."

Keeping his eye on the Russian, Remus fished the phone out his cargo pocket and complied. Right on cure, the phone began to vibrate. He pressed the green answer button and held it to his ear.

"You are extraordinarily predictable," came the first words of Alexander Pontia. "Yes, I knew you'd be here, or I suppose I should say there...in the Basilica di Santa Croce. I am also guessing you have your brother with you."

"What's this all about, Pontia?" Remus scanned the room with his eyes. It irked him that Pontia was calling him out for being predictable. Remus Crook never liked to be predictable. He walked toward the front of the chapel to join his brother. The two were just a few yards from Dimitri Bezrukov and Tess Greenway. He could now see the bodies of the two dead security guards at their feet.

"Oh, so much more than you could even guess. Now, I know time is short. So here is how this is all going to unfold. You and your brother will either join Dimitri and Tess and all four of you will walk out of the chapel with the True Cross and join me tomorrow morning. Or you will foolishly resist, in which case you will lose. Dimitri and Tess will still walk out of the chapel with the True Cross, we will take your brother with us, and you will be left behind, somewhat less than whole, I think, and then you will be arrested for the murder of two chapel security guards. So now it is time for you to make your choice."

What was this game Alexander Pontia was playing? And why? Why was he so intent on staying connected to the Crooks? And why Phin especially? Take him with them? What purpose did Phin serve? Yes, he could see that Pontia would be offended for skipping out on their deal they had made. But then again, here he was in the Church of the Holy Cross, to steal the True Cross, which were the last orders he had received before bolting. There were simply too many shadows being cast by Alexander Pontia for Remus to sort out.

"I suggest you make your decision quickly," Pontia's voice spoke again into Remus's ear.

Remus looked at his brother, who was staring back at him. He could see the look of wonder on his face, only guessing at what Pontia was saying to him. Dimitri was smiling, like a triumphant bull who had just gorged a helpless matador. Tess Greenway stared, her eyes dark pools of sinister trickery. He had to do something. Something to turn the tables in his and Phin's favor. Something...unpredictable.

Remus threw down the phone and launched himself at the Russian. "Grab the True Cross and go, Phin. Go!"

Phin was stunned as his brother barreled into the thick man named Dimitri Bezrukov. His brother was no slouch, having spent the last several years pumping iron in the yard of the Big Mac. Like two heavyweights, the men began to slug each other. Phin had no idea what Alexander Pontia had said to Remus and he had no idea what his brother was ultimately trying to do, but he made for the altar where sat the *Titulus* and the golden box. He expected that the blonde woman would race him for the items.

But she did not.

Instead, she walked coolly up to the fighting men and at just the right moment, when the two separated and before they lunged at each other again, she leaned into Remus.

Phin stopped to look on, trying to discern the strange action.

Remus stopped as well, his hands falling to his sides. He inhaled sharply and looked up at the domed ceiling of the chapel.

Tess Greenway stepped away, sliding a six-inch-long stiletto out from between the ribs where she had stabbed Remus in the upper side, into his right lung.

Phin could see the knife dripping crimson onto the marble floor. His brother's blood.

Remus lost all energy. He wavered back and forth, still staring at the ceiling of the chapel. *"I'm sorry,"* were the only words that slid from his lips as in a whisper.

"No!" Phin ran for his brother but tripped over the body of one of the guards, sprawling head first onto the marble floor.

Tess bounded up to the altar and quickly snatched the items of the True Cross. Remus collapsed forward into the arms of Dimitri Bezrukov. The beefy Russian picked him up and slung him over his shoulder like a rag doll. The two headed for the back of the chapel and disappeared around a dark corner. They had apparently worked out their own escape route.

Phin's mind spun.

He could hear commotion coming from the front of the chapel. He was out of time. The guards were coming. They'd seen the dead bodies on the cameras. They knew a theft was in progress.

Phin acted on instinct. He jumped to his feet, grabbed Remus's phone, and bounded up the steps of the clocktower.

Hopefully he could make it to Sergeant Warren and the getaway vehicle before he was captured.

Chapter 49

Phin launched the small desk against the wall. He followed the outburst by kicking over a lone chair left sitting by the wall.

"Easy there, Doc. You gotta calm down." Sergeant Warren had never seen the normally mild-mannered college professor this animated.

The two men had retreated to an isolated cabin just outside the city of Tivoli, tucked into the green forested hills of the Monte Catillo Natural Reserve. Phin had been successful in extricating himself from the Basilica di Santa Croce. Like a black cat, he darted across the courtyard without detection and scaled the stone wall to rendezvous with the waiting sergeant. The immediate commotion of the break-in had centered around the chapel itself, buying Phin the time he needed.

He hoped, he prayed, that the Russian and the woman had been caught and that Remus was on his way to a hospital. But after monitoring the newsfeeds and the police chatter on a handheld scanner Warren brought along, it was clear Pontia's people had escaped too. Phin's greatest fear, that an unidentified dead body had been found, had not been realized. That likely meant Remus was still alive.

Sergeant Warren gunned the Volkswagen minivan out of town just as sirens were descending on the church complex. They made the forty-five minute drive to the nature reserve without incident.

Phin brushed back his hair with both hands. "They took Remus, Billy. They stabbed him, this woman did, and then they just took him. Why would they do that?" Phin thought back to the brutality of the woman Remus had called Tess, how she had snapped the neck of the security guard without so much as flinching. And then the way she so casually walked up to Remus and slid her knife into his side. There was something...evil about that woman.

On the drive to the mountains, Phin had hastily unpacked the events in the chapel for Sergeant Warren. He had listened intently, only interrupting to ask a few pointed questions for clarity.

"Payback," Sergeant Warren answered Phin's question.

"Excuse me, payback for what?

"This Pontia guy sprung your brother from prison, remember? So, he owes him for doing that. And Remus bolted on him. So, payback. We're talking about a man who holds grudges and doesn't forget."

"But why not just leave him to die? Why take him with them?"

Warren scratched his crew cut. "Yeah, you got me on that one. He'd be a liability in their efforts to exfiltrate the facility but they took him anyway."

"I'm telling you, I was there. There was something calculated about the whole thing."

A buzzing sound. On. Off. On. Off.

"Shhhh...what's that sound?" Sergeant Warren was on his feet, ever alert.

"Relax, Billy." Phin walked over to the couch and hoisted his messenger bag. "It's just my phone."

But it wasn't.

It was Remus's phone. Ringing on vibrate.

Phin held the phone up and looked at the display. It was an unknown number. The ring timed out and quit. What was that about? Who would be calling his brother?

The phone began buzzing again. Unknown number.

Phin cautiously hit the answer button and put the phone on speaker.

"Hello?" he asked tentatively.

"Good morning, Dr. Crook. It is a pleasure to finally speak to you directly."

Phin knew...without a doubt. This was the voice of Alexander Pontia.

"Listen, you sonuva...my brother...Remus. What have you done to him? With him?" *Stay calm*, Phin chided himself.

There was laughter on the other end of the line. Phin's efforts failed. He was boiling. "Brotherly love is such a wonderful thing, is it not? Of course, I wouldn't know. I am an only child. But it's quaint to see in others. I'm glad you care, Dr. Crook. About your brother. In fact, I was counting on it."

"So, he's alive? Tell me he's alive, please."

"Oh, he's very much alive, you need not worry. For the moment anyway. My people are loyal, Dr. Crook. You need to know that. They do nothing that is outside of my wishes. If I had wanted your brother dead, he would be dead. And I should say that he certainly deserves to be dead for severing our agreement. But I'm not quite done with Remus. That is why he is alive."

"What's his condition? Can he speak? Let me talk to him." Phin was frantic to know more.

"His condition. Yes, well, that's another matter. I would say your brother is in *grave* condition. As in, one foot in the grave. That was a nasty wound he received. Directly into his chest cavity. His right lung has totally collapsed. Poor thing, he can barely breathe, so no, he's not in any condition to talk right now. But do not fear, Dr. Crook. I have my personal physician attending to him at this very moment."

So, Remus was alive and being tended to. Phin was only just a bit relieved. His brother's life was in the hands of what he judged to be an egomaniac. Phin looked over at Sergeant Warren, who was staring hard at the wall, absorbing every jot and tittle of the conversation.

"What is it you want, Pontia? Why are we having this conversation?"

"Ah yes, a man who likes to get to the point. Cut to the chase, as they say. I like that. You and I are going to have a productive relationship, I believe."

"Relationship? What in the world are you talking about? I want nothing to do with you, Pontia. Do you hear me?" Phin's voice rose just below the level of a yell.

More laughter.

Phin hated to be laughed at.

"And this is where the brotherly love I mentioned comes into play. You see, my dear Dr. Crook, Remus owes me. He owes me for his freedom and now he owes me for his life. He and I have unfinished business, you see. But since he is no longer in position to take care of matters himself, you are going to have to do it for him. Let's just say that I need you to finish what he started."

"Finish? I thought we were done. Remus said you had only one more job for him to do. The True Cross. You have it now, if you haven't forgotten. Your team took it. It's over and you've won. There's nothing else left."

"Oh, but there is, Dr. Crook. There most certainly is. The True Cross is the final piece to the puzzle, that is true. But the *Titulus* and the shards that were held at the Basilica di Santa Croce are not all there is of the True Cross. There is more."

More? What did he mean by more?

Phin's gears were turning. Pontia continued. "You're working it out, aren't you, Dr. Crook? Your silence speaks louder than you think."

"So why don't you just tell me?"

"Yes, I think I will. No time to waste. Poor Remus is suffering." Phin winced at the cruel tease. "The world assumes that the largest piece of the True Cross was destroyed nine hundred years ago when it was captured by Saladin the Great at the Battle of Hattin. Legend says that

Saladin had the cross of Christ burned. But that's the problem with legends, they carry only shades of truth. The fact is, Dr. Crook, that the near full crossbeam of the True Cross is very much still with us. Well, not exactly with *us*, but that's where you come in."

Phin understood. Remus was being held as collateral for Phin's cooperation. "You want me to steal it, don't you?"

"That is exactly what I want you to do, Dr. Crook." Alexander Pontia's voice had turned icy cold. "Let me say this as simply as I can: As long as you work for me, my physician will work for Remus, and your brother will live. The moment you walk away, so does my doctor. You hold your brother's life in your hands. Brotherly love, Dr. Crook, it's as simple as that."

"Where is the True Cross?"

"Perfect!" The man's enthusiasm had returned. "It's not in an easy place. But then these things never are easy, are they? That was why I needed your brother and why I now need you."

"The location, Pontia. Just tell me where I'm headed."

"Haha, my oh my, I love motivated employees! The True Cross never left the empire of Saladin. After it was captured, it was sent to Damascus in Syria. There it stayed until the death of Saladin around 1193. After that, the cross was apparently ferried to the southwest portion of the Ayyubid Empire where it made its new home. Even after the empire dissolved in the 1300s, it has stayed in the same place."

"Where, Pontia? *Please*, just tell me where."

"Jordan. The remainder of, the biggest portion of, the True Cross is in the hands of the King of Jordan."

Phin sat down on the couch and shook his head. Pontia was right, this was not going to be easy.

Chapter 50

Flying back into Jordan was not a problem. They were, after all, Jordanian citizens. At least according to their Jordanian passports, courtesy of General Omar Abdallah.

Phin and Sergeant Warren landed in Amman, Jordan, late that night on a private jet provided by none other than LaPhage Industries. Phin had once despised the conglomerate but was now grateful for the resources it provided. This also allowed Phin to stay off the radar, avoiding passing through commercial air traffic checkpoints where an image of his face might be captured and recognized.

Passport control was no trouble at all for the pair. "Welcome home Mr. Ali...Mr. Ibrahim," was all that was said by the agent after a quick glance and a stamp of their passbooks. Phin and Warren looked at each other and moved quickly to the airport exit. They crashed at a local hotel and over breakfast the next morning the sergeant had an announcement for Phin.

"I've got a little surprise for you, Doc." They were sitting under the umbrella of a small two-person table at a restaurant across the street from their hotel. They opted for the fresh outside air rather than indoors. It would be a hot day, but the temperatures were pleasant enough at the current hour.

Phin raised an eyebrow and sipped his tea. He wasn't a coffee drinker. "What's that supposed to mean?"

Warren looked at his watch. "You'll see in about ten minutes."

On cue, exactly ten minutes later, a taxi pulled up to the curb. Out stumbled what was clearly an awkward American. The young man was wearing obnoxiously bright red shorts and a Captain America t-shirt. A weak attempt at coordination had him sporting blue Converse All Stars.

"Oz!" Phin jumped up and rushed to help the computer genius/geek, giving him a big hug. "What on earth...what are you doing here?" He glanced back at Warren.

"That's what I'd like to know. The sergeant there sent me a message yesterday at noon. 911 he said. Leave immediately and fly to Amman, Jordan. You know...when the sergeant gives orders..." Oz Jenks trailed off.

"Good job, soldier!" Warren barked at the young man. He moved to stand right in front of Oz.

"Sir, yes sir!" Oz flipped his mop of brown hair away from his brown-rimmed glasses. He saluted sharply.

"Good grief." Phin was embarrassed for him. He

reached up and lowered Oz's hand. "Let's get you off the street."

They paid the cab and helped Oz with his gear – a suitcase, backpack, and a hard-shell case with a handle. "The good stuff," he said, patting it as if it were illegal drugs or some other contraband.

"I brought in tech support, Doc. I figured it would be better to have Jenks here local as opposed to being the eye in the sky, if you know what I mean. Never know what we're gonna run into and it would just be better to have him on the ground with us. He'll coordinate with Chen back at HQ in Texas."

It made sense and Phin was glad for the extra help, plus he genuinely liked the young man.

They grabbed some food to go for Oz, and then loaded up in a Mercedes SUV for the two-hour drive to the southern edge of the Dead Sea.

The Dead Sea...again, ugh, Phin thought.

He used the first hour of the trip to fill Oz Jenks in on the "mission."

After the phone conversation with Alexander Pontia ended, the man had sent Phin a text with specs on the background of the cross and the job at hand.

The crossbeam of the True Cross - the largest piece in existence stolen nine hundred years previous by Saladin - was in the basement of the Museum at the Lowest Place on Earth. When Sergeant Warren had asked for the name of the museum, Phin had to explain that that *was* the name of the museum: The Museum at the Lowest Place on Earth. Warren grunted, "Stupid name," and then let it go.

The True Cross was a problem, apparently, for the royal family of Jordan. While it was a major coup to have the famed relic, it also was a political hot potato. For one, no one knew it even existed. The legend of its capture and destruction had endured. If it was ever made public that the crossbeam of the True Cross still existed and that Jordan, a Muslim nation, had it, well, it would be a scandal and stir to a fever pitch the radicals of both Christianity and Islam. In short, it could create a modern version of the Crusades.

Jordan was at peace with its neighbor Israel, a fragile peace at best. And they were on good terms with the rest of the Muslim world, a difficult balancing act to be sure. The king just didn't need the problems that the True Cross would bring. So, in 2006, when the Museum at the Lowest Place on Earth was completed, King Abdullah ordered the relic shipped from Amman to Ghor es-Safi, on the edge of the Dead Sea, and placed as an unidentified relic in the king's personal collection located in the museum's basement.

It was now up to Phin to steal it.

Oz went to work while they drove, scouring the Internet and working to hack the Jordanian networks for any info, schematics, security, etc. on the museum.

Phin glanced out the window, watching the hot sands pass by, thinking that just a few miles to the west, he was a wanted man by the Israelis.

How am I going to get myself out of this mess?

It seemed that the harder he tried, the deeper he sank. And then there were thoughts of Remus. For all he knew, his brother had succumbed to his wounds and died. Still, he had no choice but to trust Pontia.

The Dead Sea came into view and soon they were hugging the edge of the body of water as they cruised down the Jordan Valley Highway. Phin recognized the security station that he and Sergeant Warren had been held in just three days previous. Phin wondered if General Omar Abdallah was on duty and if he'd be as accommodating if he knew what they were about to do.

Only thirty minutes later they arrived on the outskirts of Ghor es-Safi, a very small and very uninteresting farming community nestled up next to a mountain range that Phin didn't know the name of. The Museum at the Lowest Place on Earth was on the far northern edge of the town, truly in the middle of nowhere. They drove right past it just to scope it out and then kept going on into the town.

Only a few cars in the parking lot.

Not a tourist Mecca of the world.

"Boy, the king really doesn't care much about the cross, does he?" Oz asked. "This place is desolate."

The three found a small place to eat with a sign in Arabic. The food was good and they hatched their plan.

Sergeant Warren looked at the data Oz had pulled. Security was minimal. This was not a major museum and very few tourists actually visited it. The security door to the basement was the most high-tech feature of the facility.

Made sense.

That's where the King's Collection was.

Oz felt confident he could gain entry with the gear he loaded from his hard-shell into his backpack. After that, Phin would do the rest. If muscle was needed, well, they had an ex-Marine with two bionic limbs along for the ride.

They finished up and headed back to the museum. No time to waste, they decided. The sooner Phin could satisfy Pontia and get his brother to a hospital the better. They would get a closer look at the facility during visiting hours and then come back after dark, after the museum closed, to pull off the theft.

It was just after one thirty when they parked the SUV and stepped out into the scorching heat. One other car was in the parking lot. They'd stick out for sure, especially the way Oz was dressed. They should have had him change clothes, Phin commented.

A blast of cold air met them as they stepped inside and were greeted by a sleepy security guard who motioned them on through.

No checking of bags or passports.

An older lady at a booth who spoke broken English sold them tickets and handed them a piece of paper highlighting the exhibitions of the museum. The modern facility was round with circular hallways that one could walk at their own pace. The three men took their time, playing the part of being tourists just stopping by on their way through town.

At the back of the building, they found themselves alone. They also found a door with a security keypad attached. They were out of view of any museum personnel. In fact, they'd seen no one except the one guard and the ticket seller.

Oz eased an earpiece into his left ear and starting whispering to Ronald Chen back in Texas. He tapped the side of his glasses and began streaming everything he saw back to his colleague.

Sergeant Warren was picking at a stone on a pedestal with a sign that said "Do Not Touch."

Phin looked down at the keypad and studied it. It was a simple twelve button pad, with numbers 0-9 and * and a # - just like on a phone. He didn't need Oz for this, he knew exactly what to do – growing up a Crook had a few advantages. And he couldn't resist. His fingers flew over the keypad and just like that, a green light and a click. Phin turned the knob and the door opened. He looked back at the other two who had just realized what he'd done.

Before they could react, he whispered, "Be right back!"

Chapter 51

Alexander Pontia descended the few steps of his Learjet 75, Bombardier class, into the intense Egyptian heat. Even in the shade of the private hanger he had arranged at the Cairo International Airport, it was stifling.

The hangar was a beehive of activity: Dominion Safe personnel scurried about sorting and hauling military-grade equipment, all packed in duffels and Pelican hard-shells. A fleet of Humvees were parked and ready. Everything was black in color – the packing crates, the vehicles, even the military-styled uniforms of Dominion Safe employees. A secondary row of Straight Line shipping vehicles was also present, also black.

Normally, desert sand would have been the color of choice – for everything. But Alexander Pontia wasn't concerned with camouflage. The Egyptians and their pro-Islamic government had been all but too happy to assist in any plan that would embarrass their Jewish neighbors to the north and Christianity as a whole. Plus, black would make a nice contrast for the worldwide broadcast of his bold initiative.

Pontia had worked to acquire several Egyptian artifacts from Sudan for a former prime minister of the country. The man was still connected to the current prime minister and was able to arrange for Pontia's unrestricted visit to Egypt.

Two men in Egyptian military uniforms approached Pontia, flanking a tall gentleman in a suit.

"Alexander Pontia," the man said, offering his hand. "I am Sherif Mahlab. President el-Sisi sends his greetings and regrets he cannot be here to welcome you himself."

Pontia returned the handshake. He'd not expected the president to appear. Sherif Mahlab was only offering the obligatory regret.

"Please thank the president for his hospitality," Pontia said, his head moving from one side to the other, eyes taking in the whole of activity in the hangar.

"You should have no issues regarding access while you are in our beautiful country. You will be headed into the southern portion of the peninsula, I've been informed. Here is my card. If you need anything, anything at all, I've been instructed to help you."

Alexander Pontia took the card and thanked Mahlab, who gave a quick nod of the head and moved off.

Pontia smiled. Everything was falling into place exactly as he had planned. The matter with the Crook brothers had become a bit more complicated than he had originally hoped, but he was enjoying this version of the scheme regarding those two even better.

An individual approached, having emerged from a small office on the far side of the hangar. Tess Greenway met Pontia at the halfway point. She had a sly smile on her face and Pontia could read her mind. He held up a hand. "Not here, Tess my dear, it's too public."

She frowned and tried to take his arm instead, but he walked on ahead of her toward the office.

Cool air was pounding out of a small window unit and Dimitri Bezrukov straightened from a table with a large map on it as Pontia and Tess entered.

"Ah, Comrade, it is good to see you. Your flight? Is good?"

"Yes, yes, the flight was fine." Alexander Pontia was anxious for an update.

Tess pulled two bottles of water from a small refrigerator and gave one to Alexander. She cracked the cap on the other for herself, ignoring an offer for the Russian. He didn't acknowledge the slight.

"We've got one flight of gear delayed in Amsterdam, mostly video and computer equipment."

"Unacceptable." Pontia cut the security specialist off. "I was very precise on the supply list. Everything is essential."

"Relax, Comrade. The original flight had mechanical difficulties. I've already routed a replacement plane and it's in the air now."

"There can be no delays. We are on a schedule Dimitri, a very strict schedule."

This was the way Alexander Pontia operated. Precision and exactness, applied to every detail of life. Dimitri Bezrukov knew that there was more leeway in the schedule than his boss was allowing for in this moment, but he didn't push back.

"All will be well, I promise. I've updated the itinerary, figuring in the late arrival of the video gear, and we will still make the marks on the schedule. Not a minute late."

Tess Greenway took another long drink from her bottle of water. She was enjoying the minor dressing down of the Russian, whom she privately despised. Yes, he was good at what he did and was skilled, to a degree, but she viewed him as an oaf.

"Make sure you are right, Dimitri. Do whatever is necessary to get the equipment here. I'm already unhappy with how things played out in Israel under your watch. Don't disappoint me again, not now especially. We are on the precipice of something great, my friends. Something that will change the world and put a nail into the heart of religion and the Church. In just two days' time, we will wipe away two millennia of foolish myth!"

Tess Greenway and Dimitri Bezrukov both nodded.

Tess straightened her back and spoke. "And the world will know it was you, Alex. They will know that it was Alexander Pontia that did what the Romans could not do two thousand years ago. You are going to kill Jesus once and for all."

Alexander liked the way Tess said it. What the Romans could not do, he was going to do. He'd have to remember that line for the broadcast. It was good. Tess had recently taken to calling him Alex, which no one did, not even his wife, Jillian. He thought he liked it, coming from Tess, anyway. He still wasn't sure how to process the development in their relationship. But for now, he'd let her stay close to him.

"And you are ready for this new attention, Comrade?" Dimitri Bezrukov's question brought Pontia back to himself.

"Excuse me?"

"You are ready, I was asking? Once you drive the knife into the heart of the Church, you will become the most wanted man on planet Earth. And not only by the Church."

"Of course I am ready, Dimitri. I have made my living on being ready. What you are failing to calculate, *Comrade*, is that while I will create a world of enemies in what I am about to do, I will at the same time ingratiate myself to a whole new world of friends. Friends with power and money. I'm not the only man in the world that hates the Church, the opiate with which religion poisons the masses. I'm just going to be the first man bold enough to do something about it. Don't you worry, Dimitri. I've got a plan to disappear onto a beach in paradise somewhere, totally off the grid. But then I will come back. Alexander Pontia always comes back."

The confidence of the little speech was good enough for the loyal pair.

"And what about Remus Crook?" Dimitri switched gears.

"Yes, I almost forgot. What is the condition of the good Mr. Crook?"

"He's stable but in serious condition. He's dipped

some, but Dr. Potero always brings him back up. That was the latest update I received this morning."

"But not too far up. I don't want him healed; I want him in pain. I need him incapacitated and struggling for his life."

The situation with Remus Crook was the one thing that neither Tess Greenway nor Dimitri Bezrukov understood. In fact, they could not understand the fascination with the Crook brothers at all. But Alexander Pontia seemed to be certain of their purpose to what he was planning. So, they simply followed orders. Remus was not supposed to die, but neither was he supposed to recover.

"It is as you say," Bezrukov replied.

"And he too is ready for transport, correct? He must go with us to the mountain." Pontia was insistent.

"Of course. He is in the hangar with us, in fact. We've established a mobile care unit just for him across the way."

"Excellent! Then it is all set, my friends. Make sure we get that gear here, Dimitri. And then we wait for Phineas Crook to finish what he should have already started."

Chapter 52

Phin crept down a flight of stairs. A well-lit hallway met him.

Everything was immaculate and new. LED lights, white tile, the smell of new paint. The rest of the museum was in decent enough shape, but this basement space had undergone a recent renovation. Phin knew it must be used for some special purpose. His heartrate rose.

He slinked his way down the hallway past a bank of unoccupied offices and a couple of larger rooms with display tables. He paused to look, but nothing of interest was set on them, only your basic run-of-the-mill pottery shards, coins, a few ancient weapons – basic archaeological dig finds.

Phin then came to another sealed door. The same kind of keypad lock as the door above him. He entered the same code he'd cyphered out for the other, and sure enough, a green light and a click. He pulled the door open and stepped through.

He was in a vault of sorts. The room was brightly lit with fluorescents, an empty table sat in the middle. Large custom-built cabinets lined the walls on either side, each with smoked glass covering the doors. Phin could make out what was in each one as he stepped up to it. He assumed the glass was a special treatment that blocked out UV exposure and the damage it would cause, but allowed for viewing of what was inside.

The first cabinet held a helmet. Phin couldn't resist. He turned the handle to swing the door open. Amazingly, there were no locks on anything in the room. He stared at the pointed headpiece. A small index card had printing on it in Arabic. Phin's command of the language was rudimentary at best but he made out one word: Saladin.

Phin took in a sharp breath. He was looking at the battle helmet of Saladin the Great. The next cabinet held a breastplate and the next a large two-handed scimitar. All belonging, he knew, to the famous Arab sultan.

A much larger cabinet came next, this one a good five feet wide.

Was it possible?

Phin moved in front of the glass barrier and stared.

A single wood beam.

It was all happening so fast. They were supposed to wait until after the museum closed to break in and steal the True Cross. But Phin couldn't resist. He had to verify that what he was staring at was indeed what he thought it was.

He opened the door from the top and let it fold down. The beam was ancient, roughly hewn, very similar to a railroad tie. Phin recognized it as having the same look and dimensions as the Cross of Gestas, which Remus had taken from the Crook family archive just days before. The end was jagged and looked to have been broken off, perhaps destroyed or at best lost to time. What was left was over four feet long.

And sitting next to it was a little card, again with Arabic printing on it. Phin took the card and could read enough to confirm what he suspected: *The Cross of Isa*. The word Isa was the Muslim name for Jesus as it appeared in the Quran.

This was it.

The True Cross.

But it seemed so unreal. How could the True Cross of Christ be sitting in the basement of a common and little used museum in the Jordanian desert? And the simplicity of the security around the relic was stunning. Of course, the Jordanians had held the cross for hundreds of years and no one knew of its existence. If Alexander Pontia was correct, the cross was more of a burden than a blessing. It was as if...no one really cared.

But Alexander Pontia certainly cared. And Phin cared because the life of his brother was at stake.

"Ma aladhi tafealuh huna?!"

Phin whipped around, caught off-guard by the voice yelling at him. The young man in the white lab coat looked as surprised at Phin. He was skinny, maybe in his early thirties. Where had he come from?

"I'm sorry," Phin said, holding his hands up in front of himself. "I got lost...you know. I was just looking for a bathroom," he tried to articulate.

"You are American," the young man said in thickly accented English. "You should not be here. I call security."

"No, no, no! You don't need to do that. I'm leaving now. A bathroom, just looking for a bathroom."

The curator eyed him suspiciously, trying to decide if he was telling the truth. He made his decision. "You explain to security. I call them now."

The man moved toward a black phone on the wall. Phin reacted out of instinct more than thought. He rushed the man and grabbed him from behind, wrapping his arms around his torso. The stunned curator began to yell, but Phin clamped his hand down hard on his mouth. And then Phin surprised even himself as he lifted the man up and slammed him down onto the table in the middle of the room.

Whack!

The move knocked the wind out of the curator. Phin moved quickly, pulling Duct Tape from his backpack and slapping a line across the man's mouth to prevent him from crying out again. He then flipped him on his stomach and wound the tape around his hands, pulling them tight behind his back. Then the feet. It was fast and finished before the poor man knew what was happening. He struggled just a bit at first and then realized it was useless.

Phin's mind spun.

What had he just done?

There was no turning back now. How long would it be before someone came to check on him? Were there other curators in the facility? Besides the guy he'd just hog-tied, they'd only seen two other people – the guard at the door and the ticket clerk.

Phin walked back over to the cabinet and looked down at the True Cross.

He was going to do this. He was really going to do this. Now.

What choice did he have?

He reached in and gingerly laid his hands on the rough wood of the cross. What was he expecting? Lightning? A voice from heaven? But just like when he touched the Cross of Gestas, there was nothing. No revelation. No vision. Just the hard surface of a splintery beam of wood. He carefully wrapped it in the linen cloth it sat on and hefted it out. It was not light, but also not unmanageable. He threw the wrapped cross over his shoulder and hurried out of the room.

The hallway was still empty and he quickly climbed the stairs. Pausing at the door, he turned the knob and cracked it. Sergeant Billy Warren was standing about four feet away, eyes looking back and forth down each side of the hallway.

Phin pushed through the door and almost knocked Oz down.

"Hey, what were you doing down there...what is that you've got there?" And then a sudden realization. "Nooo! No, you didn't!"

"Shhhh! Keep your voice down. And yes, yes, I did."

Phin filled the sergeant and Oz in on what happened.

Sergeant Warren listened, assessing the surprise development, and made a snap reply. "Okay, time to call an audible. You guys follow me, we're gonna exfiltrate the facility now."

Phin knew enough to follow Warren's orders. They'd only gone a few feet when they came upon an exit door to the museum. It was marked for emergencies only. Before they could burst through the door, Phin called for the group to stop. He wedged open the covering on the door's upper hinge and, using a wire cutter from his bag, snipped a black cord.

"Alarm," he answered simply. "Okay, now let's go."

They pushed the bar on the door and exited the building. No alarm sounded. They sprinted around the back and then side of the museum, careful to duck under external windows.

The parking lot had three new cars.

More tourists.

That would be a good thing. Perhaps their presence, or lack thereof, wouldn't be noticed. Sergeant Warren opened the back of their Mercedes SUV and Phin carefully set the True Cross into the vehicle.

"Time to roll, boys," Sergeant Warren barked. He already had the engine started before Phin and Oz could climb in and close their doors.

Warren calmly drove the vehicle out of the parking lot and pointed it south onto the highway. No screeching of the tires, no peeling out. Just three friends touring the museums of Jordan. Nothing to see here. Once he was out of the little village of Ghor es-Safi, Warren mashed the peddle closer to the floor.

"I can't believe we just did that! In broad daylight. What are we gonna do?" Oz Jenks was clearly out of his element.

"Relax, we've got time. Doc did the right thing. If we're lucky it'll be an hour before they find the guy in the basement. Maybe longer. Then they still won't have a clue which way we went. We're only two and a half hours from the border."

"Border? Which border? Where are we headed?"

"To the closest country where Doc here isn't a wanted man. Egypt."

Chapter 53

The trek to Egypt was without incident.

Phin spent the next two hours turning to look out the back window of the SUV, but there was nothing. No lights, no sirens. They passed a few Jordanian military vehicles along the way, but that was to be expected. They were, after all, hugging the Israeli border.

One moment of tension came at the border into Israel itself. Crossing a small piece of Israeli land was necessary in order to get to Egypt. They'd have to clip the southern edge of the nation and the Israeli resort town of Eliat. Legal border crossings were not unusual, and even though Phin was a wanted man in Israel, what he presented to the border agent was a Jordanian passport. At the current moment, he was not Phineas Crook, he was Quasi Ali. And Sergeant Warren was Ahmed Ibrahim. Oz Jenks was, of course, Oz Jenks, and Phin suspected that his United States passport helped with the crossing. They were waved through and thirty minutes later they repeated the process, again without incident, at the border with Egypt.

Now the trio sat poolside in the little vacation destination of Taba. They'd checked into the very nice Movenpick Taba Resort and were now breathing easy.

They'd done it. They'd stolen the True Cross of Christ, which now sat in their hotel room, enjoying the same level of security it had for the last several hundred years. Phin couldn't believe it...how easy the job had been. Alexander Pontia could have done it himself. But he likely assumed the whole operation would have been more difficult.

Phin sat under an umbrella but had decided to keep his shirt on. He was still sunburned from the swim across the Dead Sea. He flexed his hand, which was also still rope-burned, but was beginning to feel much better.

Sergeant Warren was snoozing under his own umbrella, once again in a ridiculous looking Speedo that he'd picked up in the lobby surf shop. Oz Jenks sat next to Phin, working on his laptop.

"Oh man," the computer whiz said in a long, drawn-out fashion. "Dr. Crook, you're gonna want to see this. It's Pontia." At the sound of Alexander Pontia's name, Sergeant Warren's eyes snapped open. He joined Phin as he moved over so he could see Oz's screen. "This just posted thirty minutes ago on YouTube, Facebook, Twitter, all over social media."

Oz hit play and a video began.

Alexander Pontia appeared behind a large oak desk, hands folded in front of him. He wore a dark suit with tiny pinstripes, a white shirt, and a solid red silk tie. Behind him were an array of flags from the countries of the world. The scene reminded Phin of a national address of the President of the United States from the Oval Office. It was the first time Phin had actually seen Alexander Pontia, he realized. Whatever his image had been, it did not match the impressive stature of the man on the screen with the jet-black hair slicked back, a slight olive tint to his skin, indicating the Italian heritage of his name.

Alexander Pontia began to speak:

Citizens of the world. My name is Alexander Pontia. In two days' time I invite you to join me for a worldwide broadcast that I promise will change not only your life, but the course of history itself. You may never have heard of me but that matters not. Who I am is of no consequence. But what I can demonstrate, you will not want to miss. For too long the world has been held under the sway of the myth of religion. Does God really exist? If so, what kind of God is he and what does he want from me and you? If he is here, or there, or in heaven, why doesn't he just show himself and settle the matter once and for all? These are the kinds of questions that all people ask, no matter one's country of origin or race. And no mythology has perpetuated a belief in God more than that of Judeo-Christianity. And no one man has deceived the masses of this great earth more than the one known as Jesus.

Pontia paused for a moment, then leaned slightly forward, toward the camera:

I declare a challenge to the God who isn't there. In two days, I will challenge the God of Christianity and his self-proclaimed son, who, as the myth is told, is sitting with God right now. The dual will be held on God's home turf, the holiest place on earth to the Jewish people from whom this purported son of God came. And I invite you...all of you watching this video...to tune in live. What's going to happen, you ask? Well, it wouldn't be any fun to give it all away. Consider this a preview to the main event. But I promise, you will not want to miss it. I will destroy forever the myth of Jesus and put an end to Christianity and the cult of the Church. Where can you watch the destruction of God and religion? Don't worry, you won't be able to miss it, I am a man of great resources. Just like this preview, it will be broadcast...everywhere. You can click the link below for the countdown clock.

And a final thrust of gravitas:

My name is Alexander Pontia. I will see you in two days...for the showdown of the ages.

The trio sat in stunned silence. Phin looked up and could see others around the pool on their phones whose social media feeds had been interrupted as well. Some were scratching their heads or rubbing their chins. One woman got up quickly, grabbed her towel, and marched off. A cabana bar at the end of the pool was playing the video on a TV tuned to CNN.

"This joker is out of his mind," Sergeant Warren barked. "Who does he think he is? Ain't no way you can do that to Jesus. Just wipe him away. Can't happen."

One thing was clear to Phin, Alexander Pontia *was* out of his mind. Billy Warren was correct. But insane egomaniacs with money and power are the most dangerous people on the planet.

So, this was it. Alexander's final plan had just been set in motion. Remus had said back at Nardo's place that Pontia was going to destroy the holy relics of the Church in front of the world. Now they knew how that was going to happen. A worldwide broadcast using social media and the world's media outlets.

And the man believed that if he destroyed the holy relics at the holiest location on the planet, that would somehow destroy Christianity and the Church. It was truly insane. *He* was truly insane. The loss to the Church would be enormous for sure, but Phin struggled to see how people of good faith would ultimately be shaken.

But none of that mattered right now. This is what Alexander Pontia was going to do and Phin needed to stop him. And he needed to save his brother. And he needed to clear his own name of murder. Oh yeah, and he was believed to be the mastermind behind the thefts. He had to clear his name of that as well. Hopefully, when all this was over with, he would still have a job back in Oklahoma.

A phone rang.

It was Remus's phone, sitting on the little table next to Phin's chair.

Phin snatched it up and answered.

"I assume you've seen my little preview, Dr. Crook. Please tell me you are making progress on the recovery of the True Cross. As you can see, I'm on a clock now. Literally. I have a reputation to uphold. I am, if nothing else, a man of my word."

"You are a lunatic, Pontia," Phin spat out. "And yes, I've made progress on the cross. In fact, it's with me right now."

"Oh my! So soon. You are good, indeed. Probably better than your brother. I suppose I should have come to you to begin with and left Remus to rot in prison."

"He was scheduled for release in just months. You've ruined his life...and mine. But I've done what you asked. My brother better be alive, and if you truly are a man of your word, then I'm ready to make the trade. The True Cross for Remus. Just tell me when and where."

"Oh, Remus is alive. But not doing so well I'm afraid. The collapsed lung...yes, well, it's a terrible thing."

Phin was boiling. "The exchange, Pontia. Just tell me where to meet you so we can end this. I'm in Egypt right now and can be on a plane within hours."

"Egypt!" Pontia laughed. "How fortunate for us both, indeed. For I am in Egypt as well. You needn't worry Dr. Crook, we are most certainly going to end this."

"Where, Pontia, where?! Give me a location."

"Didn't you watch the video? The holiest place on earth, Dr. Crook. I'm surprised that you, as a biblical scholar, don't already know."

"Please quit playing games and just tell me." Phin's irritation only grew.

A dramatic pause, just for effect.

"Mount Sinai. That is where you will meet me with the True Cross. Come to the mountain of God in the Sinai Peninsula of Egypt and it is there that you will be reunited with Remus."

Of course.

It made perfect sense.

Not Jerusalem, where the Jewish temple had been and where Jesus was crucified. Holy, yes, but not *the* holiest place on earth. Mount Sinai alone held that distinction. The mountain where Moses had encountered God in a burning bush. A place so holy he had to remove his shoes. The mountain where God had brought the nation of Israel after the Exodus from Egypt. The mountain where Moses and the people met God, where the Ten Commandments had been carved by the finger of God into stone. A mountain so sacred that no one except those invited by God himself were allowed to ascend.

Phin now understood.

And then Phin laughed.

Out loud.

Into the speaker of the phone.

"You find this funny, Dr. Crook? Perhaps you don't understand what is at stake."

"Oh, I understand perfectly what is at stake. I am laughing, Pontia. I'm laughing at the man who has the resources to break people out of prison, steal the most precious artifacts of the Church, frame innocent people of murder, and broadcast his crimes to the world, but yet a man who has missed the simplest of details."

Now it was Alexander Pontia's turn to boil. He didn't like to be laughed at and no one - no one - mocked him. Ever.

"You are treading on dangerous ground, Dr. Crook. You should be very careful with your next words."

"I may be treading on dangerous ground," Phin shot back boldly. "But you're treading on the wrong ground. Mount Sinai is not located in the Sinai Peninsula. It's not even located in Egypt. Oh, there's a mountain in the peninsula *called* Mount Sinai. But that's not the mountain you want. The real Mount Sinai, the holiest place on earth, is located in Saudi Arabia. It's known on maps today as Jabal al-Lawz. And you've got another big problem, Pontia. Saudi Arabia is a closed country and that mountain, in particular, is off limits, and the Saudis don't take kindly to trespassers."

The phone was silent.

The silence dragged on for so long Phin thought the line had gone dead, but he noted that the time clock on the call continued to roll.

Finally.

"You listen to me you tiny, insignificant, little man. I am going to destroy the Church. I'm going to destroy the story of Jesus and the religion that fools like you believe in. I'm going to do it in two days' time, and I am going to do it on Mount Sinai. *The* Mount Sinai, no matter where on earth it's located. Do you understand me? And if you ever want to see your brother alive again, then you, Dr. Crook, *you* better meet me there as well. I'll find my way to the mountain. You find your way. Oh, and don't forget to bring the True Cross with you."

Pontia ended the call.

And Phineas Crook wondered what in the world he was going to do now.

Chapter 54

"You're gonna have to help me out here, Doc." Sergeant Warren stoked the small campfire they'd built on the sandy beach called Nuweibaa. "If we need to get to Mount Sinai, and we're already in the Sinai Peninsula, and Mount Sinai is that way," he pointed behind him with his thumb, toward inland Egypt, "then why are we gonna cross that, into Saudi Arabia, tomorrow?" He finished his question by extending his LaPhage Limb arm out in front of him toward the Gulf of Aqaba. Seven miles across the body of water lay the ancient mountains and desert of Arabia.

The group had hustled out of the luxury of resort life in Taba within an hour after Phin finished his call with Alexander Pontia. He quickly explained the change of plans to the men. They had to get to a remote mountain in the interior of Saudi Arabia within two days.

The Saudis don't issue foreign Visas, so they'd have to sneak in and stay off the radar. It would be dangerous, because if they were caught, they'd be arrested and deported at best, which meant being turned over to the authorities; at worst, they'd be thrown into a Saudi prison and the key thrown away.

Sergeant Warren didn't blink an eye. Phineas Crook was his friend. He was still in deep trouble. The sergeant was committed to seeing this all the way through to the end. Oz Jenks was less than enthusiastic. But Sergeant Warren gave him his version of a pep talk, and the computer whiz reluctantly changed his tune.

"It's like I told Pontia," Phin began by way of explanation. "Yes, there is a mountain called Sinai about seventy miles from here. In the Sinai Peninsula. But it's not the real Mount Sinai. It all goes back to what we were talking about at Nardo's. When Helena, the mother of Constantine, came through this part of the world on her search for the True Cross, she established churches all over the place as a way to mark the territory for Rome. But she was not an archaeologist and was working with a lot of bad information. Long story short is that she arbitrarily picked a mountain in the desert around here and declared that it was Mount Sinai. She had one of her churches built and there is even a monastery there today that watches over the mountain and perpetuates the myth. Even most Bibles have it wrong. Here let me show you." Phin fished around in his pack and pulled out a worn copy of a brown leather Bible. He flipped to the back where the maps were. "Yeah, here it is. Look right here."

Warren and Oz leaned in and could see by way of firelight where Phin's finger was pointing. Mount Sinai, clearly labeled as being in the Sinai Peninsula. Oz scratched his head and began typing on his computer.

"Well, there it is right there, Doc. It's in the Bible. So, you're saying the Bible's wrong?"

"No, I'm not saying the *Bible* is wrong, Billy. But the maps here aren't inspired by God. They're added by men, and in this case, men who got it wrong. You see, back in the late 80s, some lay archaeologists began to question the location of Sinai. The problem with the mountain on all the maps is that there is nothing around this mountain to indicate that Moses was ever there. And not just Moses, mind you. Remember he had the entire population of the Hebrew people with him, plus their herds of sheep, goats, cattle. Most scholars believe two million people at least. Now don't you think that if two million people camped out at a mountain for months on end, that they'd leave behind some kind of evidence that they'd been there? But at this Sinai," again he pointed to the map in his Bible, "there is nothing. And the topography is all wrong. It's too barren and mountainous for that many people to camp, and there's no grass to support the grazing of herds. Nope, it's all wrong."

"He's right!" Oz butted in. "There's lots of stuff here on the net on the real Mount Sinai being in Saudi Arabia. But looks like there's a lot of argument over it too."

"That's because, like I said, these were lay archaeologists, not professional scholars. The problem is that the Saudis have zero desire to cooperate with any formal archaeological work in their country. They don't want to do anything to aid the historical claims of Judaism. Remember, this is a very Muslim part of the world. But during the 80s and 90s, several groups snuck in using the same route we're about to follow. And they found it. The real Mount Sinai. It's labeled on most maps today as Jabal al Lawz. And it's about forty miles away once we cross the gulf of Aqaba here."

Sergeant Warren had been listening intently. "Well, that's another question I have. I'm not a Bible guy for sure. You know that, Doc. Don't even own one. I think some dudes in suits gave me a little red one when I was a kid in school once, but never was interested in reading it. But I've heard of Moses, see. And I know the story. He crosses the Red Sea. The Red Sea, Doc. Not the Gulf of Aqaba."

"He's right, Dr. Crook. My grandmother took me to church and I heard the same story in Sunday School. Moses led the Israelites across the Red Sea after God parted the waters."

"Parted the waters," Warren huffed. "See, that's another reason I don't believe any of this stuff."

Phin smiled. "Let me show you something." He held up the map in the back of his Bible again. "The Red Sea is south of here, see? But the Red Sea has two branches, one off to the northwest called the Gulf of Suez. Those who believe that Mount Sinai in the peninsula of Egypt is the real Mount Sinai believe the crossing happened here, across the Suez portion of the sea. But the northeast branch...you're probably already ahead of me...is called-"

"The Gulf of Aqaba," Warren finished. "Well, I'll be."

"That's right. It's all part of the Red Sea. Several years ago, one of these explorers came to my house for dinner. A man named Hector Wilde. He's like a modern-day Indiana Jones. He shared with me everything he knew about Jabal al Lawz and his own adventure in finding the mountain. He was actually captured by the Saudis and spent time in prison before they deported him. While we were driving down here earlier today, I used Oz's computer to access all my notes I took from Hector that night. I've got them stored in the cloud." He winked at Oz, who gave him a thumbs up in return. "I've got our road map, boys. Everything we need to find Jabal al Lawz and to make Pontia's deadline."

Sergeant Warren nodded as if his curiosity had been appeased. "Tomorrow morning at sunrise, the truck of supplies will be here," he said.

As soon as Warren knew earlier in the day the overview of what they were planning, he'd jumped on the phone to LaPhage Industries HQ. The conglomerate had a supply depot in Cairo. The sergeant placed his order and the truck would drive overnight to meet the trio in the morning.

"I want you guys to think about something for a minute." Phin stood and faced the sea, a not-so-mild wind hitting him in the face. "Over three thousand years ago, on this very beach, Moses of the Bible along with two million people camped out. Behind me in that mountain pass, a pillar of fire separated them from Pharoah and his army. They'd come to slaughter the people. But the next day, God performed one of the greatest and most famous miracles in the Bible. He parted the waters in front of us, and the people escaped to safety. Pharoah tried to follow, but the waters closed back in on his army."

"Whoa..." Oz let out a long sigh. "You mean we're standing on *the* place? This beach?"

"That's right, Oz. Look around you, this beachhead is massive."

And it was.

A mile up the shore was a popular resort area called Casa Del Mare.

"If you look at this area from Google Earth, you will see that this beach is unique to the entire coastline. Almost like God himself placed it here, just for his people to have a place to run to. The Bible says that the wilderness had hemmed them in as Pharoah's army descended."

Even in the moonlight of the evening, the shadow of the mountains behind them was inescapable. It was clear to see how you could be trapped on this beach.

No place to run.

No place to hide.

"Well, let's hope God shows up tomorrow, Doc. But in case he don't, I'll have a boat ready for us!"

Chapter 55

The truck arrived before the sun rose. Sergeant Warren was awake and checked the inventory. Everything he'd asked for was there. The most prominent item: a Zodiac speedboat.

Phin's heart soared. There would be no swimming today. Desert camo would be the attire of choice for their expedition. They needed to blend in as much as possible and not be seen. Phin looked at Oz, who had chosen his bright green Incredible Hulk t-shirt to wear, smiling as Warren tossed him his camos.

Three dirt bikes also appeared along with an assortment of camping and hiking gear, food rations, and plenty of water.

Everything was loaded into the Zodiac and the two drivers from LaPhage helped drag it all to the shoreline before bidding the trio of would-be explorers farewell.

The morning sky was beginning to brighten as Phin, Sergeant Warren, and Oz shoved off into the Gulf of Aqaba. All was quiet on the Nuweibaa beachhead. They would make the crossing in less than thirty minutes.

And they did.

They landed the Zodiac at Ras al Hasha, the same place that Moses and the Hebrew people would have walked up out of the Red Sea. They were now in Saudi Arabia. Illegally.

"Say good-bye to $150,000, boys," Sergeant Warren declared.

Phin's mouth dropped open. "Billy, you've got to be kidding me. I had no idea. I'll repay you and LaPhage, I promise." It was the first time he had thought about the real financial toll his personal trouble was causing.

"No worries, Doc. It's all part of the cost of the operation. You don't owe me nothin' and don't mention it again."

Phin nodded and the group began the unload and then the re-load onto the dirt bikes. The 150cc Enduro motorbike was a good lightweight choice, and a tank of fuel would easily take them all the way to their destination. Warren had wisely included saddlebags, which they would put to good use.

Oz had no clue how to ride a motorcycle despite claiming that he did. He finally admitted that he was a level 38 in some video game called Dirt Road 2000. Sergeant Warren slapped him on the side of the head and scolded him that video games don't count. He then took the next half hour to give Oz a lesson in real dirt bike riding. Fortunately, he picked up the skill quickly.

The group was finally ready to depart. Forty miles to Jabal al Lawz, as the crow flies, but the mountain terrain would take them in a further, more roundabout way to get there. They only had two days to arrive at the mountain, Phin reminded the others.

They kickstarted the three loaded-down bikes, kicking up a spray of dirt and rock as they sped off into the desert.

The going was easier than Phin would have thought. It had been years since he'd ridden, but the skill came back quickly enough. If not for the weight they carried, they could have gone faster.

Sergeant Warren's bike was especially awkward because he carried the True Cross across the back of his cycle. He'd insisted since he was the most experienced rider of the three and Phin agreed. The relic was securely wrapped in a bundle of cloth, but he didn't want to see it damaged by some mishap on his part.

Soon after leaving the beach, they found a rutted dirt road that appeared to follow the ancient migration route. Bedouins likely still used the path. This would surely have been the way that Moses had led the Hebrew people after their miracle crossing of the Red Sea. Phin so wished he had time to slow down and take it all in. They were crossing terrain in a matter of hours that it took the ancient horde of two million Israelites days to cross.

And it was desolate terrain.

The group stopped often for water and to check their coordinates. They were headed southeast and would circle back around and come to Jabal al Lawz from a southerly direction. It was either that or take the direct path, which would have them climbing over one mountain after another, extending travel time at least another week. They had neither the time nor desire for such a feat.

Just after noon, they stopped on a rise that looked down on a small village ringed by palm trees.

"Map says that's the town of al Bad," Warren declared. He pulled a blue bandana from his breast pocket and wiped a layer of dirt from his sweaty face.

"Looks like a desert oasis to me," Oz mimicked Warren, wiping down his own face. "I could sure use some shade and a break from the sun."

"Elam," Phin whispered.

"What's that, Doc? Didn't catch what you said."

"I said, Elam. That has to be the desert oasis of Elam talked about in Exodus."

Sergeant Warren grunted. "Never heard of it."

"The Bible says that after crossing the Red Sea, Moses led the people for three days and then they came to a place called Elam where there were seventy palm trees and twelve springs of water. This has to be the place. More proof we are on the right track and that the real Mount Sinai is here in Saudi Arabia."

"There's at least seventy palm trees down there. And look, you can see water as well. Come on, let's go!" Oz was eager to indulge himself.

Warren nodded at Phin. They saw no reason not to find a shady place to eat.

There were plenty of clusters of palms away from the village proper. Even though they doubted that the military would be roaming around out here, they still wanted to be careful to not attract attention.

They found a stand of palms next to a pool of water a bit of a distance from al Bad. The sergeant dug into the food bag and threw each man an MRE. "Lemon pepper tuna for lunch. Don't complain."

Phin hesitated opening his food pack. Something about this place he had never been tickled the back of his mind. He put the MRE aside and pulled his Bible from his pack, nervously thumbing through it. "I knew it!" he exclaimed.

"What?!" Sergeant Warren jumped to his feet, doing a three-sixty, looking for trouble.

Phin laughed. "Relax, Billy. This place...I'm almost one hundred percent sure this is Marah." Warren and Oz stared at Phin. The revelation meant nothing to them. "From the Bible," Phin prodded, "Exodus 15. Here, let me read it to you:

Then Moses made Israel set out from the Red Sea, and they went into the wilderness of Shur. They went three days in the wilderness and found no water. When they came to Marah, they could not drink the water of Marah because it was bitter; therefore it was named Marah.

"The word Marah means bitter. Don't you see, the people had been walking for three days across the desert we just rode through. They were parched. Then they came to Marah and couldn't drink the water. So, God told Moses to throw a log into the water - he did and then the water became sweet. Then it says that the people arrived at Elam. It all fits!" Phin was beside himself with glee. He got up and walked to the water's edge and plunged his head in. Flinging his head back out of the pool, his face carried a huge smile. "The water is perfect. Best I've ever had. You guys come drink some."

Oz rushed forward and followed Phin's example.

Sergeant Warren was more reserved, opting instead to fill his canteen and take a drink. He sloshed it around in his mouth before swallowing. Then took another long drink. "Right on," he simply said and returned to the shade of his palm tree.

"We are traveling through history guys. This is amazing." Phin realized that neither the sergeant nor Oz could appreciate the moment, but he refused to let it steal his own euphoria.

They finished up lunch, having felt renewed with energy and focus. Phin was convinced it was the water from the pool of Marah.

They skirted the town of al Bad and pointed their cycles northeast toward Jabal al Lawz. They rode out, once again, into nothing. The terrain became more challenging, as formal dirt roads were left behind and replaced with game trails and herd paths. The elevation became a game of up and then down. The going was slow and it took all day. Again, they saw no one. This truly was no-man's-land.

And then they came to a halt.

In front of them stood a fence, topped with curls of razor wire. It stretched off to the right and the left as far as the eye could see. A sign in Arabic was posted.

Warren stared at it, trying to decipher the foreign language. "What's this say, Doc? Some sort of Danger or Keep Out posting?"

Phin didn't answer.

Sergeant Warren looked over at his friend, who had dismounted his bike and was standing at the fence's edge.

"What's the matter, Dr. Crook?" Oz Jenks asked.

Phin pointed forward toward two granite mountain peaks, and even at this distance, he could see a lone tree growing between the two summits. "There it is, gentlemen. Mount Sinai. The mountain of God."

Chapter 56

They had no choice. They'd come too far to be dissuaded by a security fence.

Sergeant Warren took the honors upon himself. He snipped a nice hole in the fencing. They loaded everything they would need for the next day into backpacks and left the bikes hidden behind a stand of rocks. Phin insisted on carrying the True Cross but he knew that before they made it to the base of the mountain they would all take turns.

The sun was easing toward the horizon when they breached the barrier and hiked toward the mountain.

"I wonder where that joker Pontia is," Sergeant Warren irreverently blurted out. "Hard to imagine he made better time getting here than us."

Phin wasn't so sure. The mysterious Alexander Pontia seemed to be a man of plentiful means. Would those means extend to a quick change of staging from whatever he was planning in Egypt to the desert of Saudi Arabia on a moment's notice? They'd soon find out. The man had challenged Phin to be here inside of two days. He'd put the life of his brother, Remus, on the line as collateral that Phin would show up.

Well, he had.

The question now became: What next?

The setting sun made for darker skies which made movement by stealth easier. And being this close to the mountain, Phin was grateful. He noticed that the three of them had naturally shifted to speaking in hushed tones.

"There's a glow of light up ahead," Oz declared.

"You got a good eye, kid." Sergeant Warren applauded the computer whiz.

Warren shot forward, crouching as he ran, ducking behind a round and broken column of stone laid across the ground. Phin and Oz hurried after, coming to a dusty halt as they slid in next to him.

"A guard shack," Warren announced. "And a *lot* of movement. Way too much for a sleepy mountain in the middle of nowhere."

Phin chanced a look and took in the scene. Not just a guard shack, but guards, and vehicles. Five Humvee type transports by his count. And soldiers walking crisply between the vehicles and the shack as if having been called up to active duty. They were all carrying automatic weapons.

Phin's eyes looked down at the smooth stone his hands were resting on. Something unnatural about it.

A round column of stone.

He'd seen the broken cylinder-shaped stones as he ran toward them but thought nothing of it in the moment. But now, touching it, he knew something was off.

"This stone's not natural," he whispered.

"What are you talking about, Doc? Who cares?"

But Phin understood. And he felt compelled to share. "Exodus says that Moses set up barriers around the mountain. The people were not allowed to cross them. No one except those allowed onto the mountain."

"What are you saying, Doc?" Phin now had Sergeant Warren's attention.

"I'm saying this stone we're hiding behind is a fallen column. Carved by Moses and the people over three thousand years ago. Set in place as a marker, a barrier. I'm saying that once we cross this line, we're taking our lives into our own hands. Or maybe I should say we're putting them into the hands of God."

"Oh, man..." Oz squeezed out. "I don't like the sound of that at all."

"Relax will ya!" Sergeant Warren scolded them both. "Superstition, I tell you. Look at that guard shack and all those men. They're on the other side of this thing you call a barrier and they're doing just fine. Come on, we gotta skirt this action and find a place to hunker down so we can scout the base of the mountain."

The three of them eased back and away, blending into the shadows of a moonless night. They made their way parallel from the guards until they were a good quarter of a mile away and then they once again began their forward march to the base of the mountain.

"So, what's the plan, Dr. Crook?" Oz finally asked.

Yes, good question. What's the plan?

"The plan is to find Alexander Pontia or wait for him to arrive. And along with that plan is the goal of not getting caught trespassing by the Saudi military."

"I'm telling you, Doc. Something's not right out here. Those guards back there are on high alert. They know something's going down."

They marched on in silence, each man contemplating the truth of Sergeant Warren's statement. Phin's thoughts also drifted to his brother. Was Remus still alive or had he succumbed to the wicked wound to his lung?

Still some distance from the base of the mountain, they found a large stack of rocks to settle behind, a perfect blind and easy to see if anyone was approaching. They fished out dinner – beef stew this time – but were forced to eat it cold. Warren warned against the risk of firing up the portable camping stove. They wanted to keep their light signature to a minimum.

A phone buzzed in Phin's pocket.

Cell service out here? Amazing.

His heart leapt and his mind went to Pontia. Calling him with instructions, most likely.

But it wasn't Remus's phone that was ringing, it was the phone Sergio Nardovino had slipped into his hand as they left the smuggler's mansion. Phin stood, but before drawing the phone from his pocket, he faced the rocks, threw a thin blanket from his pack over his head and leaned in, his attempt to stay as dark as possible. By the time he pulled the phone from his cargo pocket, it had quit ringing.

Then came a text message:

Phin. I have info on Alexander Pontia. Must talk ASAP. Be very careful. DANGER.

Phin puzzled over the meaning of the cryptic message. Of course Pontia was dangerous. He already knew that. He was the mastermind of murder, theft, the stabbing of his brother, oh yeah, and an attempt to destroy the Church and Christianity. What more could there be?

Before he could reply to Nardo's text, Phin noticed something unusual. The light from the phone's screen illuminated an image on the rocks in front of him that caused him to stop. He couldn't believe what he was looking at. He killed the phone's light and tucked it away. He threw off the blanket and took several steps back from the pile of rocks.

No, not a pile.

These rocks were stacked in a very deliberate manner.

"What's going on, Doc?" Sergeant Warren asked. "Who was on the phone?"

"Shhhh, hold on a sec."

Phin walked all the way around the perimeter of the rock stack. It was a good eight feet tall and symmetrical. The top was flat. "I don't believe it," he finally let out.

Oz and Warren had joined Phin.

"Hey, this looks on purpose," Oz connected.

"Not just on purpose, Oz, but *for* a purpose. A very infamous purpose."

"What are we looking at here, Doc?"

Phin decided to throw caution to the wind. This was

potentially too important, plus, he reasoned that they were far enough away from any military activity to truly be noticed. He grabbed a flashlight from his pack and hit the button. The rock stack lit up with an array of drawings all over. All crude pictures of cows and bulls.

"Hey, Doc! Be careful and put that out."

Phin complied. "Sorry, I just had to see."

"What did we just see, Dr. Crook?"

"Gentlemen, I believe we are staring at an altar that the ancient Hebrew people built. And on it, they performed one of the most sacrilegious acts in the Old Testament. While Moses was up on that mountain getting the Ten Commandments from God, the people got tired of waiting and built an idol. A golden calf."

"I know that story!" Oz declared in awe. "From Sunday school. You're telling me this is it? *The* altar where they did it?"

"I believe so. Just like Marah and Elim, it all fits. Moses came down from the mountain, saw what they were doing, and threw down the stone tablets with the commandments on them. They were shattered. Destroyed. Then he ordered the golden calf ground into a powder and put into the water supply, forcing the people to drink their own rebellion. The people rioted and the Bible says three thousand people were killed as a result." Phin paused for a moment. The quiet of the mountain's base encompassed them. "Right here is where it all happened. Right where we are standing."

And then the stillness of the reverent moment was broken.

"Do. Not. Move!" The command was barked from behind.

"You gotta be kidding me," Sergeant Warren muttered. In their focus on the ancient altar, they'd let their vigilance slip.

"Now turn around...slowly."

They complied. Three men, dressed all in black, including head coverings, and what looked to be night vision goggles, stood with weapons pointed at Phin, Oz, and Warren.

The man in the middle walked forward and lowered his weapon. He stopped in front of Phin, cocked his head, measuring him up. And then he ripped off his headgear.

"Well, well. Dr. Phineas Crook. I've finally caught up with you."

Phin's mouth gaped.

He was staring at the smiling face of Chief Inspector Antonio Rossi.

Chapter 57

"Relax, you can put your hands down," the chief inspector instructed.

The Italian police officer motioned for the two men with him to lower their weapons as well. They complied and removed their own headgear.

"What...I don't understand," Phin stammered.

"It's okay. Come, let's move over behind these rocks and have a chat, shall we?" Rossi put his arm around Phin and led the way.

Sergeant Warren was still bowed up. He saw an opportunity to strike now that weapons had been stowed.

Phin read the ex-Marine's mind. "Relax, Billy. Let's see what they have to say." He was still confused.

The six of them took a seat, forming a ring. "This is Felix and Mario." Rossi pointed to his black-clad companions. The two men smiled back. They seemed friendly enough now that they weren't pointing semi-automatic weapons at them. "They are Eserctio Italiano – what you would call special ops. They've been assigned to me by the Italian government to aid in my investigation, which I will admit has taken some quite unexpected turns."

"I'm innocent," Phin blurted out. He didn't know what else to say.

"Yes, yes, I know that. Took some time to piece it together, but you were...well, I wouldn't say convincing, but your story under interview cast enough doubt in my mind that I had to dig just to be sure." Phin began to relax. Finally, somebody believed him. "My colleague in Jerusalem, you remember him, don't you? Commissioner Marcus Hadadd."

"Oh, yeah, I remember him. It was good cop, bad cop, and he was the bad cop."

Rossi smiled. "Let's just say it took a little more persuasion for Marcus to see the light. But his team is very good and we were able to isolate cameras in the market district that covered the entrances to the alley where the House of Reuben was located. And what we saw was very interesting." Rossi paused to fish a metal case from his breast pocket. He flipped it open, pulled out a cigarette and promptly lit the tobacco stick, taking in a long draw. "Ahhh...much better."

He offered the case to Phin who waved it off. "No thanks. I'm a pipe man myself."

"Of course, a refined college professor would indeed be one to enjoy the refined nature of the briar."

"You were saying?" Phin asked, prodding the Italian to continue.

"Yes, as I was saying. We have footage of your brother, Remus Crook, leaving the alley carrying a large beam of wood. He is calm and unalarmed. Exactly fifteen minutes later, another individual enters the alley. And just before he steps out of the frame of the camera, he very clearly pulls from a sheath around his belt...a knife. And not just any knife."

"It was the murder weapon, wasn't it?!" Phin exclaimed.

"It was indeed. We ran facial recognition software on the man and got a hit. He's a Russian."

"Former GRU. His name is Dimitri Bezrukov," Phin finished for the police commissioner.

Rossi smiled and shook his head. "We are indeed on the same page, Dr. Crook. So, it was an easy step from that point to discover that Bezrukov works for a one, Alexander Pontia. In charge of the Dominion Safe security arm of Pontia's ventures, actually. And then, of course, we have the video posted by Pontia yesterday. We were all set to move on Pontia. We couldn't wait any longer." He motioned to his special ops companions. "We just didn't know where to strike to find him. Once again, Marcus Hadaad – the bad cop, as you say – came through. As a Jew, he was able to tell us unequivocally that the holiest place on earth to a Jew is Mount Sinai. And he went as far as to kindly inform me that contrary to popular belief, the real Mount Sinai is not in Egypt, but rather right here. Or perhaps I should say...right there." He pointed up to the granite peak that disappeared into the black sky.

"And so here you are," Phin said.

"So here I am. And so, it appears, here you are as well. I must say I was not expecting to find you. I thought perhaps you were Pontia himself sneaking into the country. But that would have been too easy for me, wouldn't it? I still have so many questions that hopefully you can answer for me."

The night sky was shattered by light and thunder.

Phin whipped around, his gaze toward the peak of Jabal al Lawz where the display shot from. His first thought was of God. The book of Exodus. Its vivid description of God descending on the mountaintop in a cloud of fire and smoke and the blast of a horn, causing the whole mountain to quake.

But this was not that.

Instead, a line of spotlights and the thump of rotator blades crested the peak and moved quickly toward their group.

It was instinct that guided Rossi's men to crouch behind the altar of stones. Phin felt a tug on his collar and was yanked by Sergeant Warren into the same huddle.

It didn't matter. They'd clearly been spotted. In just a matter of seconds, a ring of Blackhawk helicopters descended around them, all bearing the symbol of the Royal Saudi Air Force. Phin counted six in all. It was an impressive show of force.

A spray of soldiers jumped out and moved into tactical positions even as the Blackhawks were finishing their landing.

The six of them were surrounded.

Wait, not six, Phin counted.

Five.

Where was Oz?

A singular man approached the five of them as they were pinned with backs against a rock wall, spotlights from the helicopters blinding them.

It was only a silhouette but Phin knew exactly who it was. The man came to a stop just a few feet in front of him.

Alexander Pontia.

"Dr. Phineas Crook!" his voice called out over the still whomping sound of the rotor blades, which showed no sign of powering down. "It is a pleasure to finally meet you in person. I am impressed at the speed of your arrival. Yes, impressed indeed. And it looks like you brought along some company. No problem at all. Soon the whole world will see and know. Your friends will have the honor of a front row seat."

One of Rossi's men must have sensed a potential advantage in what looked like an unarmed Alexander Pontia. He sprang toward the man, but his ill-fated action resulted in a single crack from an unknown direction. Phin flinched.

The special ops soldier's head sprang back, followed by his body onto the Arabian desert floor. Phin looked down at the man. It was one that had been introduced to him just a moment ago as Felix. He had a single round hole in his forehead.

The brutal display did nothing to change the demeanor of the unflappable Pontia. "Well, then, if we are done with the heroics, follow me and let's move to the staging area. We all have much to do. Very, very much to do!"

Chapter 58

Phin held the hand of his brother, tears leaking from the edges of his eyes.

Remus looked bad, very bad. His breathing was labored. He was struggling from the stab wound to his lung which was still collapsed, he'd been told. He was pale and his skin clammy. Phin suspected that he was fighting an infection as well. His brother needed to be in a hospital now.

"Remus, I made it. I'm here," Phin spoke softly. He was sitting in a plastic chair, leaned over his brother, who was laid out on a crude table. "You've gotta hold on, okay? I've made a deal and I'm going to get you out of here soon, I promise."

Remus's eyes cracked open and he turned his head. "Phin..." he whispered. "How?"

"Shhh, don't try to talk."

"Thirsty...so thirsty..."

Phin reached down for the water bottle he'd been drinking from and raised it to Remus's lips. He was careful not to pour too much into his mouth. His brother licked his dry lips. He seemed satisfied.

"Phin," he began again. "Pontia...he's not...he's...can't trust." Remus was trying to communicate but Phin couldn't follow.

"It's okay, Remus. Don't try to talk. Just rest."

"No!" Remus powered out. "Important...his plan...you...me...relics." He began a coughing fit and Phin worried he'd pushed himself too far. After he settled him back down, he eased away to leave him to his rest.

Phin exited the back room of a massive field tent. Alexander Pontia was waiting for him, along with the blonde woman who'd stabbed him in the chapel at Santa Croce. Tess Greenway was her name. She looked as sinister as ever, her face plastered with an ever-present smirk. And then there was Dimitri Bezrukov. The Russian sat on top of a folding table, his legs hanging over with feet resting on the seat of a white plastic chair. He seemed bored.

"I assume the family reunion went as expected," Pontia began. "As you can see, your brother is very much alive."

Phin was angry. What they'd done to Remus was inhumane. And here was Pontia, acting as if all was normal and well.

"What kind of man are you?" Phin began. "He needs medical care...now. He's dying, don't you see?"

"What kind of man am I? Yes, that's a good question and I think it's important that you know exactly what kind of man I am, Dr. Crook. Because only then will you truly understand why you and your brother are here."

Phin didn't know where this was about to go and it looked like he was about to get more from Pontia than he was really asking for, but he decided to let the man continue uninterrupted.

"I am the kind man that has been given nothing...nothing, in life. Except one thing, and I will get to that in a moment. My father sent me on my way when I was sixteen. It is the way of the Pontias, I was told. We are self-made people. Everything I have in life I have acquired myself. No one gave me anything. Except that *one* thing I just mentioned. And that one thing I was given has truly made all the difference as to the kind of man that I am.

"You see, Dr. Crook, the one thing I was given was a heritage. A very, very old heritage that I never asked for but I was, nonetheless, handed at birth. Behind this heritage is a story. The story of my ancestor. A man who was great. A man who was rich. A man who was powerful. He was a force in the political machinery of the Roman Empire and enjoyed an audience with Caesar himself.

"As fate would have it, this great ancestor of mine was given the governorship of a region of the empire occupied by a foolish and superstitious people. They were also a dishonest people, prone to deceit. This made governing an impossible task. Of no fault of his own, he found himself in, shall we say, a no-win situation. And then came the rebellion. Not against his governorship, he was a fine governor showing kindness and grace to these worthless people. No, the rebellion was against Caesar himself and it came on two fronts simultaneously: money and religion.

Isn't that what all trouble in the world comes down to? Money and religion?

"The economic rebellion was led by two men. Brothers as it would turn out. Thieves really. They caused the region all sorts of trouble. Orchestrated thefts from the markets and homes of the empire. The religious rebellion was led by one man. He claimed to be God if you can believe such a thing."

Phin was stunned at what he was being told. It was an impossibility that what was being suggested to him was real. That such a thing could ever, in a million chances, all come together.

Pontia laughed. "I can see it in your face, Dr. Crook. You know, don't you? Your heart sees the truth of my words, yet your mind is struggling to accept it. Yes, my great ancestor is none other than the great Pilate of Pontia. Pontia being his surname, which in Latin and in the Bible is translated as...*Pontius Pilate.*"

Alexander Pontia.

Pilate Enterprises.

Why had Phin not seen?

And Sergio Nardovino had tried to warn him but his text had come too late. Phin staggered at the revelation and was forced to steady himself.

"So, what kind of man am I, Dr. Crook? I am the kind of man that has made something truly great of himself. Not given to me by Caesar or family or anyone else. And now that I am somebody, I intend to use my power and resources to right a wrong that was done to my family."

"What in the world are you talking about, Pontia?" Phin spat the question out, sensing the mania on display in front of him. Nardo was right, Pontia was dangerous. More so than he had ever believed.

"What am I talking about? Come on, Dr. Crook! You are a man of the Bible. Surely you know your history. Pontius Pilate squashed the rebellion. He did the job Caesar sent him to do. He hung Jesus on the cross and he hung the two brother thieves on crosses next to him. Problem solved, right? But no!" A new passion had invaded the body of Pontia as he spoke. "Jesus! It's all about Jesus. It's always been about Jesus. He just won't go away. I killed him and he came back. Not to life. No way do I believe that. But the legend was born, you see. And the rebellion continued. It ruined Pontius Pilate. Caesar blamed him for losing control of the region of Judea. He was stripped of his governorship. Stripped of his wealth. Sent into exile. He was ruined. And every generation of Pontias since have known that same level of poverty and humiliation. Until now. Until me. But now it's the Church that drives the myth. I can't destroy all the churches. There's too many. But I can destroy the relics. The earthly vessels that the Church claims hold the power of God."

Phin knew crazy when he saw it, and this was crazy. Alexander Pontia had just said that he himself had killed Jesus two thousand years ago. He was clearly taking on the embodiment of Pontius Pilate. Phin was incredulous at it all. Was Alexander Pontia really the descendant of Pontius Pilate? But then again, there was Remus and himself, modern descendants of the two thieves hung on crosses with Jesus. Maybe crazy wasn't all that crazy after all. And then a thought...a very troubling thought came to mind.

"You're not planning to let me and Remus go, are you?" Phin asked. "That was never part of your plan."

Yes, Pontia's plan.

He'd chosen Remus for the plan.

He'd chosen to intentionally pull Phin into his plan.

Remus was easy, just break him out of prison and offer him a job doing something he loved. Phin was harder to bring along. Remus had helped, of course. Not knowingly so, but he'd helped enough. And once Phin was pursuing Remus, Pontia sent the letter to Rossi naming Phineas Crook as thief of the precious Jesus relics.

The manhunt was on.

And then came the framing for a murder.

And just like that, Phin was swallowed by the plan. Alexander Pontia had been pulling the strings the whole time.

And being right here...at Mount Sinai...at just this very moment...

With his brother...

With Pontia...

With the full collection of the Church's relics of the Christ...it was all planned out.

"No, I am not planning to let you go, Dr. Crook. At least not until I am done and only then if you survive. You see, Dr. Crook, I've been collecting relics. All related to Jesus Christ. And you, Phineas Crook...you and your brother, Remus Crook, are the final pieces of my grand puzzle. You two are also relics...my living, breathing relics from the past. And all the relics must be destroyed!"

Chapter 59

The ascent of Mount Sinai began.

It would be a rocky climb and Phin had been given no options but to go with Alexander Pontia and company. That company included two armed guards, Pontia, Phin, and Remus being ferried in on a mobile stretcher between two other Dominion Safe employees. The armed escort was unnecessary. Phin wasn't leaving his brother's side.

"It's a beautiful day, Dr. Crook. A beautiful day indeed, and I must say a perfect day to once and for all put an end to the greatest hoax perpetuated upon humanity."

Phin was really tired of Alexander Pontia's voice. The man, he had judged, was thoroughly insane. The idea that burning the holy relics of Christ and killing two men on a livestream to the world would destroy Christianity was ludicrous. Phin was surprised that so many people were going along with this preposterous scheme. But then again, people can be persuaded to do most anything if the price is right.

The morning was dazzling for sure. No clouds in a sapphire blue sky and the air had a dry coolness to it. But Phin didn't consider it a beautiful day. He couldn't take his eyes off of Remus, whose condition looked even more grave in the light of day. His breathing was shallow and he was unconscious.

"You're a madman, Pontia. You may have bought off the people who work for you, but you can't buy off the Saudi government. They'll notice all the activity around the mountain and send the military. There's a reason they've got security fencing around this whole area."

Pontia found Phin's comment laughable. "The Saudis? I am disappointed in you, Dr. Crook. How do you think I was able to invade this little part of the Kingdom? The Saudis are actually providing the infrastructure for this whole operation. I've done quite a bit of work for the royal family - off the books, you understand. They were all too eager to participate in anything that would bring embarrassment to Christianity and to Judaism. This is a Muslim country, remember. Oh no, the Saudis were more than happy to oblige when I called. They even provided, very generously I might add, the Blackhawks we used last night to locate you and the unfortunate Italians."

Phin thought of Antonio Rossi. The one man who knew he was innocent, who now knew the whole story. He'd been worked over viciously by the Russian - an attempt to find out if anyone else from Rome was planning to come to the rescue.

Oh, how Phin hoped it was so, but it was not to be. It was Rossi alone, and by the time his failure to check in raised suspicion, Pontia would be finished. They all would likely be finished.

Rossi had been left under heavy guard back at the base of the mountain, along with his special ops companion, Mario, the one who'd not been shot and killed, like the poor fellow, Felix. He had no idea where Sergeant Warren was.

A surge of anxiety made Phin's legs weak.

People were dead.

And if Pontia followed all the way through, more people would die today – he and his brother.

Living relics, Pontia had called them.

The group marched on in silence.

It was slow going, the whole mountain a mass of jagged granite jutting up from the desert plain toward the sky. Not a blade of grass to be seen, only a scraggly tree here or there. It would take some time to reach the 8,500-foot peak of the mountain, which, Phin could now see in the daylight, was completely black in color – very unnatural looking. He'd never seen anything like it. But then again, this was the mountain that God had literally sat down upon.

About two-thirds of the way to the top, they stopped to rest, taking advantage of the shade of a small cave.

"We are just a matter of hours away from the main event." Pontia puffed his chest as he drank from a tube attached to his Camelback. He broke open a package of granola and offered some to Phin, who declined. "Once we reach the top, we will have a proper meal before we begin. We could call it the last supper!" The narcissist laughed at his own wit.

"You realize where we are, don't you, Pontia?" Phin asked as he took a seat on a flat rock.

"Mount Sinai, of course," Pontia replied with an annoyed look.

"No, I mean here...the cave. The only cave we've come to on the hike. This is the cave of Elijah. The one he fled to when King Ahab pursued him. And it was up there," Phin pointed out of the mouth of the cave and up, "where he witnessed the power of God. You're like a child, Pontia, about to put his finger in a light socket, with no idea what he's messing with."

This brought a howl from Pontia. "You really are something, Dr. Crook. The cave of Elijah, the burning bush, the Ten Commandments, Moses camping up here for forty days. Yes, yes, a thousand times, yes! I know the stories...the legends. Why do you think we are here? If there is any place on earth where God will show up if challenged it is here. But of course, you know my feelings about the matter. It's all a hoax. Stories told by poor migrant men designed to elicit awe and wonder in the culturally deprived and ill-educated foolish – which by the way makes up most of humanity. These ancient men simply took advantage of the stupidity of the masses. But today...today, Dr. Crook, I lay down my challenge before God. Will he even bother to make an appearance? I doubt it. In fact, I'm counting on the Almighty's absence. Come on, we've wasted enough time. Let's go." He ordered the men to heft the dying Remus Crook and they continued on.

The final push was uneventful.

They arrived at the summit, however, to a bustling of activity.

There were at least two dozen Dominion Safe security personnel scurrying about in a flurry.

Two portable canopies had been erected and a third was going up as the group marched into the makeshift camp. There was gear everywhere. Two large satellite dishes pointed toward the sky and a control room of sorts sat a few meters away — a video and soundboard, a switcher, several computers and screens, it was all here. A mobile television studio on the top of Mount Sinai.

A large table was set in front of three video cameras already mounted on tripods. Hard-shell cases sat on the ground next to the table. Phin assumed they housed the stolen relics of Christ. Most alarming of all, a pile of firewood was laying next to the table. A technician was busy wiring what looked like some sort of incendiary device.

And then there were the chairs.

Two chairs on either side of the table, each with leather straps on the armrests and around the two front legs.

Phin knew exactly what the chairs were for, and for the first time he knew how he was going to die. Alexander Pontia was going to burn him and Remus to death.

It was complete barbarie. Phin was both sick and seething at the same time.

Why doesn't somebody do something to stop this madness?

All around him, men moved as if it was just another day on the job.

Then Phin's eyes fell on a pathetic sight. His heart sank. Sitting at the edge of activity in a chair, similar to the ones that were designated for burning, was Sergeant Billy Warren. He was strapped in tight, a black hood covering his head. But Phin knew it was his friend because of the missing left arm and leg. They'd removed the veteran's LaPhage Limbs. The raging beast had been defanged.

Phin felt utter pity for Billy. Nothing could be more humiliating than to have the limbs that had given him new life stripped from him. He was completely helpless without them and Phin could see the sag of his body. It was the posture of defeat.

But why?

Phin was startled back to the present by a hand on his shoulder. "I thought you'd like to have at least one friend with you in your final moments."

"You are evil," Phin spat out.

"And you continue to play the comedian, Dr. Crook! Really, you are very good at this. I think you missed your calling. There is no good or evil. Because there is no God. There is only the powerful and the weak. And you and your friend," he held out his hand toward Billy Warren, "are weak. But I am about to give you a wonderful gift. Not many people have the fortune of having their lives defined by greatness. And this is the gift I give you. In *your* death, Dr. Crook, you will be remembered as playing a key role in the death of God and Christianity."

Alexander Pontia marched off, motioning for two people to take custody of the American college professor. And not just any two people. Dimitri Bezrukov and Tess Greenway. *How wonderful.*

Phin and Remus were placed under guard beneath one of the pop-up canopies. And it was there they spent the remainder of the day.

The sun eased toward the horizon, carrying with it the last touch of day and the last embers of what Phin knew would be his life on this earth. He watched as the final preparations for Alexander Pontia's great show were put in place. He spent more than a little of the time he had left talking to his brother, unsure if he could even be heard. He recalled stories from their childhood, he asked for Remus to forgive him for not being a better little brother – for being impatient with him as he walked his own journey, struggling with issues of faith and God.

And he thought, of course, of Autumn.

His beautiful wife, restored back to life by a miracle of God. He never dreamed he would be the one leaving her alone in this life on such short notice. He could still see her standing in the driveway as he pulled out for the last time. Holding little Patrick's hand and waving with the other.

And then he prayed.

It seemed the right thing to do. Especially now. Did he believe God could show up and rescue him? Yes. But that did not mean he would. Phin knew all too well that life is cruel and that many fine people, Christians included, die horrible deaths at the hands of tyrants.

Why didn't God do something about all of that?

It was a subject he had taught to his students on campus each year. The academic answer was that God *had* done something about all of that. God sent his only son, Jesus, to die for the sins of the world. To literally conquer death and sin and put to rights all that sin has broken. But the plan of God and his son was a work in progress.

The loaf was only half-baked.

More was to come.

The *best* was yet to come.

And because of that, Phin was at peace. It was an academic answer, yes, but it was also a faith answer.

This was the moment when Phin's faith would be put to the ultimate test.

He knew that any victory Pontia might enjoy in the short term would be swallowed up by the ultimate victory of Christ when he returned to earth one day. Hopefully, that would be sooner rather than later.

So, Phin prayed. And Phin cried.

And then nightfall came.

The lights popped on.

The table was illuminated. Production staff were in place.

They came for Phin and Remus. The last supper Pontia had taunted him with never arrived.

Phin was led toward the makeshift television set. As he walked past Billy Warren, he saw that they had removed his hood. The ex-Marine only looked down at the ground. Never up at Phin.

Phin was placed in his chair first. Hands and feet secured by the leather straps. They handled Remus with less care than Phin would have liked. He was dead weight, Phin knew, but he wished they would show him more dignity. The straps were needed not to secure him but to only hold him in place. A chest strap was added to keep him from slumping over.

A doctor approached and inserted a syringe into Remus's vein. He pressed the plunger and almost immediately his brother's head raised up and his eyes opened. He had a look of wild confusion on his face. What had they done? A shot of adrenaline, most likely. Forget what it might do to his failing heart, he would soon be a dead man anyway.

Alexander Pontia was the last to arrive. He was dressed in an all silk, light gray suit and blue tie. His hair combed and nails immaculately manicured. Phin caught the whiff of some expensive cologne, the purpose of which was lost on him.

Two men came forward and popped the lids on the cases. One by one, the stolen artifacts – the relics of Christ – were laid on the table. The True Cross of Christ along with the Titulus were placed on the table last.

It was done.

The near full collection of every existing relic known to have come in contact with the physical body of Jesus Christ, all in one place, on top of the holiest mountain on the face of the earth.

There was one exception, however. Phin thought of the missing Shroud of Turin and that gave him some small measure of satisfaction.

The cameras began to roll and Alexander Pontia began to speak.

"Citizens of the world. My name is Alexander Pontia. As promised, and right on time, I come to you this evening to prove to you once and for all that God does not exist and that Christianity is the greatest lie ever put before humanity...."

Chapter 60

Phin wanted so badly to block out the ranting of the madman standing to his left.

He was trying, instead, to focus his efforts on the leather strap holding down his right arm. Phin shared a particular characteristic with roughly twenty percent of the population – he was double-jointed. The oddity had come in handy more than once when, as a child, he and Remus would practice various techniques for removing handcuffs, zip ties, and even shackles.

Pontia had threatened him at the risk of his wife and son's wellbeing to keep his mouth shut during the broadcast. But Phin had no intention of going down without a fight. If he were able to free his one hand, the real trick would be moving quickly enough to free his other along with his legs before Dominion Safe guards descended on him. And if he were able to get free, he really had no plan of what to do next except create as much disruption for Pontia's little show as possible. He doubted the ultimate outcome for him would be any different. He'd still end up dead.

"I have assembled before me the great treasures of the Christian Church. The Holy Crib where the baby Jesus lay on the night of his birth and for many days and nights thereafter. The Sudarium of Oviedo, the face cloth laid over the dead body of Jesus after his crucifixion. Stained, as you can see, with the blood of the son of God. I have here a portion of the famed crown of thorns, acquired from Notre Dame."

And on he went. Holding up each relic in turn: the Holy Coat, the Holy Lance, the Holy Sponge. He emphasized the word Holy in a mocking fashion. Then the ultimate prize for last.

"And finally, yes, I have the remnants of the three crosses used on that fateful day two thousand years ago. The day that three ordinary men were executed by order of the Roman Empire. By order of my great ancestor, Pontius Pilate!

Phin imagined a collective gasp from the viewing population of the world. Phin scanned the small group of Pontia's henchmen and found Dimitri Bezrukov and Tess Greenway standing next to each other. Bezrukov was stoic, whereas Tess had a look of triumph on her face. She was enraptured by the madness of her employer. Alexander Pontia held up the three crosses in turn.

"The Cross of Dismas, the one known as the Good Thief. The Cross of Gestas, the one known as the Impenitent Thief. And then I have...the cross of Jesus. The one known as the Christ, the King of the Jews, the Son of God."

Phin wrenched his hand further than he ever had before. He felt something tear inside and he winced. But he sensed the leverage he needed against the position of the leather strap.

"And I have two more late additions to my collection. Two actual descendants of Dismas and Gestas."

Phin imagined the camera pulling out to a wide shot that included him and Remus. And he imagined Autumn watching on her computer or television back home in horror. He was almost there; his contorted hand was slipping past the binding. He could feel his flesh beginning to rip.

"All we are missing now is God himself!"

Alexander Pontia threw his head to the sky and held his hands wide.

"Here we are God! We've all come together and we are ready. Surely if there were one place in all of creation where you would show your face, where you would grace us with your presence, it would be here, on Mount Sinai. The mountain of God — your mountain!"

Alexander Pontia's voice roared in mockery.

"The mountain where that fool Moses claimed to talk to you. The mountain where you came down from your high and lofty throne in heaven and sat down...on this very peak where I now stand. The mountain where you issued your rules for mankind to follow. We are here God! But where are you? Show yourself. And if you do not, then I will destroy in front of the whole world this time...not just a small audience of Jews in Jerusalem, but in front of a watching world...I will destroy this heap of holiness for all to see and put an end, once and for all, to the myth that the son of God ever walked on earth! Come on, God. Now is your time. Or else I will take it from you and make it my time. The time of the Great Pontia - I will finish once and for all what my ancestor began so long ago."

Phin's hand yanked free.

And then the gust of wind hit.

It blew him backward in his chair. The lights went out as they were blown over, sparks springing forth. Phin was blind, plunged into sudden darkness and the roar of a great commotion. He quickly unbuckled his other hand and moved to free his feet.

Because he was on his back, his eyes stopped on the sky above. It was a cloudless night, but what looked like a tear in the heavens was being rent, a defined glow that was growing brighter by the second.

Phin scrambled.

He was free.

The table with the relics had blown over as well and the artifacts themselves were scattered on the rocky ground.

A burst of light from above powered onto the ground. It was blinding and Phin was forced to cover his face with his hands. The wind shifted from blowing across the peak to blowing *down* onto the peak, from above. Men were launched off their feet as they tried to run away, equipment bouncing up and down, tormented by the great wind.

Then came what sounded like...yes, Phin had heard the sound before. He had *made* that sound before. From a shofar that sat on top of a bookcase in his office back in Oklahoma.

A ram's horn it was.

But the volume and power of this sound dwarfed anything Phin had ever heard before. His hands shifted from his eyes to his ears. Both burned from the abuse.

The only thing Phin could think about in the moment was his brother. He had to get to Remus and free him. He crawled in the direction that he thought Remus should be, but he was thoroughly disoriented.

His hand hit something hard.

The texture of denim.

A leg.

He felt the sheen of leather and began to work the buckles free. The light was still blinding but his eyes were beginning to tolerate a small measure of the intensity so that he could at least squint in order to see. He grabbed Remus's face in his hands and spoke to his brother over the sound of the wind and ram's horn.

"Remus! I've got you. You're going to be okay."

But it was a lie and Phin knew it immediately. Remus's skin was cold to the touch. At some point during the process his brother's heart had quit beating. The trauma to his lung and body too much for too long. Hoping against hope, he laid his head on his brother's chest.

Nothing.

He was gone.

"No!!!" Phin cried in bitter grief. He had been so close. If they could've just gotten off the mountain. If Remus could've held out just a bit longer. But then where would they have gone? And how? Phin was beating himself up for nothing. Remus had been doomed the moment the cruel knife did its work days ago.

And then a thought.

When Helena had found the True Cross.

Something about the legend he had heard a long time ago.

It was an act of desperation.

And love.

He freed Remus's body from the chair and began to drag him. He was too heavy. There was more than one way to do this. He scrambled across the granite rock on hands and knees, his hands probing the ground around him.

And he found it.

He wrapped his arms around the rough-hewn beam and dragged the cross toward his brother. Everything was harder with the wind and the light. His elbow bumped into Remus's leg and he knew he was back. He pulled the True Cross close, and then with his right arm encircling his brother's torso, he rolled Remus over on top of the beam of wood.

Phin was pounded hard on his shoulders.

Against his will he was yanked to his feet.

"You...are...not...leaving here!" Dimitri Bezrukov punched Phin in the gut, causing him to double over.

Phin was no prize fighter, but the rage inside him at that moment came spewing forth as he rose back to full height. A right cross to the jaw of the Russian, followed by an upper cut with his left fist.

Phin noticed two things in that moment. His hands hurt, and he may have broken his left one. And Bezrukov was smiling at him. Totally unphased.

Then the earth began to shake. Both men were thrown off their feet. Bezrukov was the first to regain his purchase, but only for a moment.

"Aaahhhhh!" A guttural yell came tearing into the scene and a body smashed into the Russian.

"Go, Doc, Go! I've got this!"

It was Sergeant Billy Warren.

He'd freed himself and he'd found his limbs. All Phin could make out over the blinding light was the silhouette of each. He looked on in wonder as the two men went at each other like Ali and Frazier. Each man landing blow after blow, neither going down.

Despite Warren's urging, Phin had no intention of going anywhere. Not without Remus.

He never made it.

An explosion erupted around them. The device planned for the destruction of the relics went off, in an amazingly dramatic fashion. Phin was thrown back, and then a massive gust of wind launched him off the peak of the mountain itself.

"Nooooo!" Phin screamed as he fell. All he could think about were his brother and friend in the middle of the fireball.

Chapter 61

Phin heard voices in the inky blackness.

Maybe I'm blind.

Maybe I'm dead.

His head throbbed and it hurt to move.

Pain. Definitely not dead. That was good, right?

A voice. "He's starting to move."

Shuffling sounds.

"Don't try to move, Dr. Crook. We've got you. Just stay still and we'll get you out of this cave and off the mountain as soon as it's safe."

He recognized the voice. One he'd heard before. Recently. A European accent. No, Italian to be specific.

Everything around him began to shake. Like being gently rocked...to sleep.

***

Beams of light flashed past his eyelids.

He was lying flat, bobbing up and down. It reminded him of sailing on the ocean. Up one side of a wave, down the backside.

Up.

Down.

More flashes of light.

"Hold on, Doc. They've got us. We're gettin' outta here before this whole place blows."

A new voice.

He recognized this one too. A hand grabbed his arm for a brief moment and then slipped away.

Phin tried to open his eyes. He wanted so badly to open his eyes. But the bobbing of the ocean felt so good.

He succumbed to its hypnotic power.

***

"Go, go, go!"

The shouting jolted him awake. A rumble in the distance. The rocking of the chair had ceased, as had the bobbing of the ocean.

Thump, thump, thump. It was a sound more than a motion.

He was lying on something hard now. His head still throbbed and he noticed a new pain. His shoulder blade, like a hot iron, was burning its way through the bone. He shifted to take some of the weight off of the tender area.

"Hey, our patient is stirring. Hold on Dr. Crook. *You*...get over here and start an IV. We need to get some fluids in him now!" The Italian accent was back. The name escaped him.

"He's gonna be okay, right?"

Thanks for asking Billy. I'd like to know the same thing. Am I going to be all right?

"He'll be fine. Just a bad knock to the head, I think. But we've got to go, *now*!"

A clicking sound.

Phin knew that one.

Fingers on a keyboard.

"Uh, sir, I've got incoming aircraft to our southeast. Moving fast. I think we should leave now."

Oz Jenks! You made it, buddy.

"The brother...did you get the brother?" There was stress in Sergeant Warren's voice.

"Got him out on the last chopper. Time for us." The sound of rapping on metal. "That's it, we're all on, take us up!"

The *thumping* grew in intensity and volume. Phin felt a sting in his right forearm and a swaying motion overtook him.

Time for another nap.

Chapter 62

The Learjet touched down at the Jackson Hole airport.

Before the stairs to the small jet were fully extended, Alexander Pontia was sprinting down the steps and across the tarmac to the GMC Yukon waiting for him. The driver's seat was empty with the keys in the console.

Just as he had requested. He'd drive himself.

He must move quickly. The fewer people that knew he was home the better. He was there only to collect his most important documents and then he'd be back at the airport. His pilot would refuel the plane in his brief absence and be waiting to take the now fugitive to parts unknown.

He started the SUV and drove away from the airport as fast as he dared. He didn't want to get pulled over.

His phone buzzed and he looked at the screen. Tess Greenway. Again. He didn't have time for her right now. He'd already sent word to his wife Jillian to leave the residence. "Go to the Caribbean," he told her. "Pick your favorite island and I'll meet you there in a couple of days." He sensed the concern in her voice but she knew enough to move when Alexander said move.

He'd have to solve the problem of both a wife and a lover later. He had more pressing matters at the moment. Things had spun completely out of control hours earlier. A "freak storm" of wind and lightning – is that what one would call it? – had interrupted his plans. The bitterness was palpable. He'd spent years and countless resources bringing everything and everyone together for just the perfect moment.

He'd now have to regroup.

He was still waiting to hear from Dimitri. He needed Dimitri right now. He needed to find out what had been salvaged from the mountain. Pontia had put in place contingencies in case the worst happened.

The worst had actually happened. Perhaps more than the worst.

Alexander always had contingencies, though.

Dimitri and Tess would gather the relics and each head to a separate "waiting zone" until they could safely reconnect and assess.

He came to a halt in front of his house. The Grand Tetons stood in the distance, the snowcapped range illuminating the night sky. He paused for just a moment to take it in one last time. Oh, how he loved that view.

No matter. There were other mountains in other countries. He'd regroup and start over. Maybe build one life in the Swiss Alps with Jillian and another in the Andes of Chile with Tess.

He exited the vehicle, leaving the door open, and rushed inside his house. The lights were wired to come on via a sensor...but that did not happen.

Alexander paused in the dark entryway and looked around. "Hello," he called out.

Nothing.

He hit a wall switch manually and still more nothing.

Maybe the power's out.

But that made no sense. He had spent a small fortune installing a foolproof generator system in the case of an outage.

He rushed to his study with the intention of cleaning out his personal safe. He stopped in front of the bank of windows that looked out at the mountains.

A chill moved down his spine.

Outside the house, a mere twenty yards away, was a line of figures...all dressed in black. They stood just a few feet apart and spanned the breadth of his view.

A voice behind him. "Alexander Pontia."

He turned around to face a man dressed in similar fashion, except his head was uncovered.

"My name is Lieutenant Colonel Levi Rubin. I am a member of the Israeli military. But I am not here in any *official* capacity. I have, you see, a unique heritage which has brought me, brought us, to your home. We are members of an ancient brotherhood; a guild of thieves, you might say. You are responsible for the death of Mary Gannab."

"I have no idea who you're talking about. How dare you come into my house. Do you know who I am?"

Alexander Pontia's posturing had no effect. "She was the owner of the House of *Reuben*. My house. The house of my heritage. And more importantly, she was the Keeper of the Archive. Her murder must be avenged. That is why we, myself and the brotherhood, have come."

Alexander Pontia knew it would be useless to run. The strength was already draining from his limbs. He sat down in a chair and prepared to receive his fate.

Epilogue

Phineas Crook strolled across the Oval of the Oklahoma Baptist University campus with a smile on his face.

Summer had taken its hold on the Oklahoma weather – it was sunny and hot. Phin didn't mind. The campus was quiet, just a small contingency of students taking summer term classes - not even enough to fill the parking lots plus the dorms were closed.

He took his time walking to his car, enjoying the beauty of the buildings and landscaping, waving at a groundskeeper running a mower.

He was reflecting on - and had enjoyed - the look of shock on Dean Clayton Reynolds's face as Phin presented him, and the university, his little gift. It should be more than sufficient to fulfill the school's desire to separate itself from the academic competition and put OBU on the map in a new and fresh way.

The short drive home for lunch took on a new appreciation. After all he'd been through in the last couple of weeks, driving down MacArthur and then turning onto Broadway was exhilarating, like watching your favorite show in high definition for the first time. He loved the city of Shawnee. His city.

And then his driveway. Stopping the car in front of his house. A Jeep Cherokee was sitting by the curb and Phin smiled.

They were here.

He got out and was met at the door by Autumn who greeted him with a warm embrace. "You're just in time. They only pulled up five minutes ago and lunch is all set. How'd it go?"

"Fine, fine. I'll tell you about it while we eat." Phin stepped into his living room and was met by a sight that brought tears to his eyes.

Remus was sitting on the floor playing with his new nephew for the first time. Phin and Autumn's adopted son, Patrick, had just met his uncle. The little guy had his shoebox of action figures dumped onto the hardwood floor and was explaining in detail the superpowers of each.

Remus looked up and then rose to his feet. He pulled Phin into a big bear hug. "How's the head little bro? Did we finally knock some sense into you?"

Phin laughed and hugged his brother in return. "I just can't...can't believe you're here. It's amazing."

"Hey, what am I? Chopped liver?" A toilet flushed and Sergeant Billy Warren came around the corner, a big smile on his face.

Max Allred appeared in the doorway of the kitchen. "I just pulled the burgers off the grill. Let's dive in before the meat gets cold."

It was perfect. Family and friends.

Max's kids, along with Patrick, settled down outside at a picnic table while the "adults" preferred the air conditioning of the dining room.

"Shelly had to take her sister to the doctor in OKC but she made me promise to fill her in on all the details. So, spill it, how'd it go with Reynolds?" Max asked.

"Well, its official, you are looking at the new head of the OBU Center for Modern Biblical Exploration." Autumn cheered and everyone lifted a glass of water to toast the moment.

"Is he still pushing for you to head back to the Garden of Eden?" Max asked.

"I told him it was out of the question. A total deal-breaker for me. But he let it go the instant I presented my donation to the new center - the Cross of Gestas, the Impenitent Thief. It's an archaeological boon. He was absolutely floored. Should have seen his face. Priceless. We'll begin working on the first paper on the find. Who knows what the future will hold."

"So let me get this straight," Sergeant Warren spoke up. "You don't have to return this cross thing back to some museum or whatever?"

"Nope. It was never in a museum. In fact, no one even knew of its existence. Came straight from the Crook family archive. And since Remus and I are both Crooks, we have the right to keep and preserve it." Remus smiled and took another bite of burger. Looking at his brother, alive, was still a thing of wonder. "Remus, how are you feeling, really?"

"Perfectly fine. I mean it. In fact, better than I have in years. It's like I was never stabbed in the first place. Phin, there's not even a scar." His hand reached over and rubbed the side where the stiletto had done its wicked work.

It was a miracle.

Phin called it the Miracle on the Mountain.

Remus had to agree.

Max butted in. "This is where I need some holes filled in. So, you said," pointing at Phin, "that Remus here was stabbed, had a collapsed lung, and then he actually died on top of Mount Sinai?"

"Yes, that's exactly what I'm telling you. But I remembered the legend...you know, of when Helena found the True Cross originally. The way she tested it, to see if it was the real cross of Christ, was by bringing to it a man who'd died recently. They laid him on top of it. The story goes that he came back to life. So, in that moment, when I realized Remus was gone...well, I didn't know what else to do so I..."

Remus broke in to finish the story. "Listen, I still don't know about God and all. He and I for sure have our issues, if that's what you want to call it. But all I know is this: I was in bad shape for days. I knew I was dying. I remember waking up and I was strapped to this chair and Pontia was next to me, blabbing on and on. It was hard to focus. Then it felt like my heart exploded in my chest and I was, you know...just gone. Then...I don't know how to describe it. I was standing on a road with a fork in it. On one side it was dark, and the path was overgrown. It felt...wrong. I could feel a tug, like the path was pulling on me. On the other side it was brighter, and I could feel myself being drawn to that path. But the literal tug was coming from the other one.

"Then...listen, this is gonna sound crazy, but I'm just telling you how it happened. Everything just evaporated in a massive bright light. Next thing I know, I'm lying on my back, on the ground, except the cross is under me. I can't see anything because it's so bright, but then there's this man standing over me. I can't make out anything about him. But I know it's a man, right? And he reaches down with his hand and I take it, and instantly I can fill my collapsed lung filling with breath. My pain just went away and I had this incredible burst of energy. Next, he pulls me up and I'm standing in front of him and I realize...*he's* the one that's shining. So bright. And I still can't make out anything about him except one thing...he was smiling at me. And then that was it. Just like that, he was gone."

"That's...that really is amazing," Autumn finally said, reflecting on her own death to life miracle from a year prior.

"So now you clearly believe in God?" Phin spoke up to lighten the mood.

"Let's just say...I'm getting there."

"So, when he disappeared, that's when you said you saw Billy here, lying on the ground unconscious."

"That's right. Looked like there had been some sort of big-time explosion. Bezrukov was clearly dead. But the sergeant here looked totally unharmed, like he was just sleeping. And you know another weird thing? The relics, you know, the ones I stole. They were scattered around too, but they were completely intact. I mean, all this gear and equipment was burning and had melted and stuff, but the relics were perfectly fine. So weird."

Phin shifted to Sergeant Warren. "Billy, I haven't had the chance to thank you for saving my life...again. Man, when you came bowling in to take on the Russian...I mean, that guy was about to pummel me to death. Can't tell you how glad I am you broke loose and found your robotic limbs. I think they must have made the difference. That guy was a beast."

Sergeant Warren set his hamburger down and stared at the plate, not looking up.

"Hey, I'm sorry. Did I say something wrong?"

"No... it's just." He finally looked up. "I didn't break loose, Doc. And I didn't find my limbs. They weren't even up there with me. They were back at basecamp locked in a chest."

Everyone was silent.

"Wait..." Phin spoke. "But...then how? I mean I saw you."

"All I know is...I looked down and the leather straps were gone and you were in trouble, and I came to help."

"But you had your left arm and leg. I saw."

"I know." Warren looked from Phin to Remus. "I know. And then the explosion and when I woke up, I was back to...normal, and Remus was dragging me away from the fire and stuff."

Everyone was taking in what they'd just heard. What it meant.

The Miracle on the Mountain.

"That's when Rossi showed up," Remus continued. "He and his man had apparently broken free. Told me that once the mountain started shaking, all of Pontia's men started bailing. Looks like Pontia himself ran like a chicken. So Rossi showed up at the top of the mountain to see if he could help. Gotta give it to the man for running up when everyone else was running down. He grabbed a few of the relics but says he saw Tess Greenway up there gathering some too. Then he helped me with Warren here and then we all found you in some cave about a third of the way down. Have no idea how you got there, but you'd taken quite a tumble. We stretchered you down the best we could and then commandeered a couple of Saudi choppers and skedaddled across the Israeli border before the Saudis themselves showed up."

"Oz! I remember hearing Oz's voice. When did he turn up?"

"The kid's the real hero of the whole thing, Doc. He's one slippery computer geek too. Somehow he slipped detection when Pontia's men came for us. Said he scrambled up on top of that rock altar and laid low. No one ever thought to look up there. Once we were outa there, he fired up his laptop and GPS, connected with his sidekick Chen back at HQ, and went to work on jamming Pontia's little worldwide debut."

"So that's why it never aired." Phin now understood. He was certain he would have seen news stories across all the media outlets on what happened on top of Mount Sinai. But there had been nothing - from the time he came to on the Blackhawk flight, recuperated in Israel the next day, and then headed back home. There had been zero news or social media buzz about the broadcast or Alexander Pontia's ambitions.

"Well, a little bit got out," Sergeant Warren explained. "Just the beginning of Pontia blabbing about God not being real and Jesus being a fake and how he was gonna prove it. Then the whole thing went down. All because of our boy Oz and his sidekick, Ronald Chen. Yessir, that's how it happened."

"Speaking of Alexander Pontia, did you all see the news this morning?" The question was Max's one contribution to the discussion.

"Yeah, I saw," Phin began. "Found him this morning at his Wyoming home."

"Natural causes, CNN said. Found him in his bed," Remus added.

Sergeant Warren looked at the brothers and raised an eyebrow.

"So, what's next for the Crook brothers?" Max grabbed a bowl of watermelon slices and began to help himself.

Phin went first. "Well, this Crook brother is going to take it easy. I think I've already had my summer vacation and I'm content to stay at home until fall classes begin. Assuming you're okay with that, E." He grabbed Autumn's hand. She smiled and squeezed in return.

"I'm leaving tomorrow morning for Italy," Remus went next. "Rossi and I are gonna get started on our little project."

Chief Inspector Antonio Rossi had seemingly pulled off the impossible. He declared that Phin was completely innocent of murder and theft. In addition, he brokered a deal with Remus Crook. In exchange for helping Rossi track down Tess Greenway and the remaining relics of

Christ that she had taken from the mountain, he would not only remain free from prison, but he would receive a full pardon for his original crime. Phin had no idea how the Italian pulled it off, but apparently the Vatican got involved, and then the State Department, leaving the State of Oklahoma little choice but to concede.

"Looks like I've turned over a new leaf, little brother. Gonna be working for the good guys now," Remus winked.

"Well, I just made your life easier by one artifact." Phin looked at his watch. "Right about now, Antonio Rossi should be receiving a special delivery via FedEx. I'd love to see his face when he opens it to find the Shroud of Turin."

"Thank you!" Max shouted. "Thank you for getting that thing out of the school's library and out of your life. Smartest thing you've done in a long time."

Phin agreed. He sat back, holding his wife's hand, and looked at the faces of those he loved the most.

Laughter and stories continued far longer than the food lasted.

God had given him a good life. Maybe not the life he ever expected, and certainly not a life that was always easy. But in this moment, sitting around his dining room table, all was well, and yes, he was blessed.

THE END

ACKNOWLEDGMENTS

Finishing a novel brings with it a strange mix of emotions: relief (it's finally over), pride (I think this might be a pretty good story), fear (I hope other people think it's a pretty good story), sadness (what do I do now?), excitement (I can't wait to see what other people think...I think...). But also...gratitude. Before a novel is released for public consumption, there are those special friends who are close to the project and who encourage me along the way. I am especially grateful for my first-readers: Gayla Oldham, Jill Langham, and Lee Larry. Thank you, thank you, thank you for your interest, enthusiasm, keen eye, and suggestions. The book is better because of you. My biggest expression of gratitude goes to my biggest fan, my wife, Julie. She is always the first reader before anyone else. Her skill is exceptional in knocking off the rough edges and making the story more readable and just overall, better. Thank you, my love, for *your* love and support in this crazy side-hobby of storytelling. Finally, I am grateful to you, dear reader. Novel number one was a personal project. Could I really do this? Novel number two and now number three, I owe to you. One thousand thank yous for the countless inquiries: *When's the next book coming out?* It has been a fun ride, hasn't it? I cannot express with words the gratitude and satisfaction of seeing you all falling in love with Phineas and Autumn Crook, Sergeant Billy Warren, and the host of other characters born in my imagination and brought to life in the printed word...and now in your hearts as well.

ON GEOGRAPHY AND RELICS

In 1999, I found myself captivated by a book called *The Gold of Exodus* by Howard Blum. This fascinating book told the story of Bob Cornuke and Larry Williams and how they followed the ancient path of the Hebrew people from Egypt into Saudi Arabia to the mountain called Jabal al Lawz. Before being detained for illegal entry and then escaping from Saudi Arabia, they documented the various evidences that point to Jabal al Lawz as the true location of the biblical Mount Sinai. Several years later my wife and I were thrilled to host Bob Cornuke in our home for dinner with a few close friends. We shared a great meal and even greater conversation as Bob recounted the details of his adventure to the mountain of God. I found myself thinking, "This guy is a real-life Indiana Jones!" Anyway, the story and evidence of Jabal al Lawz is so interesting and compelling I could not resist making it the location of the finale in *Thief's Revenge*. Additionally, the relics spoken of in *Thief's Revenge* are all real as are their locations in the various churches and basilicas throughout Rome and greater Europe, the obvious exceptions being the Cross of Gestas and the crossbeam of the True Cross. But that, my friends, is what fiction is for!

ABOUT THE AUTHOR

Jeffrey S. Crawford is teaching pastor and lead pastor of ministries at Cross Church in northwest Arkansas, one of the largest and fastest growing megachurches in North America. He holds a Doctor of Education in Leadership from the Southern Baptist Theological Seminary, a Master of Divinity degree from Southwestern Baptist Theological Seminary, and a Bachelor of Arts in Philosophy from Oklahoma Baptist University. He has served for over thirty years in churches across Arkansas, Texas, Oklahoma, Louisiana, Utah, and Tennessee and enjoys traveling the globe on missionary journeys and interacting with the peoples of the world. He and his wife, Julie, have raised their four children in the foothills of the Ozarks where they make their home.

Journey Into the Mind of
Jeffrey S Crawford

"Truth through story..."

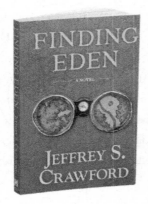

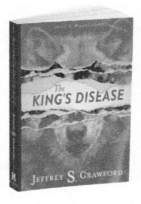

www.jeffreyScrawford.com

The Non-Fiction World of
Jeffrey S Crawford

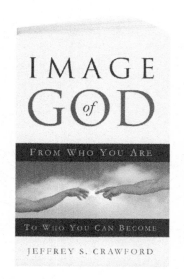

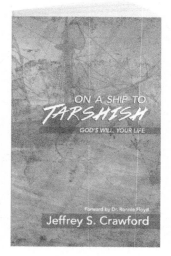

Video trailers, free samples, Jeff's blog,
Fan Connection and more at...

www.jeffreyScrawford.com

Made in the USA
Coppell, TX
20 November 2022

86713715R00267